03/23/17

PRAISE FOR LA

REGARDING ...LADY'S HONOR

"Beautiful nineteenth-century Cornwall offers a contemplative setting for this dramatic romance that involves murder, suspense, and a surprise villain."

—*Romantic Times*

—Louise M. Gouge, award-winning author of *Then Came Faith*

"A page-turning story with an in-depth knowledge of the period, an eye for detail, and an escalating mystery that will keep readers guessing till the end."

—Ruth Axtell Morren, author of *Wild Rose* and *The Rogue's Redemption*

REGARDING *LADY IN THE MIST*

"Readers will not be able to put this gem of a novel down."
—Romantic Times

"Secrets, suspense, and a sweetly told love story make this a highly rewarding read."
—Cheryl Bolen, Holt Medallion–winning author
of *One Golden Ring*

MY ENEMY
MY HEART

ALSO BY LAURIE ALICE EAKES

MY ENEMY
MY HEART

The Ashford Chronicles:

Book 1

LAURIE ALICE EAKES

Waterfall
PRESS

This is a work of fiction. Names, characters, organizations, places, events, and incidents are either products of the author's imagination or are used fictitiously.

Published by Waterfall Press

www.brilliancepublishing.com

Amazon, the Amazon logo, and Waterfall Press are trademarks of Amazon.com, Inc., or its affiliates.

ISBN-13: 9781503937635
ISBN-10: 1503937631

Cover design by Mike Heath | Magnus Creative

Printed in the United States of America

*To my agent, Natasha Kern, for believing in my ability
to write, my career, and, above all, me*

AUTHOR'S NOTE

The War of 1812 may be the most fascinating war America has ever gotten herself into. The majority of our citizens opposed it, though Great Britain was behaving badly, bullying our merchantmen, stealing our sailors, and telling us where we could and could not trade as though we were still their colonies. Yet we had no business taking on the most powerful nation in the world—again. We pitted our 18 naval vessels against their 506, our ragtag army against their well-oiled war machine. We lost nearly every land battle we fought. And yet we excelled in the water, conquering the British through their merchant fleet, and gained every concession in the Treaty of Ghent we demanded.

As with every war, however, the price was lives lost or broken, fortunes lost and won, and families torn apart. This story is about how a handful of people try to rise above enmity of nations and find common ground, loyalty, and love.

PART I

Chapter 1

Caribbean Sea
September 1812

*N*othing to worry about." Her observation of the ship on the horizon complete, Deirdre MacKenzie shoved the spyglass into her waistband, swung into the rigging, and slid down a backstay to land on the deck with a barefooted thud. "It's only a British merchantman, Captain, sir."

Daniel MacKenzie gave her a faint smile, amused to have her call him Captain instead of Father, as she had done since she could talk. Despite the smile, his face remained pale, grayish due to the ill health that had plagued him since their rough passage around Cape Horn. "If it's only a merchantman, we're safe running up the Stars and Stripes."

"Are you certain about that, sir?" the first mate, Ross Trenerry, asked from where he stood manning the Baltimore clipper's wheel. "We haven't been what one would call friends with the British lately."

"Only their navy, Ross." Father pressed one hand to his chest, and his breath rasped loudly enough to be heard above the whistle of wind in the rigging.

Deirdre bit her lip. She wanted to wrap her arm around her father's too-thin frame and lead him below, suggest he lie on his bunk and let Ross or her make contact with the other merchant ship if the British came their way. He wouldn't welcome the solicitude, though. She knew that all too well.

"British merchantmen aren't impressing men from American merchants." Deirdre spoke more to reassure herself than convince Ross or her father.

Ross shook shaggy, dark hair out of his face and snorted. "The British think they can do whatever they want. I think we're better off hightailing it out of here."

"You may be right." Father sounded as though he'd been running a footrace. "I'd like a bit more wind . . . for that. Deirdre, nip up top again and get their heading. We'll evade . . . them . . ."

"Sir—" She wanted to stay near him when he looked so poorly. But he was her father and her captain, and one condition of being allowed to stay aboard these past ten years, working as a crewman on voyages such as this recent one from Alexandria, Virginia, to Canton, China, and back was that she obey him without question. "Yes, sir."

She exchanged a glance with Ross. His eyes held the same concern she felt. He swung his glance toward her father, then jabbed a thumb toward his chest. The message was clear—he would take care of their ailing leader.

Still reluctant, Deirdre swung into the rigging and climbed to the crosstrees with practiced ease. The slanting rigging of the Baltimore clipper was harder to negotiate than a ship-rigged vessel with straight masts, but the speed with which they could sail made every other hazard worth the risk. With wind, they could outrun everything, especially a British merchantman.

One arm hooked around a line to hold her in place sixty feet above the deck, she held the telescope to her eye. A moment or two passed while she adjusted balance and vision to the increased sway at the top of the mainmast. Then the glorious view of the world came into focus through the magnifying lens—blue sky, bluer water, white lines of gently rising wave crests. Hot sun blazed down on the water, shimmering and sparkling like half-submerged gold and gleaming off the pale sails of the distant ship. Merchantman for certain, and the British Union Jack prominently displayed and unmistakable at her masthead even at that distance.

"They're on a due easterly heading," Deirdre shouted to the nearest man in the rigging, a half Seneca man called Blaze for the white streak through his black hair.

He passed the word to the deck. The other thirteen crewmen, whether on duty or not, stood to attention, sail mending or personal laundry forgotten when any moment they might need to spring into the rigging and change tack.

No order to do so came from her father. The men began to drift back to their tasks, and no one raised the Stars and Stripes. Apparently, her father had decided that the British ship would miss them altogether if they continued their own north-by-northwest course. He'd chosen that direction as the safest action. Yet he didn't order up more sail. In a moment, Deirdre realized why.

The wind was dying. What had been a brisk blow at sunrise had steadily dropped throughout the morning. Now, at early afternoon, with the sun at its zenith, its heat seemed to beat everything into somnolence—including the precious wind. Once-billowing sails began to slacken and drooped from their yards. Crewmen wiped sweat from their brows and glanced toward the west.

Dry-mouthed, Deirdre used the telescope to look to the west. The British merchantman should be becalmed, too.

She wasn't. Like a graceful sea creature, she glided across the water. Her heading changed. Instead of a tack that would take her well past their stern, she now headed straight for the *Maid of Alexandria*.

"Sweeps!" Deirdre dropped the spyglass in her scramble to reach the deck. "They've got sweeps." She sucked in a mouthful of briny air. "And big guns."

In the Caribbean especially, oars long enough they required at least three men to operate them, along with cannon ranged along the gunwales, meant only one thing: the Union Jack was a trick, a ruse to engender a sense of safety.

Ross swore and gripped the near-useless wheel with such force his knuckles showed white through his tanned skin. Behind Deirdre, old Wat Drummond muttered "pirates" as though it were the worst of disasters.

To a frail schooner like the *Maid of Alexandria*, it was a disaster. The Baltimore-clipper-style schooners were equipped to run, not fight. Without wind, they couldn't run. Their ordnance consisted of four one-pounders, a cutlass apiece for the fifteen crewmen, and a sword for her father.

Deirdre read the hopelessness of this disadvantage in her father's face, now blue-lipped and beaded with perspiration. He met her gaze with eyes the same pale green as her own. "Deirdre, get below."

She dropped her hand to the dirk sheathed at her belt. "No, sir."

"That's . . . an order."

"I'm disobeying you, sir. I'm useless below."

"You're safer below."

She crossed her arms over breasts bound to maintain the illusion that she was a tall, gangly youth of fifteen, not a woman of twenty-three. "No, sir. I am as much a part of this crew as any of the men. If they fight, I fight."

For several moments, only the flap of limp canvas and creak of timbers broke the silence that fell across the deck. Deirdre held her father's gaze in a wordless battle of wills they'd fought since she could talk. The crew looked away, staring toward the approaching enemy, faces taut, waiting for the family battle to end and their captain to give orders to collect arms, run out the guns, or raise a white flag.

Deirdre took a step away from her father and toward the nearest gun.

"You know this means . . . you will . . . never sail with me . . . again." Her father's call was labored.

Deirdre's heart staggered in aching response. She should be reaching toward him, not backing away from him. But this was not the time to argue. She could not skulk in her cabin or the hold while her fellow crewmen and, most of all, her father suffered at the hands of pirates.

"So be it, sir." Deirdre's voice sounded thick in her ears. "But right now, the men need orders to take up arms and fight." She turned her back on her father.

In that instant, gunfire split the stillness.

Deirdre raced for the nearest cannon. It looked like a child's toy compared to the gun that blasted the stillness. But she was a good shot. If she laid even a one-pounder in the right place like along a line of sweeps, or into the crowd of men on the fo'c'sle . . .

She made calculations of barrel angle as she kicked open the gunport. Yanking off the tackle rope holding the weapon secure, she ran through the steps of ramming, priming, firing.

Firing. She needed fire to light the fuse.

She spun toward the galley.

Ross and Blaze tackled her halfway down the main deck. The three of them tumbled to the planking, winded, struggling to disentangle arms and legs.

Above them, another blast from the English vessel ripped the day in two. A cannonball sailed through the bowsprit, shattering it to kindling.

"Let me go." Deirdre punched Ross in the belly with one fist and Blaze in the jaw with another. "If you're all cowards—"

"MacKenzie's dying."

Deirdre caught her breath at Ross's stark announcement. "No!"

But a glance toward the quarterdeck told her that her father no longer stood there. He lay on the deck, Old Wat and Zeb, a former slave, bent over him.

"No." Though she repeated the denial, the fight drained out of her. She stumbled to her feet on the canting deck and headed aft.

Ross and Blaze turned toward the schooner's pitiful excuse for ordnance. She pushed Zeb and Wat aside so she could kneel at MacKenzie's head. "What is it, Father?"

His breath rasped and rattled. He didn't speak.

"What is it?" Deirdre laid her hand on his brow. "What's wrong with him?"

"Apoplexy," Wat said.

"What should we do?" Deirdre didn't know to whom she posed the question.

Her father answered. "Get . . . below." He gave the order around a wheeze. "Surrender."

"Not after this. We—" She stopped. A rattling breath and glazed eyes told her that her father, her captain, had heard her argue with him for the last time.

Her chest tightened. Her throat closed. Springing to her feet, she whipped the dirk from her belt. "Why are you all just standing here? Run out all the guns. Break out the swords. We can't run, but we can fight them off."

No one moved.

Toward the bow, the enemy ship drew near enough for her to see details without a spyglass. Long guns bristled from the bow and along the beam. Men swarmed across the deck and maneuvered the sweeps, at least three times the number of men than on the *Maid*.

"We can't fight them." Wat gave her a pitying look. "Not unless we're all ready to die trying."

"Your captain died." Deirdre swallowed against the hitching lump in her throat. "Are you going to let them get away with driving my father to his death?"

In response, Blaze stepped forward and began to run a white flag up the masthead.

"Stop!" Deirdre flung herself at him.

Ross caught her by the upper arms and swung her around to face him. "You stop." His words came out harder-voiced than she thought possible spoken in a South Carolina drawl, and he gave her a none-too-gentle shake. "We don't have the men or arms to fight. We'll be prisoners, but we'll have a chance at living and even escaping. If we fight, we'll die for sure."

"Suit yourself." Deirdre tried to pull away. "I'm going to fight them."

"No, you're not." Ross spoke with utter assurance.

As though he had given a command, every one of the *Maid*'s crew closed ranks around her, hemming her in like prison walls.

"You're going to stand here and keep your mouth shut so they don't notice you're a girl, just like we do every time we meet another vessel. We don't want them to work out that you're the captain's daughter when we won't be able to protect you."

Deirdre gritted her teeth. She hated to admit that Ross was right. As the captain's daughter, she would be held for a higher ransom at best. At the worst, as a female . . .

A thud jarred the clipper from stem to stern. Without looking, Deirdre knew the enemy had grappled their ship to the *Maid*. In moments, pirates in the guise of British merchantmen would swarm aboard and take over her father's beloved vessel and the precious cargo of tea and silk. They would imprison the crew, including her, if they thought she was a boy.

Her stomach rolled with the pitch of the schooner as the first boarders landed on the foredeck. She must pretend she didn't care any more about her father's death than anyone would care about the loss of a stern but fair captain. Regardless of what they might do to his body, she must not show that he was her beloved father, who had spoiled her too much to leave her on shore.

She ceased pulling against Ross's hold, swallowed the lump clogging her throat, and turned with everyone else to watch their captors board.

They didn't look like she imagined pirates would. Their white canvas breeches and striped cotton shirts were clean, their hair short, their faces smooth-shaven. With cutlasses in hand and a few pistols in belts, most of them resembled boys playing at pirate, taking orders from an older, harder-faced man.

"Secure the prisoners," commanded the older man in a clipped English accent.

Five men swarmed toward the *Maid*'s crew. Three men with pistols drawn, two with muskets. Others dropped down the ladders to the lower deck and the hold.

Deirdre rested her hand on her dirk, tempted to draw, to avenge her father's death with one blow.

"Don't even think about it." Ross curled his fingers around her wrist.

"Drop your weapons and kick them here," one musket-bearer commanded.

Ross tightened his hold on Deirdre's wrist. "Drop it."

She dropped the dirk and kicked it between the legs of Zeb and Blaze, who stood in front of her like human shields. But that wasn't the only weapon on her person. At her father's insistence since she grew into womanhood, she had worn a stiletto braided into the thick plait of hair he would not allow her to cut. The British would never know.

"Prisoners secured, Captain," a carrot-haired youth with spots proclaimed in a voice that sounded as though it had recently broken.

The man addressed as captain stepped forward and cleared his throat. "By the power vested in us, master, owner, and crew of the royal privateer vessel *Phoebe*, by His Royal Highness, the Prince Regent of England, we declare you prisoners of war of the sovereign . . ." His proclamation blurred into nonsense in Deirdre's ears beneath the rush of confusion, then disbelief.

Prisoners of war. Prisoners of England. This was a British privateer, not a pirate ship.

The deck rolled beneath Deirdre's feet. She braced herself against Ross's sturdy arm, saw that his face displayed the same kind of astonishment she felt. She'd never in her life believed that President Madison would actually go to war with England. The United States didn't have the ships, the equipment, or the men to fight the British Empire.

"Where is your captain?" the Englishman concluded his proclamation.

Deirdre didn't dare answer for fear her voice would break if she spoke one word about her father. None of the rest of the *Maid*'s crew said a word either. Nor did any of them look at MacKenzie's supine body a few yards away.

The enemy captain looked annoyed. "I need to know who accepts our terms of your surrender."

A bubble of laughter rolled up Deirdre's throat at the absurdity of this remark. As if any of them would accept their surrender willingly. A few of her crewmates even snorted.

The *Phoebe*'s crew shifted, aligning their weapons as though preparing for a fight. Deirdre stared at the *Phoebe*'s crew. One by one, she memorized each countenance from the carrot-haired youth with spots, whose pistol looked less than steady in his hand, to the middle-aged man with silver hair referred to as captain, to . . . him.

He was the true privateer, not a fighting man or even a sailor, but the mastermind behind the adventure. Deirdre knew it the instant he appeared on the bulwark of the *Phoebe*. Tall and lean-muscled, he posed against a backdrop of the two vessels' bowsprits, one broken, one whole, and a flawless blue sky. His features were indistinct from that distance, but his straight posture and the angle of his head proclaimed "mine."

Deirdre feared if she didn't look away, she would break past the nearest guard and fling herself at this man, her stiletto in hand. Yet she couldn't stop staring—at the blue-black hair he wore in an old-fashioned queue, at the broad shoulders covered with a fine, white cambric shirt, at the long, muscled legs in buckskin breeches and Hessian boots.

Those legs began to move. They carried him forward with the unhurried precision of a cat stalking its prey.

No, not a cat. That produced images of something warm and cuddly. He was far more dangerous, a tiger ready for a feast. He passed the *Phoebe*'s crewmen as though they didn't exist, all his attention focused on one goal. The closer he drew, the tighter Deirdre's muscles grew. She sensed the tension of the men around her, as though all of them held their breath. The crew of the *Phoebe* watched him, their faces wary.

He paused beside Daniel MacKenzie's body. His face tightened. His nostrils pinched as though he smelled something more foul than a ship three months at sea.

Deirdre's body jerked. Her hand flew to her braid tucked beneath the neck of her loose cotton shirt.

Ross caught hold of her arm and yanked it down to her side. "Don't you dare." His words were barely audible above the clamor of men taking over the *Maid*.

The tiger must have heard him anyway. He raised his head and looked straight at Deirdre.

Despite the blazing sun, a shiver rippled through her. She'd never seen eyes like his, topaz gold beneath thick, dark lashes and heavy lids that lent them a sleepy look. They gave nothing away as to his thoughts or feelings. Neither did his face display any expression. With its full-lipped mouth and straight, high-bridged nose, that flawless, sculptured countenance would have been too pretty for a man save for the strength of his chin and broad cheekbones.

He broke eye contact first, addressing the *Phoebe*'s captain. "Why has this body been left here?"

His voice jolted Deirdre. It was pure English aristocrat, the sort she had heard from the boxes at the theater during their one visit to London before the relationship between the two countries deteriorated. She had been happy then, released from the boarding school where she had been uncompromisingly miserable in dresses and gloves, and so little activity her muscles grew soft.

A sob escaped her throat.

Behind her, Wat laid a hand on her shoulder and whispered, "Steady there. He's given you too much attention already."

She swallowed the lump in her throat and blinked back tears. She would not grieve in front of these strangers, these enemies.

"We thought to take care of the live ones first, Kier—Mr. Ashford," the older man said. "We are looking to see if anyone is hiding below and inspect the cargo to see what—"

"Later." Ashford gestured to her father's body. "Then take this poor man away and prepare him for burial."

They weren't going to simply dump him overboard. Gratitude softened a crumb of Deirdre's heart toward this man. Then he faced them once more, and she closed her eyes against the impact of his gaze.

"Who is he?" Ashford demanded.

None of the *Maid*'s crew responded.

"I wish to give him a Christian burial." The man's voice held annoyance. "I cannot do that without knowing his name."

A nice ploy. Once he had her father's name, he would look through the captain's log and know he was the captain. He would then know that he had prisoners without a leader, without one of them deserving, by the laws of the sea, the respect of a cabin rather than the hold. Not one of them would be up top with a chance at freeing the others.

Deirdre squeezed Ross's arm. He was the first mate. He should claim the role of captain with her father . . . gone.

He shook his head, the merest fraction of movement.

It drew Ashford's attention anyway. He fixed his gaze on Ross. "Who are you?"

Ross drew back his broad shoulders, tilted his chin. "Ross Trenerry out of Charleston, South Carolina, first mate."

"And you?" Ashford shifted his gaze to Deirdre.

"The dead man," Ross said with more speed than usual, "is Daniel MacKenzie, our captain."

The tactic worked to draw the man's attention away from Deirdre. Ashford looked back at Ross. "Thank you." He turned to two of his crew. "Find a bit of sail and sew him up. We'll bury him at sundown. Now get the prisoners below." Pivoting on his heel, he stalked to the ladder that led to the *Maid*'s cabins.

The clipper had two cabins. One belonged to the captain. The other should have gone to Ross, but Deirdre needed privacy, so received the privilege.

She thanked the good Lord that she didn't own anything female, not so much as a hair ribbon or piece of jewelry. Nothing would give away her sex to the English aristocrat turned privateer.

Chapter 2

Kieran Ashford reached the privacy of the captain's cabin before his mask of indifference slipped. He had never seen the body of a man for whose death he was responsible.

He hadn't killed him. No one aboard the *Phoebe* had killed Daniel MacKenzie. The shock of being captured had apparently brought on some sort of seizure. Daniel MacKenzie hadn't been a young man, unlike his crew.

The first mate couldn't be more than twenty-two or -three, and the tall, gangly youth beside him had barely reached his teen years. He had plenty of hair on his head though, wore it even longer than Kieran wore his, not unusual among sailors perhaps, and no longer the normal state of fashion.

Kieran drummed his fingers on the edge of the teakwood table at one end of the cabin. "I wonder why he does that."

Not for the same reason Kieran chose to be so unfashionable. He'd bet this prize on it. Another possibility . . .

But he couldn't be right about that. Merely wishful thinking or the onset of insanity from two months at sea brought that kind of notion into a man's head.

Curiosity and necessity driving him forward, Kieran began searching for the captain's log. Lunacy or not, Kieran wanted to know who all the crew were so he could ease his mind and get messages to their families if they existed. He wanted to know where the odd little ship had been and what it was carrying. His crew expected prize money. Heron wanted to retire from the sea and could with a rich enough haul from an enemy merchantman.

While the shouts of men and thud of tramping feet resounded through the deckhead, Kieran explored the captain's cabin. He found the leather-bound log on a shelf above the desk straightaway. The drawers yielded some paperwork regarding an emancipated slave and ship's stores purchased somewhere in South America. Deciding it would keep, he continued his explorations of cupboards stocked with preserves and tins of coffee, a trunk filled with neatly folded clothes, finely tailored and of high-quality fabrics, books ranging from mathematics to novels, a box on the desk complete with paper, ink, blotters, pens, and wax. Nowhere did he see a ledger. A quick scan of the log showed no columns of figures there either. Nor did Kieran find so much as a cashbox.

Kieran stood in the center of the compact cabin and made a slow pivot, scanning the teakwood paneled walls. "You would not go to sea without specie for port calls. And investors would want an accounting. So where . . ." He tapped on first one panel, then another. They sounded too solid to house a secret compartment. But he'd swear one existed somewhere in that cabin.

It could possibly be in the other chamber, yet Kieran didn't think so. Not even the most trusting captain would put his gold in the hands of the first mate.

Defeated for the moment, Kieran sat at the table and began skimming through the log. Most of the brief entries spoke in terms too nautical to make much sense to him. All that came clear was the date they sailed from Alexandria, Virginia—1 April, 1812—and the list of crew by surname and initial of Christian name. Albert, Carn, Devry, Drummond, Eider, Freeman—

Captain Tom Heron knocked on the cabin door and entered. "You all right, lad?"

Once a first lieutenant in the British Navy under Kieran's father, Heron had the right to be so informal with Kieran, even if he was owner of the *Phoebe* now.

Why would he not be all right? He had just captured a rich prize with little loss of life.

"What is the cargo?" he asked.

Heron narrowed his eyes at Kieran. "Tea and silk, sandalwood. Along with the ship itself, this will make you a wealthy man."

Kieran opened his mouth to point out that he was already a wealthy man by virtue of his birth, and the *Phoebe*'s crew could have the lion's share of the spoils. Then he remembered that turning the merchantman *Phoebe* into a privateer would probably be the last straw to compel his father to disinherit him as much as the entail on the Ashford estates allowed.

"Where do we collect this wealth?" Kieran asked. "Jamaica, Bermuda?"

Heron drew the log toward him. "England."

"England? Dash it all, man, I do not want to go back there yet."

Or ever.

"No choice." Heron flipped pages in the log. "I wonder how long it took them to sail from China to here. I've heard these Baltimore clippers are fast."

"It looks like a child's toy."

"They're not very sturdy in a blow, it's true. The draft is too—" Heron broke off on a whistle. "Sixty-eight days. Unbelievable."

Kieran rapped his knuckles on the table. "Why England?"

"Hmm? Oh." Heron raised his gaze from the log. "Prisoners."

"Prisoners." Kieran speared his fingers into his hair, dislodging it from its ribbon. "I thought we could take them to one of our colonies here near North America."

Heron shrugged. "We could, if you want to consign them to a prison hulk."

Kieran grimaced. He had seen prison hulks full of Frenchmen in the Medway. They were little more than barely floating coffins, old ships beached to house men in conditions not fit for rats. Beneath a tropical sun, those hulks would turn into death traps.

But England meant Dartmoor Prison. That it was on land and cold rather than hot were the only points that set it above the prison hulks.

Suddenly, the heat inside the cabin suffocated Kieran. Head bent to avoid the low deck beams, he paced to the stern windows and levered them open. Too little breeze rippled the surface of the sea or drifted through the open porthole. Kieran inhaled deeply, smelled only the sourness of the bilges mixed with the sweetness of sandalwood, and queasiness roiled in his stomach.

Of all the things he could forgive his father for doing to him, sending him out of England before the war broke out would not be one of them.

Kieran swallowed. "Can we not simply beach them somewhere?"

"If you want us all to hang for treason."

"No, thank you, I do not want that on my conscience, too."

Sending fifteen men to Dartmoor—if they were lucky—was bad enough atop all the reasons he stood inside a stranger's cabin.

A dead stranger's cabin.

"Kieran." Heron's voice was gentle. "You can't capture enemy merchantmen without taking prisoners or killing them. You know that."

"I did not think."

"You never do."

Kieran winced. He wished he felt as though he had the right to tell Heron to stubble it or punish him for insubordination. But Heron had applied a rattan cane to Kieran's backside a time or two in his youth, and the old habit of listening to the older man's admonitions died hard.

Heron cleared his throat. "We need to make some decisions about whether or not we'll keep the cargo aboard this vessel, who will sail this one, where we'll keep the prisoners."

A light breeze, briny, but fresher than the onboard odors, cooled Kieran's face. He could answer Heron's questions with authority. "We will hoist the cargo to the *Phoebe* and leave the crew aboard this paper boat."

"Is that wise?" Heron sounded dubious. "They know their ship—"

"Which is why I want them here." Kieran glanced around the cabin with its teakwood panels and brass fittings. "And I will stay here, too."

Heron shook his head. "I wouldn't advise it, lad. If we run into a gale, you'll be tossed around like a cork, and with your difficulty with mal de mer . . ." He returned his attention to the log.

Kieran gave him a tight-lipped smile. "You mean I will be sicker than a dog."

Heron returned the thin smile. "I wouldn't be so crude."

"Especially when you wonder how Garrett Ashford's son could cast up his accounts over a three-foot swell."

"Your father was a born sailor."

"Who gave up the sea for love." Kieran curled his upper lip. "Now I am at sea because of a lady, but not a sailor."

And Joanna had been no lady whatever her birth.

"I stay here," he said with finality.

"If you insist." Heron rose. "Do you wish me to preside over the funeral?"

"You are the captain. It's your place."

And Kieran needed his eyes free to watch the prisoners and find out which one was D. MacKenzie.

"You're the captain," Zeb said to Deirdre. "Or as good as."

She stared at him through what little light filtered through the hatchway grating to their temporary prison—the hold of the *Maid of Alexandria*. "You're mad. Of course I'm not the captain or even as good as. Ross—"

"Is merely a hired hand," Ross drawled.

Deirdre snorted. "You have investments in this cargo." She swept her arm around the bales of sandalwood scenting the air strongly enough to almost mask the stench of the bilges. "You're losing as much as the rest of us."

Ross shifted on the oilskin-wrapped bales of silk they sat upon and laid his hand on her arm. "Not nearly as much." His voice was so gentle that tears pricked her eyes.

"Don't." She swallowed hard. "I can't think about . . . my father. If they see me cry at his funeral . . ."

"They won't let us go to his funeral," Blaze growled. "He'll be buried by strangers. English strangers." He said "English" as though it were a foul curse. "Can't afford to have us topside."

"When there's fifty of them and fifteen of us?" Wat spat. "We're not likely to mutiny."

"But we'll get away," Blaze said. "We have to. If they treat Americans like they treat the French prisoners . . ." He trailed off.

Silence fell in the hold, emphasized by the clamor of hammering above deck. They were repairing the bowsprit. They'd have to sail her to—where?

She didn't care. It didn't matter. Her crew had refused to fight to protect her, and now all of them faced a British hellhole of a prison.

If only she'd gone below as her father commanded . . .

She hugged her knees against her chest and laid her head on her knees. This imprisonment was her fault. The loss of revenue for men like Ross and Wat was her fault. Ross would never have a ship of his own now. Wat wouldn't retire to the cottage he wanted by the sea on Virginia's eastern shore. Zeb would never buy his wife and children out of slavery.

"I'll get you away," Deirdre vowed.

"Only if you reveal yourself as a female," Ross said, "and I don't want you to do that."

Deirdre straightened. "It might be the best course."

"They'll find out in a prison anyway," Wat added. "And what is likely to happen to her there . . ."

"Is likely to happen to her here, too." Ross's face looked tight in the twilight dimness, the fine angles hard. "That man, the owner. Ashford. I didn't like the look of him."

Neither had Deirdre. She thought an Indian tiger was likely less predatory than that man.

"But there are rules of war or something, aren't there?" she asked. "If he harms me—"

"Who will stop him?" Ross sounded bitter. "This isn't the navy. He doesn't have to answer to superior officers. And his men won't stop him from doing anything he pleases. He's just made them rich without any of them getting a scratch."

"Aren't you judging the man too harshly?" Zeb asked in his deep, easy voice. "He was right kind about Captain MacKenzie."

Dear Zeb. He had to be the kindest man in the world.

"You're absolutely right, Zeb." Deirdre stood. "I'll call the guards." She took a step toward the ladder.

Ross caught her hand and held her back. "Deirdre, no. Think about this. We can keep your identity secret until we get to whatever English port they're taking us. Then you'll be safe with the military authorities."

Deirdre faced him.

"I'll still be a prisoner." She spoke softly, trying to think. "Noncombatant, true. I think they would put me under house arrest with a family. Remember last time we were on Guernsey? There were French women who'd escaped. They were treated kindly, but they were still prisoners waiting safe transport back to their homes."

"They escaped." Ross touched her cheek. "You could, too. You could get back to America."

"How? I don't have any money."

None of them did. For fear of losing it while climbing ladders or rigging, they kept their specie in their sea chests.

Or hidden in her father's cabin.

If she could get to that cache, she could smuggle money to the crew. They could bribe their way to freedom or at least have comfort in prison.

That made up her mind. Regardless of what Ashford or anyone else did to her, she needed to find a way to have access to her father's cabin. She pulled free of Ross's hold and strode to the ladder just as a guard drew back the grating and held a lantern into the hold. "Mr. Ashford wants you all up top for the funeral."

Relief swept over her. This would make matters easier. She could announce her identity to Ashford and say good-bye to her father.

But could she put herself in the hands of the man whose actions had hastened her father's death?

She hesitated with one foot on the ladder. Perhaps her crew was right. Perhaps she would be safer in the hands of British authorities at a port, naval authorities, than in the hands of a privateer who answered to no one.

Ross stepped in front of her, nudging her back from the ladder. "We're not coming up."

"What d'you mean by that?" the guard demanded. "The man's your captain. Mr. Ashford wants you to pay your respects."

"We respected him when he was alive," Ross said. "We don't need to do it now with the enemy reading the service."

Deirdre hadn't thought much about that, how painful hearing an English voice reading Scripture over her father's canvas-wrapped body would be.

Apparently the others had. Approving murmurs rose from the *Maid*'s crew.

"You're coming up," the guard insisted. "Mr. Ashford wants it."

"And does Mr. Ashford get everything he wants?" Ross asked in a deceptively gentle tone.

The guard's laugh wasn't pleasant. "He got this pretty ship, didn't he? And back home, he's got more. Land, you know."

"*Droit de seigneur*," Ross growled.

Right of the lord to take whatever he wanted. She knew Ross thought that would be Deirdre if he found out she was female. Remembering those sleepy, golden eyes, Deirdre shivered despite the heat of the hold, and realized he was probably right.

"Tell Mr. Ashford," Ross said, "that we'll say our prayers down here."

Would they hear the splash as her father's body went into the sea? She doubted it. That might be easier for her.

"I'll tell him, Yankee." The light vanished. The grating slammed down.

Deirdre returned to her bale and sat clasping her knees. She didn't know if she was making the right decision or not. Well, she hadn't really decided; she'd let Ross decide for her. She stood, noting the increased motion of the ship. The wind had kicked up too late to save the *Maid* from capture. But not the men.

She took a step toward the ladder.

"Where do you think you're—?"

The grating opened again, interrupting Ross's question. Two guards descended the ladder, one with a lantern, both with weapons drawn. They were big, hard-faced men who looked like they could kill their own mothers before breakfast and take a hearty meal.

Instinctively, Deirdre shrank away from them. Perhaps Ross was right, and she should remain anonymous among her crew. If these villainous-looking men got hold of her . . . To protect her and keep her from exploring on her own when they were in ports, her father had made sure she knew what evil men did to women.

The guard with one hand holding a pistol, the other a cutlass, reached the bottom of the ladder. He pointed the cutlass at Ross. "Go topside," he directed in a voice like a caged bear's growl. "Now."

Ross didn't move.

"I'll tell you and the rest once more," the guard rumbled. "Up the ladder."

No one moved except for Deirdre. She took a step forward.

"No!" Ross, Blaze, and Wat cried together—too late.

With lightning speed, the guard sprang. One arm encircled Deirdre's waist, the other held his cutlass to her throat. "Go."

Deirdre swallowed. The feel of cold steel against her windpipe nauseated her.

So did the impact of what power these men had over her crew and her.

No matter what choices she made, they seemed to be the wrong ones. How could she hope to defeat even one of these men when they could slit her throat, toss her body overboard with her father's, and claim she tried to escape or attacked one of them or . . . They did not need an excuse.

One by one, the crew ascended the ladder. The murmur of voices told her that guards met them at the top. Footfalls on the berth deck indicated them moving away to the main hatch and deck.

When the last man reached the top of the ladder, the guard holding Deirdre released her and nudged her forward. "Get up there, pretty boy."

Deirdre went, silent, head bowed to avoid the beams. The air grew a bit sweeter with every step she climbed. The main deck air felt positively fresh despite the day's heat still clinging to planking and tarred lines. She inhaled deeply and caught the scent of rain on the rising wind. The sky was still cloudless, but she'd been able to smell rain hours away since she was a child. This time of year, rain could mean a storm as severe as a hurricane. With the *Maid* in the hands of men inexperienced with handling a Baltimore clipper, the situation could be deadly.

Her crew stood in a semicircle on the main deck, an armed man behind each one of them. In the middle of the crescent, her father's body, shrouded in a piece of ragged sail into which would have been sewn two cannonballs, lay atop a mess table.

Deirdre schooled her face to show no emotion as her guard pushed her between Ross and Wat. Perhaps she shouldn't look at him. Perhaps she shouldn't think of him as her father or even her captain. She should think of him as a stranger. No, an enemy. She wouldn't show grief if that were an enemy at her feet.

She raised her head and looked at the real enemies. The *Phoebe's* captain and . . . Ashford. They looked suitably solemn. She thought Ashford looked a bit uncomfortable, but figured he was a landsman not knowing how to brace his legs against the increased roll of the deck.

The deck lay silent, with everyone facing the open starboard entry port. Above them, the sails were furled. The schooner was ready for a funeral for the first time since Deirdre's mother and the twin brothers, who had never breathed, had been sent to their eternal rest in the sea.

A strangled sob rose in her throat without bidding. The snap of a loose sheet drowned the sound from bystanders. Deirdre tensed with anxiety. She felt someone's eyes upon her and looked up at Ashford. His face was expressionless, and he didn't meet her gaze, but she knew he had been the one staring at her.

She braced herself to give nothing away until she chose to.

The captain opened the book in his hands. "I am the resurrection and the life . . ."

Deirdre closed her ears to the readings from the King James Bible and other words from the traditional sailor's funeral writings. She knew them—John, Job, Psalms, Lamentations. They were beautiful and painful. She concentrated on the creak of timbers, hiss of surf, and the snap of that annoyingly loose sheet. She stared toward the horizon, darkening on one side, brilliant with sunset on the other. She stared until movement drew her attention back to her father's body. Two burly sailors grasped hold of the mess table and tilted it until the body slipped with a quiet splash into the sea he loved.

"In the sure and certain hope of the resurrection to eternal life through our Lord Jesus Christ," the captain read, "we commend to Almighty God our captain, Daniel MacKenzie, and we commit his body to the depths . . ."

Deirdre's eyes glazed with tears. She blinked rapidly, sending one tear down her cheek. Only one, but enough.

Ashford's gaze flew to her face. His golden-brown eyes met hers before she could duck her head, and he smiled.

The sea rolled the ship with a heavy swell as though protesting the addition of Daniel MacKenzie to its depths. Deidre had never been seasick in a lifetime spent at sea, but in that moment, seeing that smile, she feared that this would be the first time for her to disgrace herself in front of her crew.

"You are dismissed," the captain announced, closing his book. "Crew to duties, prisoners to—"

Ashford held up a hand before the captain, staying his words. "No one move."

Ross swore beneath his breath. Wat sighed and bowed his head. Deirdre stood still and quiet with every muscle in her body taut as stay lines.

Ashford stalked toward her, his gaze never leaving her face. She wanted to look away, but couldn't. He mesmerized her with his grace and power and purpose. That intent brought him close enough for her to smell the lemony tang of vetiver and see the shadow of a day's whisker growth. She needed all her will to remain motionless beneath the onslaught of his steady, golden gaze.

"So, MacKenzie." One corner of his mouth twitched. "What does the D stand for? Diana, Daphne, Deborah?"

Chapter 3

eirdre." She pronounced her name in a clear, smooth contralto. Standing tall and straight, she met his gaze without a flinch.

She had beautiful eyes, a pale, silvery green like new leaves, framed in long, thick lashes with gold tips that glinted in the setting sun. Her entire face was lovely, with clear, smooth skin sun-kissed golden with a charming sprinkle of freckles across her slim nose and sharp cheekbones. Her full-lipped mouth was so kissable, and her rounded chin was so smooth, Kieran wondered how anyone thought she could pass as a boy for even a moment. He had suspected her gender the instant he saw her, but from the startled looks on the faces of the *Phoebe*'s crew, they had been fooled by her height and clothes.

"I am Deirdre Elizabeth MacKenzie." Her eyes grew hard. "You just buried my father."

He flinched. "I am sorry, Miss MacKenzie." He raised one hand, tempted to caress her smooth cheek, wanting to offer her some sort of comfort.

A hand clamped on his wrist like an iron shackle. "Don't you dare touch her."

"Ross, no." Deirdre shoved the first mate with a palm to his chest.

Trenerry did not let go. The African man gripped the mate's arm and tried to haul him back.

Kieran ignored the byplay, though his arm didn't much appreciate the tug-of-war, and turned to the *Phoebe*'s captain.

"Heron," Kieran said, "return the prisoners to the hold. Except for Miss MacKenzie, of course. She will go to the quarters."

Beside Kieran, Deirdre muttered something to Trenerry, and he released his grip so quickly Kieran staggered with the roll of the ship. One of the merchantman's men laughed. Deirdre shot him a glare that stopped his mirth.

Kieran was intrigued. Apparently the captain's daughter held a great deal of control over the crew. He stored that observation for future use and turned to the three men from the *Phoebe* striding forward, cudgels ready.

Their size and weapons gave them the illusion of toughness, but most of the privateer's crew were fishermen and farmers seeking adventure and financial gain in difficult economic times. They edged between Deirdre and her father's crew and began to shepherd them toward the main hatchway.

Deirdre took a step after them, as though she intended to follow or say something more to the first mate, but Kieran curved his hand around her arm and held her back.

"Miss MacKenzie, we will drink a toast to your father's memory." He drew her closer to his side and farther from the prisoners, marveling at the tensile strength of her arm beneath a fine cotton shirt. "Is that not what one does after a funeral?"

She didn't look at him. "I'd prefer to go to my cabin."

"And I would prefer to talk to you." They reached the companionway leading to the cabins. Kieran stepped back, allowing Deirdre to descend ahead of him.

She did so with ease, then paused beside a door to the right. "This is my cabin. I wish to be alone."

"I have no doubt you would." Kieran tried to infuse his tone with all the sympathy he felt for her. "But I need some information from you straightaway."

She curled her fingers around the handle of the cabin door. "What information could you possibly need from me straightaway?"

"The ship's manifest."

"Schooner."

He blinked. "What?"

"This is a schooner, a Baltimore clipper to be precise, not a ship."

Some vague memory of his father telling him something similar ran through his head, ignored like most things his father considered important and Kieran didn't want to know.

"Schooner. Ship. Neither matters." He held up a hand in protest. "I don't need to know about the type of vessel this is. I need to know about what is in the hold."

"Of course." Her upper lip curled. "You need to count your spoils of war."

"I need to account to the prize court back in England, and for that, I need the cargo manifest."

She shrugged. "I have no idea about that. If it's not in the log, my father didn't have one."

Although she looked him straight in the eye, she was lying. He was not the most savvy of seamen, but he knew a captain who took as good a care of his ship as had Daniel MacKenzie would have a detailed list of the cargo somewhere, probably with the specie, something else Kieran needed to account for to the prize court.

He took a half step closer to her, noticing now that they were alone how she smelled far sweeter than the average seaman. Nothing flowery, but spicy, tangy. The scent reminded him of afternoon callers in his mother's drawing room. Sweet biscuits filled with cream. Gingersnaps. She smelled like ginger. Fascinating. Enticing. He steadied himself with one hand on the doorframe beside her and focused on the issue at hand.

"You know I will find the manifest eventually, whatever you are trying to conceal."

"I'm not trying to conceal anything." Her gaze didn't waver. "We have silk, tea, and jade aboard. All legal cargoes." She lifted the door latch. "Zeb is a free man, not part of the cargo. His papers are in my father's desk." Her chin wobbled ever so slightly. "Now if I may—" She flung open the door to a small chamber bathed in light from the setting sun—light that glinted off the blades of two weapons hanging on the bulkhead.

Kieran wrapped his arm around her waist and hauled her back before she crossed the threshold. "I think not. I need to search that cabin before you are in there alone."

Once he knew the cabin belonged to the captain's daughter, not the first mate, he should have realized what he sought could be in there.

"I will be as quick as possible."

"Do as you like. I suppose I can expect nothing else." She shoved his arm from her middle and faced the aft cabin. Her shoulders rose and fell on an exhalation with too many hitches in it to be a sigh, and too even to be a sob. Kieran guessed she wanted to cry. She would not weep in front of him. Keeping her back to him, she stepped over the coaming and onto the red Turkey carpet, then went straight to the log still lying open on the table. "I need to make note of this day."

"You may." He moved up behind her. "Will you also make a list of the crew's Christian names?"

"Ask them yourself if you want them." She traced her finger along the list of initials.

"I've never seen a list of crew without more information about the men noted."

His father kept detailed notes on each of his crew in his desk at home and sent a copy with the vessel.

Kieran braced himself with one hand gripping the smooth wooden back of the desk chair beside her. "Did your father use initials to protect your identity?"

She nodded, keeping her head down. Light gleamed in her hair, a flame bright enough to shine in the dark.

Kieran tucked his free hand into his pocket so he didn't touch those bright tresses. "Why did he not simply leave you ashore?"

"I'd have just signed aboard another vessel."

"But the risk!" Kieran released the chair and began to prowl the cabin, seeking the brandy he had seen earlier. Thinking of how he would feel were his sisters in a similar situation, alone and vulnerable in the middle of the ocean, he was more inclined toward breaking the decanter against something than drinking its contents. Anger against a dead man was a ridiculous waste of energy, but he was angry with Daniel MacKenzie for risking the safety, the virtue, the life of his daughter.

Kieran yanked open a cupboard. "Did he not consider that you might get captured?"

"We didn't know England would drive the United States to war."

"That's not good enough." Kieran jerked out the brandy decanter and slammed the door. "England has been impressing American sailors for ten years." The ship rolled. Kieran staggered, banging one shoulder painfully into a bulkhead. He clenched his teeth against an exclamation and continued as though nothing had happened. "What if they had done that to you?"

"I'd have gone into the British Navy?" She sounded tired, bewildered. "I'd have been a boy named David MacKenzie. Or maybe Daniel."

"Nonsense." He spun on his heel. "You would have ended up fodder for their . . . entertainment, since you would never have passed as a boy."

She faced him and stood with her legs spread and hands in her pockets, chin jutting and shoulders back, the stance of a defiant youth.

"I've passed as a boy in a hundred ports for twenty-two of my twenty-three years."

Kieran laughed. He let his gaze flick down her body, realizing she must bind her breasts somehow. What a waste for a woman to feel the need to deny her sex.

He crossed the four feet from cupboard to table and leaned against a chair back for support. "I think every sailor in those ports need spectacles. You look like a woman to me."

She met his eyes for an instant, then ducked her head and slumped against the edge of the table, balanced with her palms flat on the surface. "I may look like one to you, but I'm terrible at acting like one."

"That missing year?" Gently, Kieran set the squat brandy decanter between the fiddle boards to hold it upright. "You said you have been playacting for twenty-two . . . Or was that your first year of life?"

She shook her head. "I was born at sea. But after my mother died, my father—" She snapped her teeth together hard enough for Kieran to hear the click. Her lips clamped together into a firm line that would have been hard save for the fullness of her lips.

Kieran lifted his hand and traced the line with a fingertip. "Keep talking. Your father what?"

She closed her eyes and shook her head. "It doesn't matter now."

"I think it does, but we don't need to talk more now." He rounded the table, intending to draw out a chair for her, remembered it was bolted to the deck, and simply stood behind her. "Sit down. I will have someone inspect your cabin for weapons so you can be private there."

Aware she remained standing, curled forward over the table, he covered the distance to the companionway in a few long strides and climbed far enough to call for Heron to send someone trustworthy down.

Heron himself appeared from what should have been the quarterdeck, but wasn't raised above the main deck. "What is it, sir?"

"I need to search Miss MacKenzie's cabin for weapons before she can be allowed in there." Sensing movement behind him, Kieran turned his head and saw her standing in the main cabin doorway. "And someone to keep an eye on her while it's done."

"I'll send down Teague." Heron looked past Kieran. "Perhaps we should take her over to the *Phoebe* now."

Kieran gave Heron a cold look and returned to Miss MacKenzie. She blocked the doorway to the main cabin, her knuckles white from her grip on the frame. "Are you going to steal my personal effects?"

"We are not thieves."

Before she cast him a look of contempt powerful enough to shrivel him, he knew that was a ridiculous claim on his part. To her, they looked like thieves. Thieves and murderers, however indirectly they had caused her father's death.

"We have a letter of marque from the Crown to take enemy ships." He leaned against her cabin door, arms crossed over his chest, as though settling for a comfortable cose, when, in truth, he was trying to maintain his balance on the strengthening roll of the deck, a problem she didn't appear to suffer. "That makes this taking an act of war, not thievery. Your country is doing the same." He laughed. "You have to have privateers. You don't have a navy."

"We wouldn't need either if Great Britain would behave like the civilized country it boasts of being." Her nostrils flared as though she smelled something foul—more unpleasant than any ship reeked, however well maintained. "I've seen the worn-out hulks you all place your French prisoners of war in. Will that be our fate?"

"We are returning to England. Plymouth, to be precise. I expect that means Dartmoor." The name of the prison built high on the barren lands in Devonshire tasted foul.

Since the prison had been built three years earlier to house French prisoners, Kieran's mother and sisters had assisted neighbors in organizing charity functions to purchase blankets and soap and other basic necessities for the men housed there probably for the duration of the war. The vicar and curate returned from making the deliveries with tales of how dank and dark the walled village of barracks appeared.

"Your crew will be sent there." He might as well be telling her that her crew was going to die a painful death. "You will be treated as a noncombatant prisoner of war and sent to live with a family approved by the Crown until you can be returned to America."

She jerked as though he had struck her. "Where? Near the prison?"

"Possibly, but you could be sent anywhere in England."

Her face paled, and she pressed one hand to her mouth. Before Kieran could ask if she were about to be ill, Teague dropped down the ladder without benefit of the rungs.

"What d'you want from me, sir?"

"Keep Miss Mackenzie down here and everyone else up top." Kieran opened the door behind him and swung himself inside.

The space was so small he could reach everything without taking a step. Bunk, chest beneath, hanging shelf above, table large enough for one made up the furnishings. The porthole was too small for anyone larger than a child to fit through. A single drawer in the desk revealed plain paper, pens, and ink. He noticed nothing like the items he had seen in his sister's desks—notebooks of friends' directions, half-written correspondence, saved letters. The shelf above bunk and table offered a wide selection of books, a miniature of a woman who looked so much like Deirdre she was likely her mother, and a green jade carving of a dragon. The chest held clothes. Male clothing. Some of it was fine, intended for special occasions, including silver buckles for the pair of well-made shoes. But not so much as a ribbon for her hair lay amid the shirts, breeches, and waistcoats. Not so much as a flower pressed between the pages of a book suggested she bore, or had ever harbored, tender feelings for a man. Her life appeared too unnatural for Kieran to comprehend. She must even go so far as to tie her plait with a length from the ball of string in the chest.

Kieran smiled at that. "Trying a little too hard not to be feminine, my girl."

Even he tied his hair back with a length of black velvet ribbon. But thinking of why she worked at minimizing her womanly appearance sobered him. Baffled and appalled that any man could allow his beautiful daughter to play the boy aboard a ship of men, isolating her from her sex, Kieran rose and removed the weapons from the bulkhead. With their jeweled handles, their value lay more in their cost than ability to attack anyone. He took them nonetheless. At the last minute, he also grabbed the dragon. It was heavy enough to smash in someone's head. Likely his.

As he had done in the main cabin, he looked for hidden compartments in search of the specie the ship was surely carrying, concealed drawers or a false bottom to the trunk. Again, his efforts proved fruitless. The trunk's false bottom was empty.

Defeated, wondering how he would explain a lack of gold or, at the least, silver coin to the prize board if he couldn't find it, he left the cabin.

Teague and Deirdre stood as Kieran had left them, still as statues, not looking at one another. Deirdre glanced from Kieran's face to the items in his hands, then shrugged and focused on something behind him.

"May I leave, sir?" Teague's spaniel eyes pleaded for mercy.

Kieran shook his head. "You will stand watch here until I arrange a schedule with Heron." He turned to Deirdre. "I will set a guard before your door—"

"Do you think I'm going to escape and jump overboard?" Her upper lip curled.

"The guard," Kieran continued as though she hadn't interrupted him, "is for your protection, to keep others out and not you in."

"I've never needed a guard before."

"And you shouldn't need one now, but you are no longer the captain's daughter." Kieran stepped out of the doorway, giving her clear access to her cabin. "Someone will bring you supper in a while."

"I don't want anything from you." Without a backward glance, she stalked into her cabin and slammed the door.

Kieran headed for what would now be his quarters. "I think you want a number of things from me—like your freedom and your ship back and your crew released."

In that moment, he wished he could give her what she wanted. Privateering was supposed to be enjoyable with its promises of riches that had nothing to do with his father's wealth. A capture was supposed to make him feel successful, proud.

He reached for a glass nested in a rack on the bulkhead and pulled the stopper from the brandy bottle. Drinking to excess was one vice he had never acquired, but this evening, he splashed a generous measure of the amber liquid into the crystal and raised it to his lips.

"A toast to Captain MacKenzie and a cargo of China silk."

"How much have you had to drink?" Captain Heron appeared in the doorway.

"None. Yet." Kieran downed half the contents of the glass and gasped. "That's terrible."

The liquor burned down his gullet and into his stomach, raw and tannic. The ship rolled in one direction and his stomach twisted in the other.

"Not another storm." He couldn't stop the groan.

Heron chuckled. "This is a moderate swell. Now what do you intend to do about this young lady?"

"Guard her." Kieran speared his fingers into the hair over his ears, felt the scar, and dropped his palms to his knees. "We want no one getting the wrong ideas about her, and we need to watch her. She's acting calm, but she's angry. Understandably. This ship was her home, her life. The crew is her family. And we have just taken it all away from her."

"You can't think of it that way." Heron poured himself a measure of brandy and sat. He merely sipped at his drink. "It's war."

"I do not make war on women." Restless, Kieran rose and prowled the cabin in the little space available. The breeze coming through the stern windows felt good this time of day, cooling in the evening. He sat on the green broadcloth cushions of an armchair, one knee drawn up. "I remembered from what we were told when receiving our letters of marque regarding prisoners, but I don't know what sort of people take in noncombatant prisoners."

Heron shrugged. "Usually tradesmen. Someone the authorities trust."

"You would think they would use those of us with land, something to lose if we consort with the enemy."

Heron cleared his throat. "I suppose some have taken in noncombatants, but not an American for your family, not with your mother being a Yankee."

"After thirty years, they would question my mother's loyalty to Britain?"

Heron shifted, poured himself more brandy, though his glass wasn't half empty. "Kieran, the loyalty of the prince of Wales has been questioned. Of course they'll wonder about your mother's loyalty now, regardless of her rank."

"I had no trouble getting this letter of marque using my father's name." Suddenly weary, Kieran covered his eyes with one hand. "We need to talk about splitting up the crew and the prisoners. I want Trenerry where I can keep an eye on him. That means here."

"On his own ship? That isn't wise. Of course, you staying here isn't—"

"And Miss MacKenzie needs to keep her own cabin."

"Kieran, with you aboard . . . ahem . . ."

Kieran lowered his hand to fix Heron with a glare. "I do not deserve my reputation with females."

But a six-month old-scar on his ear reminded him that no one believed him. On the contrary, his own family believed the worst of him.

Because he had been so irresponsible in other ways.

Even in the twilight, Heron's flush showed. "From what your father told me before he set you aboard, leaving you here with Miss MacKenzie is . . . unadvisable."

Kieran gave a rude opinion of what his father said. Then he sighed. "He's wrong, whatever you choose to believe. I've never dishonored a lady in my life."

"It's the truth people believe that is the problem."

Kieran's hand balled into a fist. He wished he could shove the words back down Heron's throat. He wished the older man wasn't right. He should return to the *Phoebe* to preserve what reputation Miss MacKenzie possessed. But leaving the prize meant someone else would stay in this cabin. Others would have access to search for the manifest and specie, one of which at the least must be aboard. Others might not be so honest about reporting its find. If coin did exist aboard and the prize court learned of it yet found none, Kieran and everyone aboard the *Phoebe* could be accused of trying to steal from the Crown. He didn't want to know the consequences of trying to cheat the Crown from its full share of a prize, no doubt far worse than his supposed indiscretions.

"I stay here." Kieran spoke with the most certainty he had felt since their lookout spotted the merchantman.

"Then Miss Mackenzie will come aboard the *Phoebe*." Heron's tone held steel.

"She stays here."

After all, Kieran would bet anything she knew where her father's ledgers and gold were hidden.

"That's an order," he added for good measure.

Heron glared at him, mouth grim. "Your father ordered me to keep you out of trouble. In this situation, that means keeping a single female as far away from you as possible."

Hurt piercing through him, Kieran wanted to lash out, break something, since he could never strike the older man. He wanted to curse everyone who doubted him. Most of all, he wanted to curse himself for allowing his reputation to go too far to save the good name of a lady who didn't deserve his fealty.

With a calm he did not feel, he rose and stared down at Heron. "You work for me." He spoke at a measured pace with a quiet voice. "You do not work for my father."

"He hired me." Heron stood, but was still half a head shorter than Kieran.

Kieran smiled. "And the moment he learns that you have gone along with my privateering scheme, he will ensure you never work for anyone else. But this prize alone should give you the comfortable retirement you want, if we make no mistakes."

"And keeping Miss MacKenzie where you are wouldn't be a mistake?" Heron glanced in the direction of the other cabin. "Her host family will never believe her fit for polite company once they learn where she's been."

"I have my reasons for keeping her here." He looked at Teague, stone-faced in the companionway. Even if Kieran closed the door, he had no doubt the young seaman would listen. Gossip picked up from an overheard conversation between the privateer's owner and the captain would doubtless earn him extra tots of rum from his shipmates. Talk of a potential cache of gold coin could get them all murdered in their beds. With coin in hand, a man did not need to wait for the prize court before he was paid his share of the capture.

"Let me think about this." Kieran wanted space to walk, fresh air in which to think. With the way the ship rolled beneath him, he would probably fall on the deck like the landsman he still was.

He perched on the bench seat beneath the stern windows instead. A fresh breeze blew across his face, smelling of salt water clean and crisp, and not bilge water, mildew, and bodies unable to bathe in more than a cursory fashion. He took several deep breaths to bring himself calm, to clear his head.

He would never dishonor a female. He had two sisters he loved dearly and would kill anyone who dishonored one of them, so how could anyone think he would do so to another lady? But he liked women, their soft voices, their smooth skin, their sweet scents. He liked to hear them laugh and never minded when they cried, other than needing to comfort them. He appreciated the different way they viewed the world, how they cared about family and children and making the world around them comfortable. He appreciated intelligent women and never doubted their capabilities.

In turn, women liked him. He was good-looking, from a fine family, and, when his father didn't withhold his allowance, wealthy. He stood to inherit more. Some ladies might even care about him beneath his appearance and noble birth. Most considered him a prize to be won like a merchantman on the high seas. They went to great lengths in their attempts to capture him, including sneaking into his bed. He had safeguarded himself against such traps as best he could, but his reputation as a roué grew until his father insisted he marry.

Miss Joanna Rutledge was perfect for his wife—or so he thought. She had turned out to be a perfect disaster for what was left of his good name. Thanks to her, association with him would ruin the reputation of any female caught in his presence except for his wife.

His wife.

No, he would not allow his mind to go there. He hadn't exchanged more than a hundred words with Deirdre. For all he knew, her reputation did not deserve to be preserved. But neither did it deserve to be harmed further. Life as a noncombatant prisoner of war would be difficult, housed with strangers who were not always kind to their charges. With an ocean between their countries, she might be stranded in England until the end of the war. He had taken everything from her, including her father, however indirectly. Giving her a future was the least he could do to make up for his actions. Preserving, perhaps even restoring, some of his honor would help his family, his sisters' matrimonial prospects, his mother's standing in the community. His father might even forgive him for turning the *Phoebe* into a privateer and bringing home a rich prize that included a female crewman.

He had really and truly lost his reason, and he saw no alternative.

He shot to his feet and strode to the doorway.

"Where are you going?" Heron asked.

"To ask Miss MacKenzie to do me the honor of becoming my wife."

Chapter 4

Alone in her cabin, Deirdre slumped on her bunk, her back to the bulkhead, her knees drawn to her chest. She hugged her legs and willed herself not to weep. If she started, she might never stop, or, worse, might begin to howl like a wounded wolf.

She hadn't felt so alone, so isolated from everyone and everything she loved, since the year she spent at boarding school, not even after her mother died. Then she had her father and crew like Wat to comfort her. Now she could reach out to none of them for solace.

For the first time in ten years, she understood why her father wanted her to learn life on shore. He wanted her to have a family of her own, a husband, children, those she could turn to when he died.

But she hated life on land, the idle uselessness of her days. She couldn't imagine loving a landsman and figured she had lots of time to find a man as her mother had, a sea captain who would take her with him on his journeys. She never expected Father to die at only forty-nine years.

Knowing the slap-hiss of the waves against the hull would cover the sound, she pounded her fists on her mattress. Her chest ached from holding in her pain. Her thoughts shredded around self-recriminations, memories, and attempts to make plans.

The disaster had been her fault. She had failed to recognize the *Phoebe* for what it was. She had disobeyed her father and not gone below. She was a woman and therefore would not be allowed to join her crew in prison, be the glue that held them together for her father's sake, organize them, lead them out of captivity and back to freedom.

The sole solution was to get the crew free before they reached England. Bermuda was the only location that made escape possible, with its harbor full of ships from myriad countries.

She had two days to get Ashford to trust her enough to leave her alone in the main cabin. She had made a start, had told him more about herself than she intended. But she didn't know what else to do. He made her uncomfortable with the way he looked boldly into her eyes and stared at her lips, touched her lips.

She touched her fingers to her lips. Why would he stare at them? They were so fat, like someone had punched her mouth or she'd been stung by bees. Hideous. Maybe that was why he stared. He'd never seen a female who looked like her.

Deirdre had seen English ladies on the visits they'd made to London before President Jefferson put an embargo on shipping between England and America. They were so pretty with their fair skin and dainty hands, their curled hair and filmy dresses. She hadn't owned a dress for six years, not since that London trip.

London, where her father had deposited funds in a British bank. Proof of that deposit also lay in the secret compartment. Once in England, if she could get to the capital and that gold, she could bribe her way to freedom.

And leave her crew behind?

No, she had to get them free first. But how could she if she were a prisoner herself? They were sailing to Plymouth. Far from London.

If all the *Maid*'s crew ended up on the *Phoebe*, she wouldn't be able to help them before they lay behind Dartmoor's walls.

She drummed her fingers on her knee. So, how could she keep the men aboard this vessel?

The schooner dipped and rolled, dipped and rolled, timbers and lines creaking to the wind that should have saved the clipper earlier. Shouts penetrated the deckhead, telling her that someone was giving orders to take in sail for the night. The *Maid* pitched and yawed, slapping the waves from stem to stern instead of its earlier even roll. Whoever was issuing the sail instructions didn't know how to manage the sails on a clipper, with its slanted masts. Few men did. Not enough of the fast vessels existed. They'd broach her if they weren't careful, snap a mast or even capsize her.

She scrambled to her feet, prepared to give orders on how to draw in the sails in a way that kept the schooner secure, its rigging intact. But a cough sounding outside her door reminded her that she had a guard who would probably not let her on deck.

In the moments she hesitated, the clipper settled back into the gentle swells, rocking like a giant cradle.

Deirdre relaxed, a plan growing in her mind. She realized that she should have listened to Heron and Ashford talking. It was possible with her ear pressed to the bulkhead that adjoined her father's cabin. But she hadn't, and now Ashford was there alone. She had heard Heron bid him goodnight.

That man, that stranger, was going to sleep in her father's bunk. The idea brought the fight back to her soul. She would defeat this man or die trying.

⁀৩

Deirdre woke to a cloudy blue sky and the feel of a blanket spread over her. Someone had covered her where she'd fallen asleep curled into a corner of her bunk. Shivering despite the sultry air, she huddled beneath that blanket and tried not to think about the man who had likely come into her cabin while she slept, kindly intentions or not. Her stomach rumbled with hunger, but she couldn't bear the idea of facing a day without her father presiding over the breakfast table. A stranger would sit there, aristocratic and self-assured of his place and ownership. She'd be tempted to toss hot coffee into his face.

Oh, but hot coffee!

She smelled it and heard the rattle of the silver service. She couldn't let this interloper take all of her father's coffee.

She tossed off the blanket and rose. She needed to comb and braid her hair again, change into a shirt that wasn't crumpled. She wished she could wash. Her face felt sticky, her eyes crusty. She must have cried in her sleep—silently, she hoped. But no one would provide her . . .

She rubbed sleep from her eyes and saw water in a pitcher, squat to keep it from tipping over, sitting atop the tiny table in the corner of her cabin.

She happily made use of the water, washing her face and torso, then opened her chest for a fresh bandeau to bind her breasts.

After struggling to tie the strip of cloth behind her back, she yanked a shirt over her head, fastened the two buttons at the neck, and grasped the door handle. An instant before she exited her cabin, she remembered she should be polite to him, the English privateer who was no sailor. She must be more than polite. She should be friendly, cooperative, whatever necessary to get him to trust her enough to leave her alone in her father's cabin.

Making her face relax, if not display a smile, she opened the door.

One of the burly young seamen from the Phoebe straightened from his slouch against the bulkhead. "Miss MacKenzie." He raised one hand as though about to salute. "Mr. Ashford said for you to go straight in to him when you woke." He tapped once on the main cabin door, then pushed it open. "Miss MacKenzie, sir."

Ashford chuckled. "Thank you, Teague. I thought the coffee would wake her. Miss MacKenzie, do come in."

Her stomach suddenly knotting, she stepped over the coaming and entered the cabin. Ashford moved from behind his chair and gave her a courtly bow, sending his hair sliding over one shoulder.

So odd, that swath of dark hair in this age of short hair being fashionable. It looked soft, too, with just the hint of a wave. Experiencing the odd desire to push it away from his face, she clasped her hands behind her back. "Good morning, Mr. Ashford."

He made a motion with one hand, and the cabin door closed behind her. "Do please sit down." He gripped the back of one chair as though he were pulling it out from the table.

The gesture was absurd with the chair bolted to the deck. It didn't sit well with Deirdre either. Men weren't courtly to her. They were mostly respectful of her because her father was the captain, but the only time politeness carried beyond common courtesy, the man wanted something from her.

This man wanted something from her.

Wary, she sidled past him and slid onto the chair. Bowls of porridge stood between sandbags that kept them from slipping, and fiddle boards held the coffeepot in place. Molasses-laced oatmeal and fresh coffee made her mouth water enough to relax the tension in her belly. Instinct encouraged her to grab her spoon and dig in, fill her mug and gulp in the event these treasures were snatched away like the life she had known for the past ten glorious years.

She kept her hands clasped on her knees, waited for him to sit.

Ashford remained behind her chair. "Did you sleep well, Miss MacKenzie?"

"Well enough, thank you."

"I was concerned when I heard you weeping."

"I have no recollection of doing anything so weak."

"Weak to cry when your father has just died? Not at all." He moved toward his chair at last, brushing the tips of his fingers across her cheek as he passed.

She dug her own fingertips into her knees. That touch brought back her taut belly. Coffee and porridge didn't smell that good after all.

He poured coffee into both their mugs. "That'll make the world look better. I'm not sure about the porridge, though. Never touch the stuff at home, but eggs won't do out here at sea."

Deirdre sipped at her coffee, appreciating its warmth. "We can be in Bermuda in two days. You can get eggs there."

"Hmm." Ashford grimaced around a mouthful of porridge, swallowed, then shook his head. "Heron does not want to go there. May I give him a reason why we should, other than the one I . . . Well, I will get to that later."

A plan began forming in Deirdre's mind. "There's a storm coming."

"How do you know?"

"It's September in the Caribbean, and I can smell rain."

"You are crazed. No one smells rain."

Deirdre shrugged and decided to make herself eat her oatmeal. She needed her strength.

"Are you ever wrong?" he asked.

"Sometimes. Storms change direction. But can't you feel the air and these swells?"

"Yes . . . I can."

A tightness in his voice drew Deirdre's attention. She glanced up to find him with his fingers white-knuckled around his spoon, and his face pale.

"Do you get seasick, Mr. Ashford?" She couldn't keep the incredulity out of her tone.

His sun-bronzed skin flushed. "Not very admirable, is it?"

His apparent discomfort made her soften her response. "Some storms make even the most seasoned sailors sick. My father—" Her throat closed without warning. She dropped her spoon and would have sprung to her feet and dashed from the cabin, but she had to stay, had to be nice. She pressed her fingers to her lips to stifle the sob wanting to emerge.

He fixed his sleepy gaze on her and reached out one hand to cover hers lying on the table. "I will not think the less of you if you weep in front of me. I would weep if I lost my father."

The idea of him having a father he considered worth weeping over distracted Deirdre enough to control her grief. She retrieved her spoon from the table and her hand from beneath his, and made herself resume eating and conversing. "What are you going to do with my crew?"

"We are setting half of them on the *Phoebe*."

"Which half?" She tried not to sound so interested.

"Which half do you recommend?"

She stared at him. "You'd take my recommendation?"

Kieran smiled. "Heron tells me that his men had some difficulty with your rigging. We could use one or two of your men to assist."

Deirdre sent a prayer of thanks to heaven.

"You're not afraid we'd sail you right into the Chesapeake?"

"Not at all." Ashford poured more coffee into their mugs. "I am not wholly useless on a ship. The *Phoebe* has a fine navigator, and he's shown me how it works. I will do the navigation here."

"You're staying aboard until we reach England?" Deirdre shifted in her chair, suddenly uncomfortable. "Do you think that's wise? I mean . . ." Her cheeks burned, and she jabbed at her oatmeal congealing in its bowl. "I'm a single female without a chaperone, and you . . ."

He kept looking at her mouth.

"Finish your breakfast, and we will talk about that."

Deirdre pushed her bowl, sandbags and all, away from her. "I'm finished." She picked up her coffee mug and carried it to the bench seat below the stern window.

That was where she always sat and talked over business with her father. She didn't realize her mistake until Ashford joined her. The seat was plenty wide enough for two people to sit comfortably, and Ashford sat a discreet six inches away. She still felt as though he sat right beside her. Ridiculous. Irrational. Uncomfortable. She couldn't move now.

"Would you disapprove of Ross Trenerry going to the *Phoebe*?"

"Disapprove?" she repeated to stall for time and work out why he'd asked that question.

"Disapprove, object to . . ." He shrugged. "Would you grieve his absence?"

"Would I—oh." She thought about Ross defending her after her father's funeral, and understood what Ashford was asking. "Of course I'd dislike him being on another vessel. He's a dear friend. We've been on ships together for seven years. But he's nothing more to me, not that that's any of your concern."

"Actually, it is. I could not ask you this if he were . . . if you and he have an understanding."

She lowered her coffee mug to her knee. "An understanding?"

"A promise, a betrothal."

"To Ross?" That made her laugh.

Ashford arched one dark brow. "I would not let him hear you laugh at that idea. It might break his heart."

"Not Ross. He's like a brother to me, and I his sister."

"I have sisters, Miss MacKenzie. No man looks at his sister like Ross looks at you."

Deirdre started to deny his implication, but oblique words of her father's came back to her, a caution not to spend so much time exclusively with Ross. She had thought her father meant she would make the crew jealous if the captain's daughter picked out one man, even the mate, particularly. Now she realized her father meant she must not give Ross hope when she thought of him like a brother.

"No promises to Ross or anyone else." She cast him a sidelong glance. "Not that it's any of your concern."

"It may be." He removed her cup from her hands, rose, and set it between the fiddle boards. Instead of returning to the bench, he stalked around the cabin, bracing one hand on a chair back, then the other on the bulkhead. He circumnavigated the room until once again he dropped onto the bench seat beside her. Closer to her.

Deirdre tried to edge away from the heat of his nearness. The cabin was too stifling for contact with a friend, let alone a stranger, despite a brisk wind blowing through the stern windows.

He gripped her hands, holding her in place with the light pressure of his long fingers and the intensity of his gaze. "Miss MacKenzie, Deirdre, I need to ask you a question to which I need a swift response. But do not act too hastily. It's important you consider all the consequences one way or the other, even though I am fairly certain you will wish to say no." Speech delivered all in a rush, he paused to draw breath.

Deirdre stared at him, eyes wide, brows elevated. "I have no idea what you are talking about, but I'm pretty sure you don't need to hold onto me like I'm going to fly out the window while you ask it."

"Perhaps you will not, but I might." He released her hands and took up a stance at the table, his back to her. His shoulders rose and fell with his audible sigh. "Miss MacKenzie, will you do me the honor of becoming my wife?"

"Will I—*what?*"

Surely she had misunderstood him.

"Will you . . . marry me?" He faced her then, his hands shoved into his pockets, his color heightened.

Deirdre shook her head, still unable to believe her ears. "You must be mad."

"Quite likely." The corners of his mouth tilted up, but the smile didn't reach his eyes.

"We don't know one another, and we are enemies by the declarations of our respective governments. I'm your prisoner."

"That is precisely why I have made my proposal." He removed his hands from his pockets and returned to sit beside her. "You are in a peculiar situation being a noncombatant, and marriage is the only way I know to protect you. As my wife, you will not have to go wherever the authorities send you. You will be free to come to my house under the protection of my family. You will have all the rights and privileges of a—of your rank."

Rights and privileges. The words sounded like gold, frankincense, and myrrh laid in her lap, gifts worth a king's ransom. Yet one observation she had made on that long-ago London visit was that married ladies in England had few rights and privileges. They seemed to travel with no less than one servant in tow, and everything belonged to their husbands.

Everything she had owned now belonged to Kieran Ashford. But if she got hold of the specie and was still independent, she could help her crew.

"From what I know," she said, "I'll be better off as the prisoner guest of some tradesman's family than as a wife."

"Not true." He drummed his fingers on his knees. "My family is somewhat above guarding our wives like a sultan's harem. That means they enjoy more freedom than those in the middle classes."

"In other words, you're landed gentry."

"We have land, yes."

"How much?"

He shrugged. "I have no idea. Enough to keep the wolves from the door."

"And outfit a privateer." Deirdre leaned against the bulkhead beneath the stern windows and crossed her arms, watching him through her lowered lashes. "In other words, you have enough wealth that your family can do as it pleases without recriminations."

He ducked his head and began to pick nonexistent lint from his breeches. "There are limitations to what we can get away with."

A light flared in Deirdre's mind, a suspicion that perhaps this man had crossed over the edge of those limitations and gotten himself sent to sea. The revelation gave her encouragement and made her warier at the same time.

"Marrying the enemy isn't crossing that line?" She pressed for more details, information that would benefit her and her men.

He kept his head bent and remained silent for several moments. Through the open windows, she heard Ross shout, "Not that sheet, you fool."

Ah, dear Ross, not the most diplomatic of men, was berating one of the Englishman on his poor handling of the schooner's sails. How she longed to run up, calm him, soothe the Englishman's no doubt ruffled feathers, make certain everyone was all right.

She kept her attention focused on Kieran Ashford.

He heaved a gusty sigh and glanced at her before flicking his gaze to the window behind her. "I have a reputation for being a . . . Lothario. That is, a debaucher of ladies."

With his looks, she could believe it.

"Is it deserved?" She asked the question, though the answer had nothing to do with her.

"I have never seduced a lady in my life." The heightened color returned to his face. "But some have lied in an effort to get me to the altar."

"I have no interest in going to the altar with an Englishman, so you don't need to worry about me claiming I've been ruined by you."

"It may not matter." He surged to his feet and began that restless pacing around the cabin again. "I need to stay aboard this ship because it is my prize, but if I do not send you to the *Phoebe*, your reputation will be ruined."

Deirdre snorted. "What does my reputation matter now?"

"How you are treated in England." He ran his hand along the teakwood bulkhead. "As the captain's daughter, you can be presumed to have been protected. As a female alone in the world, and with me this close." He thumped on the bulkhead between the cabins. "The middle and lower classes are even crueler to women they believe have fallen than the *haut ton*."

"The what?"

"The upper classes. Aristocrats. Noblemen."

"So you think I would be treated badly wherever I am housed." She studied his profile, wishing he would look at her so she could read his eyes, discover how truthful he was being. "But if I'm married to you when I get to England, I will be treated well, with rights and privileges otherwise denied me?"

"You will."

On alert for the flaw behind his claim, she demanded, "And what do you get out of marrying me?"

He turned his head and gave her a smile that reached his eyes. "I gain the right to go home with some of my honor restored."

Deirdre emitted a scoffing bark of laughter. "I find it hard to believe that this schooner and cargo aren't enough to make up for you ruining some English lady's reputation."

"It is a long story."

"We have a long voyage."

"But we need to decide before we bypass Bermuda. It is our last opportunity to find a vicar to wed us, and we must be wed before we reach England and you are taken into custody as a noncombatant prisoner."

And she didn't want to bypass Bermuda. Bermuda offered possibilities for getting free.

"That's two or three days away, and I have nowhere to go."

And every bit of information helped defeat the enemy.

He leaned on the chart table, his palms flat on the smooth surface behind him. "My father thought I should wed, so I got myself engaged to a beautiful and sweet young lady." He spoke fast, belying the casualness of his stance. "Turned out she was being a little too sweet to someone else, but accused me of being the father."

Deirdre felt a ridiculous urge to laugh at his obvious discomfort. Instead, she asked, "And you weren't?"

"I was not." He spat out the words. "But no one believed me. There was trouble, and my father said, among other things I would rather not repeat, not to darken his doorway until I had done something honorable."

"And there's the rub of this, Mr. Ashford. Is marrying me honorable?" Suddenly restless, Deirdre rose and began to prowl around the cabin, making sure she touched nothing, looked at nothing in the event her gaze strayed too long to the secret compartment. "I am not a respectable candidate for a wife for a rich Englishman. And even if I were, what happens when the war is over? You will be stranded with me and I you. Do you think I want to live on land the rest of my life?"

"As the daughter of a captain who owned his vessel, you are an acceptable enough wife." He straightened as much as the low deck beams allowed and swaggered to the window seat.

Deirdre clutched at the edge of the chart rack and waited for him to explain the rest.

"As for being stranded with one another . . ." He tilted his head as though studying something she couldn't see. "Once you provide me with an heir and a second son for security, we are free to go our separate ways. You would be socially ruined in England if Parliament grants us a divorce, but I doubt that matters to you. You can sail to India or Australia for all I care. Once the war is over, I will buy you your own ship or schooner or—"

"Stop." Deirdre flung up her hands in protest and whirled to fully face him. "What was that about an heir and an extra? Are you saying you don't intend for this to be a-a—" She choked on the next phrase, her face flaming.

He drew up one knee and rested a forearm on it, his face too bland, too innocent. "I believe the term you want is *mariage de convenable*. No, of course not. I have no intention of getting leg-shackled without some rights and privileges of my own." He rose then and closed the distance between them. "I intend to be an attentive and faithful husband until we mutually decide to go our separate ways. You will have weathered the war in comfort and a reasonable amount of freedom." His voice softened, grew husky. "And I will have done the right thing for once in my life." Shadows dimmed the gold of his eyes. He looked vulnerable, haunted, sad. The way he kept flexing his fingers against his thighs cried out his anxiety. He wasn't making an idle offer. Her answer meant a great deal to him.

Her answer should be no. Once married, he would control her life, heart, soul, and body. His notion of reasonable freedom and hers might not be the same, might not be as much independence of movement as she needed. Becoming trapped in parson's mousetrap for years, even if he didn't renege on this bargain and let her sail away, seemed risky at best. He was right in thinking she cared nothing for social ruin in England. Still, she would be laying her life into the hands of the enemy for more than the duration of the war with no guarantee that stepping into the prison of matrimony would help her free her crew from the prison in England.

She hadn't yet touched on the implications of her providing him with an heir and an extra. Thanks to how drunken sailors often behaved on the docks, she knew more about procreation than any single woman should. An image flashed into her mind, replacing couples she had glimpsed with her and Ashford, him touching her with those long, beautiful hands, kissing her, that satiny hair falling around her face—

She shivered and backed away from him. "I-I'm—let me think. I can't think." Her back collided with the door, and she pressed against it as though it were a backboard slumping girls at school had been strapped to train their spines. "Let me—think."

Surely she could find a better avenue to make up for getting them all captured and her father killed, however indirectly. She was a clever woman. At thirteen, she had managed to escape the walls of the boarding school where Father had abandoned her in an attempt to make her act like a female. She could figure out how to elude one Englishman.

"You have until we reach Bermuda to think this over." He smiled, and the deck fell away beneath her feet.

No, not from the impact of that smile on her senses. The schooner had just dropped into the trough of a wave with too little grace, and she wasn't recovering well climbing the next swell.

Heart skipping a beat, Deirdre charged to the windows. As she had focused on Ashford and his stunning proposal, the weather had begun to deteriorate. Three- and four-foot swells had turned to five- and six-foot waves with foaming crests. The wind had veered to an easterly direction and no longer swept through the open stern windows. East, the direction from which storms blew this time of year.

"What's wrong?" Ashford asked from behind her.

"Nothing yet. The wind's picking up, but the sky is still clear. It might look different from the crosstrees."

A tightness to his voice drew her attention to him. He had paled, and she recalled his mention of not being a good sailor.

For some reason, she sought to reassure him. "I think this will be little more than a squall. I don't feel the kind of drop in barometric pressure usual with a hurricane."

"Barometric pressure?" His blank look was comical. "A storm is imminent?"

"The mercury is falling, but not significantly." Deirdre pointed to the barometer mounted above the hanging shelf of books. "See that? It hasn't fallen below thirty. We're probably just catching the surf from a storm farther to our east."

"I hope so. Seeing me rolled up like a dead worm and whimpering like a baby will not incline you to accept my proposal." He braced one hand on the window frame beside her against the plunge as the schooner dropped into the next trough.

Being so close, she smelled the clean land scent of his vetiver. She turned, intending to slip away from him. The movement brought them chest to chest, him only a few inches taller than she.

Before she could dart to the side and be away across the cabin, he lowered his hand from the frame to her shoulder. "Or have you already decided your answer is no?"

"I haven't decided anything." Her throat felt strangled, her body paralyzed.

"Good," he said.

Then he kissed her.

Chapter 5

Other than the affectionate brushes of her parents' lips on her cheek or hair, Deirdre had never been kissed. Those people she had seen kissing seemed to enjoy it, but the idea of having someone else's mouth pressed to hers sounded rather disgusting. Who wanted to taste someone else's saliva, feel the heat of their breath exchanged with one's own, experience the pressure of soft, firm lips pressed against one's own?

Any woman whom Kieran Ashford kissed.

The swirling, dipping, spinning of her head, her body, the deck beneath her feet had nothing to do with the deteriorating weather. She had ridden out hurricanes with only a hint of discomfort. This contact, this melding of part of another's body to hers robbed her legs of their ability to stand on a swaying deck. She flung up her hands, grasping his shoulders for support. The schooner hurled herself off the top of a wave and dropped like a stone off a roof. Holding one another, Deirdre and Ashford careened against the bulkhead, breaking the connection of their mouths.

"I think—" Realizing her lips had formed the words but no sound had emerged, Deirdre coughed and tried again. "I think something is wrong."

Ashford smiled, his eyes sleepy. "I thought it was absolutely right."

"Not that." She shoved away from him. "I mean, that was wrong of you. But I'm talking about the *Maid*. She's not recovering like she should."

They were canted too far to port. If another wave the size of the last one struck at even the slightest wrong angle, they could capsize.

"I need to go." Not waiting for permission, she flung open the cabin door in time to see Teague racing from his guard post up the ladder to the main deck, and followed in time to find him bent double over the rail, retching. None of the *Maid*'s original crew remained on deck, but half a dozen strangers cast up their accounts into the scuppers.

She sighed. "Landlubbers. No more sense than—"

A crack overhead snapped her attention upward. A loose sheet spun in the howling wind twenty feet above. Badly tied, it allowed the mainsail to droop and catch far more wind than was safe for the rising gale.

In a shot, Deirdre launched herself into the rigging, climbing the shrouds with the ease of mounting steps. Without any rain, the lines were as dry as they ever could be. Perfectly safe. Except they weren't as taut as they should be. One sagged beneath her weight. For a moment, she swung like a pendulum, her hold jarred by the unanticipated motion.

She clenched her teeth against cursing the stupid British, who didn't know how to secure a line. If the storm worsened, those lines would come loose. Freed, sails would catch too much wind and capsize the Baltimore clipper in a heartbeat.

She paused, perched on a spar, and secured the line. Wind howled and shrieked around her. Men howled and shrieked at her, too. "Come down," she thought she heard someone shout. As if she would. She'd secure the clipper's rigging or die trying.

She reached the whipping sheet just as the first onslaught of rain struck the ship. Across two cable-lengths of water, she caught sight of the *Phoebe*, its sails properly furled, then she saw nothing but a silvery curtain of rain. Her foot slipped from a soaked shroud. For a heartbeat, it dangled in midair. She swung it hard and got a hold again. The flying sheet required both her hands. She gripped the lines with feet and knees, dove for the errant line, caught it.

"Deirdre!" Definitely her name. "For the love of heaven!"

She glanced down to see Ashford braced against a stay, scowling up at her. Even lashed with rain, his face looked green.

She grinned and tilted her head to grin at him, wondering how long he would manage not to run to the rail either.

"Get down here," he bellowed.

She shook her head at him and the half-dozen men who stood staring up at her. Ashford motioned to them, commanding them— judging by his gesticulations in her direction—to climb up and help her. Not one moved.

The schooner twisted and dipped, trying to tug the sheet from her cold hands. Deirdre returned her attention to her task. But drawing up the heavy sail alone proved more difficult than it should have, than it would have had she managed before the rain. Wet canvas weighed as much as she did, possibly more. She'd never had to raise a sodden sail alone. She needed help. A glance down told her that none of the *Phoebe*'s crew brought aboard the *Maid* were about to assist her. Kieran had even disappeared.

"Coward. You think I'd marry a man who—"

The wind caught the sodden sail. It flew to leeward, heeling the ship too far over on her beam. Water foamed over the rail, dousing the men on deck.

The *Maid* didn't right herself.

Deirdre clung to the spar and prayed for help. They were going over. Her crew locked into the hold wouldn't have a chance at survival.

Frantic, she locked her knees over a shroud and threw all her weight into hauling on the sheet. She rocked back, a line catching her shoulders and holding her in place like a chair without a seat twenty feet above a deck careening toward the sea. She had the sail furled. The *Maid* righted herself without the extra strain throwing her off balance. But she couldn't stay that way forever. Wet, the sheet slipped in her hands, tearing at even her calloused palms.

If only she had help . . .

She caught her breath. She did have help. Two long, elegant hands curled around the sheet above hers.

"Tell me what to do," Kieran Ashford shouted over the wind.

Not a coward.

Deirdre looked at Ashford with his hair whipping in the wind, his shirt plastered to broad shoulders, and wanted to be back in the cabin kissing him again. Absurd, nonsensical, dangerous thinking that. She needed to forget about those moments. She had to recover enough of her senses to give him directions. Teaching him the complexity of the knots would take too long. "Hold the sheet."

"Sheet? Oh, you mean this rope?"

Deirdre nodded, not bothering to explain that sailors never referred to lines, cables, or hawsers as ropes. At least he'd worked out that the sheet was not the sail.

Together, they hauled the line home. With a strength that surprised her in such an elegant man, Kieran—no, Ashford, the enemy—held the sheet in place while she knotted it. The sail completely furled, the *Maid* righted itself as much as it could in such a rough sea, and Deirdre prepared to descend.

"Can you manage?" she asked.

He gave her an indignant glare, then climbed down the shroud, tumbling more than jumping the last two yards. He was on his feet in an instant and staggering to the companionway beneath the quarter deck. He looked so unwell she gave him a quarter hour before she descended to the deck herself, then another five while she approached the two men at the helm.

"You can lash the wheel and go below," she explained. "There's no steering in this storm anyway. Keeping the rudder straight is the best we can do."

The men, little more than boys, exchanged glances.

"We didn't want to go without permission," the shorter of the two said.

"I'm giving you permission," Deirdre said, "from Mr. Ashford. He's unwell."

The boys laughed. "Aye, that he is. No sailor, Mr. Ashford," the taller one said.

"He's got more courage than all of you." Deirdre spoke through stiff lips.

Another exchange of glances, knowing grins.

"Aye, a real William the Conqueror." The shorter boy spoke through his mirth.

Deirdre was too cold to know if she blushed, but she didn't stay around for the Englishmen to see if she did. She turned her back on them and descended to her cabin. She needed dry clothes. When she raised her hands to unfasten her buttons, she saw that blisters crisscrossed her palms. They began to sting as soon as she noticed the abrasions.

If she suffered from the work on the sheet, Kieran's hands had to be far worse. He wasn't accustomed to that kind of labor. She could wash her hands and rub in ointment she kept for the nicks and scrapes common in life aboard ship. But he wouldn't know where it was, and infection could set in if the blisters went untreated and broke.

She flung on dry clothes, then walked into her father's cabin without knocking. Ashford had changed into dry clothes, too. Now he sat on the bunk with his head in his hands, his hair loose and obscuring his face.

"Are you ill?" she asked.

He let out a soft moan in response.

Her lips twitched. "Gets the best of us sometimes. My father always insisted tea was the best cure, but I've something better."

She opened a cupboard over the bunk and pulled out a bottle of laudanum and a jar of preserved ginger. She wished she had hot water to infuse the ginger better, but cold would have to do, and she'd have him chew the ginger. The Chinese merchant who'd sold it to her had insisted that nothing settled a sick stomach better. Going around Cape Horn, she'd tried it on a couple of the crew and found that it worked. The laudanum would make him sleep. She used a table knife to chop the ginger into a cup of water, then picked up the bottle of laudanum. It felt light. She held it up to the window and noticed that it was nearly empty. She'd procured a full bottle in Rio de Janeiro. Who had been in such pain he'd needed to use nearly a full bottle in mere weeks? Her father? Who else would have used it without her knowledge? But why?

Puzzling over that, she finished preparing the drink. At Ashford's side, she brushed back his hair and held it to his lips. Even wet, his hair was soft. His lips were white and pinched.

"What is this?" he growled. "Poison?"

"I didn't think about that."

"Too bad." He offered her a faint smile.

She forgot that she was cold.

"Drink it," she said in a husky voice.

"Yes, ma'am." He downed it, gasped, spat ginger bits back into the glass. "That was foul."

"It'll work." She took away the cup. "Now let me look at your hands."

She turned them palm up on his knees. They weren't simply blistered; the blisters had broken. She cleaned them with a cloth dipped in whiskey, which made him grumble something she was glad was unintelligible, then smeared on the salve. All the while, she tried to touch him as little as possible. Touching him wasn't sensible. She had too much of an instinct to do so. A longing to do so. That yearning was enough to keep her away.

"There," she said briskly when she was finished. "That'll do. You'll rest now."

"Will I?" He gave her a truly sleepy look and lay back on the bunk. "I believe I will."

Deirdre headed for the door.

"Wait."

She paused, not looking at him.

"Thank you."

She shrugged and left for her own cabin. There, she tucked herself into her bunk beneath warm blankets. As she buckled the straps that held her in place, she remembered that Ashford hadn't been buckled in. Well, he was a grown man. He could do it himself. She needed to be alone, to remember her father dying at the shock of being captured and her crew imprisoned. She needed to think about being stranded in England during a war that couldn't possibly last long, and would likely not end well for the United States. They would end up a British colony again, and if that happened and she helped her crew escape, they would have to become French, as America would no longer be a safe haven.

America couldn't lose. She could do her part by sending men capable of fighting back to sea . . .

A thud jerked her awake. She struggled, unable to move for a moment before remembering to unbuckle the straps. Upright, she listened for more thuds, cracks, the hiss of water rushing through a breached hull.

Nothing. Though the storm still raged, the ship rode it out with as much grace as possible. Her laden hold helped. But things happened. Spars broke free. Cargo shifted. Men fell.

"Oh." She shot out of her bunk and grabbed for the door. The guard was there, slumped on the bottom step of the ladder, asleep. She stepped past him and entered her father's cabin.

By the dim light of what the wall chronometer told her was late afternoon, she saw Ashford sprawled on the deck, motionless.

"Ashford." She dropped to her knees beside him. "Are you awake?"

She didn't think she could lift him onto the bunk if he'd knocked himself unconscious.

"I am . . . now. Winded." He rolled onto his belly and got his hands under him.

She wanted to help. She didn't want to touch him.

"I should have told you to strap yourself in."

"Never thought about it." He pushed himself to a sitting position with his back against the bunk. "*Phoebe* has fiddle boards."

"My father didn't like splinters."

"Ah, yes, that was a hazard." Ashford crossed his arms over his middle. Even in the dim light, he appeared a bit green. "Could you be so kind as to make me more of that infusion?"

"Of course." She chopped up more ginger into water and shook a few drops of laudanum into the cup. Not as much of the sleeping draft as she would have liked, but all she could get out of the bottle.

He drank it, grimacing a bit, then climbed back into the bunk and strapped himself in. "How long will this storm last?"

Deirdre glanced out the window, now frosted with salt from waves lashing the glass. "It's abating already. Nothing more than a good blow."

He groaned.

Deirdre headed for the door. She wanted to inspect the rigging, make sure nothing was blowing loose.

"Wait." Ashford spoke softly, but it was a command.

She paused.

"Will you stay and talk to me?"

She'd feel safer locked in the hold with her crew.

"Just until I fall asleep," he added.

Could she get to the gold while he slept if she remained?

Figuring it was worth a try, she pulled the cushion off the bench seat and settled on the deck. Sitting on a chair would be uncomfortable at best. On the cushion, her feet braced against the bulkhead, she sat secure enough to sway with the pitch then roll of the ship.

"You are amazing," he murmured. "You ride out this storm like it's a yachting venture down the Thames."

She shrugged. "I've barely known anything else."

"Yes, twenty-two of your twenty-three years." His tone held a smile. "What happened in that other year?"

"Nothing. That's what was so bad about it."

He chuckled. "How old were you?"

"Too old to be anything but a sailor."

"You make a good nurse."

"Not good enough to know my father was sick." Her throat closed, and she bowed her head.

"My dear girl . . ." He reached out one hand and stroked her cheek. "Tears?"

"No, I wouldn't be so weak while I'm awake."

"Don't be absurd. It's not weakness."

"But I didn't know." She heard the wail in her voice and clamped her lips shut. She took several deep breaths to calm herself. "He'd been taking laudanum. I didn't know it until I made your tonic earlier. The bottle was nearly empty."

"His heart?"

She nodded. "I saw him clutch his chest . . . He must have wanted to make it home. We were so close . . ."

"Deirdre . . ." He ran his hand down her braid, then tangled his fingers in it, pulling it apart. "I'm so sorry. I cannot undo what happened. I can't take back my actions, but I'll do my best. If you marry me, you will not entirely lose this wealth."

"My crew will still be in prison."

But she might have more freedom to get them released.

"The war won't last long. How long can your poor little country survive against the strength of Great Britain?"

He released her hair. It tumbled around her shoulders in a heavy fall that warmed her like a cloak. It felt odd and made her restless, uncomfortable. Her father would never let her cut it, though she'd begged and pleaded often. She knew he hoped that, one day, she would take up the role of a female, be a wife and mother. He wanted to stop worrying about what might happen to her in one of the ports, or the trouble that could befall her if they took on a crewman who decided not to respect her status.

"But I failed miserably on land." She spoke the words aloud she'd used to her father every time he suggested she settle down. "I tried, and I was a disaster as a lady."

Ashford said nothing for several moments, during which Deirdre noticed a discernible slackening of the wind and no rain to speak of. She suspected they would end up shrouded in fog by morning, becalmed and muffled in vaporous curtains. As long as that didn't last too long, they would come out all right, head for Bermuda and, if she managed things well, get her crew released. They could find their way to one of the numerous islands and make passage back to America from there. They would be free, and she? She would take her chances with the British. True prison, no doubt, for letting the men go. If she weren't Ashford's wife, he wouldn't be held responsible for her actions.

"Deirdre?" Her name was a rumble like a purr on his lips. "Will you tell me about that year you were not aboard ship?"

She shook her head. "It's too humiliating."

"Hmm. Then you had a poor teacher." He lifted strands of her hair and brushed them across her lips. "Who was it?"

"An entire boarding school of snobbish teachers and worse students." She licked her lips. Feeling decidedly uneasy, she started to rise.

"Oh, no, you cannot run away right now." He shifted and rested one hand on her shoulder. "I insist that you stay."

"I won't talk about school."

"All right. We'll talk about something else." She caught the flash of silver and felt as though she, too, might be suffering from mal de mer. "Like what you intended to do with this stiletto."

Chapter 6

$\mathscr{D}$eirdre squeezed her eyes shut and drew her knees to her chest. All she could do now was brazen this out. "I've always carried a stiletto in my braid. My father insisted. It's why he'd never let me cut my hair."

"Probably wise." Ashford's voice purred as though he discussed a fine Madeira. "But I insisted that all prisoners be disarmed. We accepted your honor that you had given up all weapons."

Deirdre hugged her legs. Having her honor questioned hurt like a prick from the stiletto now in enemy hands. "I didn't know if your men had enough honor to not . . . if they discovered that I'm female."

"Ah, Deirdre." He stroked her hair. "Doubting our honor doesn't excuse you not being forthcoming with us. I trusted you."

She wanted to hang her head in shame. The hank of her hair he held prevented her.

"Deirdre, look at me."

"Why should I?"

"This ship doesn't truly have a captain at present, so that leaves me to give the orders. That's an order."

Knowing she had to regain his trust, she reluctantly turned her head and looked at him. He lay on his side, propped up on one elbow. His eyes looked sleepier than usual, no doubt from the laudanum. That didn't diminish or hide the hurt. His mouth—

No, she mustn't look at his mouth and remember how it felt on hers.

She jumped to her feet, sending pain through her scalp, as she yanked her hair free of his hold. "I've obeyed, sir. I looked at you. The sea is settling, so you should feel better soon." She backed to the door. "That's all you need from me."

"For the moment." He offered her a half smile. "Go if you like."

She liked. She went. She wanted to run on deck and inspect any damage from the storm, but paused in the companionway long enough to greet the guard, who had returned to his post, looking much better. Those ill with seasickness would be missing the waves once glassy seas and a fog rolled in. She felt the cloying dampness already crawling over her skin as the clouds settled down upon the sea. But fog brought some advantages.

"We should be able to have some food cooked soon." She told the guard this because he was so thin he looked like he needed a good meal. Then an idea struck her. "Who prepared the oatmeal?"

"Riley, miss." He flushed. "Was it all right?"

"It was done well." She felt uncomfortable being called miss. "We should probably get a fire going in the galley again and make some more."

"Yes, miss. I'll ask Mr. Ashford."

"You do that." She stepped into her own cabin and shamelessly listened to the exchange.

"If Miss MacKenzie says it's safe," Ashford said, "then do so."

Good. Her plans were in motion.

She waited another quarter hour. Seated at her desk, she wrote while she waited until she smelled smoke from the galley fire, then she went on deck. No major portions of the rigging had landed on the deck, but a spar swung free, causing havoc with lines and sheets and threatening the mainsail. Her hands itched to grab a marlinespike and climb to effect repairs. No one else seemed inclined to do anything. None of the work could be executed by one person, so she activated the first step of her plan for freedom and approached the cook. No one would think a female appearing in the galley odd. Indeed, the ruddy-faced Riley didn't look in the least surprised to see her.

He offered her a shy smile. "A hot meal will go well with this damp settling in."

"Fog always makes me cold." Deirdre glanced around the galley, glad to see it was clean.

Riley hefted the broad wooden spoon with which he was stirring a pot of porridge. "Will this do?"

"On unsettled bellies, yes." She offered him her own smile. "Did the prisoners eat earlier?"

"Yes, ma'am." He looked offended. "We're not monsters. We feed our prisoners."

"Of course you're not monsters. Forgive me for suggesting you wouldn't feed them." When he appeared mollified, she continued. "Let me help you serve."

Since he didn't seem to have an assistant, Riley accepted her help, loading a heavy wooden tray with bowls of warmed oatmeal into which she suggested the cook toss a handful of raisins, and carried it up to the men gathered on deck, watching the sea flatten and mist descend like a sodden quilt. They thanked her politely, but most began to eat with tentative bites.

She retreated behind the mainmast, listening to their talk.

"When will we get rid of those Yankees below?"

"Soon as the *Phoebe* meets up with us."

"Don't see hide nor hair of her."

"Nor I."

"We won't see her neither if this fog continues, and that makes us responsible for prisoners."

Deirdre couldn't distinguish one English voice from the other, but their tones showed no sign of concern over the missing *Phoebe*. She didn't concern herself over its fate either. In fact, the more scarce the other vessel, the better. The *Maid* would have to go to Bermuda to wait.

When she descended to the galley again, she found the cook loading up another tray. "For the guards," he explained.

"What about the prisoners?"

"There's plenty for them, but you can't be taking it to them."

"No, sir." She began removing more pewter bowls from a chest. "You take that to the guards, and I'll dish this up. Then you can take it down to the prisoners when you return."

He agreed this was the way to do things and departed.

Deirdre dished up porridge and more. In one bowl, she slipped a paring knife. Two other bowls concealed tightly folded notes she'd smeared with galley grease in the hope it would preserve enough of the message from the cereal to have the notes readable. Who got what didn't matter; they would use her efforts to good effect, she had no doubt.

With only a twinge of conscience, she set the bowls on their tray and procured food for herself and Ashford. He wouldn't feel much like eating, but she'd make him try.

Having accomplished as much for her crew as she could at the present, she descended the companionway to the main cabin. Ashford was asleep. She set the bowls on the table and slipped behind it to the cupboard that held the preserves and other delicacies for the captain's table. If Ashford continued to sleep, she might be able to shift a few jars and reach the hidden key to the secret cupboard. But no, she couldn't. Because of finding her stiletto, he might distrust her so much that he searched her cabin. If he found gold and the bank papers, her game would be up.

Reluctantly, all she did was pull a canister of tea from the cupboard. When she turned, she found him watching her, his eyes far too alert for him to have been sleeping moments earlier.

She held up the canister. "Would you like tea? I know you English like it with milk, but maybe black will do."

"Black will do." His gaze passed her to settle on the cupboard. "Thoughtful of you."

He was thoughtful about something, too. She read it in his eyes. They weren't that sleepy. In fact, they appeared far too alert for a man who had drunk even a few drops of laudanum.

She had to remove the key from its canister of coffee beans before he had the opportunity to look through the cupboard. How, though, when she was out of laudanum?

Hating to leave him alone in the cabin for a few minutes, she went to the door. "I'll make this in the galley. Eat your porridge."

He shuddered.

"You should eat something, sir."

"Toast?" He looked so hopeful she hated to disappoint him.

"Sorry, sir, no bread. Hardtack is the best I can do."

"If I must." He closed his eyes. "But, Deirdre?"

She rested a hand on the door handle. "Yes, sir?"

"Stop calling me sir. If I am going to marry you—"

"I haven't made up my mind about that, sir."

If she got her crew free on Bermuda, she wouldn't have to.

She closed the door behind her, climbed past the startled guard, and descended to the galley, where she found the cook washing up the dishes. Water steamed in a kettle, and Deirdre helped herself to a generous amount, carefully pouring it into the teapot between rolls of the ship.

"Mr. Ashford feeling all right, miss?" Riley asked.

Deirdre shrugged. "Well enough to talk like a madman."

Riley chuckled. "Shouldn't be disrespectful about an Ashford, miss. They can help you out of the heap of trouble you're in."

"Or get me into more."

Her reaction to that kiss warned her Kieran Ashford was nothing but trouble for her.

She bent her head over the pot, savored the rich aroma of steeping tea leaves. "But I can keep him from casting up his accounts until he's dead."

"See that you do." Riley clattered some bowls in the pan of dishwater, and Deirdre turned to the doorway. When she was about to step over the coaming into the passage, Riley cleared his throat. "Miss MacKenzie?"

She paused without looking back. "Yes?"

"The prisoners say you're a nice young lady, even if you are dressing like a man and living on a ship of us. And we all know how you clewed up that sheet when we were all too chickenhearted to try." He hesitated, cleared his throat, splashed some water.

Deirdre waited.

He clattered a load of bowls onto the counter. "So I'm going to give you some advice." A bowl slid off the table and onto the deck with a clang like a gong. "Have a care with Mr. Ashford. He's a bit careless with female hearts, so to speak—if you catch my meaning."

"Oh, I catch it," Deirdre said through her teeth. "You can be right certain that I am not stupid about men."

Losing her stiletto in a moment of carelessness was enough stupidity for Deirdre.

"And thank you for caring, Riley."

"I got a daughter about your age," he said by way of response. "I signed on this voyage to earn her a dowry so she can leave service and marry her young man."

Deirdre flinched. She didn't want to know about the families of these men, didn't want to know that they were human enough to need the money they would gain from a rich prize. They were stealing from her and her crew. Riley's daughter would marry while Zeb's family languished in slavery.

Yet wasn't being a servant a kind of slavery, too? It couldn't be a pleasant life with little to no time off, up early and to bed late, and rarely permitted to marry.

Uncomfortable, Deirdre beat a hasty retreat.

Returning to the main cabin didn't make her any more comfortable. Ashford had risen and was in the process of pulling a clean shirt over his head. Deirdre had seen plenty of chests in her life, yet the sight of Ashford's made her feel as though the gentle rocking of the ship had turned to a corkscrewing roll.

Her mouth dry, she hastened to the table with the teapot so that she had her back to him when his head emerged from the white cambric. "I'll knock next time," she mumbled.

"No need." He sounded more brusque than usual. "The sentry should do that."

"He wasn't there." Deirdre hadn't realized it until that moment. "He must have gotten permission to go on deck and eat."

"Not from me he did not." Ashford's tone was a bit hard. "Captain Heron would have him flogged for that."

"And you?" Deirdre busied her hands with pouring out fragrant, dark tea, then adding a dollop of honey to hers. "It's common practice."

"I will give him another chance." He joined her at the table and raised the cup to his lips, inhaled deeply. "We cannot afford to have a crewman laid up, shorthanded as we are."

"Are we?" Deirdre pretended nonchalance as she opened a tin of ship's biscuit, then fetched down a crockery jar of blackberry preserves that made the tasteless and very hard flour cakes tolerable. "I thought you brought a prize crew aboard."

"The storm hit before we finished making transfers." He eyed the biscuit and preserves. "Isn't that a waste of good bramble jelly?"

Deirdre seated herself at the table and broke off a piece of biscuit. "It'll settle your stomach."

"Sailor and nurse." Ashford sat, too, but made no move to consume anything other than his tea. "And supercargo, too?"

"No, not usually." Deirdre ran her tongue around the edge of the biscuit to catch dripping preserves and soften the flour cake. "My father didn't want me having that much exposure, and I looked too young for anyone to take seriously in bargaining for supplies or cargo."

"Mmm." Ashford's eyes had gone out of focus. "Sensible. Were you not bored?"

"Rarely, and even then not as bored as I was at tea parties." She took a bite out of the biscuit with a crunch.

Ashford's eyes snapped into focus—on her mouth. "I would not get bored with you at a tea party."

Deirdre blinked at him. "You're mad. All the gentlemen there looked about to turn up their toes with boredom."

"Then they had ice water for blood if you were there." He turned his head away. "What happens with a fog?"

"We sit around and wait for it to go away. And when it does, we have some repairs to make." Since he had his back nearly turned to her, Deirdre licked her fingers of preserves and concentrated on her tea and porridge. "We should also be quiet. It's not likely there are French ships about this far north, but one never knows. I don't know if they'd free us or consider us prisoners because we're English captives."

"Now, that would be a coil." Ashford flashed her a smile. "We might also wish to concern ourselves about American privateers."

"We have privateers?"

"Oh, yes, a score or more, we learned on Jamaica. Causing a great deal of havoc among British merchants."

"That's fortunate, since we don't have a navy to speak of."

"Which makes going to war with England more than a little foolish."

"I guess we object to being treated like a market of men for your war with France."

Ashford shrugged. "Not my doing. I am just taking advantage of it."

"Why? I've heard that your family is influential. Doesn't that translate into money?"

"My father? Yes. He has pots of it. Whether or not he leaves it to me or my sisters . . ." He curled his fingers around his teacup, his face grim. "I required a separate source of income rather than depending on his largess."

"That's why my father went to sea. He shipped aboard a privateer during our revolution against Britain. Then he decided that depending solely on land for one's income was too risky, so he sold the plantation."

He arched his brows. "Your father had a plantation?"

"Just a small one along the Potomac. The proceeds from the sale bought his first merchantman. You really should eat something, Ashford."

"Later. I need to see what the men are doing."

"Nothing when I was up top."

"I will tell them to get to work on something." He still hesitated. "Heron used to be in the navy and says we need to flog the men for their laziness. Is it common practice on merchantmen?"

"Common enough. But these aren't merchant sailors. They are privateers."

"True. Still—" He glanced over his shoulder. "Did your father flog anyone?"

"Once." Deirdre busied herself with closing the biscuit tin and pushing the stopper back into the jar of preserves. She made far too much noise, so she could pretend she didn't hear Ashford's next, his inevitable question. "I'd better put these things away in case the wind kicks up and this calm—"

Ashford dropped his hand onto her shoulder, holding her still. "I asked you what for."

"Oh, well . . ." Deirdre shrugged. "The usual. Dereliction of duty. Now, if you'll excuse me . . ." She tried to step sideways to move away from him.

He moved close enough for her to feel him behind her. "Deirdre." He stroked the side of her neck with one finger. "What is wrong with talking about it? I am in charge of this ship until we catch up with the *Phoebe*, and I do not hesitate to admit I'm still learning what's appropriate."

"Dereliction of duty is cause for punishment." Deirdre's voice sounded small even to her own ears.

"Then I'd like to know about it." His voice purred far too close to her ear.

She hauled in a deep breath, spoke too fast to cover the havoc his nearness wrought on her senses. "It was my fault he wasn't paying attention on his watch. I was too young to realize I'd started to look female."

"Ah." Gently, he turned her to face him. "He got flogged, and you got sent ashore for a year?"

She nodded, trying not to meet his gaze.

"Sounds like you had the worse of the punishments."

"I thought so at the time." She stared at his chin, at the stubble of dark beard and chiseled bone. "But my father shipped him out on a different merchantman, and he got impressed by the British into their navy."

"And you think that's your fault for letting him—" His jaw hardened except for a muscle that punched and twitched on one side. "Take liberties?"

Deirdre's eyes widened at the realization of what Ashford thought. She nearly punched him for thinking that of her. With an effort, she held her fists against her thighs. "He was just staring at me because my shirt was wet from spray and I didn't know it mattered." She gestured to her bound chest.

"Too young to realize? How old were you?"

"Twelve."

Disgust twisted Ashford's features. "I would have simply thrown him overboard."

"The sea nearly did that for him. He was supposed to be manning the helm. We broached to and nearly capsized."

"So he's a scoundrel and you get punished."

"My father thought I looked too female and needed to learn how to be one, so he set me ashore."

"And you went back to sea."

"The next time he was in port." She smiled. "I was a stowaway on my own father's brig. When he discovered me, he gave me my stiletto and told me to never go anywhere without it." She held out her hand, pleading with her eyes. "May I please have it back?" She braced herself for his refusal.

Instead, he drew the knife from his waistband and held it out to her hilt first. "I think your father was right. You need some way to defend yourself. Even though I would swear by the trustworthiness of every man aboard this ship and the *Phoebe*, I am quite certain your father thought all his men were trustworthy as well, and I will not be responsible for another—" He broke off. "Will you give me your word you will use this on no one except in a crucial situation?"

"You have my word on that." She met his gaze with candid directness.

"Do not abuse my trust again, or I will withdraw my proposal." Though he smiled at her, she did not think he joked.

Hurt and not knowing why, she lashed back. "I'm not sure I want that proposal."

"Then be prepared to be transferred to the *Phoebe* once we meet up again, either here on the open sea or in St. George's Harbor, Bermuda."

Chapter 7

A fresh breeze at sunrise lifted the fog and revealed rigging snarled and broken from the storm's buffeting. It did not reveal any sign of the *Phoebe*. So Kieran charted a course for Bermuda, where they could wait for his ship, ordered those crewmen from the *Phoebe* to effect repairs on the *Maid*, and asked Deirdre to remain in her cabin.

"For your own safety."

She didn't like it. She declared she could take care of herself. She taunted him about having men he couldn't control. He repeated his order and escorted her to the cabin after their breakfast.

Her talk of what had happened when she was barely more than a child distressed him more than he admitted, and he had lost a considerable amount of sleep over it. He wanted to trust the men. Most had come from his father's lands or merchantmen. Yet they had been at sea for two months without seeing a woman. Whether she was dressed like a male or not, they all knew Deirdre was a woman, and until—unless she accepted his proposal, she was not safe.

Another reason why she should consent to becoming his wife. No man would touch an Ashford bride. Until she saw the sense of his offer, he needed to keep a watch over her or keep her confined below, no matter what she called him for doing so.

Her cabin door had no lock on the outside. Without the equipment to put one in place, he ordered Troy to stand guard. In no way would Deirdre get around Troy. He was loyal to Kieran because Kieran's father had saved him from being transported to Botany Bay after he was caught forging banknotes. Kieran's father sent Troy to sea and placed his family in a cottage on the estate.

His father seemed to be tolerant of everyone's flaws but Kieran's.

Speaking of tolerance, Deirdre had taken to periodically pounding on the deckhead of her cabin. Kieran ignored her as he took a noon sighting.

Navigation he could do and do well. He'd never fared well in math at Eton, but he hadn't found any purpose in anything beyond basic arithmetic until he sailed on the *Phoebe* and learned the trigonometry needed for celestial navigation. Reckoning by the sun with the sextant was the only thing he liked about sailing. Miles of empty blue sea and sky made him feel caged. The narrow beam of the *Maid* was even worse than the broader *Phoebe*. Three paces took him from starboard to port. He couldn't prowl the length with repairs going on.

Those repairs didn't appear to be going well. Although Heron had managed to get a few of his more experienced men aboard before the weather deteriorated and the two vessels were separated, none understood the rigging of the Baltimore-clipper-style ship. Even to Kieran's inexperienced eye, the mess of ropes on the deck resembled his mother's knitting after her collection of Pomeranians had gotten into it—tangled, twisted, and chewed.

And the ship was foundering.

"They need help, sir," a former sheep farmer named Jones said from the wheel.

Kieran nodded. "Yes, they do. We will simply sail up to the nearest hiring fair and gather up experienced seamen and carpenters."

He didn't need to be sarcastic. He had a hold full of experienced seamen, men with knowledge of this peculiar slanted rigging.

Deirdre chose that moment to remind him of her presence, as if he could forget.

"Like as not we could use some help from her," Jones suggested.

Kieran glanced at the disaster of rigging on the main deck. "If you were one of them, lad, would you take directions from a female or from a prisoner?"

"Depends, sir. They ain't got no captain. That wouldn't bother the men none." Jones scratched his thatch of carroty hair until it stood on end from more than the wind. "Captains are gentlemen. Not like you are, sir, or guess I should say, my—"

"Sir or Mr. Ashford will do. I think I'll risk a prisoner or two."

But if he dared bring Trenerry up top, that would mean pulling Troy away from Deirdre's cabin. All right then, he'd take over guard duty.

"I'll man the helm," Kieran said. "Fetch Troy to me."

"Aye, sir." Jones nipped down the ladder. A moment later, Troy and he ascended to the quarterdeck.

"Bring up Trenerry and at least one other the prisoners say is good with the rigging. We're going to be in a pickle if something isn't done about the mess."

Troy nodded. "Aye, sir. Miss MacKenzie's been trying to tell you so this half hour or more. We all saw t'other day that she knows what's what with the sail—"

"I doubt most of the lads will listen to a female giving them orders. We will manage with one or two of the prisoners."

Troy nodded. "Aye, sir. Trenerry and another. Mebbe the old man."

Kieran waited on deck until Trenerry and Wat Drummond emerged from the main hatch with Troy behind them. The two prisoners threw up their hands to shield their eyes against the glare. In two days, they'd grown unkempt and scruffy with beard stubble, uncombed hair, and clothing soiled from ballast mud from the hold. The old man's face shone as though with fever perspiration, and Trenerry's looked as hard as a bronzed mask.

Guilt plucked at Kieran's innards, twinges he couldn't put down to mal de mer on a gentle sea. These men needed access to washing water, clean clothing, and fresh air. Prisoners they might be, but they weren't worms to be kept in the dark dankness of a hold. He'd just have to watch Trenerry. If a man spelled trouble in every stiff movement, it was Ross Trenerry. He sneered at the mess the English crew had made of the damaged rigging and said something that turned their faces crimson with embarrassment or rage or both. Troy raised a hammer-sized fist.

"No," Kieran shouted.

Troy obeyed, but didn't lower his hand. Trenerry laughed and made a rude gesture.

"I'll stop that behavior right now." Kieran stalked straight for Trenerry. His men drew back, watching, faces too blank to mean they weren't anticipating a showdown. Old Wat's chest rose and fell in a sigh audible even above the whine of wind through the rigging, and Troy grinned outright, letting his fist fall to his side at last.

Trenerry took a step forward. "Your men are stupid and incompetent." The soft drawl of his voice belied the meanness of his words. "You'll have us all at the bottom of the sea if you keep this up." He swept one arm to indicate drooping sail and flapping lines. "Some of us might rather be there than enjoying English hospitality"—his upper lip curled—"but neither of us wants Miss MacKenzie to suffer." He met and held Kieran's gaze. "Do we?"

Kieran read the pain and the intelligence in the younger man's eyes, listened for an underlying message in his words, and understood.

Trenerry would do nothing stupid if it meant that Deirdre was at risk.

"Get us to Bermuda in one piece," Kieran said, "and Miss MacKenzie will be as safe as any woman ever is."

A muscle in Trenerry's jaw bunched and twitched. "What do you mean by that?"

"Get us to Bermuda safely. I will listen to any reasonable proposal of how to do that."

Kieran turned away. He had no doubt that Trenerry would get his men to straighten out the rigging, have it repaired well enough to get them to Bermuda, and sail them into the port at St. George's without so much as a hint of rebellion or mutiny.

She was in his cabin. Her father's cabin, Kieran reminded himself as he opened the door and found her holding a canister that rattled in her hand.

"Coffee," she said. "Now that we have a galley fire, I'd like some coffee." She smiled at him over her shoulder, her braid swishing across her back. "So you brought Ross up top. That was wise."

"We will see if that was wise." Kieran studied her face, seeking what he did not know. Something was different with her. Something wrong? He didn't know. Just different, a sureness to her shoulders, a brightness to her eyes.

A fullness to her figure.

She still wore breeches and a man's shirt, but nothing bound her breasts. High and firm, they were a sight fine enough to distract the most self-controlled man.

"I saw a waistcoat in your sea chest." His tone was rough. "Put it on before you go up top again."

"But I'm confined down here for my safety, you've decided, so I may as well be comfortable."

And make him uncomfortable.

He forced his gaze to her face, focused too intently on her mouth, and shifted to concentrate on the rippling blue silk of the sea. "Can I trust Trenerry?"

Deirdre shrugged. "He won't do anything to compromise the *Maid*."

"Even though he is not . . . acquiescent to his imprisonment."

"What man would be? But he thinks he's responsible for my safety, and I am your prisoner."

"Interesting." This time the twinge in Kieran's innards stemmed from a sense of more wrong than Deirdre looking more female. "He as much as said the same thing."

She shrugged. "We've worked together for a long time." She did not meet his eyes. "How about that coffee. Will you join me?"

Kieran took the canister but stood motionless, studying her face. "You seem rather cheerful for someone imprisoned below deck."

"I'm happy you've decided to be sensible about getting the ship underway is all."

He didn't believe for a moment that was all. Something was up, but for the life of him he didn't know what. She couldn't conceal a thing in the clothes she was wearing, especially without that bandeau around her chest. Still . . .

He took a step closer to her, caught the scent of ginger, so spicy for a lady to wear, yet appealing on her.

He rested his free hand on her shoulder and stroked the pulse in her throat with his thumb. "Can I trust you, Deirdre?"

She laughed and poked a forefinger in the center of his chest. "Of course you can't. You're English. I'm American. We're natural enemies."

He moved his hand from her shoulder to the side of her face and stroked her lips with the ball of his thumb. "Is anything about being enemies natural?"

She didn't reply. She didn't meet his eyes.

He felt like the one being distracted. Her smooth skin, her scent, her nearness . . .

"I want you to be my wife, not my enemy." He kissed her then to remind her of his offer, and while he kissed her, he curved his hand around the back of her neck, then tangled his fingers in her braid.

A shudder ran through her. Her breath puffed out against his lips. She grasped his shoulders, responding, and Bermuda and a wedding felt a million miles and a hundred years away.

Unfortunately, the ship was not. A cough sounded down the companionway. Footfalls heavier than necessary followed.

Kieran released Deirdre, satisfied she carried nothing more than her stiletto concealed in her braid, dissatisfied at the interruption. A quick glimpse of her face before he confronted the intruder revealed that she looked as dazed as he felt.

He turned.

Troy stood in the companionway, his face the color of ripe strawberries. "Beg pardon, sir, but a few of the men are refusing to take orders from Trenerry."

"No doubt." He thrust the coffee canister into Troy's hands. "Take this to Riley and tell him to prepare a pot for Miss MacKenzie." He tossed Deirdre a stern look over his shoulder. "Stay."

She screwed up her face. "Am I supposed to bark or wag my tail?"

Kieran grinned. He sure did . . . well, like her a great deal. Incorrigible. Indomitable . . .

"Whatever you wish, m'dear. Just make certain that it does not take you from the cabin."

She turned her back on him and flipped open the pages of the ship's log.

"Sir," Troy said, rattling the coffee beans, "I think I should stay up top and make sure the men . . . Well, sir, they're used to taking orders from Captain Heron or me. We know you're the owner, but—" His face took on the same ripe berry hue it had worn after he caught Kieran kissing Deirdre.

Kieran sighed. He knew what Troy was saying without being impolite enough to be direct. *We know you're used to loungin' about while the rest of us work. I even caught you kissing a lady while we was workin'.*

Just another ne'er-do-well son of the nobility, the kind of person that had prompted the French peasants to rebel against their aristocrats. Purposeless indolence.

But he did have a purpose—make his own fortune in the world and protect Deirdre from the consequences of his first attempt to do so.

"They can learn to take orders from me." He stalked up the companionway ladder.

"You'd better go with him," Deirdre said behind him.

He knew he should stop and command Troy to stay guard over her, but he faced potential trouble on deck. Ross and Wat balanced in the rigging, while the *Phoebe*'s crew lounged about doing nothing save for Jones at the wheel. As Kieran paused at the top of the companionway ladder, Ross shouted something about the unsavory ancestry of lazy Englishmen and started to descend. "Come on, Wat, why should we help these laggards get us to prison faster? If they don't care about their prize, why should we?"

"Because I will make them care." Kieran shot a glare from Trenerry to the lazy Englishmen. "Get up there and help."

"I ain't taking no orders from no worthless Yank." Teague spat into the scuppers.

Kieran grabbed the back of his shirt and hauled him to the nearest shrouds. "You will go aloft and listen to him if I say you will. Understood?"

"Ye-yes, sir." Teague grabbed a ratline.

"Very good." Kieran showed his teeth in an unfriendly smile. "From now on, you can join the prisoners in the hold if you continue with this behavior. Any of you."

"They'd kill us," one man nearly sobbed.

"And if I or Troy tells you to listen to any one of the men from this ship, we mean for you to do so," Kieran continued. "Understood?"

Shifting eyes, shuffling feet, a few grumbles came in response.

"I believe," Kieran purred, "the appropriate response is, 'Aye aye, sir.' Or do you want to get friendly with the Yankees in the hold?"

The men straightened, touched their fingers to their brows.

"Good. Troy." He spoke to the man he sensed standing close behind him like an upright mast. "Carry on. Ensure that these men obey my orders." He plucked the coffee canister out of Troy's hands and descended to the galley.

The scent of bean soup and salted pork mingled with the effluvium of the ship, and he swallowed, tried to remember how ginger smelled on Deirdre's skin, and approached the cook.

Riley sweated over the enormous cooking pots, wielding a spoon that looked long enough for supping with the devil.

Kieran smiled at the allusion to the old saying about using a long spoon if one supped with the devil, and knocked on the bulkhead. "Riley?"

The man jumped, spraying soup broth across the stove, where it sizzled and stank. "My—Mr. Ashford, I never expected to see you down here."

"Only a mission for a lady." Kieran held out the canister. "She has a desire for coffee."

"I can do that for her. Just finished roasting some beans."

"Just finished roasting beans? But how, if this is the only coffee aboard?"

"We have bags of it in the stores."

Yet Deirdre had been holding the canister when he found her, and claimed she wanted coffee.

Brows knit, he set his mouth in a thin line. "Then make a pot for Miss MacKenzie. I will wait."

He would return her canister unopened and take coffee and full canister back to Deirdre for an explanation. That she needed to give him one he had no doubt.

~∂

Deirdre guessed she had five minutes between Ashford's departure for the galley and his return to demand why she had sent her father's canister of coffee. If Ross carried out his part, as she had explained in the slips of paper in the oatmeal, five minutes was all she needed.

Holding her breath, she watched and listened as he and Wat directed the *Phoebe*'s crew in how to lower the sail needing repair, and how to secure a new one. Wat he sent forward to help make more secure repairs to the bowsprit. The way was clear.

With a speed born of long practice and many races among the crew, Deirdre sprang up the companionway ladder and leaped into the shrouds. Before anyone noticed what she was doing, she had scampered to the crosstrees and settled herself astride a spar in front of Ross. "Don't talk. Listen."

Ross nodded and handed her the end of a sheet. If someone forced her to let go of this one too quickly, it would create havoc with the sail. And someone would force her soon. Below, Troy was shouting and gesticulating, trying to get one of the *Phoebe*'s men to climb up after her. The ruckus would bring Ashford in a moment.

"Waistband. Back. Paper knife." It wasn't much, but it was what she could find in the cabin and hide in the log. "Get it."

Ross hesitated.

"Now."

He reached behind her and drew the small, but sharp, blade from her waistband. Odd how his touch did nothing to thrill her or make her forget what was important.

A glance to the deck told her that Ashford had emerged from the galley. He would come after her if no one else did.

"I got the key from the coffee canister," she told Ross, speaking in a rush. "I'll manage a chance to get into my father's secret cache and smuggle gold to you all. When we get to Bermuda, I'll help you all escape."

Ross snorted. "On an island?"

"An island with a harbor full of merchant ships and fishing boats elsewhere this time of year. Someone will take you on."

"They'll hunt us down."

"Deirdre," Ashford called from the deck, "get down here now."

Deirdre waved the end of the sheet at him and grinned. "They won't come after you. I'll promise Ashford that I'll marry him if he leaves you all alone."

"You'll do what?"

"Marry him. He thinks he's honor-bound—"

Ross clamped his hand on her arm. "You'll do no such thing."

"Do you have a better idea?"

A fast idea? Ashford was heading up the shrouds, his face pale in the sunshine, but determined.

"You escape with us."

"Then who will distract him?" Deirdre spoke through her teeth, feeling tension stiffening her muscles with every foot Ashford climbed.

In moments, he'd be close enough to hear their conversation.

"We won't do it," Ross said. "We won't leave this ship without you."

"But, Ross—"

"We would never abandon MacKenzie's daughter to an Englishman, and I won't let you marry one."

Ashford glanced up at them. Had he heard that last?

Deirdre looked from his set face to Ross's and wondered which of them was more stubborn. Ross's tenacity she knew. Ashford's was still an unknown quantity, though she guessed that he would come after her. He would be concerned about her safety.

Rightly so, she had to admit.

A compromise? A bluff?

"All right," she snapped to Ross, "I'll do it."

Ashford paused just below her. "You'll do what, Deirdre, m'dear?"

She gave him a sweet smile and handed Ross back the sheet so he could splice the end he'd deliberately shredded with a marlinespike. "Marry you, of course."

Chapter 8

Laughing at the expression of astonishment on Ashford's face, Deirdre swung off the crosstrees, dropped freefall into the futtock shrouds, then swung onto the backstay and slid to the deck. That was an exhilarating descent she hadn't performed in years. From the purposeful way Ashford paced toward her across the deck after his conventional descent, she guessed she wouldn't perform it again any time soon. He looked as though he intended to pick her up and toss her over the taffrail and into the frothy sea.

He did pick her up as though she weighed five stone rather than ten. But he didn't toss her over the taffrail. He tossed her over his shoulder.

"Put me down, you English—" Her middle squeezed over his shoulder, cutting off her wind.

But not her hearing. The English crewmen were laughing as though she were one of the puppets in a Punch and Judy show. Her cheeks warm from more than her exertions or the subtropical day, she kept her head down so they didn't see her face, her humiliation. She didn't care if they saw her pummel his back with her balled fists.

Ashford didn't speak. He stalked across the deck to the companionway, leaped down the short ladder, and pushed his way into her cabin. There he dropped her onto her bunk, then stepped back to the doorway.

"That," he said through deep breaths—was she too heavy for him after all? "—was nothing less than a stupid, irresponsible, childish action. You could have been killed."

"It wasn't likely."

Except that with inexperienced men manning the braces, Kieran was all too right that she could have been killed. With her father's men in the rigging, she knew how the ship would perform in a sea like this one, but one line pulled too far or not far enough—

She shivered. "You're right. I could have, since your men don't know what they're doing."

"And what, may I ask," Ashford purred, "were you doing?"

He lounged against the bulkhead as though he had all day.

Deirdre drew her knees up to her chest, wishing she hadn't given in to the mischievous impulse to leave off her binding that day. "I went to visit Ross. We're friends. I hadn't talked to him—"

"So you sent me on a fool's errand with the coffee."

"Oh, well, that." Deirdre realized that her braid had come loose. She began running her fingers through her tangled hair, combing it out so she could plait it again before she lost her stiletto. "I wanted to tell him not to do anything stupid."

Ashford laughed. "Deirdre MacKenzie, I think I can throw you farther than I can trust you, and after carrying you down here, I don't think I can throw you very far. But I give you credit for planning. And if Trenerry behaves . . . If Trenerry does not . . . uh . . . er . . . mutiny . . . Do you own a hairbrush?"

"On the table behind the fiddle board." She glanced up at him. "Your hair is a mess from the wind, but you have your own. I saw it—"

"I'm not referring to my hair." He caught up her hairbrush and knelt on the floor. "Turn around."

She thought about refusing to do so. No one had ever brushed her hair for her since her mother died, and she didn't intend to let him touch her long enough to do so. But the proximity of his face to hers, his eyes glowing like sun-warmed amber, compelled her to look away, turn away, present him with her back, as she sat cross-legged on her bunk. "Why would you want to brush my hair? It's absurd."

"It's beautiful." He lifted a handful of her hair and began to work the brush through it. "Like trapped fire."

"It's unlucky for a ship. Some men won't"—she swallowed—"wouldn't sail with my father because I'm a red-haired woman."

"I do not believe in such nonsense." He worked the brush through another strand, holding it so that he didn't pull at the roots. "It is pure superstition and completely untrue."

"Is it?" The brush and his fingers reached the nape of her neck, and she flinched away from her shiver of response to his touch. "We were captured. My father died."

"You were captured by someone who has the best of intentions toward you." He drew her hair back from her face, smoothing his fingertips across her brow and temples. She closed her eyes, fighting the urge to lean back against him, call on his strength. She wanted to believe his intentions were good, that she could get her men away in Bermuda and count on Ashford to do nothing that would harm them.

The brush slid through her hair in long, smooth strokes. She doubted Ashford's words.

"If you had the best of intentions toward me," she said through stiff lips, "you wouldn't expect me to marry you. I mean, you'd at least make it a marriage in name only."

"I'm a selfish brute on that one." She felt him gather her hair together at the back of her neck and begin to braid it, his fingers warm against her skin. "I think a ribbon would look much prettier here than that twine. Green to match your eyes. I will look for some on Bermuda. A dress as well?"

Deirdre jerked her braid from his hands and turned on him. "Why in the world would you want to waste your money on buying me a dress?"

He laid one hand on her cheek. "I am not marrying a female in breeches."

"I'm not marrying you—" She caught herself in time. "If I have to wear a dress."

He laughed, a low rumble in his chest. "We will see about that, m'dear." He sat back on his heels. "Now, tell me about what you and Trenerry were discussing."

Deirdre rose to fetch her twine from her sea chest so she had an excuse to keep her back to him as she responded. "I told him to behave himself is all. Oh, yes, and that you were insisting that I marry you."

"He didn't look like he took that well."

"He wouldn't." Deirdre shrugged. "Will you cut this for me?"

"Of course." He stood behind her and reached around, a knife flashing in the bright light from the porthole. He took his time cutting the thin rope, standing too close to her, laying his cheek alongside hers.

"Why do you not want to wear ribbons or a dress?"

"Females wear ribbons and dresses."

"M'dear, you are very much a female."

"Purely an accident of birth."

And a curse at that moment with the way she was reacting to his nearness, wanting to lean against him, ask him to make all the bad things go away like some swooning heroine in one of the novels that turned up on the ship now and again.

"I should have been a boy." She tried to pull away, but she had nowhere to move in the tiny cabin. "My twin brothers died and killed Momma. Papa didn't deserve to lose both of his sons and get stranded with me. I wouldn't be here now. He wouldn't be dead . . ."

She would surely have the strength to prevent the sobs that rose in her throat, choked her until she had to let them out.

"Shh." Kieran turned her in his arms and cradled her head against his shoulder. "It's not your fault you are here and he is gone and your crew are prisoners. It's the fault of the men who make wars and men like me who take advantage of wars to make our fortunes. You . . . Deirdre . . ."

His voice trailed off. He simply held her, stroking her hair, while the ship around them took on the normal roll of a vessel through a gentle sea with all its rigging properly set. Jury-rigged, of course. They'd need more extensive repairs in Bermuda, but for now, they were sailing as well as they could. Ross was doing a good job because Kieran Ashford, despite his claims to the contrary, trusted her enough to take her word that the ship needed men with the right kind of experience. He held her because he cared enough to know that she needed comfort she would never ask for because she'd never asked for it, never dared ask for it.

He was kind to her, and she was going to betray him.

Her stomach knotted as she realized that she was caught between loyalty to her crew and a growing respect for her enemy.

～۹

Kieran hated leaving Deirdre in her cabin with Troy posted as a guard outside her door. Yet he couldn't bear the idea of seeing her dropping from the rigging again.

Nor in Ross Trenerry's company.

After the crew took in sail for the night, Kieran sent Trenerry and Drummond back to the hold without showing the reluctance he felt to do so. On the morrow, he would allow each of the prisoners up top for a while, two at a time would be safe, to enjoy the fresh air and get some exercise. During that time, he would guard Deirdre himself.

Deirdre!

Kieran stood at the weather rail, allowing the spray to cool his face. It helped with the feeling of illness that never completely left him while aboard ship. It helped him forget his reaction to holding Deirdre close, the tenderness toward her, the longing for her to forget who he was—her enemy.

He wanted to be her husband. She attracted him as no woman had since Joanna . . .

But Joanna was a subject closed for discussion with anyone, including himself. He'd erred there, thinking his rank and the things he would inherit would win the most beautiful and intelligent of eligible ladies of the Season. He was expected to marry. Her family expected her to find an advantageous alliance. A match made in—

He clamped down a lid on those memories. But that left thoughts of Deirdre roaming free. Marrying her felt right, too. It was the honorable thing to do. It would salve his conscience and, when they reached England, his pride. He would have close companionship for the rest of the voyage. What happened between them after that depended on time and nature.

But as the *Maid of Alexandria* plowed through the sea toward Bermuda, doubts assailed him. He doubted Deirdre had intended to agree to marry him perched atop that spar.

Yet she made no complaint about being stranded in her cabin except for the two hours a day Kieran allowed her on deck. When in her cabin, she remained quiet, only asking for books to read and more writing paper. When Kieran invited her to share his meals, she refused.

For his part, the boredom weighed heavily upon him. Other than performing navigational adjustments twice a day, he had nothing to do. On the *Phoebe*, he had Captain Heron with whom he could pass many pleasant hours playing cards, talking about Garrett Ashford's years in the navy, life. But the *Phoebe* never appeared, something that concerned Kieran and the other crewmen. She was a sturdy merchantman that had weathered worse storms. Still, things happened to ships, during war especially. She could have been captured by the French or Americans, capsized in a battle, sunk with all hands lost.

His father would never forgive Kieran if that happened. Kieran would never forgive himself. When they had learned of the war between America and Britain preventing Kieran from going to the plantation in Georgia that his mother had inherited, he should have simply changed course for the West Indies, for Jamaica, instead of becoming a privateer. Fortune under his feet or not, that had not been one of his more intelligent actions.

"You make a muck of your intelligent choices," his father had accused him after the fiasco with Joanna.

Would he make up for some of his errors by bringing both ships safely into Plymouth Harbor?

First, they had to reach Bermuda safely and pray that the *Phoebe* joined them there. For the time being on the *Maid*, the crew had settled into a routine, working out the different maneuvers with the Baltimore-built ship and, if with many a grumble, followed directions from the American prisoners.

Kieran tried to lose his troubled thoughts in literature. He liked to read, and Daniel MacKenzie had carried a sizable library with him on the voyage. But the difficulty of focusing his eyes on a page while the world rolled beneath him increased his mal de mer so badly he dared read nothing more than the ship's log.

He was trying to find a clue to the whereabouts of MacKenzie's specie. That he had it aboard Kieran knew. But where baffled him. He'd had the crew's belongings searched for weapons and come up with a not insignificant amount of money among the men, money he would let them keep to ease their life in prison, but it was not enough to account for notes in the margins of the log that indicated MacKenzie was carrying a small fortune back to America beyond his cargo.

A hidden compartment still seemed like the most logical answer. Where that compartment was, Kieran could not work out. The bulkheads just didn't sound hollow anywhere. Somehow, he must convince Deirdre to show him for the sake of his honor with the prize courts. She might, if she found marriage pleasing.

Marriage. He had surely lost his reason. He almost hoped they would somehow sail past Bermuda by a miscalculation. But at the end of the third day since the storm, the lookout spotted land. By evening, they were sailing into the harbor at St. George's, Bermuda, the Union Jack flying from the masthead of an American merchantman. Cheers rose from the decks of English ships anchored in the calm waters of the bay. Kieran felt like cheering, too. For the first time since leaving England, his innards settled down so that food sounded like something he wanted to eat instead of needed to eat.

"I'll have eggs for you for breakfast, sir," Riley promised when he brought Kieran's dinner. "And fresh bread for the crew."

"For the prisoners, too," Kieran said. To Troy, who stood in the open doorway, he added, "We'll draw straws to see who gets to row us ashore tomorrow."

Shore. Solid land. How he wanted to go now!

"Aye, sir. Who'll be goin' ashore with you?"

"Miss MacKenzie and you."

Troy's face lit up, making his scarred countenance appear almost pleasant. "That sounds right fine. Fresh food and all."

A market where Kieran could buy trinkets for his mother and sisters, and ribbons and a dress for Deirdre.

"Troy, you may go have your dinner now," Kieran said. "I will see to Miss MacKenzie's dinner."

Troy nodded and followed Riley up the companionway ladder.

Kieran knocked on Deirdre's door. To his surprise, she opened it and stepped into the companionway. "I'm done feeling sorry for myself, Mr. Ashford, if I may join you for dinner."

He gave her a bow. "Please, enter."

She grinned at him. "You look ridiculous bowing to me." She stepped over the coaming and into her father's cabin. "You're getting a nice breeze through here. My cabin is horribly stuffy now that we're at anchor."

She moved to the table and Kieran watched her, admiring the grace of her movements. It was not a grace that would be accepted for a female in a London drawing room. Her stride was too long, too sure in an age when ladies minced about. At the same time, it was too fluid to be masculine. It was unique.

It was Deirdre.

His chest tightened. He ached to reach out to her, smooth wisps of fiery hair away from her brow, and feel the fine texture of her skin, taste her lips . . .

"I really dislike harbors," she said. "The air is foul. May we stay on land while we wait for the *Phoebe*? We are waiting for the *Phoebe*, aren't we?"

"Yes, we are. We will stay here until we have made repairs before sailing on to Plymouth with or without the *Phoebe*." A tingling of wariness at the back of his neck made him choose his next words with care. "As for staying ashore . . ." He moved to the table and began dishing out the bean soup flavored with salt pork, far from the most appetizing fare he knew and hardly the stuff for an intimate dinner. "I thought you disliked the land."

"I dislike living on the land." Deirdre sat and dug into her soup as though she were starving. "Visits to ports around the world are part of the pleasure of being a merchant sailor. The markets and the food—may we buy oranges? I think I'd commit a crime for fresh fruit right now."

"Of course we can buy oranges." Kieran sat across from her, but barely touched his food. Settled stomach or not, this was enough to make it bad again. "Would you like me to purchase oranges for your crew, too?"

"Would you?" In the dim light from the harbor and last of the day's radiance, her eyes shone bright and her smile brighter.

He reached across the table and laid his hand over hers. "You keep looking at me like that, and I will buy you anything you want."

She shoved her half-finished bowl aside. "Just fresh fruit and meat will do." She stood and moved to sit on the seat below the stern windows. "There's a fine inn ashore here and a church. I'd like to get to the church and pray for my father's soul, whatever that's worth."

Kieran turned in his chair to face her. "We will be going to the church when you marry me."

"Oh." She started as though receiving a shock from one of the electricity machines. "I thought you'd change your mind by now."

"I am more determined than ever." He moved to sit beside her and take one of her hands in his.

Her fingers were ice cold despite the heat inside the cabin.

"Frightened?" he asked.

"Of course I am. Marriage. To you. To the enemy . . ." She rested her head on the bulkhead beside the windows and closed her eyes. "You'll want your wife to wear dresses. I can't marry you if you insist that I wear dresses."

"What is wrong with a dress?"

He saw the shudder pass through her. "I look absurd in them. I cross my legs and take long strides and can't breathe or climb, and I have to wear shoes. Kieran, I'll marry you, but not if it's in a dress."

He laughed and kissed her. He couldn't help himself, though the contact made him want to marry her that night.

"You do not have to wear a dress on the ship," he assured her, "or any other time except for during the ceremony, whenever I arrange that."

"And in England?"

"You would have to wear a dress no matter whether or not you married me."

"I suppose so." She heaved a sigh. "But while we're here, I can go to the inn and eat fresh food dressed in my own clothes? And go shopping in the market in them, too?"

"I suppose there is no harm to that."

"And we'll stay ashore. I mean, after we're married, we won't . . ." Even in the dim light he could see her blush.

He understood what she was having so much trouble saying—the ship, her father's cabin, was no place for their wedding night.

He touched her cheek. "We will stay ashore until we are able to sail."

"Thank you." She turned her head and kissed the palm of his hand.

Now he felt like he had received a jolt from one of those electricity machines. Such a small gesture of affection. Such a great reaction.

He stood. "I think I will take some air on deck before I turn in. Do you wish to join me?"

"No, thank you, I'd rather stay here. That is, if you don't care if I do."

At that moment, he doubted that he would care what she did.

"Of course. I will return in a quarter hour or so."

He left her alone in the cabin. Troy had not returned, but that didn't matter. Even if she dashed up to the deck, she would have no one to talk to with her crew battened down for the night. Anything that could possibly be construed as a weapon he had locked away. She could get into no mischief alone in the cabin, and he needed what cooling breezes he could find on deck.

He found enough to clear his head from thoughts of the aftermath of marrying her and to realize he had been a fool to leave her alone.

At sea, she could get up to no mischief alone in the great cabin, but in a harbor of calm water with shore only a few hundred yards away, she could slip out of the stern windows and swim to shore.

If she could swim. Not that many people could, but he would not put that skill past her abilities.

He took the companionway ladder in one leap and shoved open the cabin door he had not closed.

As he feared, the cabin was empty.

Chapter 9

*D*eirdre disliked herself for the games she was playing with Kieran. For a man who had been dishonorable enough to become a privateer—nothing more than legalized piracy, as far as she was concerned—he was proving touchingly honorable with her.

Part of her yearned for that connection, that closeness, that sense of being protected. All her life, except for that one year, she'd had her father's protection and the guardians of the crew. With her father dead and her crew prisoners, she understood her vulnerability.

She couldn't afford to feel completely female right now.

For that reason, she needed to win back Kieran's trust, the trust she'd sacrificed in order to get the key to her father's cache from the canister of coffee beans, and get another message to Ross. For that reason, she needed to show Kieran that she could have escaped. But he worked that out faster than she anticipated, clever man, and charged past her before she could let him know where she was—on the main deck preparing to join him and enjoy what breeze blew across the harbor.

"Deirdre?" His voice held a note of panic.

She leaped down the companionway ladder and met him face to face in the cubicle between the cabin doors. Dim light filtering from above showed his face taut, concerned, a little wild.

She laid her hand on his arm. "I'm right here."

He grasped her shoulders. "I thought you'd gone. Where were you?"

"I was coming on deck to join you." She laid her hands on his shoulders, inhaled his scent. For a moment of weakness, she wanted to lay her head on his shoulder again, not to cry, just to rest there and forget about the thirteen men in the hold. But she had to help them escape at the cost of betraying this kind and honorable man.

She kept her spine straight and looked him in the eye. "Where did you think I'd gone?"

"I thought you had escaped." He sounded vulnerable, not angry.

She made herself laugh. "On an island? Where would I go?"

"I put nothing past your ability, Deirdre MacKenzie." He brushed his lips across her forehead. "Where's Troy? I am afraid . . . I am sorry if it's uncomfortable, but you will need to stay in your cabin tonight with a guard."

"You don't trust me?" She tried for the kind of pout she'd seen young women on shore use on men.

He laughed, and his didn't sound forced. "I am removing temptation. Island or not, land is too close."

"Presuming I can swim. Most sailors can't, you know."

"And I note that you did not include yourself in that." He gently nudged her toward the open cabin beside her. "Go."

She stepped over the coaming and closed the door.

"I know it is hot in here," he said from the doorway. "But you'll be in an inn tomorrow night."

With him, if the escape failed, as his wife.

Knowing that she needed her rest, she tried to sleep, but plans, ideas, dangers swept through her mind in an endless parade. She also felt too conscious of Kieran in the next cabin, quiet, but awake. She heard him moving about, cat-footed, prowling in the darkness.

Her mind turned to wondering what disturbed his mind. What could make him, the conqueror, endure a sleepless night?

She thought she must have slept somewhere near dawn for she woke to the sounds of an anchor being raised on a nearby ship. Reflexively, she rose, ready to go on deck and watch. She always loved that sight of sails rising into the morning sky, catching the wind, bellying out as graceful as wings, like a bird flying toward the freedom of open sea.

She remembered before she opened the cabin door that Troy would be in the companionway.

She had never minded the narrow dimensions of her cabin. It was sufficient for someone who spent little time there. But imprisoned, she thought she would suffocate from lack of air. With the door closed, the porthole allowed little of the breeze to enter, though the temperature had lowered to a comfortable level during the night. That her crew was worse off in the hold reminded her of the responsibility she bore that day.

She rose, washed in the little water left in the pitcher on her table, and dressed in her shoregoing clothes of white cambric shirt, black breeches, a black silk vest with silver buttons, and black leather boots. When she brushed her hair, she remembered Kieran brushing it for her, how that made her feel . . . well . . . protected. Cared for. She wondered about brushing his hair. It was soft, thick and heavy, so black that blue lights shone in the sunlight. If he had blue eyes . . .

He had amber eyes, feline and feral.

She shivered, though wearing shoes always made her feel hot regardless of the temperature. Honorable or not, kind or not, Kieran Ashford was determined to get his prize home and reconcile with his family. What she was about to do would ruin that for him.

She must not care. After today, she would never see him again.

The seat of the commonwealth's government, St. George's, appeared to offer all the vices and amenities of civilization. Doxies for anyone's taste ranging from Nordic blondes to Guinea ebony swarmed amid the sailors and stevedores crowding the wharves. Cheap grog shops and boardinghouses gave way to King's Square, where the town hall and a few houses, respectable inns, and a public garden revealed the inhabitants' wealth. Golden sunshine illuminated the prosperous scene, and breezes kept the heat from being oppressive.

Deirdre and Troy in tow, Kieran paused in the shade of a building where a beautiful amber-skinned woman presided over a table of embroidered ribbons. Before Kieran opened his mouth, she was already holding up a length of green satin ribbon the color of Deirdre's eyes and embroidered along the edges with scallops of gold thread.

"Perfect, yes?" the woman asked in a lilting voice.

Deirdre looked shocked.

Kieran smiled. "I'm not the only one who knows a woman despite the clothes."

Deirdre looked away.

Kieran turned back to the proprietress. "It is perfect, thank you. How much?"

She told him, then began holding up other colors. Beside him, Deirdre stood mute and tight-faced until the merchant held up a ribbon of pale pink.

"If you buy that color for me, Ashford," Deirdre said through her teeth, "I'll strangle you with it."

The merchant laughed and tucked the pink ribbon into the growing pile.

Deirdre snatched it out. "Enough. I'm not wearing ribbons in my hair like a simpering miss."

"My sisters do not simper—"

"I'm not a lady and have no intention of being—"

"And where may I find a dress?" he asked the ribbon seller over Deirdre's protests.

The merchant began to laugh. "You'll need to have one made for a lady that tall, mon." She gestured to a point past the inn. "There's a seamstress down thattaway."

Deirdre began sidling in the opposite direction.

Troy laid one of his ham-sized hands on her shoulder. "Mr. Ashford wants you to stay here."

"I will if he stops giving me ribbons."

"Just the green and the blue," Kieran said. "And we'll see how we can bribe the seamstress." He paid the ribbon seller and turned in the direction she had indicated for the seamstress's establishment.

He allowed Deirdre to follow him with Troy in charge. She simply looked too attractive in her vest, breeches, and boots for him to concentrate, and with her on land, he needed to concentrate. She had not escaped the night before, had merely shown him that she could and had chosen not to. That scarcely set his mind at rest.

Yet she talked positively about going through with the wedding.

He concentrated on maneuvering through the increasing crowd in the square, glancing back now and then to make sure that Troy still followed with Deirdre, and seeking the seamstress's shop. Food vendors distracted him. Fresh fruit glowed on long tables, and meat that had not been pickled in brine for months roasted over braziers.

He paused for a moment beside a wizened man with baskets of oranges and lemons. "How much for a bushel?"

"Bushel? No, mon, you pay each." The man hefted an orange. "See. Big. Juice." He sliced the fruit in half with a dubiously clean knife. The pungent sweetness of orange dominated the scents in the air, and, indeed, juice did run down his arm.

Deirdre reached past Kieran and plucked one half of the fruit from the man. "Don't tell me his knife is dirty." Peels flew. "I haven't had an orange in months."

"You pay," the man shouted.

"Of course we pay . . . for that orange. As for the others . . . Deirdre, is it any good?"

She shrugged and swallowed. "Good enough for now, but a little sour. That stall over there may have sweeter ones."

"No, those are old. Husks only," the orange seller protested. "I'll give you a good price."

"It'll have to be very good." Deirdre dropped a quarter of the orange onto the ground and crushed it with her boot heel. "We can't feed the crew that kind of swill."

Troy snorted.

Kieran stepped on one of his toes and began to bargain, with Deirdre lending just the right amount of support. When they finished, they had purchased several boxes of oranges and lemons.

"We can't carry them around with us," Deirdre said. "Can Troy take them while we get some dinner? Or, wait, you need your dinner, too."

"I'll just buy a meat pie here," Troy said. "Fond of meat pies, I am."

"But the Royal George has a fine taproom and good food," Deirdre said. "They'll have salad and fresh bread."

Kieran's stomach growled at the mention of fresh bread.

Troy shook his head. "Not much of one for salad or fresh bread."

"But I will need you to . . . stay with Deirdre while I obtain a license," Kieran said. "Perhaps this man will hold our boxes—"

"Yes," the old man shouted.

"No," Deirdre said at the same time. "He'll take your money and sell them to someone else." She took on a pout that would have looked ridiculous on a woman with any other kind of mouth. On her . . .

Kieran had to look away. "You can hire a boat to send the oranges back. Just have them put in the main cabin."

"Yes, the main cabin," Deirdre agreed. "It's coolest in there out of the sun, but with a breeze."

"Aye, sir." Troy hefted a stack of crates in his arms and headed for the harbor.

Kieran grasped Deirdre's elbow and steered her toward the seamstress shop once again. The closer they grew, the more stiff-legged she walked. Her arm felt rigid beneath his hand. He could not see her face, but did not doubt that it too looked frozen.

They reached the shop, a narrow establishment so dim that Kieran wondered how anyone could choose a color there or how the workers managed to thread needles. However, it did lend relief from the heat outside.

A woman whose slender proportions suited the constriction of the shop bustled forth on a rustle of taffeta petticoats and greeted them at the doorway. "Gentlemen—ah, no, madame and monsieur. How do I help?" Her accent sounded genuinely French.

Deirdre relaxed and began speaking to her in that language. "He thinks I need a dress today, but I hate them. So please tell—"

"Deirdre," Kieran interrupted. "I know enough French to understand you."

She sighed. "I should have guessed."

The petite seamstress had round black eyes that danced and sparkled in the dimness. "I am afraid that madame will have her way, monsieur. I have nothing even half-finished that will do for a female of her tallness. Four days, perhaps three with enough of the advance payment. But sooner . . ." She shook her head.

"Could you not add a flounce or something to the bottom of a gown?" Kieran asked. "I am not marrying a female in breeches."

"A flounce on her?" The seamstress fairly shrieked. "It would be absurd. Inelegant. She is too tall, too much of the slenderness. Bands of ribbon to cover the join of the same fabric?" She tilted her head to one side. "*Oui*, that would do. But today? No. With the right fee, tomorrow morning." Her eyes danced again. "You can wait that long for the wedding, monsieur?"

He didn't want to. Another day might bring the *Phoebe* into port, and Heron, not at all in favor of Kieran marrying Deirdre, would put up a fuss Kieran did not wish to contend with. And, of course, other reasons compelled him to want to marry her now. He wanted to spend the night on land and did not dare leave Deirdre on the ship without him. At the same time, he would not stay at an inn with her even in another room. The impropriety did not sit well with him regardless of the conditions they shared on ship being less acceptable. If only he had connections on Bermuda, knew someone with a house where he could impose upon their hospitality, he could set Troy to guard Deirdre . . .

But he did have connections there. He had not considered that his father and mother knew a family who had settled there after the last war with the American colonies.

"Tomorrow morning will be soon enough," he agreed. "Deirdre, go with Madame here and get yourself measured and pick a color. No, not a color. White. It's becoming the color for wedding dresses in England. It'll do well for you."

The seamstress nodded. "Come with me. I have the private room so you can remove—" She gestured to Deirdre's bound chest. "Come." She turned toward the back of the shop.

Deirdre did not move. Her hands clenched and unclenched at her sides, and her jaw looked as rigid as a bowsprit.

Kieran opened his mouth to order her to follow the seamstress, then shut it again as he realized that she was frightened, not defiant.

"What is it?" he asked. "Marrying me or wearing a dress?"

She licked her lips. "The dress." Her movements jerky, she turned her back on him and stomped after the seamstress.

Waiting in the shop, Kieran listened to the two women chatter in French. More accurately, Madame chattered about the benefits of muslin over silk in warm weather, the elegance of Deirdre's figure, the glory of her hair. Deirdre responded with grunts and mm-hmms and an occasional protest about a pin sticking her. She sounded unhappy, tense.

Kieran crouched on a chair meant for a female and one half his size at that, and speared his fingers through his hair. What was he doing to her, forcing her to go through with something she disliked so much? Was this simply for his pride? What mattered about her being his bride in a proper gown? Being his bride was what counted for him. The dress could go, could it not?

No. His wife would need to wear female clothes once they landed in England. She needed to arrive equipped for a life she did not even know existed.

He knew he should tell her. He knew if he did, she would refuse to go through with the wedding. That was not a risk he was willing to take. Let her simply be Deirdre Ashford. Plain Kieran Ashford suited him just fine away from home. There, it afforded him privilege and license, yet neither had worked with Joanna . . .

Joanna was gone.

Her memory hurt only a little, more because of how his family had reacted to the tales that reached them before he did. The pain lessened when Deirdre emerged from the fitting room. She seemed more relaxed, even gave him a smile that made him think that she might help him forget Joanna even existed.

"You'll need to settle with Madame," she said. "It'll cost you."

"It will be worth every farthing. Madame?"

The seamstress bustled forward, and more bargaining ensued. When both of them were satisfied with the price, and Deirdre looked about ready to have an apoplexy at the figure, Kieran led her out of the shop and toward the inn. "Will they have a private parlor at the Royal George?"

"Private parlor?" Deirdre sounded bewildered. "What for?"

"You to eat in."

She laughed. "I have never eaten in a private parlor in my life except for at boarding school."

"But you said that the food is good here." He paused a few feet away from the inn doorway through which gentlemen, sea captains, and tradesmen alike entered and exited in a steady stream. "How do you know if you have not eaten here before?"

Deirdre stared at him for a few moments, then laughed even harder than before. "Ashford, I eat in the taproom."

"But you are a—"

"Boy, as far as the world is concerned. I'm your cabin boy. A little old, but no one really cares about that." She pulled free of his grasp. "C'mon. I'm starved."

Kieran supposed a female who admitted to being starved could tolerate the roughness of an inn taproom.

He followed her into the common room, then seated them at one of the long tables and introduced himself as the owner of the *Phoebe*, expected at any time, and presented Deirdre as MacKenzie.

Some of the other men merely nodded. The man directly across from them introduced himself as Dennison, the captain of the *Marianne*. A burly man with a strong Suffolk accent, Dennison gave Deirdre the merest of nods, then turned his attention to Kieran. "Hear you're to be congratulated, Mr. Ashford. Not too many English ships can catch a Yankee schooner, and what a prize! Heard those Baltimore clippers are the fastest thing on the sea, but you caught her."

Deirdre squirmed beside him.

"Pure luck." Kieran turned to a hovering waiter to order as English a meal as the inn could provide and Deirdre the size meal a growing lad would enjoy. From the renewed tension of her face and body, he wondered if she would eat despite her claim earlier that she was starved.

"Mebbe 'twas only luck," Dennison said. "Still and all, it does an Englishman good to see an American merchantman captured after what they've been doing to ours these months past."

"What do you mean?" Kieran asked.

Beside him, Deirdre leaned forward, eyes suddenly bright, lips parted.

"Devastation," Dennison announced. "Been sailing rings around our merchant fleet and picking 'em off like weevils from hardtack."

One corner of Deirdre's lips twitched upward.

Kieran pressed a warning hand against her thigh. "How can they? They have not anything we would even call a navy."

"Eighteen ships," Dennison agreed. "Not even ships. All of 'em. Nothin' bigger'n a forty-four-gun, if that."

The waiter set down bowls of savory onion soup. Once he left, Dennison continued.

"They don't need a navy. They've got privateers coming out of New England and the Chesapeake like somebody smoked a hornet's nest. The *Decatur* took eleven British ships in forty-five days. The *Saratoga* eight, the *Comet* twelve. One American took eighteen, another fifteen. The list goes on. It's almost too fantastic to believe."

"I believe it," Kieran said. "My father fought the Americans in the last war. He took French prizes, but never an American."

"Peace by Christmas?" Deirdre murmured. "Ha!"

"Course we'll have peace," Dennison shouted. "We won't stand for anything else." He slammed down his tankard.

Deirdre smiled into her empty bowl.

The next course arrived. As if she'd never eaten, she tucked into half a roasted chicken with asparagus, potatoes, and tomatoes sprinkled with fresh basil.

Kieran looked at his own beefsteak with far less appetite than he should have possessed. He knew why. Dennison's report spoke of threat. The threat Kieran might lose his prize, thus making Captain MacKenzie's death pointless. Except the man might have died soon anyway.

But if the *Maid* were recaptured, Kieran would lose Deirdre. The idea disturbed him more than he would have imagined there on land with the prospect of feminine companionship all night.

Lifting his own tankard, he asked, "Have they sailed this far east yet?"

Dennison shrugged. "Only seven hundred miles from their coast. Like as not they'll be hovering off the Bermudas any day now, if they ain't a'ready."

"Then why do you not sail back to England with us?" Kieran said. "There's safety in numbers. Protect us from Americans and French."

"That's the rub of it," Dennison grumbled. "Can't see how we'll fight off both the frogs and the Yanks."

"Because we have the best navy in the world," Kieran said.

"Yeah?" Dennison sneered. "And where is they when we're needin' 'em?"

"Saw a frigate and a sloop weighing anchor as we made landfall." A rail-thin man farther down the table spoke for the first time.

Deirdre jumped. Her fork clattered to her plate.

Kieran touched her hand beneath the table. He had not seen the warships either.

"Won't do us no good if they're leavin'," Dennison said. Again slamming his tankard onto the table, this time adding a shilling, he lumbered to his feet. "I'll be ready to leave day after tomorrow."

"We will sail when we effect some repairs and the *Phoebe* arrives," Kieran told him. "Heron, the captain, made post captain before he left the navy. He knows how to fight."

"Thank you, sir. I'll see if anyone else would like to join up with a convoy." Nodding, Dennison departed.

"Well," Kieran drawled. "Who would have thought a fledgling nation like America could make such a show of force? It is rather like one of Mama's Pomeranians biting one of Father's horses."

"If it strikes the right vein," Deirdre said, "even a Pomeranian can damage a horse." The smile she gave him ignited such a hunger he attacked his meal with renewed vigor. He liked seeing her happy, even if her happiness might stem from his and England's expense.

"They'll never win," another man insisted. "The very idea is preposterous."

"So," Deirdre said, "was the very idea of the United States winning the Revolution."

Kieran nudged her—too late. A dozen hostile glares turned on her. She met each with defiance.

Kieran shook his head. "He has got a Yankee mother."

The assembled men made comments about American mothers that made Kieran want to batter heads together, since he had one, too. Instead, he laughed, then ordered port and cheese to finish his meal. Deirdre asked for oranges. When they came, she ate three.

"You are going to have a stomachache," Kieran warned her.

"No, I won't. I always eat them like this when I don't know when I'll get another one."

"We just sent dozens back to the brig."

"Yes, but—" She stripped some of the white from the inside of the peel and ate it.

Kieran grimaced. "Please do not do that in front of me when we have a rough sea."

"Sorry." She took the serviette from the fruit basket and wrapped up her peels. "I like them dried. We had some candied ones, but my father ate them before we reached Cape Horn."

"Time we were leaving." Kieran stepped over the bench and all but dragged Deirdre out the door. "Do not talk about being around the Horn. People will ask questions."

"Sorry. I didn't think—oh, Kieran, look!" She darted forward to inspect a display of silver jewelry glistening in the sunshine. "Aren't these bracelets pretty? You should buy some for your sisters."

If she had not been dressed like a boy, he would have bought one for her, she so obviously enjoyed the bangles with their feathery etchings and inlays of semiprecious stones. Malachite for her. Amethyst for the girls. Mama would like lapis.

He caught the salesman's look of greed and shook his head. "I never purchase the first thing I see. There will be other gifts for the girls at better prices." He left the man shrieking after them that he would reconsider the prices.

Deirdre started to laugh. "You're awful. You'll go back, won't you?"

"Possibly."

"And pay half the price."

"Nothing wrong with being frugal. Now, look at these shawls. You will need one to go over your dress." He picked up a gossamer silk confection with silver embroidery around the edges.

Deirdre snatched the shawl away from him. "Buy gifts for your mother and sisters and father and friends, but don't buy me anything."

"When we are wed—"

"You may buy me anything you like, but not before." She glanced back at the inn, looked about to say something, then paused as church bells rang. "I'd like to go to a service. Vespers?"

"In those clothes?"

She made a face at him. "I always have before, though a real bath would be nice. And don't you need to find a bishop or something for a license?"

"Nothing that formal here in the colonies, but I do need to make an arrangement for that and a place for me to stay tonight." He turned them back to the Royal George, leaving behind the colorful and crowded market with too many things that would enhance Deirdre's beauty.

Once inside, he bespoke private rooms and was given exactly what he wanted—a chamber with an antechamber where Troy could unobtrusively keep guard over Deirdre. The room being on an upper floor, she could not escape through the window, not even Deirdre, who climbed like a cat. Troy arrived while Kieran was making inquiries about Mr. and Mrs. Willoughby.

"Oh, yes, sir, we know them well," the landlord assured him. "I'll send a lad with a message straightaway."

Message written with paper and ink supplied by the landlord, Kieran sent Deirdre and Troy up to the room.

"May I go to vespers, sir?" Deirdre asked from the foot of the stairs.

"No," Kieran said.

The landlord and even Troy looked shocked that he would not allow a young person to go to a church service. He felt his face heat and sighed. "All right, if Troy does not care about going with you."

"Of course I don't, sir." Troy glanced at Deirdre, then back to Kieran. "I'll see to MacKenzie's safety, sir."

"Thank you." Deirdre's voice was soft, her eyes bright. She blinked twice, then turned and dashed up the stairs, Troy in her wake.

Kieran had nearly reached the governor's offices when he realized that the brightness in Deirdre's eyes had been tears.

Chapter 10

*D*eirdre leaned on the windowsill and watched Ashford depart from the inn. The trade winds caught his hair and ruffled it like playful fingers. A handful of finely dressed ladies perusing the stalls turned from the displayed wares and watched him instead, their parasols coquettishly shading their eyes. He seemed not to notice them as he stalked straight ahead, a man with a purpose, a commission of great importance. If he'd glanced back just once, Deirdre would have waved to him. But he didn't, so she watched him until he disappeared from sight.

Her last sight of him.

"Does his family dislike him?" she asked Troy, who sat just outside the open doorway between both rooms.

"No, Miss MacKenzie, I'd say they love him right well." The straight wooden chair creaked beneath Troy's weight as he shifted. "His sisters adore him, and his mama is the kindest lady in the world."

"His father?"

Deirdre needed to know what kind of homecoming he would receive after his seafaring adventures. Or would they view them as misadventures and make him suffer because he'd lost the prisoners?

Troy cleared his throat. "Well, his . . . father can be a stern man. He was a naval officer and expects to be obeyed."

Deirdre perched on the edge of the high four-poster bed. "And Ashford disobeyed his father, so the man sent him to sea?"

"I can't say, Miss MacKenzie."

"Oh, yes, you can. You just won't."

Deirdre bounced up and began to prowl around the chamber, running a finger over the surface of the armoire, tracing a leaf on one of the pineapples gracing the tops of the posts, looking out of the window again to see if it really were too far a distance and hard a landing to jump. She doubted Troy would jump after her. And by the time he got outside, she would have lost herself in the crowd.

The church bells reminded her that she had a better plan.

"Do you mind me going to vespers?" she asked.

"No, miss, if you still wish to go."

"I do." She wandered to the window and rested her elbows on the sill.

She caught no sign of Ashford in the square, not that she'd expected one, but she did see a hundred other people. They ranged from black to white to brown, even to ivory. Some looked poor and others wealthy. She noticed some large blond men she thought might belong to a Russian vessel, and noted where they headed. A lad in fancy green-and-gold livery rushed toward the inn, a packet in his dark hand. She and her crew could blend into a throng like that and lose themselves.

If she could get them away.

A knock sounded on the door. Troy closed the door to Deirdre's room and went to answer it. She snatched up the pillows.

Troy opened the door. "That was a lad from the Willoughby plantation. Mr. Ashford will be taking dinner with them and staying the night."

Deirdre's heart began to pound, but she kept her voice calm. "Then we can leave for vespers."

"Yes, miss, but I'm holding your arm the whole time."

"When we're outside, yes, but not in the church. I want to pray alone and take communion."

And pray for forgiveness for all her lies.

Troy nodded his assent, and they made their way through the crowded square to St. Peter's Cathedral. Only a handful of persons occupied the mostly wooden church, and those looked like they had come in for the cool shade rather than to worship.

Cold rather than cool, Deirdre slipped up the aisle and into one of the pew boxes. Between the high back of the pew and the door to the box, Troy couldn't see her well. When she knelt, she knew he couldn't see her at all.

Lord, give me strength, she prayed as the mass began.

Trying not to fidget, she followed the service, though she didn't have a *Book of Common Prayer* with her. With so few persons present, no one seemed to be reciting the congregation's part in voices anyone could hear outside their own boxes. That made the mass seem longer, the droning voice of the priest coming too close to putting her to sleep. Fingers tense on the latch to her door, she waited for the signal for communion.

When it came, she bolted from her box and then forced herself to take a sedate pace up the aisle to the altar. A glance behind her showed a line of worshipers, and Troy hanging back in the church doorway.

She accepted the wafer from the vicar, but before he reached the line of supplicants at the rail, she dropped to all fours to be below the line of pews and thus Troy's sight, and crawled like an overgrown infant toward the door behind the altar.

A few people gasped. Someone made a noise as though intending to call out, but no one would interrupt Holy Communion—

At the door, she reached up, turned the door handle, and crawled through. On the other side, she stood and ran down the steps to an alleyway. In moments, she was racing for the wharves.

She grabbed the first sailor she saw near a long boat. "Quick. I need to get to the Russian boat before my captain catches me."

The man laughed, exuding the stench of rum on his breath. "Been where you aughtn't a' been, eh? I can help, but it'll cost you."

Cost. Of course it would cost, and her gold still lay hidden on the *Maid of Alexandria*. She had no silver.

But yes, she did.

She twisted off one of her vest buttons. "Solid silver. You can have another one when I'm home free."

"Well, now." The burly seaman took the button and bit it with teeth that looked too rotten to bite a pudding. "Seems you're tellin' the truth. Get in."

She dove in, then crouched low on the thwarts to make herself as invisible as possible.

The sailor untied the painter, then jumped in before the boat drifted away from the dock. He looked as weather-beaten as a deck and smelled soaked in rum, but he pulled the oars with sure, strong strokes that sent them skidding across the calm surface of the harbor waters and straight for the Russian ship.

Perhaps because they anchored in a safe harbor and this was broad daylight, no man stood sentry on the Russian brig. Her oarsman wanted to pull off, muttering something about this being a deserted ship and bad luck.

"Don't be ridiculous." Deirdre could hear the chink of coins and thud of tankards on wood coming from the stern cabin. "They're below."

With no time to waste, she scaled the chains and landed on the deck with a thud that still brought no one up to investigate. The echoes of raucous laughter drew her aft, and she swaggered down the companionway ladder and into the cabin.

The laughter stopped. Men stared. One dropped his hand to a cutlass tucked into his three-inch-wide belt.

"Ami," Deirdre spoke in the French most Russian seamen knew.

"I'm a friend. I need to get away from my present berth at once. Will you take me on as your cabin boy?"

The man stared at her with bloodshot blue eyes. "I do not need a cabin boy. Got too many crew as it is." Lifting his tankard, he tossed down a handful of cards and cursed in Russian.

One of the other three men at the table scooped up a coin from in front of the captain.

"A passenger then?" Deirdre pressed. "I can pay."

The men around the table laughed.

"A boy like you can't afford to pay," spoke a man with eyes so close together they almost met at the narrow bridge of his nose.

"I can—" Deirdre began.

"Go away." The Russian captain hunched his burly shoulders against her and began shuffling cards.

Desperate, Deirdre offered Ashford a silent apology and played her best hand. "Please, monsieur. You must understand, my captain wishes to use me as his—" She didn't know the French word, and blushed at the English one, despite having heard it in many a dockside tavern.

All the men understood her hesitation and blush. Tankards were suspended halfway to mouths and the deck of cards fluttered to the table.

Five minutes later, she had made a bargain and plans.

Kieran barely noticed that the tea was weak and the sandwiches a little stale. It was food cooked on land and, like the noonday meal, divine for that alone. He liked the surroundings, too. Mrs. Willoughby had chosen to serve her refreshments on a shady terrace with roses and jasmine scenting the air in heady profusion. Mrs. Willoughby wore perfume, too, the same violet scent his mother applied with a far lighter hand, and every move her daughters made sent lily of the valley blending with the floral bouquet of aromas until he had to suppress more than one sneeze.

But they were pretty and charming, all three possessing huge dark and sparkling eyes and complexions they had managed to keep flawless and creamy despite the subtropical sun.

Unlike Deirdre's bronzed yet flawless skin.

He pushed thoughts of Deirdre aside. She disturbed him and was better left out of his brainbox until tomorrow morning.

He turned to Mrs. Willoughby, née Moira Kate McIntyre in Savannah, Georgia, when it had been a colony. "So, madam, you do remember my parents?"

"I knew the instant we learned that an Ashford had captured that American ship that you had to be related." She preened. "I was composing a message for you when yours arrived. So thoughtful of you to pay us a call. My husband will be delighted. And my daughters always enjoy company."

They looked as though company frightened them to death, as they hid their faces behind their teacups and blushed.

He smiled at them, which made them blush even darker and bow their heads.

"My husband doesn't like them meeting the military men," Mrs. Willoughby explained, "which means they meet few gentlemen at all. I was going to send them to my family in Savannah, but then this wretched war began . . . But you're not interested in our troubles. Tell us about capturing that American schooner."

He shrugged. "It was nothing. They were not prepared to fight and surrendered easily."

"But their vessel is so odd looking," the elder daughter whispered. "The masts look about to fall down."

"She is fast," Kieran said.

He felt oddly defensive of the *Maid*. She was not odd; she was graceful and beautiful.

But they would think Deirdre was odd, when he thought she was also graceful and beautiful.

"They were becalmed," he added, "or we never would have caught them. We had sweeps."

And three times as many men.

"Will they all go to prison?" Mrs. Willoughby asked.

"I am afraid that will be so."

"Your father must be so proud of you," the younger Willoughby daughter murmured.

"Mama has told us that he was in the British Navy." The elder daughter—Mary?—grew a little bolder. "But you chose not to go into the military?"

"My mama would never have approved," Kieran said.

That made the ladies laugh.

"She always was a peace-loving little thing." Mrs. Willoughby reached for the teapot and rose to refill cups, her silk gown swishing like the breeze through the wisteria vines giving them shade. "Is she still shy?"

"No, madam, she is the friendliest lady in the county. Our house is constantly filled with guests."

She, at least, would welcome Deirdre with open arms. His sisters would, too. But his father? He would be polite at the least.

"Ah, yes, she was kind." Sadness crossed Mrs. Willoughby's face. "I hated putting her on that naval vessel with your father practically a stranger to her, but it was for the best."

"Apparently so." Kieran smiled when he considered his parents' marriage. "They are devoted to one another."

"Wonderful." Mrs. Willoughby's face lit. "Your mama has written, of course, but letters do not always tell a true tale. Now do tell us all about your home and your sisters."

Kieran obliged, remembering what he could about current fashions, since the ladies seemed to like that topic best. The early evening lazed on. He would have felt relaxed and comfortable except for concern about Deirdre.

When the ladies went upstairs to dress for dinner and prepare for the imminent arrival of Mr. Willoughby and a handful of guests, Kieran went for a stroll through the gardens. The clean scent of pine refreshed his nose after all the floral perfumes, which helped to clear his head enough to think of what about those last moments with Deirdre nagged at the back of his mind.

He paused at the end of a crushed-shell path and gazed toward where a distant sparkle spoke of the sea not far off.

Why else would she have tears in her eyes when saying good-bye to him if she did not fear the marriage? If not fear, at least regret its necessity. Yet if she did not want it, why did she not simply say so? Deirdre was not shy or afraid to state what she did or did not like. Yet when she had said good-bye to him—

"Good-bye," Kieran cried aloud. "God be with you. Farewell. Oh, Deirdre, you would not."

But of course she would.

Spinning on his heel, he loped back to the house to make his apologies to the Willoughbys and ask for fast transport back to St. George's.

Since the sailor rowing the longboat looked about to lose consciousness from his consumption of rum, Deirdre used all but one of her buttons to make a trade with him—a supply of rum, a dagger, and the use of his boat. She used the last button to send the bottles of rum to the *Maid* with a note supposedly from Kieran stating that he would be away and for them to enjoy themselves despite being stranded on the schooner. She hoped the men were bored enough and resentful enough for not being allowed to go ashore that they would not reject the rum.

She didn't want to physically harm any of them to achieve her goal. Getting them drunk was a far lesser crime. Kieran wouldn't punish them for that, especially with the forged note to justify their actions.

She hated waiting another hour before returning to the clipper, but needed time for the rum to take effect. With every moment that passed, she feared that Troy would arrive or go out to the *Maid*. She counted on him not expecting her to return to the vessel, and she calculated that he would go for Kieran at once.

At the end of the hour, with the sun beginning to slope toward the sea in red-gold glory, she rose from her crouch on the bottom of the longboat and began to row. She'd never done that alone, and the strain made her muscles ache, then quiver with fatigue. Her shirt became soaked with sweat, and she discarded her vest. Only half a dozen more yards. Three. Two . . .

The longboat bumped against the *Maid*'s side. A blurry-eyed Jones leaned over the rail. "Whozh there?"

"Deirdre MacKenzie," she called up. "Mr. Ashford is occupied for the evening, but Troy'll be along soon."

She hoped she was wrong in that.

"Did the oranges arrive?" she asked, as she grabbed the chains and clambered aboard.

He made a face as though about to be ill. "Stinkin' up the main cabin."

"I'll go fetch some then. Mr. Ashford wants the prisoners to have some right away. Will you escort me down with them?"

"Aye, if 'tis what Mr. Ashford wants." Jones sagged against the rail.

Deirdre glared at him. "You being drunk on watch is not what he wanted when he sent the rum. Give me trouble and I'll tell him. I'm going to be his wife, you know."

Shock twisted his homely features, and he took a long pull at the rum bottle. "Mercy on us, Mr. Ashford marrying you."

Unreasonably annoyed, Deirdre turned her back on him, stalked down to the cabin, and locked the door behind her. She could scarcely move for the crates of oranges and lemons stacked on table, chairs, bunk, and deck. No matter. She didn't need to move far. Only to the cupboard behind the table.

With her heart pounding, she removed several bottles of preserved fruit, slid the tip of the borrowed dagger between the panels, and pushed open the concealed door. Inside, a tin box glowed with a dull sheen. The key she'd managed to remove from the coffee canister and hidden in her stiletto sheath now in hand, she unlocked the box that was affixed to the bulkhead and popped up the lid. Copper tubes wrapped in oiled cloth and sealed with wax snuggled inside. In two of those tubes, wrapped in more oiled cloth, lay bank certificates for institutions in London and Alexandria. A copy of her father's will enjoyed the same watertight treatment. Two more tubes held specie— gold in one, silver in another.

After removing the cylinders, shoving the first three down her shirt, Deirdre pushed the cupboard door back into place and set to work. A quarter hour later, she returned to the deck lugging a box of fruit. Jones still slumped against the rail gazing toward St. George's. Three other men on watch ranged about the deck, their backs to her, a clear message that Englishmen weren't going to help an American.

"Too bad for you," she murmured.

Maneuvering down the ladders with the crate was even more difficult than rowing the longboat alone. Determination kept her going, breath ragged, arms aching, splinters driving into her arms and hands. At the ladder to the hold, she had to stop, light a lantern and carry it down, then return with the crate.

Thirteen startled faces stared up at her in the feeble light.

"What the deuce are you doing here?" Ross demanded.

Deirdre dropped the crate and drew her dagger. She couldn't help grinning. "I've come to free you."

"Much good that'll do on an island," Blaze jeered. "Leave it to a woman—"

"Listen to her," Wat interrupted. "Are those oranges in that crate, Deirdre? I'm like to die of thirst."

"Can't eat an orange tied up," Blaze grumbled.

Deirdre decided to cut him loose last. She went to Ross first. The instant his hands were free, he grabbed her arms and shook her. "What have you done?"

"I gave Troy the slip. There's money in that fruit. Gold in the oranges, silver in the lemons. The only weapons I could get you are dinner knives, belaying pins, and marlinespikes, but—"

"Dash it all, Deirdre." Ross shook her harder. "You know that we're not going anywhere without you."

An uneasy murmur rippled through the men.

Deirdre held up her hand for silence. "I've arranged it all." Though half of what she was about to tell them was a lie, she made certain to look Ross in the eye so he'd believe her. "I've found a Russian captain who'll take me aboard as a passenger. He's heading to Philadelphia before the English sign a treaty with the tsar, so I can get to Alexandria from there."

"You can't go aboard a Russian ship," Wat objected.

"His wife's along," Deirdre assured them in complete falsehood. "I'll be safe. As for you—" She continued to slice ropes. "If you go inland and across the island, you'll find a way home with one smuggler or another."

"I didn't know a girl could be so smart." One of the newer men spoke in a loud whisper.

Deirdre decided to untie that man second to last.

"How we gonna go free, Miz Deirdre?" Zeb asked. "They got slaves here, don' they?"

"You'll be all right if you stay with Wat or Ross," Deirdre assured him. "Act like their servant."

Deirdre freed Blaze. "Now get moving. There are only four guards aboard, and they're drinking heavily. We'll manage them easily." She began passing out fruit. "Tuck them into your clothes. Hurry."

"Wait." Ross stopped her. "Do you think we'll go without knowing you're safe?"

"We'll see her safe off." Blaze snatched up several pieces of citrus and a marlinespike.

"The Russian boat is waiting for me below the stern windows." Deirdre leaped onto the ladder and started up.

With only minimal chaos, the men sorted themselves out, collected weapons, and followed.

Deirdre wanted to sing, shout, dance with joy. Her heart raced so fast she could scarcely feel it. Freedom! Her men would no longer have to be concerned about her at their own expense. They could escape. Go home. Fight.

She fairly flew up the ladders, soared over the coaming—

And came face to face with Kieran Ashford.

Chapter 11

$\mathscr{D}$eirdre slashed her stiletto toward Ashford. He jumped out of range. She darted around him and sprinted for the companionway. She must reach the cabin. She had a few moments' advantage.

Behind her, the deck erupted into a maelstrom of shouts and pounding feet, orders, a scream.

Deirdre skimmed down the companionway and into the cabin. *Slam the door. Lock it.* No, better than that. She flung boxes of oranges against the door.

"Deirdre!" Ashford's voice sounded beyond the door. Fists pounded on the panel.

He would kick it in. He was strong and could move the crates.

Deirdre leaped onto the window seat. Right on schedule, the Russian boat hovered below her. She swung her legs over the windowsill.

The cabin door crashed inward. "Stop!"

Deirdre dropped. Huge, calloused hands caught her, set her on the thwarts.

Ashford leaned from the window, tried to grab her. A Russian lashed at his arm with an oar.

Deirdre gasped. "Don't. Get away. Hurry. *Vite, vite, vite.*"

The Russians began to pull away from the *Maid of Alexandria*.

"Don't do it, Deirdre," Ashford shouted.

"See you at home, Deirdre," Ross called from the deck where he stood with Blaze and two other of her men. "My love."

"Get away," Deirdre shouted back. "They'll stop you."

"I'll stop you," Ashford roared. He swung his legs over the window ledge.

She cast a frantic look at the Russians. "Faster."

"He can't catch us," one man said in a voice slower than any Southerner's. "We'll get you safe."

Of course they would. No one could jump into the harbor and swim to the boat.

Ashford didn't jump. He stood on the window ledge and launched into a dive that carried him yards away from the schooner.

Yards closer to her.

He still couldn't catch her. No one swam that well.

Ashford cut through the water like a dolphin. Swift.

Graceful.

Not too swift. Oars were faster than swimmers.

The Russians seemed to row as if the water were jelly, slow, ponderous. Ashford gained on them. She swore. He would catch them. Take her back.

If her men were safe it wouldn't matter.

Anxious, she glanced toward the quarterdeck. Only Blaze remained, glowing like a mahogany figurehead in the sunset. One arm raised, swung. Metal flashed.

Deirdre screamed. "No!"

Too late. The marlinespike swooped toward Ashford.

"Look out," Deirdre cried.

Ashford raised his head—too late. The marlinespike struck. He went down. The harbor water closed over his head.

And stayed closed.

Deirdre sprang to her feet. Rough hands dragged her back. She elbowed one man in the belly and kicked another in the groin. The second man bellowed, dropped back, landed against his companion.

Freed, Deirdre dove. Harbor water engulfed her. Green. Murky. Foul. She saw nothing. She felt nothing but cold deeper inside than the water reached. Searing pain in her lungs. Roaring in her ears. She had to surface.

She had to find him. If he drowned, it would be her fault.

She was going to drown, too. Another heartbeat and her lungs would burst. She would breathe in water . . .

Her foot struck something solid. She twisted in the water, reached out, felt long, wet strands. Seaweed? The bottom of a ship? Or Ashford's hair?

His hair. She grabbed a fistful and hauled him to her. Wrapping her arms around him, she kicked her legs, trying to drag him to the surface. Her legs were gelatinous lumps. Useless legs. Useless arms. Searing lungs.

His weight dragged her down. Down to death, not up to air, to life. She had no more breath, no more strength. She could let him sink and save herself or go down with him.

She couldn't let him go. One more try. One more kick.

His weight lifted from her arms. She still clung to him, but he was buoyant, drawing her upward. The water lightened. She saw sky. Her head broke the surface.

Hands grabbed her, lifted her over a gunwale, then bent her over that same gunwale while she spewed up harbor water.

"Thatta girl, cough it up." Ross's voice.

Deirdre whipped around. He knelt beside her, drenched to the skin, his hair hanging in sodden clumps around his face. On the other side of the *Maid's* longboat, two English seamen held Ashford over the gunwale. His hair streamed down his back like black seaweed threaded with a scarlet ribbon.

"Dead men don't bleed, do they?" Deirdre murmured.

"He's still alive, but he's in a bad way." Ross touched her face. "I'm sorry."

"No, I'm sorry." Deirdre dropped her face into her hands. "It's my fault. You wouldn't have given up your freedom if not for me. If I'd gotten away . . ." Her voice shook, but she didn't weep. Her pain ran too deep for tears. "Did anyone escape?"

"Blaze and Zeb. They swim almost as well as Ashford. A good thing, too. If they caught Blaze, they'd hang him."

"He shouldn't have done it." She doubled over. "What have I done?"

Ross squeezed her shoulder. "You're going to have to figure that one out for yourself, my sweet."

The boat bumped against the ship. Curses rang down on them like hailstones, preventing Deirdre from asking Ross what he meant. She couldn't be concerned with herself now. She had to think of Ross, her crew, and Ashford.

Shaky, she rose and reached for the chains. Her hands wouldn't grip. Ross lifted her up high enough for one of the Englishmen to haul her aboard.

"I'd like to throw you back," the man ground out.

"I don't blame you," Deirdre answered.

He looked startled and released her. "Get below before I'm tempted, missy."

"Help me with Mr. Ashford." She forced her muddled brain to think. "Hot water. Fresh water. Lots of it. Lemons. We've lots aboard. And rum. Rum helps fi-fight—" She couldn't say it, that dreaded word that could result from swallowing harbor water. The disease that killed too many sailors.

She was safe. She had lived through typhoid. One didn't contract it twice. But what about Ashford? Highborn, pampered, rich enough to drink wine and tea instead of water . . .

"And something for bandages." She concluded her list of necessities and turned aft. The deck dipped and swayed beneath her as if the ship rode out a storm. She flung out a hand for balance.

A solid arm appeared beneath her hand. "I've got you, miss," Troy said. "I'll get you to your cabin."

She shook her head. "Ashford."

"We'll see to him."

"No, I must. My fault." Her vision blurred. She blinked to clear it. No time for tears now. "Please. I know I did you wrong at the church, but let me see to him."

"You get yourself into dry clothes first. Then we'll see."

Troy's kindness nearly broke Deirdre. She had to force herself to place one foot in front of the other. Inside her cabin, the temptation to collapse onto the bunk nearly overwhelmed her. The sound of men carrying Ashford into his cabin stiffened her spine.

After stripping off her sodden clothes, she tucked the cylinders into the false bottom of her sea chest, dried off on her coverlet, and yanked on shirt and breeches. Her braid was half unbound, but she left it as it was and stumbled the few feet to the captain's cabin.

Troy and Jones were tugging off Ashford's clothes. Ashford's face was ashen, his eyes closed, his body inert. He looked dead save for the blood soaking through a pad of linen and into the pillow.

"Jones, fetch a doctor," she commanded.

Jones, apparently sober now, turned on her. "Don't you order me around, you—"

"Fetch a doctor, Jones," Troy said. "She can help me."

"It ain't right," Jones objected.

"Go," Troy shouted.

Jones stomped from the cabin.

Deirdre went to Troy's side. Without a word, she began to dry Ashford. Hot water arrived, and she bathed him while Troy cleared away the crates of fruit. She touched all of him, face, chest, legs. Smooth skin over refined muscles. A dusting of dark hair, thicker on his legs and chest. A beautiful man. A strong man. A man who neither moved nor spoke.

She replaced the makeshift bandage on his scalp. Where it wasn't sticky with gore, his hair was soft. She combed her fingers through it, brushing strands stuck to his face, and felt the scar on one ear. What was left of one ear. No wonder he wore his hair long. That disfigurement would damage his good looks. She started to wonder how he received the wound, but jerked her hand away and concentrated on staunching the bleeding from his newer wound. Once, Deirdre laid her head against his chest to assure herself of his heartbeat. It was too weak for such a big man. It couldn't keep him alive. She and her crew would have given up their freedom for nothing if he died. She had sacrificed her crew to save the enemy, and no good would come of it. Even if Ashford lived, he would not be grateful to her.

She should have let him drown. They would all be free if she had. Yet she had accused him of causing her father's death and could not turn around and be the cause of his.

She must keep him alive to protect her crew, to keep them all alive. She pressed a pad of cloth to the gash on his scalp. "The doctor will have to shave part of his pretty hair."

"He's got enough to cover it." Troy laid his hand on her shoulder. "Go to your own cabin, Miss MacKenzie. You look worn to a shade. I'll see to him now."

"No, I must do it. I have to do it."

"You'll make yourself ill if you don't get some rest."

"I won't rest knowing he's in danger."

Deirdre had the same conversation with the doctor who came to stitch up Ashford's head, pronounce that he was concussed, and predict that he'd likely end up with a fever. She had the same conversation with Troy a dozen times during the next two days. "This is my fault. I will nurse him back to health."

She didn't realize how difficult that would be. Oh, she had done her share of nursing. She didn't grow faint at the sight of bloody bandages or gag at cleaning up from sickness, both of which she had to deal with taking care of Ashford. She even managed on little sleep. When she grew fatigued, she reminded herself she had only herself to blame, and kneeled on the hard deck beside his bunk, bathing his face with cool cloths and holding his hand, spooning tea and broth between his lips, and reading to him whether he heard her or not.

Two days after Blaze's attack on him, Ashford opened his eyes and stared straight into hers. "Fool me once, shame on you. Fool me twice, shame on me."

"I'm—" She stopped the apology before it slipped out.

She was sorry he was injured. She was sorry she and her crew had not gotten away. She was not sorry she had tricked him.

"I had to try to free us. Please understand."

But he was already unconscious again.

With a sigh, she rested her head on the bunk beside him and must have drifted to sleep, for his voice jerked her awake sometime later.

"You have got to believe me, sir. I never—I never—"

His head tossed hard enough to dislodge the bandage.

"Hush." Deirdre stroked his face, trying to calm him enough to replace the dressing. "I believe you."

"You will regret this." The words were clear, the message surely meant for her, yet his eyes remained closed.

Deirdre tied the white linen strips back around his head, combing her fingers through the thick tangle of his hair, then settled beside him again. "Sleep now."

"Ah, so sweet." A smile curved his lips. "So beautiful."

Deirdre's solar plexus tightened. "How can you say that when I—"

"Joanna, my dear."

Deirdre rocked back on her heels as though he had struck her. He hadn't been talking about her. He was dreaming of that other lady who had betrayed him. She, Deirdre, was neither sweet nor beautiful, especially not to him. She was a fool for thinking he had been, even for a second. And yet, for that moment, she had hoped he meant her.

Only because that meant he had forgiven her for her treachery, nothing else. The sound of another woman's name on his lips merely annoyed her.

He didn't mention the sweet and beautiful Joanna again. His fevered ramblings focused on trying to convince someone to believe him, to understand. Deirdre considered asking him about whom he fretted so much, and maybe even ask him about his scarred ear.

Then he awoke the evening of the third day and fixed his eyes on her with sorrow dimming their golden depths. "You had tears in your eyes when you said good-bye at the inn."

"Nonsense." Deirdre laid her wrist on his brow to test for fever. "Your fever has broken."

He caught hold of her wrist. "I came back because you had tears in your eyes when you said good-bye."

"But you're still concussed."

"I am perfectly well." He tried to sit up, but fell back against the pillow. "And weak as a kitten."

"Rest." She collected a full bottle of laudanum. "You need rest."

She spoke briskly to mask her joy in seeing him in his right mind and not cursing her for her actions—yet.

"No medicine." He closed his eyes. "Cannot trust you out of my sight for a moment."

"I have scarcely left you for a moment." She returned to his side.

He clasped her hand in his. "Do not go."

Later he roused and asked about the *Phoebe*.

"No sign of her yet." Deirdre brought him a cup of broth. "Maybe tomorrow."

"Either way, we will settle this tomorrow."

Deirdre blinked. "Settle what?"

"Your future."

"My future is settled. I will be treated as a noncombatant prisoner."

"Not if you are my wife."

Broth splashed onto the sheet. "That blow to your head addled your wits. I nearly got you killed."

"You saved my life at great cost to yourself. The least I can do is protect yours." He levered himself up on one elbow. "So my offer of marriage still stands."

Deirdre stared at him. "I would be as mad to accept your offer as you are to give it."

"You could end up in prison for what you did."

A possibility she hadn't taken the time to consider.

"So I marry you to stay out of prison, and you marry me to pay a debt—"

"My life is worth a great deal to me." He touched his right ear hidden beneath a swath of dark hair. "Especially after nearly losing it this second time."

Deirdre seized the diversion from marriage talk. "I noticed it. What happened?"

"A farce of a duel where the seconds lied." He waved one hand as though shooing off a fly. "It's not important at present."

"It is if it's another reason for your loss of honor."

"It is, but if I take home a bride, my father will see me and I can prove the truth—about that at the least."

If not what had happened with his fiancée.

"Between you saving my life and giving me the entrée with my family," he continued, "I will be eternally grateful to you."

"I don't know much about the subject, but I don't think gratitude is a good basis for marriage."

"I think we can find more to a union than gratitude." He gave her a sleepy-eyed smile that curled her toes and sent tension coiling deep in her belly.

Needing to break the impulse to touch him, Deirdre backed to the window seat still clutching the cup of broth as though it were her good sense. "You don't trust me."

"Another reason why I would prefer to have you where I can keep an eye on you." He dropped back onto his pillow. "To have to leave you to your own devices when I am responsible for capturing you is a frightening idea."

Deirdre laughed with relief. "You aren't serious."

"I am perfectly serious. I expect an answer tomorrow by the time the *Phoebe* arrives or our repairs are effected and we sail."

The next morning, when Troy descended to the cabin to inform her that the *Phoebe* had just limped into St. George's Harbor, Deirdre had not yet made up her mind. She would be better off as Ashford's wife, especially if otherwise she would end up in a prison. Yet marriage to him sounded like it would be just as confining as stone walls. She still might end up with a tradesman's family to guard her, a situation she surely could escape now that she possessed money and the means to more. She would not escape Kieran Ashford again.

Nor, she feared, would she elude Captain Heron's wrath. With Kieran still asleep, she followed Troy on deck to meet her next hurdle.

The *Maid of Alexandria* lay under a pall of unnatural silence as Captain Heron and two of the *Phoebe*'s boyish-looking seamen climbed aboard. All three of them appeared exhausted, with shadows beneath their eyes and hollow cheeks. Their clothes were crumpled and streaked with salt stains, and Heron sported a bandage around his left wrist.

Troy beside her, Deirdre stood at the top of the companionway and watched the Englishmen climb aboard.

Heron glanced around the too-quiet deck, then approached Deirdre and Troy. "Where's Ashford?" His voice rasped as though he'd been shouting too much.

"Below, sir," Troy said. "There was a bit of trouble three days ago and he's . . . er . . . injured."

"Injured?" Alarm crossed Heron's face. "How? Where?"

"His head, sir." Deirdre's own voice came out raspy. "May I please explain after you've had some breakfast? We have eggs and fresh fruit and—"

"You will explain now," Heron commanded, looking at Troy. "Why is she not locked in her cabin? She's a prisoner."

"She's been helping me nurse Mr. Ashford, sir."

"Why is that nursing necessary?" Heron glared at Deirdre. "Start with when you arrived here."

"Three days and a night ago," Deirdre said. "We had some damage from the storm—"

"Does Troy know what happened in those three days?" Heron interrupted.

"Yes, sir, I do," Troy said.

"Then I want the report from an Englishman."

Deirdre opened her mouth to protest, but shut it without saying a word. She didn't need Heron's reminder that she was not English, and therefore the enemy, to let her know that she stood in an untenable situation. A dangerous situation for her crew and herself.

Troy told his version of the incident that had culminated in two prisoners escaping and Kieran Ashford lying injured. The men from the *Phoebe* stood swaying, looking so fatigued they might fall over at any moment. And Deirdre stood with her legs braced apart, her arms crossed over her chest, expecting Heron to command her to be carried to the privateer and locked up somewhere, and her crew flogged.

She had only one option to spare them all if Heron chose the course he had wanted to before the storm separated the two vessels.

At the moment, his face remained impassive. He didn't so much as flick a glance her way.

"Miss MacKenzie did save his life," Troy concluded his story, bless him. "None of us could swim."

"Huh." Heron didn't sound impressed.

"And some of my crew pulled us out of the water," Deirdre added, "rather than escape as they could have."

"Huh," Heron said again. He rubbed his red-rimmed eyes. "Is Kieran awake?"

"He may be now," Troy said.

"I'll see." Before either man could stop her, Deirdre leaped down the companionway and dashed into the cabin.

"So the *Phoebe* has arrived." Kieran sat on the edge of the bunk, his shirt on and a sheet covering his lower half. The bandage glowed white against his dark hair, a stark reminder of the assault on his life. "Is all well?"

"Well enough." Deirdre dropped to her knees beside him. "Ashford . . . Kieran . . ."

Before she gathered her scrambled wits to speak further than her first use of his Christian name, Heron stomped into the cabin.

"At least I don't have to face your mother and tell her I couldn't keep you alive." His tone was gruff, but the look he cast Kieran was affectionate. "Of course, the report to your father—"

"What took you so long to get here?" Kieran broke in.

"Storm hit us hard." Heron stepped over Deirdre's legs as though she weren't there and settled on the window seat. "We will need to hole up here for a bit and effect some repairs. The *Phoebe* lost a topmast and took some other damage in that blow. Looks as though you rode it out well enough."

Kieran gave out a rusty laugh. "Not well, but we rode it out, thanks to Deirdre's quick actions."

"Yes, well—" Heron harrumphed. "She needs to be guarded strictly while we're at sea and the authorities notified about her antics once we are on land, too. According to Troy, she is a menace to your safety."

"She saved my life," Kieran said.

"She would have been hanged if she had not." Heron reached down and grasped Deirdre's upper arm. "Troy, remove her—"

Kieran closed his hand around Heron's wrist. "Let go of her, Heron. Under whose authority she will be here at sea or on land is not yet settled, is it, m'dear?"

Deirdre gulped and stared at the rumpled sheet covering his legs.

"Deirdre?" Kieran cupped his hand beneath her chin, gently compelling her to look at him.

Beneath his half-mast lids, his eyes held that sleepy look Deirdre now knew meant he was at his most intense. She braced herself.

"What is the answer to my question?" He spoke in a voice like a purr. "Are you going to marry me?" He brushed his thumb across her lower lip. "Speak the truth this time."

PART II

Chapter 12

Devonshire, England
November 1812

*E*ngland was cold. It was wet. It reeked of too many men packed in dark, dank quarters upon the half-dozen naval vessels anchored in Plymouth Harbor along with countless brigs, schooners, and single-masted pinnaces. Garbage floated on the murky water around which bung boats steered, selling wares ranging from fresh vegetables to doxies.

Though her only coat proved inadequate to the damp chill permeating to her bone marrow, Deirdre stood amidships in the tumbling rain and watched yet one more kind of boat draw away from the *Maid of Alexandria*—longboats. Rowed by men in the tarred hats, striped shirts, and white duck trousers of British sailors, the two craft carried her crew toward shore, toward prison.

Tears blending with the rain, icy on her face, she waved until the boats vanished around the looming hull of a seventy-four-gun ship-of-the-line. They couldn't wave back. Their hands and feet were shackled. Neither did they look at her.

Not one of them had looked at her in the six weeks since she had gone ashore with Kieran Ashford at St. George's and returned two days later with his ring on her finger. She had tried to talk to Ross once.

"I did it for your sakes." She had pleaded for Ross's understanding.

Ross spat into the sea. "You're lying with the enemy."

"I'm his wife. He has a right to me."

"And you look like you hate every minute of it." He had walked away from her without a glance back.

With that, and with every head turned away from her, her heart had torn and her resolve to free them had hardened. All but two of them had given up their chance to escape there on Bermuda in order to rescue her and Kieran from the harbor waters. They had saved her and Kieran's lives. Freeing them was the least she could do. Once she was settled, once she knew the lay of the land, she would get her men out of prison if it killed her. If the English didn't hang her for treason, now that she was wed to one of their own, her conscience might.

Movement behind her drew her attention seconds before an arm slipped around her shoulders. Kieran, the cause of her divided conscience, drew her close to his side.

"Prisoners at Dartmoor can have visitors, you know. You will get to see them."

"They don't want to see me." She hugged her arms across her chest and stared ahead as though she could see through the massive war ship. "They want nothing to do with me."

The tightening of Kieran's hold reminded her that he wanted her, and, the good Lord forgive her, she wanted him, too. By day, though she and Kieran clashed over their views on the war or toddled toward finding common ground in books they had read or in his interest in the places to which she had sailed and languages learned, each glimpse of her crew reminded her that she had married the enemy. Reminders that slipped an invisible barrier between her ever wanting to befriend her husband. Nighttime, however, found them together in her bunk, as physically close as two people could be, satisfying a soul-deep hunger she hadn't known existed until her wedding night on Bermuda.

She slipped out of the curve of his arm. "At least I can provide them with some comforts. If you will allow it, of course."

"Of course I will. I told you I will be generous with your pin money, and I intend to keep my word." An edge crept into his voice.

Deirdre understood—she must keep her word as well.

She must be an exemplary wife and help restore him to the bosom of his family, English society, respectability. She must provide him with an heir and, for good measure, a second son, to continue the family line of Englishmen. More Englishmen to suppress and imprison Americans, if the United States could not win this war or, if they did, win the next, or the next. Just like the succession of wars between England and France, so would England and her former colonies proceed.

"I will keep my word." She faced him. "I will not shame you in front of your friends and family as far as I am able to avoid doing so. I owe you that much."

"You are capable in any way you need to be." He cupped her elbow in his hand. "Come along. Let's get ashore and into hot baths. And I'll buy you a warm cloak. You're freezing."

"I am, and a hot bath is one of the few things I love about being on land." She followed him down to the cabins.

Her sea chest was already aboard the cutter that would carry them ashore. Besides her clothes and a handful of favorite books, the only personal items she took were the two decorative daggers her father had given her as gifts, the jade dragon, and the family Bible. She had written in that Bible twice since the *Phoebe* captured the *Maid*—once for her father's death and once for her marriage. The next time would be to record the birth of a child, if that day came.

She glanced around the chambers that had been her home since her father bought the schooner six months ago. They were little different from those in previous merchant vessels he had owned. Many of the furnishings were the same, moved from one vessel to the other, bigger or faster ones, but always just the one. Sailing vessels were the only home she had ever known, but by the end of the day, she would enter a home on land.

With one last glance at the bunk they had shared, she retraced her steps up the companionway ladder and back into the rain. "I have nothing else to bring."

"I thought of this." Kieran held up the coffee canister and shook it.

Nothing rattled. The beans were gone. The key to the strongbox was in his pocket. Inside the strongbox lay the specie recovered from the recaptured crew, and the fruit, all but what Deirdre had managed to hide.

She gave him a blank look. "Why would you save that?"

"A reminder to myself to pay attention to small matters." He offered her his arm.

They strolled together to the entry port, where someone had rigged a bosun's chair.

"For the lady," one of the boatmen said in an accent as thick as Riley's porridge.

Kieran and Deirdre laughed.

"I have never used a chair in my life." Deirdre grabbed the chains, swung over the gunwale, and dropped down into the boat.

Six pairs of eyes stared at her with varying levels of astonishment and disapproval.

Kieran lowered himself beside her and directed the men to push off. Then he turned to Deirdre. "One last time."

"Yes, sir." Her stomach rolled at the idea that she might have descended from a merchantman in the fashion of a crewman for the last time. She did not want to leave that life behind. It was the only life she knew save for that year in a girls' school, a year of despair and loneliness.

She twisted around and gazed at the beautiful, graceful Baltimore clipper with its steeply raked masts and clean lines that gave her so much speed. Deirdre would certainly never sail on the *Maid* again.

Her vision blurring, she turned her face toward shore and a future so uncertain she would not allow herself to think of it in any specific detail. She thought of only one step at a time.

"So we'll go to an inn to make ourselves presentable?" She addressed their first actions on land and no further. "Will they have fresh bread and eggs as well?"

"Yes, and lemons, maybe even oranges." Kieran clasped her hand. "We will not be able to tarry there too long. I would like to reach Bishops Cove before nightfall."

"We have to go today?" The cutter was sailing beneath the bowsprit of the seventy-four, and she realized her fingers were crushing Kieran's.

The United States didn't own a single naval vessel that could fight something that big.

Kieran rubbed his thumb on the back of her hand. "If we do not leave here today, Tyne will come here, and I would rather meet him with Mama there."

"Tyne?"

"My father."

"You call him by his name?"

"I do now."

"I only called my father captain when I was on duty."

And she had disobeyed his last orders to her as her captain and as a father who wished to protect her.

"My father never became a captain, but I think there has been a time or two he would have liked to take a rattan cane to my backside as though I were a midshipman."

"He wouldn't dare do that." Deirdre eyed the filthy harbor water, wondering about her chances of escape if she leaped into the murky depths. "You're a grown man."

"A grown man who is wholly dependent on his largess until the prize court comes through with the assessed value of the schooner and cargo and paid out."

Paid out wealth at her expense.

"And you're too much of an English gentleman to get a job." She wrinkled her nose. "I don't understand this expectation of laziness."

"I am supposed to have work as . . . as my father's heir and all that entails—" He broke off and laughed without humor. "He will change his mind now that I have decided to be a respectable married man."

Deirdre was dubious about that, but not because she wouldn't do her best to make the Ashfords happy with his choice. It was the devil's bargain she had made with him.

The cutter swept past a bumboat laden with fresh fish. Despite the powerful stench, Deirdre realized she was starving. Earlier, she had been too distressed over her men being taken away to eat breakfast. She should be distressed now over the impending introduction to Kieran's family. Yet all she could think of was some lovely warm bread, butter, eggs, and fish or beef or chicken, anything that hadn't been preserved in brine for months.

"I need dinner and then a bath." She needed sustenance to face the upcoming ordeal.

"I'll order refreshments sent to your room. I sent Troy ahead to set everything up for us. The George is waiting for us."

Another inn named for the king—or the previous king, or the one before that.

The cutter bumped against a flight of stone steps leading into the pier. Kieran leaped out first and held out his hand. Deirdre started to refuse for the sake of one last bit of independence, but with the seamen watching, with half a dozen females in sight, even if they were not the respectable sort, she took the proffered assistance and stepped onto English soil.

It rocked beneath her worse than any ship in a gale ever felt. For a moment, she feared she would overbalance and land in the water. In an instant, Kieran's arm slipped around her waist, drawing her close to his side despite a few jeers from passersby.

"It's his wife, you fools," one of the oarsmen shouted to the scoffers.

Deirdre laughed, and the world settled. "I suppose I had better get into that dress before your reputation is ruined."

"Indeed." Kieran was laughing, too.

They climbed into a waiting carriage. Sticky from weeks at sea, Deirdre only perched on the edge of the leather cushion. "Is this from your family?"

"No, it's hired. Ours have velvet squabs because Mama gets cold easily."

"I can see why." Deirdre rubbed her upper arms. "I don't think I was this cold coming around Cape Horn."

Nor was she bounced around this much at sea. The iron wheels of the carriage jounced over cobblestones or dropped into holes where the pavers were missing. Through the grimy window, everything looked gray save for a few colorful signs and the red coats of soldiers. Enemy soldiers and naval officers seemed to flood the streets of Plymouth. Except they weren't the enemy. This was their country. She was the outsider.

Deirdre shivered.

"A hot bath and hotter fire will set you right." Kieran leaned down and kissed her. "And this."

"Don't do that in public." She turned her face away. "I need to concentrate on being a lady."

The carriage drew up in front of a brick structure that was a fine inn, possibly the finest she had ever seen. It rose several stories and sprouted chimneys from every corner. Smoke issued from each of those chimneys and feathered into the sky, which was still gray but no longer dousing the world with rain. She caught a whiff of roasting pork and baking apples and groaned aloud.

"We look too disrespectable to be admitted."

"My dear, we could walk in there wrapped in torn sails and they would give us a room." Kieran opened the door and leaped to the ground before anyone came to let down the steps.

A man in dark livery approached from the inn. "Welcome home, my—"

"You received my message then?" Kieran spoke over the man's greeting. "Are our rooms ready?"

"Yes, my—"

"My wife will need assistance dressing." For a second time, Kieran cut off the man's words.

And he had left Deirdre in the carriage. She could have easily leaped down in her boots and breeches, but knew he wanted her to act like a lady regardless of dress, now that they were on land. So she stayed put while he led the liveried man back toward the inn, speaking softly and earnestly. She could not see their faces, but caught the exchange of coin between Kieran and the footman.

Annoyed with being left behind, Deirdre jumped down and strode up to Kieran. "I beg your pardon, but I would like that fire and bath you promised."

The footman jumped and scurried toward the inn.

Kieran's look was unfriendly. "You should have waited for me to assist you down."

"Do not leave me in a carriage like that again." Deirdre stalked past him and into the warm, fragrant embrace of the inn.

A plump, middle-aged matron in black dress and white cap and apron dropped a curtsy. "I'm Mrs. Sparks. You're to come with me. I've my best girl Maggie ready to help you."

Before Kieran stepped over the threshold, Mrs. Sparks was ushering Deirdre up two flights of steps to a chamber bright with light from fire and candles, where two footmen were pouring steaming water into a copper bath. Deirdre nearly plunged in clothes and all. She managed to remain motionless and dignified until the footmen and the innkeeper's wife departed, promising food and a maid shortly.

Food arrived as Deirdre was wondering how she would rinse her freshly washed hair.

"I will pour the water for you," the maid offered.

"But I'm, um, I have nothing to put on but my dress." No one had ever helped Deirdre bathe or wash her hair before.

"Like this." As she stepped out of the tub, the maid wrapped a length of toweling around Deirdre's hair and offered her a velvet dressing gown warmed from the fire. Behind a screen, Deirdre dried off and donned the robe, then leaned over the tub while the maid poured fresh water over her hair until the water ran clear.

"I'll brush it while you eat, madam. I'm Maggie, by the by."

"I'm Deirdre."

The girl giggled. "I know, but I won't be calling you that. Now sit and eat. It's simple fare, but we didn't have much notice."

It was ambrosia fit for a king as far as Deirdre was concerned. While Maggie brushed her hair, Deirdre indulged in a pork pie with pastry as light and flaky as meringue. She followed that with an apple tart frilled with cream and washed it all down with new cider. Several slices of warm bread and fresh butter accompanied the food, and she consumed every one of them.

"So nice to see a lady with appetite." Maggie smoothed the brush along a length of Deirdre's hair. "This is so beautiful it'll be a pleasure to pin it up for you."

"I just braid it."

"No, no, His—your husband has sent up combs."

They were silver studded with seed pearls. Deirdre stared at them with eyes narrowed and jaw set. She didn't want such fripperies from Kieran because now she had to wear them. Not to do so would make people question her fitness to be his wife, as no lady turned down pretty baubles—except for her.

"They won't hold up my hair."

The maid's eyebrows shot up. "I have pins for that."

"And I'm going to freeze in that dress." Her tone was sharp, her guilt emerging.

"You have a warm cloak." Maggie stopped brushing Deirdre's hair long enough to lift a spill of deep blue velvet from the bed.

White fur edged the hood and made up the matching muff.

"You won't be cold in this cloak and with that man as your husband." Maggie's bright blue eyes sparkled.

Deidre thought perhaps the girl was speaking out of turn, but recognized the friendliness for what it was—kindness to a stranger in a strange land—and tears filled her eyes.

If Maggie knew how Deirdre intended to betray England, she might not be so nice.

Annoyed, Deirdre dashed her eyes on her sleeve. "I'd better get ready then and not keep him waiting."

"No, madam. He's downstairs pacing already."

They hurried as fast as anyone could when two dozen hooks marched up the back of Deirdre's dress, for all its simplicity, and her hair needed further brushing to dry it. But in the end, Maggie declared her beautiful. Deirdre thought herself more like a sow's ear someone tried to pass off as a silk purse, with nothing to be done about her height and rolling stride.

She descended the steps to find Kieran was indeed pacing the lobby between taproom and coffee room. He stopped at her approach, stared for a moment, then smiled and came forward, hands outstretched.

"You will do better than well, m'dear. Shall we anon?" He tucked her hand into the crook of his elbow and led her to the waiting carriage without anyone so much as mentioning the reckoning.

A footman waited for them to climb in. He let up the steps and closed the door, bowing as he did so. Then the carriage set off to the east with the sea on one side of the road and the land on the other.

Deirdre suddenly wished she hadn't eaten quite so much. She crossed her arms over her middle and pressed her back into the corner of the squabs. "Is your family expecting us?"

"They are." Kieran waved a creased sheet of parchment at her. "This is my father's response to my message announcing our imminent arrival."

From his grim expression, she knew the response was not good. "He's not happy about us?"

"He is not happy about me." Kieran balled up the letter and tossed it across the carriage, where it landed on the opposite seat. "He does not know about our marriage yet. I thought I should deliver that news in person."

"You aren't delaying because you're ashamed of marrying me?"

"No." He laid the back of his hand against her cheek. "I am ashamed of obtaining a letter of marque. I am ashamed of having caused your father's death. I am ashamed that I am the cause of eleven good men now heading to Dartmoor. But if anything will redeem me in Tyne's sight, it is marrying you."

"So you've said." Deirdre blinked back too-ready tears. "But he may reject me out of hand."

"You are a lady bearing the Ashford name. I cannot guarantee that my father will love you. You are hindered a bit by being my wife, since he does not love me. But I can and do promise that he will protect you with his life because you are an Ashford."

"How could a father not love his son?"

"Because he finds me feckless and lazy and immoral."

Whatever she thought of his status as her enemy, her benevolent jailer, if Kieran were all that immoral, he would have tried to seduce her without benefit of marriage. She liked to think she wouldn't have succumbed, but couldn't be sure. Much to her shame, she hadn't resisted his attentions once his ring was on her finger.

"What does the message say?" she asked instead of sounding like his champion.

"Nothing new."

Deirdre switched sides and picked up the parchment, smoothing it out on her lap.

> *Of course you may bring this young woman to Bishops Cove. Whether or not you may stay depends on how I assess why she is in your company in the first place. Your behavior is, once again, reprehensible, and I shall deal with it accordingly.*

That was all. No greeting. No affectionate or even courteous close, just recriminations and promises of unpleasantness and a grudging welcome to her.

Deirdre screwed the paper into a tighter ball than Kieran had and thrust it into her muff. "What if you are wrong and leg-shackling yourself to me makes him more angry with you?"

"Mama will bring him around. To him, I have been an abominable son, but Mama thinks all her children are angels." He glanced out the window. "And there is Bishops Cove."

Deirdre looked out of the window, too. All she saw were acres and acres of rolling pastureland with a clump of sheep and a distant patch of woods. "I don't see any house."

"That is not for another four miles. We have several thousand acres here."

"Several thousand—" She clasped her knees, unfamiliar beneath velvet, muslin, and petticoats. "Here?"

Kieran sighed. "Yes, and another monstrosity of an estate in Northumberland and a small one in Hampshire."

"And your mother's plantation in Georgia? Oh, dear." Her head spun. She lowered her face to her knees. "I didn't know you were that rich," she mumbled into her lap.

"I am not. My father is. I have nothing that he does not give me." Bitterness tinged his voice. "Except for the prize money from the *Maid* and her cargo."

Deirdre made herself breathe slowly, deeply. "It's a generous dowry."

"More than generous." He leaned across the carriage and took her hands in his. "Whatever the circumstances, I will try to keep you from being unhappy here."

At that moment, as the carriage slowed and turned between two tall, iron gates, Deirdre doubted that anyone could keep her from being unhappy. Her head felt as though someone were using it for bowling practice.

Kieran seemed to grow a bit pale, too, though between the mist and the bare, yet heavy, branches of trees stretching up on either side of the long drive, she couldn't be certain. When the carriage stopped and he jumped down, she could be sure. He looked as he had when suffering from seasickness. Her own heart pounding faster than the hooves of a racehorse, she took his hand and allowed him to assist her to the ground at the foot of three fan-shaped steps.

Behind those steps rose a wide oak door with long windows on either side of it and a fan-shaped window above it. Broad wings stretched in either direction, gray stone covered with green ivy and soaring to meet the leaden sky.

Deirdre could not breathe. Black spots danced before her eyes.

The front door opened, and she gasped. Three men emerged. Each wore fine blue-and-gold livery and hair powder. Each bore some kind of infirmity. One sported a peg leg, one an eye patch, another a pinned-up sleeve. Yet their posture was straight and their faces strong and warm.

"Mr. Kieran, that is, my—"

Kieran waved the man with the peg leg to silence. "We will see to the greetings later, Addison. Please let us get this lady inside. She is not used to our climate and is freezing."

She wasn't sure her shivering was entirely due to the cold.

"Of course." Addison held the door open and motioned the other two men in their blue-and-gold livery to stand aside. "Go on into the gold salon. Everyone is waiting there."

Deirdre gripped Kieran's arm as though it was all that could hold her upright as her head began to swim. He covered her fingers with his and proceeded into a hall that, upon first impression, seemed large enough to fit the entire *Maid of Alexandria*, including the mainmast. The air inside the hall was a degree or two warmer than that outside. It smelled of lemon oil, damp stone, and—

"Dogs?"

Kieran smiled. "Yes, Mama usually has half a dozen or so. She will have them locked away until you are settled. Unless you do not like dogs, in which case she will keep them away from you."

"I don't know if I do. I've never been around one much. We had a ship's cat, but it disappeared in Canton."

"Uh, yes, well, do not tell Mama that." He headed for a staircase wide enough for an army to climb in formation and led her up the green strip of carpet in the middle. She would have preferred walking on the stone edges where she could grab hold of one of the carved mahogany railings for support.

They reached the next floor, the first floor, she remembered the English called it. Kieran pushed open a carved oak door to the right. Warmth, color, and a chorus of voices met them on the other side.

Two young ladies, who looked nearly identical save for their eye color, swooped forward and flung their arms around Kieran's neck. "You are home, you terrible, handsome, adorable brother."

"Did you bring us any presents?"

"You are in such trouble."

"Papa should absolutely beat you, but I will not let him. Oh, I am so happy you are alive."

Laughing, he hugged them back, then held them off at arm's length. "Give over, children. Let me present you to our guest."

Instantly, the girls backed off.

"Deirdre, these scapegraces," Kieran said, "are my sisters." He indicated a golden-eyed beauty. "Chloe, the elder, and Juliet, the baby."

The girls curtsied, though gave their brother quizzical glances.

"Pleased to meet you." Lightheaded, Deirdre managed a smile and an inclination of the head. She had learned to curtsy ten years earlier, but didn't dare attempt it at that moment for fear she would land on her backside.

Her lack of the curtsy met with disapproval, for the young ladies flicked their glances to her, their expressions changing from curious to astonishment, as though she had grown an extra head.

"Who is she?" Chloe leaned toward her brother to speak sotto voce. "A foreign princess?"

"You are all forgetting your manners."

Chloe and Juliet stepped back to make a path for a tiny, middle-aged lady with lovely gold-brown hair with touches of silver and Kieran's golden eyes. She came forward and hugged him around his waist. "You're still in one piece with all your limbs attached." She spoke in a gentle drawl, then a sob broke from her lips.

Kieran shot an anxious glance to an older man who hadn't moved or yet spoken from his position ten feet away, then wrapped his arms around his mother and held her close. "I have all my fingers and toes, too."

"Perhaps not once Papa gets hold of them." Juliet giggled. "You are so beyond the pale."

"And we are beyond rude." Kieran's mother stepped away from him and turned toward Deirdre. "Do present this young lady to your parents."

"This is Deirdre." Kieran took her hand and drew her a step closer to his mother and, presumably, father. "She is the daughter of Daniel MacKenzie, who was the captain of the schooner we captured."

Deirdre held her breath, expecting him to add "And my wife." But he heaved a gusty sigh. "And since you don't know this and my sisters have already marked that I broke protocol in how I introduced you, you may as well find out now, m'dear, that my parents are the Earl and Countess of Tyne."

Earl and countess. His father was a peer of the realm.

Blood roaring in her ears, Deirdre turned on Kieran, a demand for him to explain why he hadn't told her surging to her lips. But the gold and cream of the room, the five Ashfords, and the slate-gray sky beyond the long windows began to spin like a bouquet in a whirlpool, faster and faster until she was sucked into the vortex and the world went black.

Chapter 13

*K*ieran caught Deirdre the instant she began to fall. The girls cried out. Mama's hand flew to her lips.

"What have you done now?" A white line around his mouth, Tyne started forward at last.

Mama stepped between them. "Not now, Garrett. We need to get this young lady upstairs."

"That was unkind of you not to tell her Papa has a title." Chloe scowled at him.

"Why would you not?" Juliet looked bewildered. "Have you acquired revolutionary ideas and are now ashamed of our titles?"

"My reasons are my own and good enough." Kieran picked Deirdre up in his arms. "Which bedchamber have you prepared for her?"

"You should just lay her on the sofa," Juliet said. "That's what they do with the heroines in—"

"It's too short for her, you goose," Chloe said.

Deirdre in his arms, Kieran turned and headed toward the salon door.

"The Duchess Suite." Mama hastened ahead of him to open the door.

Chloe and Juliet started to follow.

"I will see you in my study as soon as she is settled," Tyne commanded. "Chloe, Juliet, this is none of your concern. Stay right here."

"But, Papa . . ."

Kieran left the salon and headed up the steps. Part of him looked forward to the confrontation with Tyne. The rest of him—

Felt like the ne'er-do-well to which his father could usually reduce him in a few words.

The Duchess Suite was the farthest bedchamber from his own. He would have to remedy that, but not now when Deirdre looked so ghastly pale. The past two weeks of mist and rain had begun to rob her of her bronzed tone, and he did not like her new, if fashionable, pallor.

She was a heavy female for all her slimness.

Her eyes opened. "What happened? Why are you carrying me?"

"You fainted."

"Deuce take—"

"Shh, Mama is coming."

Deirdre struggled in his arms. "Let me down."

"I think not. If you fainted again on the stairs—"

"I've never fainted in my life."

"You have now." He continued up the next flight of steps and down the corridor to the suite of rooms named for the one visit of his aunt, the Duchess of Worthington.

Better not tell Deirdre she now had an aunt by marriage who was a duchess. She might swoon again. Then again, if she gave him trouble . . .

"I was startled is all." She glared at him. "You didn't tell me your parents are titled."

"And you may as well know now that so am I."

She closed her eyes. For a moment, he feared she had indeed swooned again. Then she spoke through clenched teeth. "I am going to kill you."

"Not if I get to him first, Miss MacKenzie." Mama darted ahead of him to open the door and turn down the bed. "These are freshly aired sheets. I'm so glad you let us know ahead of time that you were bringing a . . . guest."

Her hesitation over the word "guest" and the concern in her eyes asked Kieran a score of questions.

"Stop treating me like I'm fragile and tell me why you didn't warn me." Deirdre's green eyes blazed up at him, though her pallor remained.

"I will—later." He laid her on the bed and backed away. "Right now I had best settle matters with Tyne, or neither of you will have the opportunity to make me a corpse."

"You're going to leave me here?" Deirdre shot upright, then grabbed her head and slumped back onto the pillows. Perspiration beaded her brow, and she took several deep breaths. "I must be coming down with something. I am so sorry to come into your house ill."

"No need to apologize." Mama smoothed her hand across Deirdre's brow, then tugged the combs from her hair. "I think you are exactly where you belong. You just rest there for a minute. I'll be right back with some tea."

"I can't stay here." To Kieran's horror, Deirdre began to cry.

He returned to her side and brushed the tears from her cheeks with the tips of his fingers. "You can and you will stay here." He wanted to kiss her, but Mama was already glowering at him as much as someone with a face as sweet as hers could glower. He settled for pressing two fingers to Deirdre's lips, then drawing the coverlet to her chin before following Mama into the corridor and closing the door behind him.

The instant the latch clicked, she seized his lapels. "Tell me the truth, Kieran, is that young lady *enceinte*?"

"Most likely." He kept his tone bland to disguise his elation.

"Most likely?" Mama jabbed a forefinger into his sternum. "If she is, are you the father?"

"Most definitely." He couldn't stop his grin. His feet seemed to hover a foot or so above the floorboards.

"Why are you smiling? Have you learned nothing after Joanna? Did we go astray in teaching you right from wrong? Oh, Kieran." Tears swam in Mama's eyes.

They slammed Kieran back to earth. "It is all right, Mama. She's my wife. We married on Bermuda seven weeks ago, before I ever touched her."

"Then you should have told us." Mama set her hands on her hips. "Your father is already raging against you. This is only going to make matters worse."

"I have no doubt." Kieran's tone was cold. "He will draw the same conclusions as you and think the worst."

"When you didn't tell us of the marriage, what do you expect?"

"Some faith in my honor?" He laughed with more bitterness than humor. "If he were not so determined to think the worst of me, he, of all people, should realize that I could not have brought home a noncombatant prisoner without having married her."

"And you didn't make matters clear to us because you want to egg him on." Sighing, Mama shook her head. "This feud between you two has got to stop."

Kieran crossed his arms over his chest. "He can start taking my word for the truth. All of you can." He turned away. "Please see to Deirdre. She hasn't had a mother since she was ten or so and not a great deal of female contact since then. I need to beard the lion in his den."

"Tell him straightaway that she's your wife, Kieran."

Mama's admonition followed Kieran down the hallway. Of course she was right. He should walk into Tyne's presence and make the announcement of his marriage straight off. That would take the wind from Tyne's anger-filled sails, especially if he suspected why Deirdre had fainted. By the time Kieran reached the ground-floor study, he resolved being up-front after all was the course he would take for the sake of peace—or at least a truce—between Tyne and him.

He paused outside the study door and knocked.

"Enter." The voice of Garrett Ashford, Earl of Tyne, still held the resonance that had made it audible along the deck of a frigate.

And instilled fear and trembling in those he summoned to his presence.

Kieran entered and made himself pace to the chair across from the desk with the languid amble of a feline too lazy to move any faster. Tyne watched him the whole time, his deep blue eyes as cold as the lapis they resembled. Kieran shivered and sank onto the leather chair, his legs sprawled out before him, his prepared speech a jumble of nonsense in his mouth.

He had persuaded a beautiful, headstrong woman to marry him. He had kept a ship full of sailors and prisoners under control and gotten them safely back to Plymouth. He was five and twenty and about to be a father himself, and the icy disapproval of the man across the desk from him reduced him to the state of a recalcitrant schoolboy about to be caned by the headmaster.

He was not worthy to be Deirdre's husband, nor the father of any boy or girl with which she presented him. For her sake, though, he needed to try.

He started to sit more upright. "Sir, I need to explain—"

"You need to explain a great deal." Tyne's voice lashed with the crack of a cat-o'-nine-tails. "Do you know how your actions of the past six months have shamed your mother and me, how they have pained your mother especially, and hurt your sisters?"

"A great deal, I know."

No concern for how their actions had hurt him.

For Deirdre's sake, he held his tongue in that regard. "I am trying to make amends."

"By bringing that young woman here when she is obviously more to you than a hapless victim of war?"

"She is indeed more—"

"Have you no more honor than to treat her like the spoils of war?"

"Tyne—" Kieran's resolve snapped. Before he could spew out the fury, the anguish of the past six months in a stream of vitriol that would surely leave more scars, he shot to his feet. "Thank you. I do not mind if I do have some brandy. It's dashed cold here after the tropics."

"Sit down."

Kieran ignored the command and stalked over to a table where a variety of decanters and glasses ranged. Liquor that would dull his wits in front of his parent was the last thing he needed, but he wanted something to do with his hands.

"That you would buy letters of marque in my name after the scandal was bad enough, but now you bring home this poor young woman."

Trying to block out Tyne's voice, Kieran splashed cognac into a glass before he faced his father, leaning back against the table. "Tell me, sir, what was I supposed to do with myself? You banished me from England. The Americans declared war on us, so I could scarcely go to Georgia after that. I was not welcome here. You have seen fit to allow someone else to live at Bishops Down and run that estate—"

"Because I prefer to keep it profitable rather than a den of iniquity—"

"And," Kieran pressed on despite the stab of pain in his chest, "Uncle David's widow and daughters are cluttering up Tyne House, not that they would have wanted me there."

"With good cause." Tyne's voice rose in volume. "No sensible mother—"

"What am I forgetting?" Kieran fairly shouted down Tyne. "Oh yes, I was not allowed in London either, thanks to Joanna's brother."

"With whom you fought a dishonorable duel."

Kieran glared at Tyne. "You were so convinced I must be dishonorable, were you not? You took rumors for truth and wrote me those scathing letters without asking. I—" Brandy glass or not, he began to shake. He thumped it onto the table, yanked the ribbon from his hair, and scraped the waves back. "I was the one who was wounded. See that?" He turned his damaged ear toward Tyne. "See how close he came to ending the Ashford line?" He did not look at Tyne in case he showed no concern, no reaction.

"Rutledge and his seconds said you shot early." At least Tyne's voice was softer, less certain.

Or was that wishful thinking?

"Even your seconds agreed."

"Seconds who were no friends of mine."

"But what did they gain by lying?"

"Bringing down an Ashford for not being a dupe."

"Are you saying you did not fire early?" Tyne's tone held a challenge.

"Yes, dash it all, I did shoot early. I fired into the air. But I never even turned around. My wound proves that." With a curse, he shoved the brandy glass onto the floor, where it landed with a satisfying crash. "My shot never went near him. But of course you do not believe me, so why do I trouble myself explaining?"

Turning his back on Tyne, he paced to the fireplace, where he stood trying to warm his hands and calm his breathing.

"That was a rather childish display," Tyne said in a conversational tone.

"I suppose it would have been far manlier if I had thrown it at your head. And I suppose I would have been more honorable to shoot Rutledge over his slut of a sis—"

"Kieran Ashford," Tyne bellowed, "you will never call a lady that again."

"Joanna Rutledge," Kieran said through his teeth, "is not a lady."

"Thanks to you."

If he had not agreed with Tyne about smashing the glass being childish, Kieran might have smashed something else, something even more satisfying like the ormolu clock on the mantel or one of the French windows.

Instead, he sighed. "I denied it before, not that you would listen to me, and I will deny it again. I was not responsible for Joanna's downfall."

"You were found by several people with her in a grotto, and her clothes were awry."

Kieran speared his fingers through his hair. "We were walking in the garden as betrothed couples are wont to do. She fainted."

"As females in her condition are wont to do." Tyne's voice held a coldness that made Kieran flinch.

He inclined his head in agreement, swallowed. "Joanna was further along that night than I could have managed in the weeks of our acquaintance, but we will never know that, with the way her family packed her off to Greece with that scholar who preferred their money to his wife's virtue. He should have been a proud papa two months ago or more, giving his fine name to a footman's bas—"

"Kieran."

He did not just flinch this time; he jumped. Then, his ears growing hot, he gripped the edge of the mantel, feeling as though he could rip it from the wall, took a deep breath, and plunged. "But you are not interested in the truth, are you, my lord? You are interested in anything that confirms your belief that I am—"

He could not finish the thought that his father considered him feckless and without direction. Tyne might agree.

Silence fell in the study save for the hiss and crackle of the fire. Outside, mist had turned to rain that beat a monotonous tattoo against the windows.

Then Tyne's chair creaked. That was the only warning Kieran received that his father approached him. At eight and fifty, Garrett Ashford could still move without a sound.

He paused directly behind Kieran. "I have sent a messenger to Greece to learn of the actual date of the child's birth."

"Sir." Suddenly, Kieran felt the fire's warmth.

Tyne had believed him enough to go to the expense of sending someone all the way to Greece to learn the truth.

"Your mother wishes to take Chloe to London for another Season and launch Juliet into society in the spring," Tyne continued. "She cannot go back into society with everyone believing that her brother is a debaucher of young ladies."

So he had done it for Chloe's sake, not his son's.

Kieran gripped the mantel until his fingers hurt.

Tyne sighed. "So tell me about this young person upstairs."

Kieran would have been taken aback by the abrupt shift in subject, but he knew where Tyne was going and that it was not a true shift at all.

He should tell him now that she was his wife.

He could not. He simply could not miss this opportunity to show Tyne how unjust he was.

Kieran shrugged. "She was the captain's daughter. The man died, not from any fighting. They surrendered without a true fight. So I took her under my protection."

"And Heron did not try to stop you?" Tyne sounded shocked.

"He had no choice. The *Phoebe* got separated from us in a storm."

"I see."

This time, Tyne chose to cross the room and pour something liquid into a glass. He did not smash his; he drank its contents.

The glass thudded onto the table. "Just tell me, Kieran, did she faint because she is with child?"

Kieran relaxed his grip on the mantel. He knew the rules to this game.

"More than likely."

"Is it yours?"

Kieran faced Tyne, smiling. "Most definitely."

177

Tyne's back went rigid. "That you would take actions that are little better than piracy is bad enough, but to . . . to take advantage of a female without a protector—" He tramped to his desk and sank into the chair, looking all of his years. "Get out. Get out of my sight before I say or do something I will regret."

Kieran gazed at the lines etched around Tyne's mouth, the increased gray in his hair, the shadows of fatigue beneath his eyes, and remained where he was. The game was over. He regretted having played it. Watching Tyne, his father, age before his eyes took away any pleasure he thought he would gain from exposing how badly he thought of his only son and then laying down his trump card.

"Sir." He returned to the chair across from Tyne and perched on the edge. "Deirdre was my wife before I ever touched her."

Deirdre wanted to crawl under the covers and hide. No, under the high bed would be preferable. If only she didn't suddenly feel so utterly fatigued, she would have raced after Kieran and yanked out every strand of his hair for not telling her just how powerful a family he came from, he was a part of.

She had read about the English in books, in old pamphlets from the Revolution, in newspapers that made their way into foreign ports. The English nobility like Kieran's family ruled the country by right of birth, not common election. They carried privilege beyond anything the wealthiest Americans possessed. Their wars with America and France proclaimed how fiercely they intended to hold on to what was theirs and take what they wanted.

Now she was a part of them, but wholly intended to betray them by getting her crew out of prison. Surely her rank in the ruling class would make treachery all that much worse.

She rolled onto her side. Tears flowed onto the pillow that smelled of something sweet and clean.

Kieran had been wrong. Their marriage wasn't going to make matters better with his family; it was going to make them worse. English noblemen's sons did not marry the daughters of Yankee merchants. He must be up to something else, and she didn't like not knowing what that was.

The door opened. Silk whispered. "You poor girl." A cool, smooth hand tugged the pillow away and caressed Deirdre's cheek. "I've got some nice chamomile and mint tea coming up. It'll help you rest. Do you have a nightgown you can change into?"

Deirdre shook her head.

"That's all right. Chloe isn't that much shorter than you. One of hers will do until we can get you some of your own."

"I'm sorry to be such a bother." A sob escaped Deirdre's efforts to hold it back. "To come into your house ill like this . . . without warning . . ."

"You're our son's wife. You're more than welcome."

Deirdre pushed herself up on one elbow. "He told you?"

Lady Tyne smiled. "He told me, and we can both pray that he tells his father before things get much worse between them."

To Deirdre's surprise, Lady Tyne hoisted herself onto the edge of the bed and covered Deirdre's hand with hers. "But Kieran can't help but stir up trouble with his father, and Garrett is weary of Kieran's lack of interest in anything useful—but never you mind all that now. I need to ask you some questions."

"I married him for protection, not to be a pawn in some game with his father."

"I'm sure you did, and Garrett will see the reason of the marriage for your protection eventually and that will ease this battle between them." Lady Tyne squeezed Deirdre's fingers. "But that isn't what I wish to discuss right now. I have some female issues to discuss with you."

Deirdre gave her ladyship a blank look. "What sort of female issues?"

"Have your courses been regular?"

That kind of female issue. Momma had explained all that when she had become expectant on her last voyage. Only ten at the time, Deirdre had been horrified and disgusted. But when the changes came in her twelfth year, she was prepared and able to discreetly manage the regular event—

Regular until recently.

Deirdre's face felt as though it must blaze as red as her hair, but her heart began to thud like a bass drum. "I'm late." Her throat closed. "I've never been late."

"By how much?"

"Five weeks." She began to shake. "I've missed twice. But my life has been so disrupted."

"That it has." Lady Tyne stroked her cheek. "Do you always cry a great deal?"

"Not like lately." Deirdre's eyes filled with tears. "Everything makes me cry these past few days or so. I've just seen friends go off to prison. I lost my father not so long ago."

"And your husband hasn't been exactly up-front with you about his family connections." Lady Tyne had the sweetest smile Deirdre had ever seen. "But he has been attentive as a husband."

Deirdre ducked her head, mortified to even hint at how attentive, especially not in a conversation with Kieran's mother—a conversation whose conclusion Deirdre did not want to hear, for she feared she already knew the answer.

"As he should be." Lady Tyne slid off the bed and crossed the room to where a cherrywood stand held a china pitcher and basin. She wet a cloth in the water and returned to the bed to wipe Deirdre's face. "Have you been sick in the morning?"

Deirdre shook her head, hope trying to ignite like a spark on wet flint. "I haven't much felt like eating breakfast, but I haven't been sick at all."

"Well, let's hope that continues. I thought I was going to die for the first three months I was carrying Kieran."

There, the truth was out. Deirdre met Lady Tyne's sherry-colored eyes. For a moment, her heart soared with elation. She might already be carrying the heir, one step toward ending this passionate but loveless marriage.

Now, with the reality of her bargain staring her in the face, she wondered what sort of unnatural woman would agree to carry a child and then abandon it to land and riches and—now she knew—a title simply because his father's land and hers were at war.

Beneath the coverlet, she curved her hand over her flat belly as though to shield the spark of life inside. Whatever she had or had not been thinking when she made her deal with the devil, she needed to find a way to change it now.

"Did you not suspect?" Lady Tyne's smile was gentle.

Deirdre shook her head. "The wh— the strumpets on the docks never . . . that is . . . I am so very sorry. I'm not used to being around ladies or talking about . . . about . . ." Words failed her.

Her ladyship laughed. "When I was your age, we talked about these things much more freely than is done nowadays, but I'd have died rather than discuss my marriage bed with my mother-in-law. It's the sort of thing you should be able to talk about with your mother, but since you don't have one, please feel free to ask me anything."

"Thank you." Deirdre barely managed to choke out the two words around the lump of gratitude in her throat.

"Good. Shall I send Kieran up here?" Lady Tyne asked. "Or would you prefer to rest?"

"I'd prefer to rest, and you'll want to be with your son."

"I have missed him." Lady Tyne half turned toward the door. "I'll send a maid in with a nightgown."

"No need. I'm not wearing stays." Deirdre slid down in the bed so warm and soft and fragrant, pretending a fatigue she no longer felt.

She needed to be alone to think, to plan out a new future.

And work out how a lady bearing the next generation of Ashfords was going to manage to get eleven men out of Dartmoor Prison.

Chapter 14

Tyne stared at Kieran until he felt like a butterfly on a pin beneath a magnification glass. With the sun beating down on it. He applied all his will not to squirm. That look shaved a dozen years off his age. Once again, he was a schoolboy caught planting moles in the neighbor's bowling green, or trying to smoke a pipe, or dipping Chloe's braids in ink. The thrashings he'd received had been a relief, for they turned him away from the spine-chilling coldness of that look. When Tyne took a step toward him, Kieran nearly backed into the fireplace.

"You married an American prisoner." Tyne's tone was as cold as his eyes.

Kieran nodded. "Yes, sir, I did. On Bermuda."

"Why?" Tyne's voice didn't warm a degree. "So you could bed her?"

Kieran clenched his fists. "So I could protect her, my lord. I thought it was the honorable action." He bowed his head to hide the pain piercing through him. "I thought you would approve."

"She would have been comfortable as a noncombatant prisoner here in England. You did not need to bring the enemy into our household."

"Enemy? You call her the enemy?" Kieran's head shot up, anger replacing anguish. "Mama is an American. Do you call her the enemy now that we are at war with her countrymen again?"

"Your mother is married to me."

"And Deirdre is married to me."

With those words, he suddenly missed being near her. He wanted to hold her, to know how she felt about the likelihood that they had created a child together.

That knowledge strengthened his resolve to make his father understand, to make peace in the family for Deirdre's sake, for all their sakes. He no longer wished to fight with his father, but sought the kind of love and understanding Chloe and Juliet shared with their sire. He wanted his son or daughter to have a grandfather they could love.

"Deirdre is my wife." He spoke the words with pride.

Tyne's expression did not change. "Phoebe was not a prisoner, combatant or otherwise. When I met her, her family was known to be loyal to the Crown."

Kieran sidled over to one of the chairs facing the desk and perched on its arm. "I met Mrs. Willoughby on Bermuda."

Tyne paled and dropped onto his chair, looking suddenly old and tired. "Did she tell you anything about your mother's family?"

"No."

But his father's reaction made Kieran suspect more to that existed.

"Good." Tyne relaxed. "She was always a terrible gossip. And I will not be diverted from discussing the inappropriateness of your marriage, nor you turning my merchantman into a privateer, nor you corrupting my best captain with the promise of gold."

"Which we acquired." Kieran shot his father a rueful grin. "Deirdre's dowry."

Tyne made a noncommittal grumble in his throat, rose to catch up the poker and stir the fire into a greater blaze. "Sit here by the fire and tell me what happened."

The directive emerged more as a command than a suggestion, but Kieran's insides uncoiled just a little. He settled on one of two wingback chairs set at angles facing the fire. Tyne took the other. They sat, not quite facing one another, and yet not separated by the massive mahogany surface of Tyne's desk.

"You do not want the whole story." Kieran began to talk, measuring each word with care. "I am not a sailor, which is another black mark in my copybook, I am certain. I do not like death either. The sight of Captain MacKenzie's body . . . It was an apoplexy that took him, so no blood. But to know I had caused a man to die . . ."

That made Tyne smile. "Your mother would approve. When we heard you fought a duel, she was overset. If you had come home, I would likely have forgot that you are five and twenty and thrashed you."

"Perhaps you will believe that I could never shoot anyone." Kieran sipped his brandy, waiting.

Tyne did not move.

Kieran sighed, then continued his story, emphasizing Deirdre's courage, her strength, her cleverness. "So, instead of escaping as she could have," he concluded, "she dove into the harbor and pulled me out."

"How altruistic of her." Tyne did not sound complimentary.

Kieran bristled. "All but two of her crew did not escape either because they chose to help me. It *was* altruistic of her. She sacrificed a great deal to save my life. Marrying her is the least I could do to repay that."

"But where do her loyalties lie, Kieran?" Tyne asked. "Can you trust her not to betray England?"

"What can a lady in her condition possibly get up to?" Even as he asked the question, Kieran felt a prickling of concern that Deirdre could get up to anything. "We have the family to watch out for her," he said with an edge of defensiveness. "And Dartmoor is a bit more difficult to get men out of than a ship with a drunken watch."

"Do not," Tyne said in a constricted tone, "even jest about that ever again, not even to me. You cannot imagine—"

A gentle tap sounded on the door, and Mama slipped into the study.

Kieran and Tyne rose.

Mama looked from them to the smashed crystal, then back to them. "Where's the blood?"

"No blood," Tyne said. "Just trouble."

"Have the two of you been fighting all this time?"

"We have been having our usual sort of discussion." Tyne smiled—for Mama, his whole demeanor softening.

"I have been telling him about how Deirdre saved my life in Bermuda." Kieran bowed his head to show the scar from the marlinespike.

"Oh my." Mama paled. "But your hair has grown out nicely around it. Surely you can cut it to a respectable length by now."

"We have had that discussion," Tyne grumbled. "He intends to spend the rest of his life looking like the pirate he is."

Kieran stiffened. "My letters of marque were legitimate . . . sir."

"Legalized piracy is still—"

"That is enough." Mama laid her hand on Tyne's arm. "I'm sure Kieran regrets what he did."

"I do," Kieran hastened to affirm. "Except for meeting Deirdre. How is she, Mama?"

Phoebe smiled. "She's an interesting girl, told me that she didn't guess her condition because the ladies on the docks never got that way."

Kieran and Tyne groaned.

Mama's eyes twinkled. "She apologized quite prettily. But she's not happy with you, Kieran. I was coming back with a nightgown for her and heard her repeating her intention to kill you."

"Perhaps she and I can discuss the best method," Tyne muttered.

Mama poked him in the ribs, probably the only person in the world who would ever dare do so. "You should have more respect for your heir."

"I should have a more respectable heir."

Kieran turned his back on his father. "Is it all right if I go see her?"

"I'd let her rest if I were you," Mama said.

Kieran's mouth went dry. "She is all right, is she not? I mean, she fainted."

"That is normal under the circumstances." Mama's soft hand patted his arm. "You should have shown a little restraint."

"When," Tyne asked, "has he ever shown restraint?"

"He's been spoiled by his good looks and charm just like you. Now, Kieran, get upstairs and have your father's valet do something about your hair and clothes."

"The clothes, yes," Kieran said, glancing down at his rumpled shirt and salt-stained breeches. "The hair stays. Refreshments in the gold salon at five of the clock as usual?"

"Yes, but your hair—"

Kieran bowed without turning around. "Good afternoon to you then. Tyne can explain the hair."

He exited the study, but he did not go upstairs immediately. For a moment, he paused outside the door, listening to the quiet voices beyond the panel, waiting, hoping, that his father would say something kind about him.

"Is her being here going to make difficulties with the Admiralty?" Mama asked.

"I am afraid so," Tyne said. "She already helped her crew escape once. If she tries again, we could all end up in prison."

Deirdre knew she had to face Kieran's family. When she awoke, she felt too well to make the excuse of illness to hide in the enormous four-poster bed with its blue silk bed hangings.

Silk, just draped off a bed! The same sea blue adorned the long windows and reflected in the border of the carpet, velvet of the chaiselongue cushions, and stripes in the chairs that formed a cozy area to read or talk in the adjoining sitting room.

No one was there to talk to. In fact, the room was disturbingly silent after shipboard life. Low, the fire hissed, and outside, a rising wind rattled the branches of the trees. No timbers creaked. No sails snapped. No one laughed or coughed or banged down a hatch.

She had never felt more alone in her life.

Shivering outside the bedclothes in a white batiste nightgown that reached just above her ankles, she strode to the fire and huddled before it. She had no idea what to do next. Her gown was missing, and she needed help donning it anyway, with all those nonsensical hooks up the back. Her sea chest stood at the end of the bed, but she could scarcely don her salt-stained breeches and waistcoat and slide down the banister like it was a backstay.

One thing she could do was hide the gold and bank certificates tucked into the false bottom. As she withdrew the gold, a knock sounded on the door.

"One moment, please."

In haste, she tucked the bag beneath the mattress up against the headboard. Later, she would find a better hiding place for it and the certificates still in the chest.

"Deirdre?" Lady Tyne's soft voice came through the heavy door. "Are you all right?"

"Yes, ma'am." Deirdre hauled the counterpane over her shoulders.

Lady Tyne entered, carrying fabric over her arm. A maid followed with a tray on which resided combs, brushes, ribbons, and—

"Scissors?" Deirdre squeaked.

Phoebe smiled. "We're not cutting off that lovely hair of yours. The scissors are for cutting the basting threads if these alterations are right. You can set that tray on the dressing table, Sally."

The maid, a pretty girl of no more than sixteen, nodded and did as she was told.

"I've raided Chloe's dressing room," Lady Tyne continued to Deirdre. "We'll get into Plymouth and have a real seamstress work up some things for you, but this will do for a day or two. You just can't continue to wear that other dress."

Deirdre made a face. "Yes, the white is ridiculous for me, isn't it?"

"For anyone on the English Channel in November. I don't care if filmy fabrics are the fashion, no lady needs to freeze herself. Now then, go into the dressing room and put on these things and the dressing gown while we get this fire built up."

"Dressing room?" Deirdre looked around.

Sally crossed the room and opened a door beside the hearth. Painted the same cream color as the walls, it wasn't noticeable.

The dressing room was larger than Deirdre's cabin. Shelves, hooks, and drawers lined the walls. Another door opened from the opposite side. Deirdre opened it and found another bedchamber, one dark and cold, its furniture draped in cotton and liberally sprinkled with lavender. Kieran was not going to be moving into that chamber. She was going to be alone in these quiet rooms with that big, silk-draped bed large enough for four of her.

Chilly in the unheated dressing room, she turned her thoughts to donning the undergarments Lady Tyne had provided. Except for the lace and ruffle leggings, the stockings, garters, chemise, and petticoat reminded her of her one year on land. For a moment, she considered throwing them on the ground and stomping on them. Her breeches, like her freedom, were lost to her. That made her cry.

Sinking onto a low stool, she buried her face in her hands and wept for her loss of freedom, for her imprisoned crew, for her father. She cried over the weakness of tears, which made her weep harder.

Finally, Lady Tyne entered with a handkerchief and soothing noises, then a small but firm hand on Deirdre's arm.

"That's enough of that now. The rest of the family is waiting to meet you properly, and Kieran has been pacing about wanting to see you for hours. They'd have all stormed in if I hadn't told them that you deserve to look your best first. Here, do you need some help with the pantalets? They're a bit silly looking, and these will be too short for you, but they keep one's legs warm. And Sally and I have been working to lengthen one of Chloe's gowns. I still had some of the fabric in my studio, so we made a flounce. I used your gown to measure things. You're a bit smaller here"—she gestured to her bust—"but taking in is easier than letting out."

Phoebe's chatter and Sally's quiet competence got Deirdre through having a gown tucked, pinned, and stitched around her, her eyes bathed in lavender water to remove the redness, and her hair snipped—"Just a bit so you can have some curls around your face"—curled, twisted, and pinned, then finally adorned with her own combs.

"Two pieces of silver," Deirdre muttered.

"What was that, my dear?" Phoebe presented Deirdre with a cashmere shawl of a creamy fragility that looked like sea foam over the lavender silk gown. "Now, you look lovely. Take a look."

"No, thank you." Deirdre turned her back on the dressing-table mirror.

"Are you warm enough?" Lady Tyne asked. "I can fetch you a warmer shawl. A pelisse would be better, but a bit difficult to alter quickly."

"I'm warm enough," Deirdre assured her.

"Good. We'll go down then. You may go have your dinner, Sally."

"Thank you, my lady." Sally curtsied. "And you do look lovely, my lady."

The girl had dropped another curtsy and left the room before Deirdre realized that this compliment was directed at her.

She stared at the blank panel of the door. "Why did she call me my lady?"

"You are now Lady Ripon. It's a courtesy title given to the heir to the Tyne earldom and his wife. A viscountcy. You will now be introduced as Deirdre Ripon."

Deirdre continued to stare throughout Lady Tyne's brief explanation. When her ladyship fell silent, Deirdre shook her head, wincing at the unfamiliar curls brushing against her face. "I can't use a title. I'm an American."

"My dear." Phoebe looked grave. "You are English now. You have to use the title. We can't toss them away or give them away at will."

"It seems like treachery."

Lady Tyne looked Deirdre in the eye and all the softness left her face. "For you not to use the title could be construed as treachery, and the last thing any of us needs is another scandal." An edge to her voice added to the illusion of her face hardening to stone. "My family has been hurt enough this past year. I will not allow anyone to be hurt again. Do you understand, Lady Ripon?"

Deirdre understood. Lady Phoebe Tyne might be as fragile-looking as sea foam, but her core was razor-edged steel. If harm threatened her family, she would fight to the death.

Deirdre understood the sentiment. She felt the same way about her family, the crew. Yet now the Ashfords were her family as well.

"I understand," she said.

Lady Tyne smiled, and the gentleness returned. "Then we will get along just fine. Shall we go?"

Lady Tyne led the way down two corridors and a half flight of steps to a smaller, warmer room in reds and gold. The two gentlemen rose at their entrance, and Kieran strode forward, devouring Deirdre with his eyes, his look assuring her she wouldn't be alone in that big bed. But she just might strangle him afterward.

Kieran curled his fingers around hers. "Let me properly present you to my father this time. Lord Tyne, allow me to make you known to my wife, Deirdre Ripon."

"Allow me to welcome you properly, Deirdre." He glanced at Kieran. "Now that I know you are part of the family."

"Thank you . . . sir . . . my lord . . ."

"Tyne will do." He smiled, and she realized that all of Kieran's charm hadn't come from his mother.

"Thank you."

"Do come sit down." Tyne led her to a chair nearest the fire. "I'll get you some refreshment before the girls descend upon you."

"I will get her some refreshment." Kieran's tone was possessive. "Madeira? Tea?"

"Tea, please."

"And don't give her ladylike portions on her plate," Lady Tyne said. "I have no doubt that she's starved, even if I'd scold the girls for admitting such a thing."

Kieran smiled. "Oh, I know Deirdre's appetite." He brought her a cup of tea and a plate filled with tiny sandwiches, a scone oozing cream and jam, and a slice of seed cake. "That will do for starters. Eat up. We keep town hours for meals, so dinner isn't for another three hours. And here come the girls."

Chatter beyond the door heralded their imminent arrival. Although she wanted to reach for that slice of seed cake and cram it into her mouth, she forced herself to sit still with her hands folded in her lap.

"You did come down." Juliet, her hair bouncing in glossy ringlets down her back, darted to Deirdre's side. "Kieran, she is lovely. I wish my hair were that color, and my eyes are just plain old blue."

Nothing about Juliet Ashford's eyes were plain. They were the same lapis blue as her father's, sparkling with gold lights and fringed in impossibly long lashes. She was tall, too, with a prettily rounded figure, though not quite as full on the top as her sister.

"You're so kind." Deirdre thought that was the right response.

"No, we are not," Chloe said. "We will ask you all sorts of annoying questions and be frightfully intrusive."

"We never thought Kieran would marry after—"

"Juliet," Kieran interjected, "do get yourself something to stuff in your mouth." He moved up behind Deirdre's chair and laid his hand on her shoulder. "Let her enjoy her tea and cake."

"Perhaps she will enjoy it more," Juliet pressed on, eyes dancing, "if she learns how she has tamed a rogue like you."

"I expect she already knows," Chloe said.

"Some." Deirdre liked the idea of Kieran's sisters talking about his past rather than asking about hers. "But I expect he's left out a great deal."

Juliet slid to the edge of her chair. "Did he tell you about—"

"This is not appropriate conversation." Lady Tyne's soft voice still managed to override Juliet's excitement.

"But, Mama," she protested, "Deirdre is bound to meet Amelia and—"

"Take the wheels off your tongue and get some tea." Chloe steered her younger sister toward the tea and sandwiches.

"But I do not understand why we are not to discuss—"

"Juliet," Lady Tyne's tone sharpened. "Remember your manners."

Deirdre decided to remember her manners and not go against her ladyship's wishes by asking about Amelia—and others, apparently, besides the scandalous Joanna and her homicidal brother.

Her sister pushing her along, Juliet slipped over to the table where trays of food lay in casual elegance.

Kieran rounded Deirdre's chair to perch on the arm.

He felt warm and solid and familiar beside her. She barely stopped herself from leaning her head against his sleeve.

And what a fine sleeve! Of blue superfine, it fit him without a crease as did his buff pantaloons. His Hessian boots glowed in the firelight, and his hair was so smooth she wanted to mess it up with her fingers—

Before she yanked it out by the roots.

His smell reached her nostrils, and the urge to draw his head down and kiss him left her shaken and ready for a dozen tiny sandwiches.

She ate three, noticed that the Ashford ladies held no more than two apiece on their plates, and shoved the plate at Kieran without taking the desired seed cake.

"If you're done eating," Juliet said, "and since I am not allowed to talk about my brother, will you tell us all about yourself? I mean, to grow up on a ship and sail around the world must have been so exciting."

"She is not finished eating." Kieran broke off a piece of seed cake and popped it between Deirdre's lips, preventing her from answering Juliet. "I saw you eying that like a cat at a mouse."

"Kieran, do not be so vulgar," Chloe said. "Papa, can you not make these two behave themselves? Deirdre will think we're all common."

Deirdre thought the sisters charming.

Tyne strolled over and joined Chloe on a settee. "I believe the less said about Deirdre's background the better."

Deirdre choked on poppy seeds, and her skin began to heat.

Kieran shot to his feet and glared at his father. "Are you ashamed of my wife's background . . . my lord?"

"No." Chloe emitted a groan. "Do not start fighting again. Kieran, you know he meant nothing of the sort."

"No, Chloe, I do not."

Deirdre closed her eyes and wished she had remained beneath the bedclothes after all. She didn't want to give these people a broadside, but a female only had so much self-control.

"Garrett and Kieran," Lady Tyne said, "do try to maintain the peace for at least another quarter hour."

Deirdre stood. "Will you please excuse me? I need some air."

"Sit down," Tyne commanded.

Deirdre recognized that tone. She'd heard it from her father often enough to know it meant the one in authority would not tolerate disobedience. The last time she had disobeyed such a command, her father had died, and that had landed her crew in Dartmoor and her there, the wife of an English nobleman. She should be a good daughter-in-law and sit.

She spun on her heel and bolted from the chamber. Broad steps lay before her. She raced down them, slipping on her leather-soled shoes. She jumped the last three steps despite her dress and landed in the cavernous entryway, a chamber cold enough to clear her head, cool the hottest temper. Best of all, the air smelled of the sea.

A footman appeared from nowhere. "My lady, may I assist you?"

"Air." She headed for the front door.

Looking alarmed, he sprang after her and yanked the portal open, held it for her, bowing, until she reached the bottom of the fan-shaped steps. She didn't know where to go from there. Someone would catch up with her soon. She heard raised voices, then a bang before the footman closed the front door. She had maybe two minutes' head start, enough time to move away from the house. She was running away when she needed something to run toward.

Darkness had fallen early at that season and that far north, but torchieres blazed on either side of the front door and around the court for carriages. Beyond them lay the drive. It drew her. It led to the road and the sea. She could smell the salt tang on the wind. Though she shivered in her silk gown and filmy shawl, she welcomed the flowing air and moved herself. Forward, along the carriageway. Gravel dug into her thin slippers. She didn't care. Years of mostly going barefoot for the ease of climbing the rigging had toughened her feet enough to withstand a little rock.

"Deirdre." Kieran's voice rang out behind her. "Wait."

She kept going. He would catch her. He had a longer stride and wasn't hampered by a skirt.

A skirt!

She might be thousands of miles away, but she may as well be back in Virginia with the headmistress of the school waving her hands as though she could erase Deirdre from the world as one erased chalk marks from a slate.

"Deirdre." Kieran's boot heels crunched on the drive.

Without intending to do so, she slowed.

He caught up with her in a minute and tucked his arm through the crook of her elbow, drawing her to his side.

"What are you doing?" He was trembling, and he sounded furious. "It is blacker than pitch out here, and you are walking along like . . . like . . ." He gave her arm a little shake.

She pulled her arm free and increased her pace. "Smelling the sea. Breathing real air. Getting away from all those rules about whom we can and cannot discuss. Not you. Not me. What will be next? The state of the weather?"

"Do not be ridiculous." Kieran breathed as though he'd been running. "It is simply that our histories are not fit for my sisters' ears. They are young ladies—"

"And I'm not a lady—young or otherwise." Her throat closed a little more with each word. She felt strangled on the last words. "Kieran, I can't go through with this. I'm never going to be a lady. I hate female things."

Kieran drew her to a halt and faced her, though even the bare branches blocked out what starlight lit the night, and she couldn't read his expression.

"You do not like my mother and sisters?" He sounded uncertain, bewildered. "I can understand not liking my father, but Mama and the girls are—"

"Perfect," Deirdre said. "Your mother and sisters are utterly perfect. They're beautiful and warm and friendly and dainty. They ate two sandwiches, and I saw embroidery. I don't know how to sit still long enough to embroider. I hate skirts and stays and having my hair pinned up. I hate the idea of eating just two sandwiches when I'm hungry. And they're such ladies. Your mother, with three children, still blushed when she told me about . . . this." She pressed her hands to her belly.

"Another female thing you hate." Kieran's voice had gone flat, quiet.

"No, no, not that. I'm not that unnatural of a female. But I'm going to be confined to stitching tiny garments and eating tinier cakes when my crew is suffering. I can do nothing to help them."

"You will be safe from any harebrained schemes." He laid his hand against her cheek. "Which is why I did what I could and prayed for nature to take its course."

The warm, caressing hand against her face may as well have been a slap. Deirdre swayed. Flailed at the air for something to hold onto besides her husband.

"You just wanted to stop me from helping my crew."

"I wanted—I want—to keep you safe from your own misguided loyalties."

"They are not misguided."

"They are if they go in any direction but toward this family."

"I can't—" She stopped, fearing she would begin to weep.

"Deirdre, I am sorry, but I cannot have my wife haring around the countryside consorting with the enemy." He cupped her chin in his hands and stroked her cheekbones with his fingertips, stirring longing deep inside her, distracting her with his touch.

She backed away from him. "Then you shouldn't have married me."

"I had to. We were alone on the *Maid* for days, and the scandal would have harmed my family further. And you." He touched her elbow, trying to steer her toward the house. "You suffered enough losing your father and everything you knew. I could not abandon you to strangers."

His voice held such tenderness she wanted to throw herself into his arms and beg him to love her.

She planted her feet. "You said marrying me would also improve matters with your father. Was that a lie?"

"No. I thought if I did the right thing by you and came home respectable, the rift would heal. A baby, a grandchild on the way, would cement a new bond." He sighed and looked away.

She crossed her arms over her chest. "It hasn't worked."

"I'm afraid it's made things worse. I do not know why, but there is something in their past I do not know that has Tyne overset. In truth, Deirdre—" He dug the toe of his Hessian into the gravel. "Seems like my marrying you was a mistake."

Chapter 15

*D*eirdre stared at Kieran, the word "mistake" reverberating through her head like a ship's bell clanging through a fog. Marrying her was a mistake to him. Considering the condition she was probably in, marrying him was a mistake for her, too.

"C-can your father have the marriage set aside?" She had begun to shiver and wanted to huddle next to one of the fires wafting smoke from the chimneys. Yet she did not wish to go back to the home where she was unwelcome. "Will he have the marriage set aside?"

"Not without a great deal of trouble and even more scandal. A vicar married us, so it has to go through the ecclesiastical courts and Parliament. And if you are carrying the heir, nothing would even be considered until after we know if the child is a boy or girl." He spoke as though he had memorized the explanation.

Deirdre began to walk toward the house. "Then no sense standing outside here freezing. I expect your family will accept me as your wife whether they like it or not, just as you must."

"Deirdre, no." He caught up with her and tucked his hand through the crook of her elbow. "Don't think we don't want you here."

"I will do without facing them all at dinner."

"Coward." The word held enough affection some of Deirdre's chill dissipated.

She took a deep breath as they reached the front steps. "All right, if you think it's all right, I'll stay for dinner."

"Of course it's all right. We won't be eating *en famille*. We usually do not."

"You have guests?"

Deirdre nearly accepted defeat at that idea and reconsidered the tray.

"Not guests. My father's secretary Burnham and his steward Leith, and Miss Pruitt, who was the girls' governess. She is mostly a companion or chaperone now." He stroked his fingers down the inside of Deirdre's forearm before hurrying ahead of her to open the door.

Warmth and light greeted them along with the delicious aroma of roasting beef. Deirdre's stomach growled. "How long until dinner?"

"Two hours. Would you like me to show you around the house?"

"Yes, please. I'll get lost if you don't, but can you sneak me a half-dozen more sandwiches?"

"I will be happy to do so, m'lady." The one-armed footman hastened forward and bowed.

Deirdre wanted to sink through the floor. She had forgotten that servants lurked everywhere.

"Have them sent to the music room, Rochester." Kieran offered Deirdre his arm. "We will start with the ground floor. Here we have all the public rooms—dining room, drawing rooms, Father's study, and the estate office for the steward and secretary." His voice was low, gentle, friendly, but not warm.

Most of the rooms weren't warm either. Dark and closed, some with furniture shrouded in cloth covers, the chambers ranged from one or two anterooms not much bigger than her father's cabin to rooms the length of a naval frigate.

"The ballroom." Kieran introduced this last one.

The music room was next door. Someone had lighted a fire and several candles. Before the hearth stood a low table with a tray bearing far more than a few sandwiches.

"Whoever Rochester is, I adore him." Deirdre nearly fell upon the bread and butter and little cakes dotted with tinier black seeds.

Kieran poured them each a cup of the steaming tea. "He has apparently taken a liking to you. Probably because he was once a sailor himself."

"Did he sail with your father?" Deirdre sank her teeth into a thick slice of brown bread liberally smeared with butter. Fresh, rich butter.

She nearly swooned from the pleasure.

Kieran just stared at her, not answering.

She set the bread down. "Is something wrong? I thought it all right if I eat like this when we are alone."

"Just not enough alone." Kieran rose and lifted the lid on a pianoforte. "Nearly every servant on the estate, especially the ones with some kind of infirmity, either served with my father or someone who did. They get tossed on the beach once they aren't fit enough to serve, and most die shortly if they have no families to take care of them. So Tyne does his best to find them work."

Deirdre's opinion of the earl rose. Surely a man who cared so much about the plight of injured sailors carried a heart inside that breastbone of his. The contrast between that and his treatment of his son did not connect in Deirdre's head.

"Your father has a great deal of kindness."

Kieran shrugged, then ran his fingers along the keys. "Ah, the girls have been practicing. This is in tune."

"Do you play?"

"Not as well as Chloe or Juliet, but well enough. Shall I serenade you while you eat?"

They couldn't talk then, but she didn't care. Music might distract her enough that she wouldn't walk into the dinner of strangers ready to run and scream.

He played something gentle and quiet and full of trilling notes. He got a few wrong, grimaced when he did so, but didn't stop. Finished eating, Deirdre wandered around the room, finding a harpsichord and a harp beneath brown linen cloths and a violin in a leather case.

"Do you play any of these?" She plucked a string on the violin and started at its tuneful response.

"My great-aunt played the violin, though it's not a lady's instrument, and Chloe is trying to learn it. Mama taught us all the pianoforte and harpsichord, and Juliet is rather accomplished on the harp. Tyne couldn't so much as sing a right note to save his life." Satisfaction rang in his tone. "Are you musical? I never heard any music on the *Maid*."

"My father couldn't tell one note from another, and singing irritated him because of it, so I didn't grow up with music aboard. I like it, though."

"I could teach you."

She gazed at him in wonder, but before she could ask if he was serious in his offer, Rochester knocked on the door and announced that the time had arrived to dress for dinner.

Deirdre looked down at the pretty lavender silk gown she was wearing. "I have nothing nicer."

"Mama will have found something by now." Kieran rose from the piano stool and offered her his arm. "I shall show you how to get from here to the front hall and from there to your room. If you can get to the front hall, you will always find a footman, if one eludes you elsewhere."

They traversed corridors and climbed steps to more hallways. When Deirdre saw her bed, she just wanted to fall upon it and rest. But a blue velvet gown lay atop the coverlet, and Sally stood by the dressing table. With a promise he would return for her, Kieran retreated.

If this was her life, Deirdre thought two hours later, she was going to die of boredom. Life at sea had its stultifying moments, but one always needed to trim a sail or prepare the next meal—something. She needed to do nothing. Doors were opened for her, chairs pulled out, and dishes set before her. She was supposed to only take a spoonful from each of the dishes presented to her, all the while listening to Juliet's lively but shallow chatter on one side, or risk conversation with Lord Tyne on the other. When he asked her about the *Maid*'s speed, Deirdre was happy to talk with him about the raked masts and how, yes, they reached China in ten weeks. To Juliet's undisguised disgust, Deirdre and Tyne talked sailing until Lady Tyne rose and indicated the ladies should follow her into the drawing room. The governess looked through fashion magazines with Chloe and Juliet, Lady Tyne read from a book of William Blake's poetry, and Deirdre fell asleep in her chair before the fire.

A forefinger caressing her cheek woke her. She opened her eyes to see Kieran standing beside her chair, but not really looking at her.

"I will take her up, of course, sir." He addressed his father, then turned to Deirdre. "Let us get you some rest."

Though he offered his hand to help her rise, not that she needed it, he released it as soon as she stood. She bade goodnight to the Ashfords and their entourage of lackeys, then followed Kieran to the door a footman held open.

"Miss Pruitt, perhaps you can teach her how to curtsy." Juliet's sweet, clear voice rang out through a portal not closed quickly enough behind them.

Deirdre shot Kieran a panicked glance, but he shook his head, took a proffered taper from another footman, and led the way up the steps. Once she was certain they were alone, she touched his arm. "Should I have curtsied there?"

"It is not necessary *en famille*, but you will have to learn before we have guests."

"I did learn once. I just forget where I'm supposed to put my feet."

"You will learn." He sighed. "A whole lot of things."

Deirdre stumbled over the edge of a hall runner and slapped her flattened hand against the wall.

"Am I an embarrassment to you? Do you want to lock me up so I don't humiliate you in front of your neighbors? Or maybe you've already done enough of that for yourself with all the indiscretions you haven't told me about. What kind of a father is this baby going to have?"

"One he or she can be proud of." His voice husky, Kieran drew her against him. "You are not an embarrassment to me. I even think Tyne likes you. And anyone who can learn what all those lines, hawsers, and cables on a ship are and where they go is capable of learning how to curtsy and all those other social affectations."

Her body ached to melt against his warmth. Her stupid head longed to accept his compliment and leave matters be, but she understood his affection and flattery for what they were—distractions. He was good at distracting her with caresses and kisses and sweet words. So good she might not be able to free her crew until after she delivered her baby.

She pressed her palms against his shoulders. "You're not going to talk about your past, the reasons why your father was quick to believe the tale Joanna's brother put about."

"I find the subject embarrassing." He clasped her elbow and started forward. "And it makes me sound either vain or a weakling for blaming the ladies involved, but . . ." He sighed. "Some females whose birth entitles them to be considered ladies will go to great lengths, even ones that compromise their reputations, in an effort to entrap one of England's most eligible bachelors."

Deirdre rolled her eyes. "And you didn't always resist temptation."

"To my shame, I did not." Color high, he faced her, his eyes blazing in the light from a wall sconce. "But I never debauched an innocent lady, and offered for Joanna to show I had changed my ways."

"Which proved to be an error." Heaviness settled inside Deirdre's chest. "Just like marrying me to prove your turned leaf turned out to be a mistake."

"It should not have been." An ache rasped through Kieran's voice.

They reached her room. A fire burned in the grate, a nightgown lay across the bed, and the coverlet had been turned down.

"There is no bell in this room. I will bid you goodnight and go send your maid up." Kieran stood in the open doorway making the offer without attempting to depart.

Deirdre thought of how her presence in the Ashford household, as Kieran's wife, was a mistake, and opened her mouth to wish him away from her, then she thought about a night alone in a strange house, a strange bed, and turned her back to him. "Or you can provide the service for me."

"I thought you would never ask." The door closed. The key grated in the lock.

Deirdre woke up alone in the big bed. Kieran had been gone so long his pillow no longer held his warmth, only his scent. She wrapped her arms around it and buried her face in the soft linen.

She was such a fool to succumb to passion. So weak to hunger for intimacy with the enemy just to avoid being alone. Now that marrying her had only confirmed his father's belief in the irresponsible behavior of his heir, the only good she was to Kieran was to satisfy his physical needs. She managed that just fine now, quite happily, but, unless they were all wrong about her condition, if the signs were misleading, he would not find her attractive in a few months when she grew big-bellied and unwieldy.

The door opened. Soft footfalls whispered across the rug. China clinked and water splashed. Then the aroma of hot chocolate drifted to Deirdre's nose.

She sat up, glad she had pulled her nightgown back on sometime during the night, and gazed at the tray Sally held. "Chocolate?"

"Yes, m'lady. All the Ashford ladies have a pot of hot chocolate to start their day, along with some bread and butter."

"I approve." Deirdre leaned forward so Sally could slip several pillows behind her, then rested against them to receive a tray across her lap.

A china pot glazed in deep blue and gold issued steam from its spout. A matching cup waited to receive the hot chocolate, and a small plate had been piled high with slices of fresh bread and creamy butter. At one corner, a tiny pink rose had been pinned to a folded slip of paper.

"Roses this late in the autumn?" Deirdre lifted it to her nose.

"It won't have much smell." Sally poured the dark brown liquid into the cup. "It's from the hothouse. But his lordship wanted you to have it with his note."

His note.

Deirdre sipped her chocolate, waiting for Sally to stop hovering before she opened the message from Kieran. At last, murmuring something about fetching a gown for Deirdre, Sally departed.

Deirdre opened the note.

> *My Dear Lady,*
> *I have had to depart for Plymouth for business having to do with the cargo. Mama and the girls will bring you in later for some shopping. See you at dinner.*
> *K*

Other than the "My Dear," the note was cool, impersonal, signaling how they would go on when not completely alone.

She should be glad of that. With only physical attraction between them, remembering that she was loyal to her crew remained easy.

Wishing she didn't feel like giving into the too-easy tears, Deirdre drank her chocolate. Like everything else in the Ashford household, this was perfection—sweet, but not too sweet; hot, but not too hot; creamy, but not too creamy. The bread and butter were the same, but she had no appetite. She nibbled a slice then set the tray aside and slid from bed. She wanted to wash before Sally returned. She wasn't about to live her life under that sort of public scrutiny.

By the time Sally returned with yet one more altered gown, Deirdre wore her stockings, pantalets, and shift. Sally had also brought stays, but Deirdre refused to put them on. "Wearing a dress is enough torture without that contraption inhibiting my movements."

"But, m'lady, you must. If anyone should discover you weren't wearing them, they would be scandalized." Sally looked so distressed Deirdre nearly gave in.

Not nearly enough.

She crossed her arms over her chest and took up a spread-legged stance. "I either wear the dress without stays, or I stay in this room."

"But it's expected." Sally's big brown eyes grew bright with tears.

Deirdre picked up her dressing gown and took a seat before the fire.

"The carriage leaves for Plymouth in half an hour." Sally had apparently decided on a different tack.

"And I won't be in it." Deirdre picked up a book bound in blue leather to match the room.

More poetry, this by John Donne.

And we together prove . . .

The only thing she and Kieran would prove was the utter rightness of the proverb about marrying in haste and repenting for a lifetime.

Her own eyes flooded.

The door opened. "Deirdre, what's the delay? Does the dress not fit right?" Lady Tyne breezed into the room on a cloud of sweet scent and filmy fabric.

"I'm ever so sorry, m'lady." Sally leaped into the breach first. "I can't get her ladyship to wear her stays."

"Then she won't wear them." Lady Tyne studied Deirdre from beneath her long golden lashes. "Of course, if she doesn't, we will look stingy in the dressmaker's shops like we couldn't provide her the most basic needs for decency."

"Then I won't go," said Deirdre.

"And let everyone in Plymouth, everyone in Devonshire, think we are ashamed of you?"

"Aren't you?"

"Not yet, but your inability to follow convention and wear stays may lead in that direction—"

"Oh, all right." Deirdre slammed the book of love poems onto the table and rose. "You Ashfords are all masters at manipulation."

"For your own good, my dear." Lady Tyne patted her arm.

"Kieran said something like that when he married me, and that isn't such a good idea in the execution, is it?"

"Is it not?" Her ladyship smiled. "We leave in twenty minutes." She sailed out of the room.

Deirdre submitted to the torture of having whalebone bands marched around her rib cage to hold in her nonexistent excess flesh. Then further torment occurred with the styling of her hair, but at last, Sally declared Deirdre ready to face the world.

Within the hour, she thought she should have stayed home and let the world think what it would. Juliet talked of nothing but what colors and fabrics would suit Deirdre, how sadly dark was her complexion, how surprisingly dainty her feet. Deirdre wished the family was ashamed of her and didn't want to dress her fit for company.

And if the carriage ride was torturous, the fittings were worse. The dressmaker made disparaging remarks about Deirdre's complexion, but cooed over Deirdre's hair. Deirdre might have ordered two gowns. Her ladyship ordered ten.

"That will get you started until we can send to London for something better."

Deirdre's head spun, but not, as she wished, fast enough for her to faint and get out of the rest of the excursion. The rest entailed hats, gloves, slippers, and walking boots ordered, silk and lisle stockings, and hair ribbons.

"I have lots of those." Deirdre looked at the display and such a yawning need to be back at sea opened inside her, she walked from the shop for fresh air.

And saw the prisoners.

Ragged, filthy, some barefoot despite the cold, three dozen men or more shuffled along the street between red-coated guards. The guards carried muskets and bayonets. The prisoners wore chains. Those chains rattled and clanked in rhythm with the slap of feet and shouts of the soldiers to move along. One man stumbled. A guard yanked him upright by the links binding his hands, and Deirdre saw the man was old Wat Drummond. Ross marched behind him, shoulders back, head up, chin jutting forward in defiance of the ignominy of his situation.

Deirdre's eyes blurred before she saw the rest of her crew. Nonetheless, she knew they were there amid other Americans or Frenchmen or both. They would not, however, remain imprisoned even if she died freeing them.

She took a step toward the edge of the pavement and the line of soldiers and prisoners.

An arm slipped around her waist. "I can see you are as impatient with all these fripperies as I am." Chloe's hold was firm as she turned toward Deirdre's mother- and sister-in-law and the wide-eyed dressmaker. "I am going to take her back to the inn for some tea and cakes. The rest of you may continue shopping."

Deirdre stood rigid, silent as the last of the prisoners passed.

"There's the carriage." Chloe steered Deirdre to the vehicle trundling along the street in the prisoners' wake. "Some tea will set you right in a trice."

Nothing would set her right until her crew was free.

With all the grace of an automaton, Deirdre climbed the steps of the carriage and dropped onto the velvet cushions. She clasped her hands in her lap and willed herself not to scream.

"Were some of those men from your crew?" Chloe settled onto the seat beside Deirdre and a footman closed the door.

Deirdre nodded. "The old man who stumbled? I've known him all my life."

"How could anyone shut a man that old in prison." Chloe clasped and unclasped her hands around her reticule. "It's barbaric."

"He's the enemy."

Chloe made a rude noise, and Deirdre decided she liked this new sister, but that didn't mean she would trust her with her opinions.

She straightened, face composed. "I can return on my own if you wish to keep shopping."

"I do not." Chloe groaned. "If I hear Juliet squeal over one more dear little bonnet, I think I will start screaming."

"You mean you don't enjoy shopping?"

"I would rather climb a tree and read a book in peace."

Deirdre scanned Chloe from the brim of her blue straw bonnet to the tips of her dainty blue slippers and shook her head. "You never climb trees in that getup."

"No." Chloe winked. "I keep a set of Kieran's old clothes in a trunk in the attics and change into those, then hide in the parkland in a tree to read or watch the sunrise. I love my sister, but her constant chatter and romantic notions are a bit too much at times."

Deirdre laughed and realized she had perhaps found her first female friend.

The men joined the ladies for dinner at the inn, where they had earlier made arrangements for three bedchambers and a private parlor. Juliet and Chloe rushed from the fireside to join them, Juliet waving her new bonnet under Kieran's nose. Deirdre remained by the fire with the older ladies, waiting for Kieran to come to her, uncertain as to whether or not they formed a united front before his father, or if their closeness was confined to the middle of the night.

For the moment, his sisters held Kieran's attention. Tyne, after kissing each of his daughters on the cheek, went straight to Phoebe and took her hands in his. The tenderness on his face when he looked down at her made Deirdre's throat close.

Then, all of a sudden, Kieran was at her side, his hand on her shoulder. "Are you well, m'dear?"

"Well enough." She smiled up at him with feigned tenderness. "Did you enjoy your day disposing of my inheritance . . . er . . . your prize?"

Someone gasped.

Kieran's fingers flexed on her shoulder. "I had to go on the water. That does not make any day pleasant."

"I have seen more turbulent baths," Tyne said, "than that harbor today. How did you manage to cross the Atlantic and back without starving to death?"

"I kept him dosed with ginger and laudanum." Deirdre offered Tyne a sweet smile. "He probably wouldn't have married me if he'd been in his right senses."

"Deirdre," Kieran said through his teeth.

Tyne's lips thinned, but his eyes held those dancing lights, as he gave Deirdre a bow, then turned back to Phoebe. "You have bespoken dinner? We did not have much in the way of a noonday meal aboard the *Phoebe*."

"We had a lovely nuncheon," Juliet said. "Except we saw some prisoners being marched through the street."

Chloe clapped her hand over Juliet's mouth. "Will you ever learn when to keep your tongue inside your teeth?"

"I have bespoken dinner," Phoebe said a little too quickly. "I told them to begin serving as soon as you arrived."

Deirdre's head spun, and she leaned back in her chair.

"Are you all right?" Kieran moved to crouch beside Deirdre's chair, his eyes holding concern.

Deirdre drew as far from him as the chair allowed. How dare he act the caring husband when her men were on their way to hell on earth?

He covered her hand with his and squeezed. "They are at Dartmoor. I am sorry."

Her only hope for the crew now lay in either freeing them or praying the war would not last for long. Except the brevity of the war would likely mean America would lose, making them all British subjects again.

She gripped the arms of the chair to stop herself from springing up and racing from the room.

Kieran laid one hand over hers. "I went to church today and asked the vicar to pray for them."

"You went to church on a weekday?" Juliet swooped down on her brother and pulled his hair. "Does impending fatherhood make you truly repentant?"

Phoebe moaned. "Where did I go wrong as a mother?"

"You needed more discipline," Tyne said.

"Oh, Papa." Juliet giggled. "You never needed to discipline me."

"He most certainly did," Chloe muttered.

The entrance of inn servants with trays of food ended that discussion.

Kieran rose and drew Deirdre up after him. "Are you up to eating some dinner?"

Deirdre wasn't sure, but the scent of warm, fresh bread drew her to the table on Kieran's arm. He pulled out the chair to the right of his father's, then moved around the table to the other side and his mother's right and Chloe's left. Juliet sat to Deirdre's right and tried to engage her in conversation, but Tyne shot her a look that shut her up more effectively than did words or actions from anyone else.

"I enjoyed looking over your schooner today." Tyne dipped his spoon into a bowl of lobster bisque. "I can see why she's so fast. What a beautiful design. But she cannot carry much cargo with such a shallow draft."

"She's so fast we don't need to carry a great deal of cargo." Deirdre knew too little about fashion for Juliet, but Tyne knew ships and cargo, and so did Deirdre.

"So you concentrated on a light, high-profit cargo." Tyne leaned back so the servant could exchange his soup plate for a plate of oysters.

Deirdre shook her head at the waiter. "Since the Embargo Act five years ago, my father"—she swallowed the burning at the back of her throat—"concentrated on the China run. It has proved profitable."

Tyne looked thoughtful.

The hairs on the back of Deirdre's neck prickled, alerting her to be cautious about mentioning much more about profits. By law, that money belonged to Kieran as her husband, and she didn't want him to find out where or how much she still possessed. To free her crew, she would more than likely need every last coin.

Tyne pushed the oysters aside and picked up his wineglass. He gazed down the table at either Phoebe or Kieran, Deirdre couldn't tell, with the former talking to Juliet and the latter to Chloe. Then Tyne turned his full attention back to her. "Kieran said you had land in Virginia."

"Yes, but it was only a thousand acres." Because she knew these things mattered to Englishmen, she decided to give him her lineage. "My father's family ended up there after the Jacobite rebellion in 1715. My mother's family are descendants of Lord Fairfax."

Tyne smiled. "That sounds more prestigious than the Ashfords. Do you have relatives living? I can probably manage to get a message to them regarding your whereabouts."

"Some distant cousins in the western part of Virginia and into Kentucky. I've never met them, but they may wish to know about my father."

"Yes, your father." Tyne touched her hand. "Please accept my condolences. As you have discovered by now, I know, Kieran has not been an exemplary son, but becoming a privateer is the worst of his transgressions, and depriving you of your only parent in doing so is unforgivable."

Deirdre looked at her husband, now laughing with his mother and elder sister over something Juliet had said, and shook her head as she turned back to Tyne. "I can't wholly blame him for my father's death. He would have died soon anyway, I'm afraid. According to the log, he was having such bad headaches and pains in his chest that he had been dosing himself with laudanum. I think he wanted to get me home safely."

Tyne sighed. "And my son kept him from fulfilling his wish. The least we can do to make up for it is keep you safe."

"As long as I keep my mouth shut about being from Virginia."

That was probably not polite, as the man was being genuinely kind to her, yet she couldn't resist.

He gave her a grim smile in acknowledgment. "It would be best as long as this little conflict with your country is on. Please. We have some . . . associates who are not fond of Yankees. I will know more about the situation when we return from London."

"We?" Deirdre crushed the rest of her bread roll. "You and Phoebe are going?"

"Kieran and I are going. I still have some friends in the Admiralty . . . Ah, I smell fricassee of chicken. Will you take some of this, m'dear?"

She would. The creamy sauce made her mouth water.

At the far end of the table, Kieran was regaling his mother with the story of meeting her old friend from Savannah. "I do believe she intended me to make an offer to carry her daughters back here to England."

"Perhaps we should invite them," Phoebe said. "They can't meet many men there on Bermuda who aren't military."

"We will see how the war goes," Kieran said. "Both wars."

"Are they pretty?" Juliet asked.

Kieran shrugged. "I did not notice."

That made his sisters laugh and scoff in doubt.

"One matter I am seeing to in London," Tyne said to Deirdre alone, "is the fact that I wish to purchase the *Maid of Alexandria* for myself rather than turning it over to the naval prize courts. Someone needs to start making regular runs of goods to the New South Wales colony, and that takes a fast vessel. But I am concerned about piracy in the Indian Ocean. Can she carry more ordnance than you have aboard her?"

With the hairs on her neck prickling again, Deirdre thought before answering. "More ordnance would slow her, sir. And she lies so low in the water now, it might make her outright dangerous in a storm, especially when fully laden. Speed is your best weapon."

The waiter entered again and began to carve a joint of beef.

"As long as the wind does not fail you." Tyne looked thoughtful as he sipped from his wineglass.

Suddenly, Deirdre thought she might fall asleep where she sat. Pushing back her chair, she glanced from Tyne to his wife, not sure whom to ask. "I know this is terribly rude of me, but may I be excused?"

At once, Kieran was on his feet and around the table, assisting her to her feet. "Are you ill? Faint?"

"Merely tired." She forced herself to remain upright.

"Take her up to your room, Kieran," Phoebe said. "We dragged her about far too much today."

"No, no, Kieran," Deirdre protested. "Stay with your family."

She wanted to be alone, think about any benefit she could have given the enemy with her answers to his questions, fall asleep before

Kieran returned and she had to be alone with him again, knowing his solicitude was because of guilt over displeasing his family and not caring for her.

"Nonsense. You cannot go up alone." He slipped his arm around her waist and ushered her from the room.

When they were inside their chamber and he had added some coal to the grate, Deirdre expected him to leave. As weary as she felt, she would not undress for bed until he returned to his family. She stood by the fire and waited for him to go.

He began to prowl around the room, toying with her hairbrush on the dresser, lifting a swath of ribbons off the table beside the bed, rearranging the bed pillows. Finally, he reached the door.

Deirdre opened her mouth to assure him he need not hurry back.

He turned the key in the lock. "Tyne told you that we are going to London tomorrow, did he not?"

"Yes." Deirdre's mouth was dry. "Are you going to petition the courts or the Church or whoever is in charge of these things to have our marriage set aside?"

His eyes widened. "That would be Parliament, but why would you think I would do that?" He paced toward her. "You are my wife."

She crossed her arms over her chest. "Your wife you don't want."

"That is not true." He placed his hands on her shoulders and leaned toward her.

She flattened her palms against his chest and held him off. "That's not what I mean, and you are well aware of the fact."

Kieran covered her hands with his, pressing them hard against his chest so she felt his heart racing. "One purpose of this journey is to ensure Chloe will have a successful Season in the spring."

"Because of the scandal." Her own heart rate matched his.

Kieran nodded.

A chill stole through Deirdre's limbs. "You won't fight another duel, will you?"

"I did not fight the last one." He released her and turned away. "But to reassure you, no, I will not fight any duels. Nor will I resume the behavior that got me into trouble the first time."

She thought she said she didn't care what he did in town, but she did—for the sake of the baby, of course. Kieran's child deserved a father he could be proud of, not a ne'er-do-well nobleman with too much money and too little responsibility. Boredom had driven him into activities that had persuaded his father the worst of him was true. As long as she was his wife, she didn't want to be the recipient of others' pity because her husband was a rakehell.

"Your father should set you up in business so you have something to occupy you." She spoke to his broad back.

"I have business." Those shoulders suddenly rigid, he began to unbuckle the straps of his valise.

"Of course you do." Deirdre clasped her upper arms, cold despite the fire on the grate. "You've brought in a rich prize. Will the Admiralty congratulate you even if you did marry the enemy?"

"My father will take care of the Admiralty business." The valise opened. Kieran reached beneath a pile of clean shirts. "I am going to take care of this."

He faced her with a sheaf of papers gripped between his hands.

She didn't need to look at them to know that he had found her father's will and the certificates for Drummond's Bank in London.

Chapter 16

*D*eirdre's eyes widened. Her mouth opened, and for a moment, Kieran feared she would scream or begin to pummel him with her fists. He braced himself for an onslaught of sound or assault.

She turned away, her flounced skirt swishing around her feet. "Get out." Her voice was harsh, but barely above a whisper. "Get out before I smash something over your head."

Kieran didn't move. He would risk the head bashing in order to talk to her, to explain.

"I could not let it go, Deirdre. Tyne suggested I look for banknotes or certificates in your possession. He said it was highly unlikely your father didn't have those aboard if the schooner was your home."

"So you looked through my sea chest." She reached the windowsill and leaned her palms upon it, her brow against the frosty glass. "When? Last night after you shared my bed? Is that why you shared my bed?"

"Why not?" Kieran glared at her back, his body shaking, but his voice low and even. "You were not going to stick with our bargain. You were going to run off to London, collect cash for these certificates, and leave me. Were you even going to wait for the birth of our—our, not your—child?"

Deirdre's shoulders stiffened. "I'd have done what I needed to see my crew not suffer in an English prison." Her voice was cold. With her brow against the window, he couldn't see her reflection in the glass.

Her words said enough.

Kieran returned the certificates to his valise. "I have established pin money for you. Tyne's steward will give it to you when you return to Bishops Cove. I will also pay your dressmaker's bills and the like, so you may use the pin money to send your crew any incidentals they may need in prison, but it will not be enough to bribe them into freedom. Nor, in the event one or all of them find their own means of escape, will you visit the prison and connect the Ashford name or earldom and viscountcy to the prisoners. I am sorry to renege on what I said earlier about you visiting them, but I cannot risk seeing us all hanged, including you, and our lands attaindered because we're traitors. Do you understand?"

Her response was short and vulgar, and he almost laughed. That was his Deirdre, the sailor maiden he admired so much.

"They will be all right, Deirdre." He would leave as she wished him to, but he could not walk away without touching her hair, without inhaling her sweet, sharp scent of ginger. "You will thank me in the end." He kissed the side of her neck, the only bit of her flesh he could access, then left their bedchamber.

The taproom was nearly empty at that hour. Kieran ordered brandy, then found a seat on a banquette in the corner and prepared for a long, uncomfortable night knowing he had protected Deirdre from her own loyalties, and perhaps begun the steps to restore his place in the family, all at the cost of harmony with his wife for whatever length of time they needed to stay together.

Not for the first time in his life, he wished for the oblivion of inebriation. But it never came to him. As much brandy as he consumed throughout the night, long after the barkeep left for his bed and the fire burned down to mere winking eyes, he met his father at the coach that would take them to London tired, rumpled, and stone cold sober.

Tyne's valet traveled with them in the carriage, so Kieran felt no obligation to speak with his father during the five days of travel to London. During the evenings, however, at a posting house, the Ashford estate in Hampshire, and more inns, Kieran sat across from Tyne at supper tables and grates and wondered if he and his father had ever spent this much time together. When Kieran was not at school or university, Tyne seemed to be traveling between estates or sitting in Parliament. During the holidays, the family was together, and the girls held their father's attention.

But Chloe was five years younger than Kieran, and Juliet eight. What had happened in the intervening years?

"Did you and Mama keep me locked away in the nursery until I went to school?" he asked one night over brandy and day-old London newspapers.

Tyne set his paper aside. "Of course not."

"There is no 'of course not' about it. Most parents do."

"Your mother is not most parents."

"But you would have preferred to keep me shut away."

Tyne gave him a long, thoughtful look. "I did not trust anyone else to teach you to ride or fence. Do you not recall?"

Kieran stared at him, his mind blank. Why could he not remember the patient man who had put him on his first pony, the master who had handed him his first foil, as his father?

He covered up his confusion over this with a laugh. "I expect I am not terribly good at either of those activities."

"Why do you think that?"

Was that hurt in Tyne's eyes?

Kieran shrugged and raised his newspaper. "You gave up teaching me to ride about the time Chloe was born and fencing when Juliet came along."

Tyne remained silent for so long Kieran thought that he was not going to continue the conversation. Then he folded his paper altogether and refilled their glasses. "When you were two years old, my elder brother died, making me the heir apparent. My father was getting on in years and had been relying heavily on David's assistance with things. I took on that role along with my other two estates. While I was in Northumberland, your mother delivered a baby a month early—a stillborn boy." He cleared his throat. "We nearly lost her. I thought you might be the only child we would have, so arranged matters to be in Devonshire as much as possible, to ensure you rode properly."

"But Chloe was born when I was four."

"That she was, and she was a demanding baby, but such a blessing." Tyne's face was soft. "I did not have as much time for you as I would have liked, but I did begin your sword training shortly before Juliet came along two and a half years later."

"I do not believe you trained me for long before I went up to school." Kieran could not release a memory of Tyne's attention disappearing from his life.

"I suspended your training and sent you up to Eton when Phoebe's confinement was near." Tyne's brow creased. "We had concerns, and I did not want to leave Phoebe's side. I neglected a lot of things right before and after Juliet's birth."

"I never knew Mama was in such danger in childbearing." Kieran felt humbled and ashamed for not thinking that his parents' lives had not always been rosy.

For a moment, a twinge of apprehension for Deirdre squeezed his heart. But Mama was small and delicate. Deirdre was a big, strong girl. Surely she would be all right.

"You were too young to understand." Tyne gave him the gentle smile he usually reserved for Mama and the girls. "You may understand a bit more now that you are going to be a father. Of course, a great deal can go wrong this early. Childbearing is a risky business for the ladies and those of us who love them."

"Our marriage has nothing to do with love." Kieran managed a cynical twist of his lips to go with the declaration.

Tyne laughed. "Neither did ours. But things change until every day away from the object of your affection makes you feel like someone is hollowing you out. And when the children come, you love her even more."

"If the children come." Kieran held his brandy glass and spun it between his palms, watching firelight dance in the golden-brown liquid. "If she does miscarry, would it be better to have the marriage dissolved?"

"There are a number of reasons why that might not be a worthless idea." Tyne rose and squeezed Kieran's shoulder. "But I would rather think about having a healthy grandchild in another seven or eight months."

Kieran's head shot up. Although he knew if he stood he would be at least as tall as his father, he felt young again, smaller, looking up at someone he had once considered all wise and powerful and good instead of just all powerful. "You do not mind about the baby then? Even though Deirdre is an American?"

"How can I mind?" Tyne smiled. "I have three beautiful children from an American lady."

Kieran coughed, then laughed. "Yes, well, the girls are diamonds of the first water, are they not? Juliet needs to learn to curb her tongue, but she will by the time she is old enough for a Season. And why Chloe has not taken yet just shows how stupid most of us *ton* bachelors are."

"Chloe is a bit bossy. She will run her husband ragged, and he will love every minute of it." Tyne retrieved his paper and brandy. "I believe I will turn in. We may have a long day tomorrow if we push through to London." He went to the door of the private parlor. "Just remember, Kieran, I said three beautiful children."

Kieran remembered. He simply did not know how to respond to that kind of compliment, to any kind of compliment from his father. He had thought Tyne considered him nothing more than a sluggard, a scoundrel, a blot on the family honor.

Kieran touched his ear. He would never be beautiful with that mangled appendage showing, and his hair was going to look ridiculous in London. Yet Tyne had indeed said "three beautiful children." That made Kieran feel a warmth toward his father that had died—when? After he had been sent down from Eton at eight, shortly after arriving at that august institution, for . . . for . . . oh yes. Writing a naughty poem, the meaning of which he had not wholly understood, and posting it on the back of some duke's son. Of course, the back of his cousin Dante, speaking of wastrel sons. Kieran had sworn he did not know that the poem meant what the headmaster told him it did, but he was caned anyway because no one believed in his innocence. When he got home, Tyne had been distracted, paid little attention to Kieran's protestation of unjust treatment, and sent him to the stable to spend his extra holiday mucking out stalls.

Juliet was born that week.

Now Kieran understood why his father had been distracted and simply wanted Kieran out of the way. It was not because he did not care; it was because he had indeed been full of apprehension for his wife.

And Tyne wanted Deirdre's baby to be born. That placed even more burden on Kieran to make certain Deirdre did nothing risky to her health, the baby's safety, the family's future.

❦

"Non, non," cried Madame, the dressmaker, who was about as French as Dolley Madison. "There is nothing wrong with my sewing. Her ladyship insisted I leave fabric for the expansion." She shot her hands

out from her bosom. "You must not yank it on so. Pull the garments on slowly so the seams lie flat."

After three days of fittings, Deirdre thought she was going to indulge in either a ladylike fit of hysterics or an unladylike fit of raucous cursing. And if her bosom expanded to the proportions Madame indicated, she would never get close enough to Kieran to strangle him.

"Why can't you sew the extra fabric flat?" she asked.

Madame's hands shot into the air. "Oh, you colonials are so ignorant of the fashions. The stitching would show."

"Better than me squirming about and itching because I'm being tickled." Deirdre yanked the offending garment over her head.

"Ah, *les mesdames enceintes*, they are so much trouble. But I will make right for the oh-so-kind Lady Tyne."

"Not like the oh-so-unkind Lady Ripon," Deirdre muttered.

That was just weird, the use of her title. When people heard Lady Ripon, though, they began to bow and scrape. She wanted to laugh.

She never would have married Kieran if she'd known about it.

That and a few dozen other items like the fact that he possessed more loyalty to his family than to her. The problem with that was she couldn't blame him. They were kind and warm and so popular among people in Plymouth she couldn't believe for a minute that they had done anything so terrible that one slip-up from her would send them to prison.

Meanwhile, her crew was in prison, and Kieran had made getting them out more difficult. At the moment, she barely liked her ladyship for continuing to drag her about Plymouth to find shoes, hats, shawls, and gloves, of all the abominable inventions. She thought perhaps she should be wearing black to mourn her father. Gently, kindly, Kieran's mother explained that Deirdre must not draw attention to her father's identity with such an open display.

"I would mourn for Papa forever," Juliet declared. "It must hurt terribly."

"It does." Deirdre's eyes began to water. "I want to go back to sea, back home. You are all very kind, my lady, but this isn't where I belong."

"We're leaving after luncheon." Phoebe handed Deirdre a handkerchief. "You need to start carrying these with you. And start calling me Phoebe when we are in private."

Deirdre wiped her eyes. "I need to stop acting like a-a"—what was the expression Chloe used?—"watering pot."

"It's natural," Phoebe assured her. "Are you hungry?"

"Starved."

Juliet exclaimed in exaggerated horror. "You should never admit such a thing."

"Remembering all the rules is too difficult."

Everything seemed more difficult. She was tired most of the time and hated feeling as though she had to run to the chamber pot every quarter hour; thus, once back at Bishop's Cove, she retreated to her bedchamber. She scarcely left for a week. The Ashford ladies left her alone most of the time. They seemed occupied with their needlework and callers. Phoebe, Deirdre learned, spent much of her time in an attic studio, painting, or out in the garden playing with the dogs.

Her gold hidden six inches beneath her feet, Deirdre stood on the balcony, enjoying the sea-scented breeze and weak but definite sunshine, and watched Phoebe tossing a leather ball for the entertainment of six dogs not much larger than rats and looking like white dust mops.

Chloe, who had taken to visiting Deirdre in the afternoons, joined her on the balcony. "They are all descendants of our Great-Aunt Bess's dogs. She used to name them for Greek characters. Oedipus, Lysander, things like that. Mama has started giving them silly names like Fluffy and Snowball."

"She looks so young playing with them." Deirdre leaned on the rail, wondering how long she would have the agility that had allowed her to hang upside down in the middle of the night and affix a bag of gold coins between the underside of the balcony and a beam that gave it support. "How old was she when she came here?"

"Twenty-three, I think." Chloe laughed as a puppy took a summersault over the ball. "It was an arranged marriage during the first war with the colonies. She and Papa knew one another for only three or four days before they got married, so none of our neighbors think it odd that Kieran married you so quickly in order to bring you here."

"Did Kieran come along right away? No, he couldn't have been. He's not old enough. And I'm probably not supposed to discuss my condition with a single lady like you."

"Pooh." Chloe made a face. "I am a country girl. I likely know more about it than you do after visiting the tenants in all stages. I was there for a birth once, but Mama does not know that. We are not supposed to know about that or we will never marry and bear children because it is so awful. Labor, that is."

"Is it?" A frisson of fear ran down Deirdre's spine and forward to her belly, where she swore she now felt a fullness, though that wasn't possible; her abdomen remained flat. "I suppose I've seen women who are *enceinte*, but I'm more used to the male side of talk about—oh, dear, I'm not supposed to discuss that topic either."

"Actually, Mama would probably make me stay home if she knew what I have learned about that. And with a brother like Kieran—" Chloe bit her lip.

"You don't need to hide it from me. He has been quite forthcoming regarding his misbegotten past."

"At least he's done that right." Chloe pounded one fist on the railing. "He had no cause to say we can't go to Dartmoor."

"He promised me I could if I married him." Deirdre gripped the iron railing, her knuckles whitening, her mind racing as she wondered how far she could trust Chloe. "How long will he be in London?"

"Perhaps as long as until Christmas. Papa wants to ensure I can have another Season, since last spring did not work out, as you know."

"Because of Kieran."

"Last Season, yes."

"Has he damaged your reputation?" Deirdre asked. "I mean, is that why you haven't married?"

"Last spring was not my first Season." Chloe twisted up her face as though smelling something unpleasant. "The gentlemen were simply boring. I had offers, but none were suitable. Last Season was just the same."

"I don't think I would like a London Season the way Juliet talks about it, though I did enjoy the theater the time I was able to go."

"The theater is grand, but I expect after the life you have led, you would hate London during the Season." Chloe's eyes sparkled like topaz in the sunshine. "Now tell me more about your life now that Papa is not around to stop you."

"Tut-tut, Chloe, you wouldn't disobey your father, would you? Not the great Lord Tyne."

"Ha! Papa is a pussycat where Juliet and I are concerned, and Mama, too. And there she goes in with the dogs. She will likely be up soon. We are not having guests today, so do come down. Or better yet, come out with me when I make my rounds. Do you ride?"

"A horse? No."

"Then I will have one of the grooms clean up the pony cart. We can talk with no one to overhear."

"I don't know what you wish me to tell you that is so secret."

Chloe grinned. "We will start with a visit to Dartmoor."

"You'll help me get there?" Deirdre entered her bedchamber, sank onto the chaise, and covered her face with her hands. "It's all right. Everything upsets me these days. I miss them. They're my family."

"But—"

Phoebe walked into the bedchamber.

"Good afternoon, Mama. Deirdre is having one of her fits." Chloe made the tears sound like something ordinary, something to mock. "She needs a distraction with Kieran gone. So I am taking her with me on my calls this afternoon."

Phoebe looked concerned. "There isn't any illness on the farms, is there?"

"No, Mama. I would never risk her or Kieran's heir."

"It might be a girl," Deirdre said.

"Then the fresh air will do her good." Phoebe smoothed her hand across Deirdre's brow. "You need other distractions, too. Do you sew, knit, paint?"

Deidre looked at her mother-in-law and smiled. "I paint tar on deck seams. I tie the best knots a sailor ever saw. And I can sew a patch on a sail. That is the extent of my talents, unless you count my ability to bargain."

"Hmm, well." Phoebe plucked at the sleeve of her pelisse. "We'll have to teach you something."

"Watercolors, Deirdre?" Behind her mother, Chloe stood gripping her sides as though holding in the mirth that danced in her eyes. "But no, you should be making lace for tiny garments."

"Lady Chloe Ashford," Phoebe scolded, "mockery is unkind."

"But amusing." Deirdre welcomed the image of herself hooking lace like a Breton matron. "I will settle for lots of fresh air. I love fresh air, you know."

"Then we will plan to be gone for simply hours." Chloe winked behind her mother's back and darted from the room.

"Part of the difficulty with Juliet is," Chloe said as they tooled along in the little pony cart she drove with ease, "she is bound to run off with the first romantic stranger who comes along and think things will work out because Mama and Papa love one another so much. But that man is likely to be after her dowry. I worry about that myself. You are so fortunate that was not a concern for you."

Deirdre turned her face toward a distant sparkle that was the sea, straining for the hint of a sail. "I didn't have to concern myself about it because Kieran stole it from me."

"Oh, of course. I am sorry. It is vulgar of me to ask, but were you rich?"

"Not compared to the Ashfords. But, yes, I think so. You know that's part of why Kieran went to London. He is taking my money out of Drummond's Bank there."

"The rascal."

"So he can pay for another opera dancer or whatever they're called?"

"No, Kieran never went in for light skirts that I heard of. He had enough highborn ladies chasing after him. Do you want me to stop so we can go walk out onto the cliffs?"

Deirdre barely waited for Chloe to pull up the little spotted pony along the side of the road before she climbed down and headed toward the sea with her usual stride. The folds of her purple muslin skirt hindered her so much she finally pulled it up above her half boots.

Chloe was laughing and breathless when she caught up with her. "You must not do that. It is too unladylike even for me."

Deirdre gripped her straw bonnet to keep it from flying away on the stiff breeze blowing off the Channel. "Until these past two weeks, I haven't had a dress on in years, not since we went to the theater in London. Well, except for my wedding. I can't walk in them and—oh, isn't she beautiful?"

"She" referred to a frigate in full sail heading toward Plymouth or even beyond the Isles of Scilly to the open sea. She rode at the head of a convoy of merchantmen with smaller naval vessels holding the flanks like collies beside a herd of sheep.

"And the formation. What seamanship." She blinked her eyes. "This war has got to end soon. We can't possibly fight that kind of might and preserve our nation as it is. Chloe, there are nearly as many ships guarding that convoy as we have in our entire navy."

Chloe touched her arm. "You do not agree with the war?"

"Of course not. I am a merchant's daughter. We didn't even know we were at war when we were captured. But that doesn't mean I want us to be British colonies again. Virginia has been the home of my ancestors for nearly a hundred years. We were nearly home. Another week." She faced Chloe. "I say home, but it wasn't really. We usually stayed at a boardinghouse in Alexandria when we were in harbor. My real home was out there." She gestured to the sea. "The men I sailed with were my family, the schooner was my true inheritance. Now I've lost all of it. And for what?"

Chloe drew her eyebrows together. "You do not believe marrying my brother was right?"

"It is—" Deirdre chose her words with care. "Convenient. He gives himself respectability, and I have a safe haven."

More like a luxurious prison.

Deirdre touched the black fur trimming the stand-up collar of her cloak, the opulence of the woolen garment itself. "This isn't even a percentage of what luxuries I have, while my crew is starving and cold up there on the moor."

Chloe slipped her arm through Deirdre's and began walking back to the cart. "We can get food and blankets and things to them. I know some ladies at the church have been collecting things for the French prisoners since the prison was built three years ago and taking them up to the moor. We can do it, too."

"But how, when Kieran has ensured no one will take me?"

"Kieran does not need to know." Chloe looked grim.

"And your parents?"

"Neither do they."

"How? If I am supposed to disguise the fact that I am an American, I can scarcely walk into the prison and announce I am Lady Ripon. Even if we made up names, we would be recognized."

"We shall work on that. For now, let us start the first step and get on with these calls. We can talk about this more later."

They got on with the calls. Deirdre appreciated the fresh air more than she did meeting a score or more of strangers, who stared at her, cast knowing glances at her middle despite its narrow proportions, and winked. They would be counting backward from the birth to the wedding. If it didn't add up to nine, Kieran would have added to his scandals. They all loved Chloe with her packets of tea for the women, sweets for the children, and tobacco for the men too old to be working.

"Some physicians disapprove of the stuff," Chloe told Deirdre on their way back to the house. "But why deprive them of a pipe on their stoop in their old age? They do not have much else to do. Tomorrow I will take you to meet Sally's mother. She is the local midwife and will tell you anything about childbearing you are too shy to ask Mama."

Between the fresh air and the exertion of talking with strangers, Deirdre slept long and deep after returning to Bishops Cove. She woke to firelight and the silence she doubted she could ever get used to—silence and aloneness and wondering if Kieran were spending his evenings, his nights alone.

She didn't need to be alone. A note propped up on a book beside the bed informed her that she could find the Ashford ladies in the gold salon and that she could have her supper any time she liked. She simply needed to ring for assistance dressing.

Assistance dressing indeed. Who invented clothing a woman couldn't don herself?

She wrapped herself in a dressing gown and traversed the corridor until she found a footman to send for Sally. Instead of the maid, Chloe slipped into the room, carrying a tray. "I was waiting up for you."

"You shouldn't have done that. I didn't realize it was so late."

"I was going to wait up anyway."

"Why?"

"Eat this lot, and I will tell you."

Obediently, Deidre sipped the tea and wolfed down bread and cheese. When she could eat no more, Chloe grabbed her hand and headed for the door.

"I'm not dressed," Deirdre protested.

"No one will see you. That is why I waited this late. Now, be quiet and follow me."

Deirdre obeyed, too bemused not to. With only a single candle lighting their way, they traversed two corridors, ascended another flight of steps, tiptoed down a narrow, nearly windowless hallway, and mounted yet one more flight of steps, these steep and narrow, and passed through a doorway. Once that was closed and locked, Chloe set down her candle and darted into the shadows.

"Do not move. I know my way around here, but you may trip over someth—*hechew*. Dratted lavender. It always makes me sneeze."

"Then what are we doing up here?" Deirdre sniffed the air. It smelled of lavender, turpentine, and years of dust. "What is this place?"

"One of the attics. Mama has her studio in the other. Here we are." Something scraped along the floor. "Come this way. I cleared a path. Bring the candle."

Deirdre picked up the silver holder and made her way past towers of trunks and a wardrobe with a padlocked door. She paused beside Chloe, who knelt on the dusty floor beside a trunk with its lid thrown back.

"Look." Chloe plunged her hands into the trunk and held up several garments. "Kieran's old clothes."

"I see that." Something about the jacket and trousers that must have belonged to an adolescent Kieran wrenched at Deirdre's heart. "What are they for?"

But of course she knew, and she began to smile.

Chloe looked up, her eyes glowing golden in the candle flame, her smile broad. "For us to wear when we visit Dartmoor."

Chapter 17

White's fell silent the instant Kieran and Tyne walked through the front door. Though London was lean of company at the end of the Little Season, White's enjoyed a comfortable number of visitors that evening. To a man, they stopped speaking, held glasses, cards, and newspapers poised as though performing a tableau titled *Astounded Man*. Eyes stared and mouths hung open.

The reaction was not as bad as Kieran feared when his father proposed that they pay the St. James Street club a visit the day after their arrival in London. They actually planned their entrance and strategy together for the first time in their lives. For the first time since Kieran could remember, they were not in opposition on a subject. Side by side, they were far from an insignificant force with which to contend.

Rutledge would have to contend with them. They had made certain that Lord Rutledge would be present before they made their entrance.

Scanning the faces of the assembled company, Kieran felt his gut tighten and his resolve to maintain an air of sangfroid slip.

Tyne looked as cool as ever as he bowed. "Good evening, gentlemen."

A handful of gentlemen nodded. A few others cleared their throats and appeared as though they might rise and return the bow.

One man stood, looked directly at Kieran, then turned his back on the Ashfords. "I thought this was an exclusive club, not a Cheapside gaming hell."

Kieran sucked in his breath. Every nerve in his body quivered with the desire to slap his gloves across the man's face. But he had already caused trouble by engaging in a duel with Freddie Rutledge.

"Steady," Tyne said from the corner of his mouth. To the assembly, no doubt waiting to see if Kieran or Tyne would rise to Rutledge's bait, he offered another bow. "It is so cold in here, I do wonder if the weather in Greece is warmer."

Kieran choked on a laugh. He did not think the atmosphere in the room was cold at all; his father's words had just warmed him straight through.

Others did not hold their laughter in. Above his stiff shirt collar, Rutledge's neck turned crimson, and his hands balled into fists against his thighs, one fist holding a pair of leather gauntlets.

Challenge the scorned younger son Rutledge might do, but not the respected and powerful father, a man twice his age. Kieran understood now why Tyne had warned him to keep his mouth shut at all cost to pride and leave the introductions to him.

Rutledge, however, was not without friends. Two young men from the back of the room strode forward to flank him. "Let us go, Ruttles," one of them suggested. "I do believe the servants have forgot out which door to remove the trash."

In a phalanx, they headed for their door. Kieran recognized the men as Rutledge's seconds and did not wish to let them go.

He stepped into their path, forcing them to halt. "Just the . . . er . . . gentlemen I wish to see."

They turned their faces away, but none could pass Kieran without bodily thrusting him out of the way.

"We have some unfinished business." Kieran smiled. "Like who shot whom."

"You shot before the signal," one of the seconds declared in a rather squeaky voice. "Your own seconds agree."

Kieran met and held his father's gaze over the other men's heads. If he could not get this to come out right, he lost something far more precious than his reputation—his father's trust and respect that he was just beginning to gain.

"Yes, my seconds." Kieran scanned the club, seeking someone who had been a witness to that night. "I do believe I had to rely on men I scarcely knew, Lord Rutledge here being in such haste to make an end of me—I beg your pardon, have an end to the affair—"

"Sir—" Rutledge raised the hand holding his gloves.

Kieran managed not to flinch and continued with an air of bored indifference. "The honorable meeting, if you prefer. Not that much honor was practiced there with all the seconds friends of yours."

"You were the dishonorable one." Rutledge's handsome but dissolute face reddened. "You fired early."

"And?" Kieran pressed.

"That is the kind of dishonorable action we expect out of an Ashford," Rutledge said.

"Careful, lad," someone spoke from the back of the room. "Don't wish to make Tyne angry."

Tyne looked as tense as a ship's figurehead on a vessel named *Avenger*.

Kieran propped one shoulder against the wall and shoved his hands into his coat pockets. "Tell me, gentlemen," he addressed the room at large, "is it dishonorable to decide that the whole affair is a farce and discharge one's weapon into the air and without ever turning around?"

Men straightened and looked at one another. Eyebrows rose.

Rutledge and his friends shuffled their feet.

"And," Kieran continued, "is it then honorable for the other man to fire at his opponent's back?"

Gasps and murmurs of protest rose like storm winds.

"You're lying." Rutledge's voice wavered between the same drawl Kieran affected and a strained squeal. "You will take it back."

The gloves waved in the air, and Kieran more than half expected them to slap against his cheek. From the expressions of others, they expected it, too. When Rutledge seemed to think better of the blow that would signal a rematch on the field of honor, Kieran raised his own hands, tugged the ribbon from his hair, and pulled the waves back to expose his damaged ear. He turned his back to the other men so they could see that, if the ball had struck him from the front, it would have gone through his skull, too.

"Fortunately," he said to the silenced room, "I have rather large ears." Returning his attention to Rutledge and his friends, he offered them a warm smile. "So may we have the entire truth now, Lord Rutledge?"

Rutledge's mouth opened and closed like that of a landed fish. Then he pulled himself to his full height, a head lesser than Kieran's. "It don't change the fact that you ruined my sister."

"But he has ruined you, too," someone spoke from the room.

Again, voices rose like a storm. Illegal or not, rules of dueling needed to be followed. Kieran had broken them, which was a bit questionable, yet was nothing in light of the other man shooting at his opponent's back.

"If this is true," one of the seconds asked with a sneer, "why did you not come forward sooner 'stead of fleeing the country like the coward you are?"

"I was unwell," Kieran said. "I had a fever from the wound."

The lies had reached his father by the time he recovered, and he had been ordered to board the *Phoebe* at Southampton and not to come home. Hurt and angry, he bought his letters of marque and sailed for the Caribbean. But now he had the chance to set things right, his father's apology for believing the worst.

He smiled. "I can provide you with the name of the apothecary who attended me if you like."

"You will pay for this." Rutledge spat on Kieran's boots, then stalked from the club, his friends in tow.

Kieran bent his head to replace the ribbon in his hair and looked down to clean the toe of his Hessian on the carpet. When he looked up, his father stood right before him, a glass of brandy in his hand and on his face an expression Kieran never expected to see directed at him—pride.

"You did well," Tyne said. "I knew his father well. He was a fine man. How his heir turned out so badly I cannot work out."

"Happens to the best men," Kieran said with a self-deprecating laugh. "Or have you forgot that Rutledge is right about his sister? I can prove nothing about Joanna."

How he wished that his father would say that of course Kieran was telling the truth about Joanna.

"Rutledge's behavior certainly casts doubt on his sister's honor," Tyne said.

Better than nothing. Not what Kieran wanted. Yet what else did he deserve? He had not lived a virtuous life until his betrothal to Joanna.

Yet Tyne was right that no one wondered about whether or not Joanna Rutledge was as virtuous as her brother claimed until Kieran Ashford, Lord Ripon, came along. If not friendly, the men at White's that evening were at least polite to Kieran, congratulating him on his marriage with only slightly raised brows. He knew those brows would climb higher once word got out that he was to be a father by the end of June or middle of July. For now, however, he enjoyed the camaraderie of his peers and the fact that Tyne did not altogether think him an embarrassment of a son.

The next day, however, he went out on his own, first to a solicitor with Daniel MacKenzie's will, then to Drummond's Bank. There he discovered that MacKenzie had deposited ten thousand pounds. Not a princely sum. A third of what the Ashford estates and other holdings brought in annually, but nothing to turn one's nose up at either. If Deirdre had gotten hold of it, she would have been able to bribe any number of prison officials and fishermen to get her crew out of England. As matters stood now, she could not possibly have enough gold in her possession to make much trouble.

The letter Deirdre received from Kieran did not in the least induce guilt over the plans she was making with Chloe. Maybe if it had been warm and loving or even personal, she would have experienced a twinge of guilt for being disloyal to him in setting up arrangements for getting to Dartmoor for a visit to her crew. The note was worse than something she would have felt free to read to his mother and sisters. It was too impersonal to read to them.

> *My Dear Lady,*
> *Our journey has been uneventful, even pleasant. If all continues to go well, we will be home for Christmas and probably before. I have sent instructions for you to receive extra pin money for Twelfth Night and Boxing Day gifts.*
> *K*
> *PS: Pet the dogs for me. I forgot to tell Mama to do so.*

Deirdre burned it so his family would not find it and see how little he cared about his troublesome wife, then she descended to the sitting room where Phoebe kept the dogs in an effort to prevent their long, silky fur from invading the entire household. Deirdre had been making friends with the canines over the past three weeks. In the event she needed to slip past them in the night, she wanted them to recognize her as family and not bark.

They did not bark at her knock on the door.

Phoebe called for her to enter, and she stepped inside. Two of the dogs ran over to paw at her skirt and gaze up at her with beady black eyes and puppy grins. The rest of the pack swarmed around Phoebe, who perched on a low stool, the dogs' brushes beside her in a basket, and a letter on her lap. One dog, the oldest female, also sat on her lap licking away the tears running down Phoebe's face.

Deirdre closed the door and stood gripping the handle. "Bad news?"

Had Kieran kept something from her?

"No, no, good news." Phoebe turned a radiant face toward Deirdre. "Garrett and Kieran are actually getting along. Listen to this. *Either five months at sea has greatly changed our son, or we have been doing him an injustice. Either way, he has an intelligence of which we can be proud and a streak of kindness he certainly inherited from you, my . . . '* Well, um—" She blushed. "Did you have a nice letter?"

Deirdre stooped to run her hand along Snowball's back. "He told me to pet the dogs for him because he forgot to mention that to you. So here I am."

"I'm certain he misses you greatly." Phoebe picked up a second letter from her lap. One corner looked a little chewed. "He says he's looking forward to Christmas pudding making. And . . . Oh, how nice. He and Garrett were invited to the Cantrells'. I'm pleased to see that Liza is going out into entertainments again. She was one of Chloe's friends in town, and the poor girl lost her fiancé in Spain three months ago. Not that her parents thought a mere captain good enough for their daughter. I expect her parents will push for her to ally herself to a title this time."

Phoebe and Tyne had probably intended her for Kieran.

Deirdre petted two more dogs. "I'll leave you to your letters."

She fled to a gallery in an older part of the house where family portraits were supposed to hang. Instead, with the Ashford family seat in

Northumberland, the gallery in the house Tyne had purchased with prize money he made while a naval officer displayed Phoebe's paintings. Deirdre had already been there and admired them, the color, the detail, the way she captured facial expressions in her portraits of humans and dogs alike.

Deirdre stopped in front of one of Kieran as a youth of perhaps sixteen. His hair was fashionably short then, his body a little gangly, but his eyes already bore that sleepy look that made a female with weaknesses like hers think of soft pillows and smooth sheets.

"Are you making Liza Cantrell think along those lines?" Deirdre asked the painted Kieran. "Will you still want your mistake of a wife when you return?"

Mrs. Barnes, Sally's mother, had assured Deirdre that she would still have her figure at Christmas, though Deirdre hadn't asked for the information. "Truly you will have more of one, my lady." Laughing, she had gestured to her own abundant bosom.

Kieran might find her new shape unattractive. Her American accent would surely be repugnant and crude after the cultured tones of an English lady, especially after what she had said to him that last night, applying all the sailor cant she could muster to tell him what he could do outside of her presence. English ladies never said such things. They probably never knew such things. She was beyond the pale for the wife of a viscount, heir to an earldom.

But she had been in such pain, her tongue was her only defense.

The impersonal letter dampened more than the merest twinge of guilt the following morning when she and Chloe set out early allegedly for a day of visiting some families at the farthest corner of the estate. Instead, they stopped at an abandoned cottage along the way and donned the male attire Chloe had smuggled there on previous excursions. Kieran's old clothes fit both of them tolerably well, though they needed to pin the waists on the trousers to keep them up, and wear more than one pair of socks to make the boots fit. A heavy mist made wearing broad-brimmed hats practical and acceptable for hiding their hair. Since they would never be inside a building, they would not need to take off their hats. One difficulty Deirdre encountered was wrapping her chest. She had done it for years without a twinge, but now the binding made her gasp.

"I can't do it, Chloe, I won't flatten." Her heart raced while her spirits plummeted. "At the most, I'm not quite three months along, and already—this."

Chloe patted her shoulder. "Put on the greatcoat with the capes."

"It's too big for me. I'll look like a scarecrow."

"You are selling sweets and tobacco to prisoners at Dartmoor. No one expects you to be fashionable."

"I suppose not." She huddled into the greatcoat, and she and Chloe headed for the pony cart and the fifteen-mile drive to Dartmoor.

Upon seeing the barren land stretching out around the gray stone fortress, Deirdre doubted that she could ever get her men out. The walls were too high, the hiding places too few, the gorge leading from the coast to the high moorland too narrow. Yet the gates stood open, and others, as did Chloe and she, passed in and out with baskets and boxes of wares. Red-coated Somerset militiamen guarded the entrance, muskets and bayonets ready, and inspected the visitors. Still, with some coin, guards could be bribed.

Chloe had used a little of Deirdre's gold to learn the days of the market and get a message to "anyone from the *Maid of Alexandria*" that they would have callers on the tenth of December. The smell of unwashed humans, wet wool, and other filth met Deirdre's nostrils. Ships never smelled good, but the sea breezes kept the worst of the odors away once one was on deck. This was only the prison yard, the market area, open to the sky. The barracks in which the men lived would be far, far worse.

Kieran did this to them.

The reminder felt hollow. She had done this to them. Yet she could not have watched Kieran die in the filthy waters of St. George's Harbor.

"Take this basket." Chloe thrust a wicker container of wrapped sweets into Deirdre's hands. "We must be quick."

Deirdre followed her sister-in-law through the prison gates and into the thick of the milling throng. The men were pasty-faced and ragged. Their hair hung long and lank, often in greasy clumps, as though they either had given up or had no way to bathe. Up close, their stench brought on a nausea she hadn't before experienced. She swallowed.

"Not here." Chloe's voice was a mere hiss.

Deirdre swayed.

A hand far larger than Chloe's encircled her arm. "What's wrong, MacKenzie? Does the sight and smell of us make you sick?"

"Ross." Deirdre gripped her basket with both hands to keep herself from throwing her arms around his neck. "Are you all right?"

He looked anything but. He seemed to have made an effort to comb his hair and wash his face, but he was bearded and sported a black eye. Grime encrusted the edges of his coat sleeves, and one sleeve was nearly torn off.

"You've been fighting," she said.

He shrugged. "Wat objected to me calling you a whore."

"He should have knocked your teeth down your throat," Chloe said with pure Ashford haughtiness.

"You didn't hurt him, did you?" Deirdre stamped down the pain of learning that Ross still despised her.

"No, of course not. Who's with you?"

"You don't need to know, but you can trust her."

"When she talks like that? I don't think so." Ross snatched two packets from Deirdre's basket and held out some coppers. "So this looks like a legitimate transaction. Or do you want to rob us of what coin we have left, as well as our freedom?"

"Don't be a beast." Deirdre dug beneath her packets and lifted the false bottom of the basket. "I've brought you more." She thrust two specially made up packets into Ross's coat pocket. "More coin and some messages for everyone."

"We appreciate the money." Ross started to turn away. "But don't think this will salve your conscience. Nothing but our complete freedom will make up for us being here while you sleep with the enemy in a clean bed."

"Then you've got to trust my companion," Deirdre said. "She may have to come with information if I can't."

Ross shot Chloe a withering glance. "She's dead if she betrays us." As silently and swiftly as he had appeared, he vanished into the throng.

"Well," Chloe said with a shaky laugh, "we had best be on our way home."

They skirted the worst of the refuse in the prison yard and nodded to the vacant-faced guards at the gate.

"Not too much in the way of sales, eh," one of them called.

Deidre and Chloe shrugged. "Too many people and too little coin."

They reached the pony cart before Deirdre lost her composure. While she wiped at the stream of tears that would not stop flowing down her face with the mist, Chloe drove the shaggy moorland pony in silence until halfway down the rock-strewn gorge.

"How old is Ross?" she asked in a quiet voice.

"My age. Twenty-three."

"I suppose his anger is justified."

"He came sailing with us," Deirdre said, "because he got caught helping slaves escape from South Carolina. His family helped him evade prison. Now he's there after all."

"He could not have been very old when he did that."

"Seventeen."

"Oh." After that, Chloe again fell silent until they reached the track that would lead them to the abandoned cottage and their female clothes. "How long has he been in love with you?"

Deirdre laughed. "You sound like your brother. But, truly, he is nothing more to me than something akin to a brother."

"Why? I mean, what is wrong with him?" Chloe smiled. "I mean, other than being rude and foul-mouthed and hot-tempered?"

"Nothing. He's usually a gentleman. The Trenerrys are a wealthy family, and he was well educated. Was supposed to go up to William and Mary College in Virginia, but he liked the sea."

"Did you say Trenerry?" Chloe sounded too casual as she turned the cart into the yard of the cottage. "Is he related to the Cornish Trenerrys?"

"Probably. I think his grandmother is English."

"We should find out. They might be able to help us."

"I don't think you should be helping me, let alone enlisting the help of another English family."

Chloe leaped from the cart and tethered the pony before assisting Deirdre to alight, much to her protest. "The Cornish Trenerrys are reputed to be smugglers. Legend has it that they have waterways that go right under their house. We have only caves and a cove not big enough for anything but a few fishing boats." She winked. "But fishing boats can get away with carrying all sorts of cargoes."

"Chloe—"

"Hush. After seeing that prison, do you think I can, for a minute, leave those men you call your family there?"

Deirdre waited until they were inside the cottage, shivering as they changed their clothes, before she asked, "What about the danger to your family?"

"Danger to us?" Chloe laughed as she tugged her gown over her head. "No danger if the authorities know nothing of who helps these men."

"But if anyone does—"

"Turn around and let me hook up your gown. We need to get home before Mama misses us much."

Deirdre acquiesced.

On the way home, they spoke only of what they should have seen that day. Phoebe was in her studio when they arrived at Bishops Cove, and Juliet curled up before the library fire reading, Miss Pruitt knitting on a nearby chair.

Juliet gave them a vague smile and distant look and returned to her volume.

"More romantic drivel?" Chloe prodded.

Juliet glanced up, frowning. "It is not drivel. It is showing me just what kind of man I will want for a husband."

Chloe snorted. "Let me guess—handsome and dashing and probably a lawbreaker who wants nothing but your dowry."

"Hmph." Juliet slammed the book closed.

Deirdre read the title, *Domestic Affections*.

She considered retreating to her chamber, but Phoebe came in then, and they spent the evening playing whist and reading aloud from a book of Sir Walter Scott's poetry.

That night and the subsequent days of Kieran's absence passed more quickly than Deirdre thought possible in the company of three females. Rather than bored day by day, she joined in the bustle of life on a large estate, and liked it most of the time. But some nights, such as after excursions to the farms with Chloe or working with Phoebe learning the art of the stillroom, Deirdre dragged herself up the stairs and down the corridors to her chamber. Most nights, she was glad she was too weary to think about the reality of the prison and how much Ross disliked her now.

As usual, Deirdre entered her bedchamber to find Sally sewing by the fire, waiting for Deirdre's arrival so she could help her out of her gown and into a nightgown. On nights like this, when she was cross-eyed with fatigue, Deirdre appreciated the pampering, even allowing Sally to brush out her hair.

This night was no exception. Sally sat by the fire with some mending in her lap. She sprang up at Deirdre's entrance. "Milady, did you hear?"

"Hear what?" Deirdre's fingers convulsed around the door handle, mind racing around thoughts of something having happened to Kieran or Tyne the servants learned of first. "My husband?"

"No, no." Sally clasped her hands in front of her as though she were trying to rein in her excitement. "Some Frenchmen escaped from the prison."

"What? How?" Deirdre sank onto the nearest chair.

"No one knows for certain how, but those Somerset militia are so stupid anybody could fool them."

"Are they now?" Deirdre worked not to smile. "I suppose that is unfortunate."

"Yes, milady. Cook's afraid we'll be murdered in our beds."

Remembering her role as lady of the manor, Deirdre rose to pat the girl's shoulder. "Don't fret yourself over that, Sally. They'll be too busy getting back to France to worry about us. Besides, we have locked gates and high walls around us to keep strangers out."

"Yes, milady. But I wish we had guards."

Deirdre didn't. Guards kept people in as much as out.

She allowed Sally to unfasten her gown, but sent the girl off without brushing her mistress's hair. Deirdre needed the repetitive motion to calm herself for sleep.

If Frenchmen could escape, so could Americans.

Usually Deirdre fell asleep the instant she climbed into the big bed. Tonight, however, her head whirled with possibilities and excitement too much for rest. And the house seemed to join in her restlessness. Something disturbed the stillness more than the usual cracks and pops of a house or dripping of moisture off the eaves. She heard a clang of metal on metal, then a click. A blast of cold, damp air sent her shooting upright in bed, reaching for her stiletto.

"Who's there?"

The click sounded again. The cold air flow ceased, and the silhouette of a man moved between her and the fire. "Did I wake you—my lady, is it now?" asked the mocking voice of Blaze Eider, second mate of the *Maid of Alexandria*.

Chapter 18

$\mathcal{K}$ ieran wanted to go home. While enjoying the company of the ladies who flocked around him, so long as they kept their distance with tapping fans and pouty lips, he longed for home and Deirdre.

She had finally written to him. Bold and full of loops, her handwriting looked just as he imagined it would. Her letter smelled of ginger, which put him in mind of warm, tropical nights, and made him want to bolt for the nearest post chaise and depart, despite his father's request that he remain in London.

Not that she said anything that encouraged him to believe all was well between them. She wrote of riding out with Chloe, which made him happy to learn they were becoming friends. She wrote of feeling well and how Juliet had actually ripped a seam on her gown she laughed so hard over Deirdre's first attempt to knit something. She wrote of making friends with the dogs and of rebelling against Phoebe's insistence that she help with the church fete.

I'm weary of having people look at my middle instead of my face as soon as I'm introduced as your wife.

He squirmed like a schoolboy caught in a misdemeanor over the fact that he wasn't with her to ease the humiliation of that kind of scrutiny. Fortunately, as far as he knew, nothing should show yet. That would ease her way a bit. People could be so mean about these things, and if anyone learned of her life aboard a ship with only men for company, someone was bound to raise questions regarding the child's parentage.

He did not doubt for a moment that the child was his. Deirdre might have had more knowledge of intimacy than most females on their wedding nights, but her body was innocent.

Sometimes, Kieran doubted those words of his father's he had overheard in the study and wondered if Tyne wanted to keep Deirdre's background a secret for her sake rather than the family's. But Tyne was spending most of his days at the Admiralty, and that concerned Kieran.

It also left him with far too much time on his hands—as usual. No one expected a viscount with money to do anything useful other than perhaps dabble in the funds now and again. He was supposed to pursue pleasure and had for all his adult life. But gaming had bored him, excessive drinking of blue ruin in the slums had given him a headache, and females got him into trouble because he liked them the best.

The fact that he was married now did not seem to stop them from pursuing him. "It is only a *mariage de convenable*," Liza Cantrell had the audacity to claim when he refused to dance with her at a party that had ended up far too small for his comfort. "Was it not simply to get some colonial to England with honor and safety?"

"Actually, no," Kieran said. "My wife is—"

But he could not tell a single young lady Chloe's age that his wife was already with child, or even that their marriage was far from one in name only. It just was not done.

When someone, apparently weary of the same people and the same gossip, decided to have a little fun with the guests at a dinner party for a mere twenty, Kieran knew he had to go home regardless of what his father wanted him to do. Let these people cavort beneath a sprig of mistletoe stuck in the lintel of the drawing room doorway. Before Deirdre, he would have done the same. Now she was the only female he wished to kiss.

He had to pass beneath it to reach the front door and would have made it except that a young man waylaid him with some tale of them being up to Oxford together. The man looked familiar, but Kieran knew neither his name nor anything about him.

"We suffered through writing the same papers for the same don," the gentleman proclaimed. "But I can see you do not remember me. Too many ladies addling your wits. Ha, ha, ha!" He burst into gales of mirth as Liza Cantrell sidled up and kissed Kieran full on the lips. "Your face, Ripon. Oh, your face!"

Kieran had no idea what his face looked like—disgusted, he hoped—but he could see his father's from across the room—thunderous.

Liza laid her hand on Kieran's arm. "You are not moving away, my lord. Do you wish me to kiss you again?"

"What I wish," Kieran said, brushing her hand away, "is for you to remember that I am married, and for your father to lock you up until he finds you a husband of your own."

That is what his father would do to Chloe or Juliet if they acted in such a forward manner.

Seething like a keg of gunpowder with the fuse growing near, he slammed out of the house without waiting for a footman.

Nor did he wait for the carriage. He walked from Upper Brook Street to Grosvenor Square despite a driving rain. Once at the Ashford townhouse, he ordered a servant to pack his bags.

"You're never leaving tonight, sir," the man protested.

"Daylight." No, that came too late this time of year. "Six of the clock."

Still dripping from the rain, he stood before the library fire and steamed himself dry. Tyne would be home any moment. Kieran wanted to make certain he was still wearing his evening attire to face his father and discover how much of their newly built ground Liza's actions had cut away.

He did not have long to wait. Carriage wheels sounded in the square. A door banged, then footfalls sounded on the steps, brisk. Determined.

"I did not plan it," he greeted Tyne.

Tyne shed his greatcoat and laid it over a chair back. "I know."

"You do?" Kieran felt deflated with the wind yanked from his sails. "But you looked like you wanted to thrash me right there."

Tyne offered him a tight smile. "Not you, that friend of Rutledge's."

"Rutledge?" Kieran thrust his shoulders back, his chin out. "Are you saying that Rutledge set that up?"

"Precisely."

"And Deirdre is just going to happen to find out." Kieran ground his teeth. "Why?"

"Petty revenge." Garrett moved to the drinks table and filled two glasses. "I suspected he would get up to something, so I have had him followed. I knew this little trick would occur, but I did not know when. And, to be frank, I did not suspect Liza Cantrell to be in on it. She seemed like such a nice young lady when she went about with Chloe."

"But she gains nothing by putting a rift between Deirdre and me."

"Except for Rutledge." Tyne strode to Kieran's side and pressed a glass into his hand. His face was full of concern. "And why are you so certain word of this will place a rift between you and Deirdre?"

Kieran drank before answering. When he did, he looked into the fire. "From the beginning, I have done nothing to endear myself to her. I perpetrated the death of her father. I took her ship and imprisoned her crew, her true family. I would not settle for a marriage in name only." He shoved his fingers into his hair. "And I told her our marriage is a mistake."

Tyne remained silent for several moments, so long Kieran knew that if he looked at his father he would see disapproval. He had done one more thing wrong.

He set his glass on the mantel, prepared to leave the library.

Tyne laid a hand on his arm. "Why did you tell her that?"

"She needed to know." Kieran retreated a step from his father's side, but turned to face him. "I overheard you telling Mama that if there was trouble about the marriage, we could all end up in prison. Deirdre needed to know that so she would think before she did anything foolish like trying to make contact with her countrymen or free her crew from Dartmoor."

Tyne looked thoughtful. "Would she do that?"

"The first opportunity that arises." Kieran shoved his hands into his coat pockets, felt Deirdre's letter now crumpled and damp. "Two of her crew escaped because of her. The rest would have if she had managed to get away, too. But those men went to prison rather than abandon her to me on the ship. She will want to repay that kind of loyalty."

"That takes money and a contact."

"I am afraid that she has the money. I found her bank certificates and some specie on the ship, but that might not be all of it. As for contacts"—he shrugged—"she can find those with enough gold. I do not want to see her suffer for her own loyalties. Nor can I abide the notion that I could be the cause of the rest of you suffering because I brought an enemy into our midst. If . . . if I did not misunderstand you."

"You did not." Tyne paced to the door, opened it, looked into the corridor, then closed and locked the portal. "Sit down, Kieran. It is long past time you learned the truth behind my marriage to your mother."

Blood drained from Deirdre's head. The room spun, and she put her head between her knees. A dream. She was having a dream. No, a nightmare.

She moaned. "You're not really here."

Blaze laid his hand on her hair. "I am."

"Why? How? What do you think you're doing? Oh, you fool, you were free."

"We are free. Zeb is in France helping a captain from Maine outfit his privateer. I slipped over here with a smuggler helping some frogs escape."

"Why? No, wait." Aware that she wore only her nightgown, Deirdre reached for her velvet dressing gown and pulled it on. She made certain that both doors into her bedchamber were locked, then settled on the hearthrug and began shoveling coal onto the fire. "How did you know how to find me?"

Blaze settled beside her, nibbling one of the savory biscuits left on Deirdre's bedside table each night. "Everyone knows that the Ashford heir married an American. Seems your husband's father is a powerful man in Devonshire."

"And Hampshire and Northumberland." Deirdre shoved her hands up the sleeves of her dressing gown to warm her fingers. "I didn't just marry a title; I married a man whose father made so much prize money in the Royal Navy he bought two estates."

"Then why did he need to steal from us?" Blaze's dark eyes glittered.

Deirdre sighed. "He and his father had a falling out. He thought he was going to be disinherited. But I think he wanted to prove he could accomplish something on his own, or gain his own money not dependent on his father."

"Of course he wants his own money." Blaze gave out a bark of mirth. "Has he worked out the money might not be worth getting leg-shackled to you?"

Deirdre grabbed his streak of white hair and yanked as she had been doing since she was six and he signed on board her father's merchantman. "We don't need to talk about me. Just tell me why you're here."

Chuckling, Blaze broke her hold with a thumb to her wrist. "I see the lady is in name only."

"Yes, now talk. What are you doing here?"

Blaze sobered. "It's not my first time I've been here. I needed to find you in this pile and make sure that that . . . person you married doesn't share your bed like he did on Bermuda."

Deirdre's cheeks heated. "I made a bargain to save your hide. But he's in London right now."

"Good." Blaze gave her an intense look. "You're all right?"

"Yes."

"You look different."

Deirdre snorted. "I'm wearing something female. Now tell me why you're here. You never liked me well enough to take this kind of a risk for my sake. You do know that they'll hang you for what you did to Kieran."

Blaze shrugged. "They'll hang me for escaping, for being here . . . Can only hang a man once. And I had to find out about the crew. We need to get them out. America needs men to man the privateers. That's the only hope we have of winning this war."

""I don't know how we can ever win this war." Deirdre clasped her forearms. "England is too wealthy. Its army, its navy, they're all better than we are. I've heard our army is a disaster in land battles."

"Have they turned your coat?" Orange flames glittered in Blaze's eyes.

A shiver ran through her despite the fire. "Not at all. I don't want to see the United States become British colonies again any more than you do. But England's might frightens me. I've seen their navy at work."

"But you haven't seen our privateers at work. What navy we do have has acquitted itself well. Our ships are so much faster. And now we have you inside, so to speak. You can work for us."

"I'm trying." She drew her knees to her chest and wrapped her arms around them, wondering how much longer she would be able to sit like that. "I saw Ross at the prison the other day."

"So you can get in?" Excitement rang in Blaze's voice despite its low tone. "Do they know how to get out?"

"We don't know yet. Men manage it, as you know. We're working out a system for exchanging information. And I know where to hide them if we can get them to escape. But we'll have to get them out of the country after that."

"That's why I'm here." Blaze stretched out, leaning back on his elbows. "If you can get them out of Dartmoor, I can get them out of England."

"How will I let you know our plans?"

"On the other side of the woods out here"—he gestured beyond the balcony—"there's an oak whose branches extend over the wall. It's high, but not for someone who can climb like you. I loosened one of the stones in the wall beneath it. Leave messages behind that stone. I'll find them or leave my own there."

"It's a great risk."

"You're not game?" His dark eyes challenged her.

She took a deep breath. "Of course I am. But I'll need time."

"Not too much. We need them." Blaze stood. "When do you go back?"

"December twenty-second. The other ladies of the house are attending a village fete. I'll feign illness and cry off."

"You, ill?" Blaze snorted. "They're fools if they believe you."

They would believe her, the one blessing of her condition.

She shrugged. "They don't know me that well. They'll leave me alone to rest, and I'll slip back to the prison. I'll leave you a message that night."

"Until the twenty-second," Blaze said, then was gone back through the balcony doors and into the night.

The locked door warned Kieran that he did not want to hear what his father was about to tell him. He had known that his parents' marriage was arranged. Most marriages were alliances for wealth and social standing. That Mama was a colonial seemed a bit odd, yet her father had been well off, and Tyne was simply the Honorable Garrett Ashford then, never expecting to inherit title, lands, and wealth. Younger sons had made far worse contracts with English ladies. Yet Kieran also knew that his parents shared a devotion few married couples enjoyed, a devotion he could only dream to have in his life.

"Sit down," Tyne repeated.

Kieran sat, cradling his glass between his hands.

Tyne did the same. "You know I was stationed in Savannah, Georgia, after we took that city, do you not?"

Kieran nodded. "You met Mama there."

"Yes, but how I met her . . ." Tyne stretched out his legs and gazed at a point beyond Kieran's shoulder—a point over thirty years in the past. "My ship caught on fire one night. I was supposed to be on watch. But I was sleeping."

Kieran stared at him. "And they didn't hang you?"

"Erwine, my captain, threatened to at the least have me court-martialed. I doubt they would have hanged me. I was an earl's son, and those are so few and far between in the navy, they are a bit cautious with our hides. Still, I could have been imprisoned on the ship until we got back here to England. And my father . . ." He smiled. "Suffice it to say that compared to him, I look like the most indulgent of fathers. I would rather have hanged than face him with a court-martial blot on my copybook, and Erwine knew it. I was wholly under his thumb, and I knew I would pay for him overlooking my dereliction of duty."

Kieran sipped his brandy to fill the ensuing silence, then prompted, "And you did, pay for it, I mean?"

"Not for weeks. Then one night we got called out to search for a young woman who had helped a rebel escape capture. We suspected that this was an American who was causing havoc with the ships and troop supplies in the city, including the man who set my ship on fire. We hoped she would lead us to him if we caught her. But she was alone when we found her." Tyne's face softened, and he smiled.

Kieran stared, his glass at his lips. "Mama?"

"Yes, your mama, Phoebe Channing." Tyne straightened in his chair, looked at Kieran now. "We all thought her father was a loyal Englishman, so no one wanted to put a lady like that in the guardhouse with the prostitutes. But her parents wanted her out of Savannah before she did anything else foolish."

"Why did she do it?" Kieran asked. "Help the rebel escape?"

"He was her fiancé."

Kieran choked. "Mama was betrothed to a rebel?"

"He was a privateer captain."

"Oh, my—" Closing his eyes, Kieran leaned his head against the chair's winged back. "I must have hurt her deeply going off like I did."

"If you had come home much sooner, I probably would have barred you from Bishops Cove."

"I bought the letter of marque, sir, because you had barred me from Bishops Cove."

"Yes, well, you did pound a few nails in your coffin last spring, you must admit."

Kieran bowed his head. "Will I ever be forgiven for that?"

"You already have been." Tyne's voice was gentle, a balm to Kieran's spirit.

They sat in silence for several moments, both watching the crackling flames licking around a pile of coal.

Then Tyne sighed. "This is not getting the rest of this out. And in light of some things . . . About Phoebe and me . . ." His tone grew brisk. "The best way for her to get out of Savannah was on a naval vessel sailing. We were sailing. So Erwine, who owed Phoebe's father rather a lot of money for gaming debts, blackmailed me into marrying her."

Kieran choked on his brandy. "Blackmailed you? If he was sailing back to England, why would he care about debts to a colonial?"

"I will get to that." Tyne sipped his own brandy. "I tried to get out of it. But once I was officially introduced to her, I realized how badly

Phoebe was being treated by her father, and I wanted to help her. I was more than half in love with her before we reached Portsmouth. But she hated fighting men. She hated war. Still does. She wanted nothing more than a nice home and a loving family. I could have given her that. I had a nice home, and Aunt Bess was one of the kindest people I've ever known. But Phoebe did not want a family with me, a killer of men, I believe she called me. I preferred to think of myself as a defender of the kingdom."

"Was that why you resigned your commission?"

That was what they had all believed. Even as he asked the question, Kieran knew it was not the whole truth.

Tyne pinched his nostrils together. "I should have, but I was ambitious and had to prove something to my father, who tried to keep me from promotion in the navy. So I accepted a commission as commander of my own little sloop. My assignment was to find the identity of the spy who was passing information to American privateers regarding our merchant and supply transport convoys in the Channel."

Kieran's heart skipped a beat, then began to gallop. He leaned forward, wanting to hear the rest, guessing the rest, afraid of the rest.

Tyne inclined his head. "I can see that you have worked that out. It took me a few months, but the clues were there. The spy was your mother."

Despite seeing it coming, Kieran felt poleaxed.

"Why?"

Tyne rose, set his glass aside, and stood with his elbow propped against the mantel. "She wanted to end the war with the fewest people harmed. That meant having America win. But she made a mistake."

"Only one?" Kieran tried to lighten the tension in the room.

Tyne did not smile. "She made a few, but her biggest one was to recognize that her spymaster did not care about who won the war so long as he got rich off the conflict. And she fell in love with me."

"How was that a mistake, sir?" Kieran asked, surprised.

Tyne smiled then. "Thank you for that. I will accept it as a compliment." He sipped from his glass. "She was supposed to run away with her spymaster, her fiancé before she married me, when she completed her mission. But she refused to continue her work, so he threatened to kill me if she did not give him more information."

Kieran caught his breath. "He tried, did he not?" He had seen the scar on his father's shoulder.

Tyne nodded. "He tried. Phoebe went along with him, but I was on to her by then and knew I either had to turn her in or find another way out of the fix."

"Since Mama is alive and still wed to you, I presume you found another alternative."

"Oh yes." Tyne's lips tightened. "I made a bargain with my father. He would get Phoebe a pardon from the king if I would resign my commission."

"You loved the navy," was all Kieran could think to say.

"I did. I still do." The tension around his eyes and mouth relaxed into his full, warm smile. "But I love your mother more and would never go back and change a thing."

"I believe you."

But what did this have to do with him and Deirdre?

"Why are you telling me this now, sir?"

"Because you have a wife who could easily betray England, too." He returned to his chair. "For the weeks we have been in London, I have been trying to find ways I can get her crew paroled so she is not tempted to help them escape again. I have been unsuccessful. My father was friends with the king, as much as any man can be, and I inherited some of that power. But the king is hopelessly mad, and Prinny is no friend of the Ashfords. With this new war with America and your mother's history, as closely guarded a secret as it is, and now you bringing home an American wife . . . Our loyalty to the Crown is being questioned.

The *Phoebe*'s crew talked. They know about how Deirdre tried to help her crew escape. Dartmoor is a bit more difficult to manage, and escapes do occur more often than the military would like us to know."

Kieran's chest tightened. "So I was right. My marriage was a mistake."

"Yes."

He did not realize that he hoped for a different answer until his father spoke that single affirmation.

"Just another blot on my copybook."

He rose and began to prowl the room, picking up a copy of *Waverly* he had tried to read, setting it down again. Checking the locks on the windows, rearranging the drape of the curtains. Tyne watched him, he knew, though he did not look around. When he reached the door, he considered bolting. Yet he knew he had to stay, finish talking this out. Somehow, he would make up for being such a disappointment of a son to this man, who deserved even more admiration than Kieran previously believed.

He leaned his back against the door. "How can I untangle things? How can I make up for risking all of you, my family." His voice broke like a youth's, and he felt foolish.

Tyne's gaze was so understanding that Kieran's throat closed. "That she is breeding helps, regardless of what you think. Her own body will keep her close to home in a few months. Meanwhile, if you truly do not trust her to be loyal to us, we have no choice but to keep her virtually a prisoner."

"She will hate me for it," Kieran said, and sadness descended upon him like a sea fog. "But it is for her sake, too. I plan to leave in the morning. Will you join me?"

"Yes. My work here is done." Tyne rose. "If the roads are not too bad, we should be home on the twenty-second."

Chapter 19

The knowledge that Blaze and Zeb were alive and well and free eased some of Deirdre's sadness after her visit to Dartmoor. That, unlike Ross, Blaze did not despise her, helped a great deal. So she woke far more cheerful than she had previously felt. The brighter spirits lasted throughout the day, until Phoebe announced that Deirdre must assist with the fete.

"As Kieran's wife," Phoebe explained, "you will have to do these sorts of things often."

As was their practice in the evenings, they sat around the fire in the gold salon, the other ladies sewing, knitting, or embroidering. On the evenings Miss Pruitt joined them, Deirdre took turns with her reading to the Ashford ladies to have something to do. Reading was one part of her education her father had not neglected, unlike the feminine arts.

Now, with Phoebe's remark, Deirdre set the book she had been about to open aside and exchanged a concerned glance with Chloe.

"What do I do? You saw what happened when I tried to knit a scarf."

Juliet giggled.

Phoebe shook her head. "Laughing is not kind, Juliet. You have been knitting since you were small. Deirdre had a different kind of upbringing."

"Which we are not allowed to talk about," Chloe murmured.

"We have all the scarves we need," Phoebe continued as though Chloe had not spoken. "One for each child. On Monday, we will set up trestle tables in the gallery here and arrange the items for the children. Tuesday, we will make the sweets and sandwiches to feed the parents and children." She smiled. "I know you don't cook either, but Cook and the maids are competent. They will show you what to do. I imagine that you can stir a pot of fruit juice for jelly."

"I imagine so." Deirdre did not need to feign a grimace.

"And you can cut pieces of cake," Phoebe added.

"I cut things quite well," Deirdre couldn't resist saying. "I used to carry a stiletto in my braid."

"Oh, how amusing!" Juliet, who, being only seventeen, still wore her hair down, began to plait it. "What happened to it?"

"Kieran doesn't like me carrying it, so it is in the chest beside my bed."

Phoebe set her needlework in her lap. "You may wish to carry one on your rambles with Chloe. I expect she does."

Chloe said nothing, bending low over her needlework.

"How would she carry it? She does not wear her hair plaited any longer," Juliet said.

"I should." Deirdre touched the coil on the back of her head that took so many pins to hold up it gave her a headache. "Much easier than all the work poor Sally has to do every morning and ten times in between."

"May I pin my hair up for Christmas Eve, Mama?" Juliet asked. "I am almost eighteen, and Papa and Kieran will be home and we will have all those guests."

Christmas Eve was not something to which Deirdre looked forward. She wanted to see Kieran, more than she wanted to admit, but his arrival would make visiting the prison more difficult. Worse than that, she could not avoid the hordes of visitors the family expected that day. Apparently, all the local gentry paid calls on the Ashfords, and several returned to the house after the midnight church service to consume the pudding.

Her need to rest would help her avoid some of the visitors, but not all of them. She had wifely duties to perform, demonstrations that she was a proper wife, if not a devoted one. She needed her marriage not to be a mistake for Kieran. Now that she had seen her men in the prison, even more so did she recognize the importance of making her husband and his family happy with her, giving them reason to trust her, so she could find a way of freedom for all of the crew.

One way she showed her commitment to the family was to write Kieran long letters filled with details of her life. She talked of playing with the dogs and meeting local children, of learning household management from Phoebe, and of listening to Chloe and Juliet play the pianoforte. In all her words, she tried to sound content with her life, not sad that she enjoyed comfort while her men suffered and lonely with the stillness of the house and emptiness of her bed weighing down upon her each night, especially after she received one of Kieran's notes scrawled as though they were an afterthought penned in between social engagements.

But sometimes she was content, even happy within the circle of Phoebe and her daughters' warmth. Juliet made her laugh. Chloe understood Deirdre's need for movement and fresh air, and Phoebe was endlessly patient and thoughtful.

This matter of the Christmas fete, however, dragged up all Deirdre's restlessness.

"The Trillings will help us set up for the fete on Monday," Phoebe was saying. She looked at Deirdre. "You have been hiding away so much, you haven't yet met Alicia, Mrs. Trilling. She is my oldest friend here in England."

"And her eldest daughter is a cat," Chloe announced.

"That isn't nice, Chloe," Phoebe admonished her.

"I have failed in my duties to teach her this, my lady," Miss Pruitt murmured.

"Amelia," Chloe drawled, "wanted to be Lady Ripon."

"I heard that she had a temper tantrum when Kieran got engaged to Joanna."

"Imagine the hysterics she must have had when she learned he married Deirdre." Chloe's eyes danced. "Perhaps that is why she has not yet come to call."

"She has been visiting her grandparents in Hampshire," Phoebe said. "But she will be here along with Jane."

"Jane is her younger sister," Juliet said. "She is Chloe's age and exceedingly kind and pretty."

"Amelia is a lovely girl, too," Phoebe said.

"Of which she is well aware," Chloe grumbled. "Perhaps I can find a way for you to carry your stiletto before Monday, Deirdre. You may need it."

Miss Amelia Trilling didn't look like a formidable opponent, Deirdre decided upon having the young woman presented to her. She was nearly as tiny as Phoebe, with huge cornflower-blue eyes, hair the color of sunshine, and a flawless complexion as pale and smooth as fresh cream.

Deirdre became all too aware of her height, her changing figure, and an odd rosiness that had taken over her skin in recent days. She also reminded herself that she was the second lady of the manor. However uncomfortable she found that position, others envied her for it.

Amelia gave her a languid hand and a bored glance before moving on to gush over Phoebe's latest painting hanging in the gallery. Later, when Deirdre found herself alone with Amelia as they covered a table with a linen cloth and ribbon rosettes, Amelia unsheathed her claws. "I heard that Lord Ripon had married." She sounded as though she were about to yawn. "At first I thought it a jest. Now that I have met you, I see that it must be."

Deirdre wondered if she could shove the rosette pin into Amelia's hand instead of the tablecloth. She simply had no idea how to respond to female games like the one Amelia apparently wanted to play. She glanced around, hoping for assistance, and caught Chloe's eye.

Chloe dropped her bough of holly and sauntered over to the table. "That is a lovely gown you are wearing, Amelia. But do you not have a matching cap?"

"A cap?" Amelia lost her languid air. "For what would I need a cap?"

Chloe shrugged. "It is only proper that you wear a cap once you are declared on the shelf."

That broadside struck home. Deirdre witnessed the hit in the way Amelia's shoulders went back, her chin up.

"I am not much older than you," Amelia declared. "That is scarcely on the shelf."

"Oh." Chloe laughed. "And here I didn't think you were Kieran's age. I beg your pardon. Deirdre, I never told you this morning how pretty you look in that pelisse."

Amelia sniffed. "It's pink. It clashes with her hair."

"I thought so myself." Deirdre managed a smile. "But the Ashford ladies and Miss Pruitt disagreed with me, and you know how formidable they are."

"They lied to you, my dear lady." Amelia sighed so loudly, it was nearly a groan. "Revenge, you know, for Kieran feeling he needed to give you the protection of his name to bring you back here." Her gaze swept Deirdre's body. "If that was why he felt obligated to marry you."

Deirdre felt her flush deepen and the front of her gown and pelisse cling to her no longer perfectly flat stomach. She also saw Amelia's gaze sharpen as a giggle escaped her lips.

"I do believe Miss Pruitt needs my assistance with that holly you abandoned, Lady Chloe." Amelia danced away.

Deirdre met Chloe's eyes. "I gave it away, didn't I?"

"The fate of a redhead." Chloe sounded cheerful. "You blushed. But nothing shows, and since you got married over three months ago, no one will have cause to question your virtue."

Deirdre bent to her task of affixing rosettes to the tablecloth. "She said that my marriage to Kieran must be a jest. How do I respond to something like that?"

"You use your left hand for tasks so she can see your wedding ring. Here, do you need to sit down?"

Deirdre glanced around the long chamber now filled with fashionable ladies from ages ten to sixty, chattering, laughing, giving one another instructions, and casting curious glances Deirdre's way.

She shook her head. "If I go all over faint or ill now, the cat will be out of the bag." She lowered her voice and leaned toward Chloe under the pretext of straightening the cloth. "But what about tomorrow?"

"All arranged. I will receive an urgent message that Mrs. Barnes needs me for her youngest two, who do have the grippe at the moment, and you will be too worn from today to work in a hot kitchen."

"And give the truth of my condition away to everyone."

"That will just be the family and the—oh, I understand. The Trillings will be there." Chloe propped her chin on her fist for a moment, then shrugged. "What does it matter if everyone knows? You are right and properly married to my brother, and he adores you."

Deirdre swallowed against the sudden and unnecessary lump in her throat. "Is that why I scarcely get a word from him while he's dancing attendance on the London ladies?"

"He never takes his eyes off you," Chloe said.

Deirdre snorted. "I don't believe devotion has anything to do with his watchfulness."

"You'll see I am right." Chloe squeezed Deirdre's hand. "His last letter says he will be home by Christmas Eve. Now come help me with the holly. Amelia is making a muck of it." She raised her voice. "It needs to be higher so the little ones do not try to eat the berries."

Sticking close to Chloe's side, Deirdre managed to survive the day of female gossip and sidelong glances. She discovered that she liked Jane Trilling, who was even prettier than her sister and far more sweet-natured. She said little, but laughed a great deal. When she took out her embroidery over a late nuncheon of tea, sandwiches, and cake, the way she sought Phoebe's approval touched a chord in Deirdre that brought the ready lump back to her throat.

She was the kind of daughter-in-law Phoebe deserved—petite, pretty, accomplished in the feminine arts. Not a great gawk like Deirdre, who looked better in breeches than gowns, who couldn't knit a row or sew a seam straight. A daughter-in-law who intended to betray her.

After refreshments, Deirdre wanted to sleep. She didn't dare ask to be excused, though, so stumbled back to the gallery and began sorting scarves and embroidered handkerchiefs to give away to the children and their mothers. Others set out small toys, and Chloe and Jane Trilling practiced a Christmas pageant some of the children would perform. Jane played the pianoforte and sang beautifully. If Kieran had gotten engaged to Jane, or even Amelia, he never would have found himself in a pickle over Joanna, never would have been sent to sea, never would have brought the enemy home as his bride.

The need to move, to take a brisk walk along the gallery surged through her, and she stood too quickly. Dizziness overwhelmed her, and she sank to her knees, head down. At once, half a dozen females surrounded her, twittering, questioning, giving her speculative glances.

She wanted to simply crawl under the table and hide.

"How long have they been married?" Amelia asked sotto voce.

"Three and a half months," Chloe snapped. She offered Deirdre her hand. "Come along. You look worn to a shade from meeting all these people at once."

Willingly, Deirdre let Chloe lead her from the gallery and up the stairs to the second floor. She had to pause on the landing and blink away spots before her eyes.

"Are you ill?" Chloe asked.

Deirdre shook her head—a bad idea. "I stood up too quickly, and everything went spinning." She leaned against the cool, plastered stone wall. "Nothing like making an announcement to the world."

"What does it matter? You have been married well long enough, especially since you are not showing in the least."

"But I am."

When they reached Deirdre's room, she took off her pelisse and pulled her gown tight. "Look."

Chloe shook her head. "I do not notice anything. But, Deirdre . . ." She gnawed her lip for a moment, studying Deirdre with a grave expression. "Does this not make you happy? I mean, Mama told us nothing is more joyful than providing your husband with a child."

"I'm an unnatural female, you know that. I rarely considered that I'd marry, let alone provide a man with a baby."

"Why ever not?" Chloe perched on the edge of the bed.

Deirdre smiled. "I spent a year on land. The married ladies all looked so bored."

"Mama never seems bored. But I think I understand. I would be a lunatic if all I did was gossip and embroider all day. Kieran will not expect that of you either since he knows how you grew up."

"He does expect that of me. That's why I am this way." Deirdre pressed both hands to the definite thickness below her waist. "He seemed truly happy about it at first, but I'm not sure that he is now that he seems to have been accepted back into society." She sank onto her chaise. "If I weren't an American and our countries weren't at war, maybe things would be different. Now, though, it's an inconvenience for both of us. The marriage can't be set aside without an act of Parliament, and either I get my men out of Dartmoor before I do start to stick out, or they'll have to wait until afterward, and that's months off. I wish I could be happy and the right kind of wife and daughter-in-law, but I'm not and never can be like Jane."

"Jane? You are jealous of Jane Trilling?" Chloe looked shocked.

Deirdre startled. "Of course I'm not jealous of Jane or Amelia or anyone else. Why would I be?"

She had to want her husband's regard at the least to envy another female's beauty and talents. Right then, weighed down by anxiety for her crew and Kieran's determination to keep her away from her crew, she doubted she could want him to so much as like her. A disgust of her would keep him away once he returned to Devonshire, and that suited her plans best, even if his indifference toward anything about her other than her good behavior left her hollow.

"I've been jealous of some men for their greater strength and freedom of movement in port," Deirdre plunged on, "but never of another woman."

Except, to be honest with herself, she did envy the Trilling ladies for their poise and beauty.

"Deirdre, you are far prettier, and Kieran chose you."

"He felt obligated."

"Did he"—Chloe blushed—"take advantage of you before he married you?"

"Not in the least."

Unless kissing her until she lost her good sense counted.

"Well, then, he was not obligated. He made a choice, and, my dear sister-in-law, Kieran does nothing he does not want to do." Chloe stood. "I must return and shut up that cat Amelia. You get rested up for tomorrow."

Deirdre slept for several hours. After she woke and ate the light supper Sally brought up to her, she lay in bed with her hands on her belly and, in the dark emptiness of the night, found herself, for the most fleeting of moments, wishing she were more like Phoebe and happy to be presenting her husband with his heir. How pleasant would life be if Kieran gazed at her as Tyne did Phoebe? Would she feel so empty and restless if she and Kieran created children from love and not merely mutual passion?

That was a fantasy she couldn't afford to dwell upon. That was for other females, ones without the lives of eleven men on their consciences.

With that thought, she rose at dawn, dressed, then made a show of merely picking at her breakfast.

"You still aren't feeling well, my dear?" Phoebe asked.

Deirdre shook her head. "I'm so tired."

"Amelia was beastly to her," Juliet pronounced. "She is so jealous Kieran never even looked at her she could probably pull out your hair, which is prettier than her boring blond."

"Juliet," Phoebe cautioned, "don't you be mean, too."

"But she said the most horrid things about Deirdre." Juliet pinched up her face. "She said, 'I hope it is a girl so the succession is secure when he does get a son and can be sure it is his.'"

Chloe's cup clattered into its saucer. "She never dared say such a thing in front of everyone."

"That is precisely what she said," Juliet insisted. "And in front of everyone."

Phoebe sighed. "I'm afraid she did. In a whisper, of course."

"She would not have dared if I had been there," Chloe ground out. "I know a thing or two about her she would prefer kept secret."

Juliet's blue eyes sparkled. "Like what?"

"Like the time I caught her and—never you mind. What is it, Addison?"

The butler stood in the breakfast room doorway. "You have a message, Lady Chloe. One of the Barnes children is waiting in the kitchen."

"I will be right down. Deirdre, you find a good book in the library and go to your room. We have managed the food for the fete without you in the past. We can do it again." She squeezed Deirdre's shoulder.

Deirdre cast Phoebe a hopeful glance. "May I, ma'am?"

"Of course." Phoebe smiled. "But the truth was bound to come out soon. You are starting to look radiant. Kieran will be bowled over when he sees you."

Phoebe was the one who radiated happiness. Deirdre was glad that she was taking pleasure in the upcoming happy event.

When she and Chloe reached the abandoned cottage an hour later, Deirdre discovered that she no longer needed to pin the breeches to make them fit at the waist, and couldn't be happy about that at all. She could never visit the prison again unless she found a disguise that allowed her to be female.

"Can I go as a widow?" Deirdre asked as they headed up the gorge. "Don't they wear veils?"

"Yes. I expect we have one or two in the attic. But, Deirdre—" Chloe steered the cart around a boulder jutting over the track. "Deirdre, what if Ross—Mr. Trenerry—sees you are . . . *enceinte*. Will it not overset him?"

"He might be tempted to kill Kieran, yes. But he won't. Given the opportunity, he'll simply get out of England."

"To fight us."

"I expect so."

Chloe fell silent. The day was clear, so only the jingle of the pony's harness and rumble of the cart wheels disturbed the stillness of the barren moorland. Uncomfortable in breeches for the first time in her life, Deirdre shifted on the hard seat and sought for distraction.

"So what did you catch Amelia Trilling doing with Kieran?"

"Kissing in the hayloft over the—oh, drat." Chloe snapped her teeth shut.

"The hayloft? How crude."

"What is crude is me telling you."

"Why?"

"You do not need to know about all my brother's indiscretions. They are simply not as bad as everyone says they are. He was seventeen." Chloe glared at the track. "Kissing was all. It meant nothing to him. He has kissed all the pretty girls around here."

The prison hove into view.

Chloe drew up the pony. "We will park the cart here. Be careful climbing down."

Deirdre ground her teeth and descended from the cart. She had decorated her basket with holly for a festive air and planned to give the entire thing to Ross with its contents of woolen scarves, soap, and peppermint lozenges. Too little to bring them Christmas blessings, but all she could manage. At least she could tell them that Blaze and Zeb were near at hand, operating on a privateer in the Channel. That would bring Ross pleasure.

But Ross did not meet them; Wat did. He stumbled from the crowd a bent and gray-faced old man Deirdre barely recognized. She knew he wasn't young, but two months in Dartmoor had made him ancient with completely gray hair, rheumy eyes, and a deep, hacking cough that shook his fragile-looking body.

Deirdre's own chest felt tight. "Ross?"

Wat shook his head. "He didn't want to come. You broke his heart, lass."

"I never pretended to love him for more than friendship."

"Aye, but young men have dreams." Wat took the basket. "We thank you for what you're doing."

"I saw Blaze."

Wat's hand tightened on the basket. "A prisoner?"

"He's free. He and Zeb both. Privateering."

Though he started coughing again, Wat left them smiling.

Chloe and Deirdre were not as they left the prison yard. Neither spoke on their way down to the coast. Chloe kept her face averted, but an occasional sniffle gave away the fact that she was crying.

"If you cannot," she finally spoke at the end of the track, "I will get them out of there, whatever it takes."

Deirdre understood why Chloe felt so strongly. She had seen it often enough aboard ship to know that Wat was dying.

"It's my fault," she said. "I'll do it."

Fine, though cold, weather made the return journey easy going for the last twenty miles, and Kieran and Tyne arrived at Bishops Cove in the middle of the afternoon. Carriages and horses filled the stable yard, a reminder that their ladies would not be alone. That fact stabbed Kieran with disappointment, but the mere possibility of seeing Deirdre, even if he had to do nothing more than give her a chaste kiss on the hand until later, sent him leaping from the carriage before it came to a full stop and loping to the house, Tyne's chuckle rumbling behind him.

Addison opened the door with the announcement that all the ladies were in the kitchens. "They are making the jellies and things for the fete tomorrow."

Kieran muttered a rude word about the fete, shed his greatcoat, and headed for the back of the hall.

"My lord," Addison called.

Kieran paused. "Yes?"

"You may wish to tidy your hair."

Kieran grinned. "Thank you." He smoothed the waves back from his face and retied the black velvet ribbon. He knew his cravat was a bit crumpled and that he probably smelled a bit of horse from being in such a hurry at Barnstable that he helped the hostler back the team into the traces so the coachman could get himself some refreshment. Nonetheless, he did not care.

He missed his wife.

He shoved open the swinging door into the back passage and took the steps down to the kitchen two at a time. Light, fragrant steam and female chatter drew him forward. Deirdre must be drowning in such a feminine enclave. Poor girl. He would rescue her.

He leaped the last two steps and entered the kitchen.

Talk and motion came to a halt, presenting him with a tableau of maids and ladies alike rolling out pastry on the broad deal table in the center of the room, other maids and ladies stirring huge kettles at the new cooking stove, and the cook pulling bread from the hearth oven. Like a miniature general, Mama stood in the midst directing it all.

She reacted to his arrival first. With a wordless cry, she glided forward and clasped both his hands in hers. "My dear, you are home early. And your father?"

Kieran heard footfalls on the steps behind him. "On his way." He stepped aside so she could greet Tyne, and scanned the room for Deirdre.

One glance was enough to tell him she was not there. Amelia Trilling was. She started in his direction, but Juliet pushed her out of the way and flew into his arms.

"My dear, dear brother, you were away far too long. Did you bring me something nice from London? Fashion plates perhaps? Did you clear your name? Why—"

"Give over, Jule." Kieran set her from him. "Where are Chloe and Deirdre?"

"Chloe is off with the Barnes children, who have the grippe, and Deirdre is resting."

Kieran tensed. "Is she all right?"

Juliet leaned close to him. "She is actually avoiding Amelia, the vicious cat."

"Thank you." Giving the room a general nod, he turned sideways to move past his parents, who were gazing at one another like young lovers, and then raced up the steps—

To find Deirdre's bedchamber empty.

The bed was rumpled with a discarded nightgown tossed upon it, as though someone had recently slept there, but the fire had died to mere coals. A chill hung over the chamber, and the candles had burned long enough to gutter out.

No one had been there for some time.

For a full minute, he stood motionless scarcely able to breathe, his heart stuttering. All he could think was that she had left him, escaped, taking his unborn child.

"Deirdre, no."

He sped down the stairs again and burst into the kitchen. "Sir." He grasped his father's shoulder, turning him to face him. "Deirdre's gone."

Alarm flashed across Tyne's face. "Steady, lad." His voice remained calm.

Tyne led Kieran up into the hall, Phoebe following.

"She couldn't go far," Phoebe said. "She was so worn to a thread yesterday that she nearly fainted in front of everyone."

Despite his concern, Kieran smiled. "That will provide grist for the gossip mills."

"When was the last time you saw her?" Tyne asked.

"This morning." Phoebe wrung her hands. "I've been so preoccupied—oh, I am sorry."

"Never you mind that," Kieran said. "You should have been able to trust her."

He should have warned his mother not to trust Deirdre out of her sight.

"But where could she go?" Phoebe asked.

"And how do we find her without making this public knowledge?" Tyne added.

Kieran pictured Deirdre in male attire seeking passage on the nearest vessel. But could she still get away with wearing male attire without looking ridiculous? More than likely. She was not that far along. But if a day preparing for a fete fatigued her to the point of fainting, she could not walk far, not far enough to find more than a fishing boat, and the fishermen would not be at their boats in harbor in the middle of the day. She needed assistance for anything else.

"Where is Chloe?" he asked again.

"Helping Mrs. Barnes," Phoebe said. "Why?"

"From their letters, I presume she and Deirdre have gotten friendly."

"Yes, but—" Phoebe's hand flew to her lips. "Chloe would never help Deirdre leave us."

"Let us go find her and learn for certain." Tyne spoke through stiff lips. He kissed Phoebe on her brow, then led Kieran from the house.

In grim silence, they rode to the Barnes holding. Smoke rose from the chimney and children and chickens played in the yard. They scattered at Kieran and Tyne's arrival, and a plump woman with a round, cheerful face opened the cottage door.

"My lord, sirs, what is it?"

"We have come to fetch Chloe home," Tyne said.

Mrs. Barnes's eyes widened. "Um, she-she's gone a'ready."

"How long ago?" Kieran asked.

She shrugged.

He exchanged a glance with his father.

Tyne nodded. "Thank you, ma'am." When they were out of earshot, he turned to Kieran. "We will head for the cove, but let us take the back road around the estate so that Phoebe's guests do not see us."

"Yes." Kieran kept his back straight and his face stiff.

Please, let us find her before it is too late.

Tall hedgerows lined the road, keeping the sheep in their pastures, so he could not see the source of the sound he heard, only acknowledge that it was the jingle of harness on a road where no one but his father and he traveled.

And Chloe.

The pony cart rounded the curve, and Kieran came face to face with his wife wearing a caped greatcoat, top boots, and trousers.

Chapter 20

Kieran stared at Deirdre with cold eyes—flat and cold and hard. He had been angry with her in the past, but not like this spine-chilling too-calm rage.

She wrapped her arms across her chest and clutched the sleeves of the greatcoat as he and Tyne dismounted and stalked to either side of the pony cart. Tyne looked as full of controlled fury as his son. Deirdre shivered. Beside her, Chloe had gone tense and still.

"An odd way to dress to make calls on the tenants." Tyne spoke first.

"And you have been on a rather peculiar rest, m'dear." Despite the endearment, Kieran's voice held no affection.

Deirdre caught his gaze and remained silent.

"Where have you been?" The words cracked out of Tyne like whiplashes.

"Dartmoor," Chloe and Deirdre answered together.

Kieran closed his eyes. His hand dropped to the side of the cart, looking as though his fingers gripped it hard enough to wrench off the board. "I should have known. But to drag my sister into this-this . . . treason—" The cart panel creaked under his grip.

"It was my idea." Chloe made the declaration with her chin high, her own golden eyes bright. "While they are locked in that hellhole dying, we are warm and clean and free—"

"Not now you are not." Tyne took the reins from Chloe's fingers. "Go get on Kieran's horse."

"But my clothes—"

"Now."

Head bowed, Chloe scrambled from the cart and trudged over to one of the horses.

Without a word, Kieran climbed into the cart and took the reins from his father. "The side gate, sir?"

Tyne nodded, then returned to his own mount.

Deirdre laid her hand on Kieran's arm. "Kieran, I—"

He shook off her touch and snapped the reins to get the cart moving behind the two horses. "Do not talk to me right now. I am likely to respond with words I will regret later."

Deirdre considered playing Juliet and talking nonstop all the way back to the house. Yet this side of Kieran disturbed her, frightened her. She had never realized that he could be so much like his father— autocratic, wintry, inflexible. She feared what he might do to her. Not physical harm. He would never be cruel that way. But he could curtail even the semblance of freedom she enjoyed now. In fact, from Tyne's words, she suspected that he would.

She huddled in the greatcoat, trying not to touch Kieran where he perched on the narrow seat of the cart, and prayed that she would be wrong.

In too short a time, they reached the wall that surrounded the house and parklands of Bishops Cove. An even narrower track than the one they had been on led to a postern gate just wide enough for the cart, carefully maneuvered, to pass through. Tyne carried the key. After they all entered the grounds of the estate, where towering trees formed their own barrier on either side of the lane, and he locked the gate behind them, he remained dismounted and indicated that Chloe should do the same.

"Kieran, help Deirdre down. We walk from here to draw as little attention to us as possible. The stock can graze until I send a reliable man back to fetch them."

Deirdre didn't wait for Kieran to help her down. She scrambled off the cart and moved to Chloe's side.

Chloe caught hold of her hand and squeezed. "They love us," she whispered. "They will not hurt us. And Bishops Cove does not have any dungeons or towers to lock us in."

"Just our bedchambers."

Of course, she could descend from the balcony without too much difficulty until she got too big.

"Christmas is coming," Chloe said.

Then the men flanked them on either side, and she fell silent.

"My study," Tyne said. "It is on the far side of the house from the kitchen and any guests who might still be there."

"Mama will want to know that they are safe," Kieran said.

The walk from gate to house took no more than ten minutes. Deirdre felt as though an hour passed. Her feet hurt. Her head and legs ached. Her breeches felt like a corset cutting off her breath. The cold wind off the sea made her eyes water. The ache, the fear, in her heart turned that water to tears, which ran down her face. Maybe this feminine reaction to distress would soften Kieran.

He merely handed her a handkerchief. "I have two sisters. Crocodile tears do not move me."

"Not to mention all your experience with ladies." Chloe's taunt sent a charge of anger into Deirdre, setting her resolve.

God bless Chloe.

In silence, they reached Tyne's study by a circuitous route. Tyne indicated the ladies should sit in uncomfortable chairs in front of his desk. He settled behind it. Kieran stood by the hearth, one hand, glove removed, gripping the mantel hard enough to whiten his knuckles.

"Our journey to London was not for our pleasure." Tyne leaned back in his soft leather chair as though intending to lecture. "We had a little matter to clear up for Kieran, some business transactions to see to—"

"Taking my money away from me," Deirdre interrupted.

Chloe gasped. Kieran rubbed one temple as though his head ached.

Tyne snapped his teeth together, then he sighed. "That money is Kieran's by law."

"The law should be—"

"Deirdre," Kieran interjected with an air of weary resignation, "shut up and listen. We can all get baths and hot food sooner if you do."

That was so sensible, Deirdre complied.

"Kieran," Tyne said, "will you go find your mother?"

Kieran didn't move. "I would rather stay with my wife, sir."

Deirdre's heart gave an odd flutter at a possessiveness in his tone.

"I understand," Tyne said. "But I promise not to harm her while you are gone."

Kieran smiled, then departed.

Deirdre felt cold, bereft, alone in a court where Tyne was judge and jury.

"Those men are dying up there, Papa," Chloe said. "And we had to do what we could to help."

"We only took them some—" Deirdre caught herself before mentioning money. "Luxuries like soap and sweets and the like. They're my family. I can't just abandon them."

"We are not just abandoning them," Tyne said, more gently than she thought he could be under the circumstances. "I have spent much of the past weeks using what influence I still have in the Admiralty in an attempt to get them paroled."

Deirdre stared at him. "You . . . care?"

"Deirdre, you are my daughter now, too. I could do nothing less." He sighed. "I am afraid that I failed."

"Oh, Papa." Chloe jumped up and ran around the desk to hug him. "You are so kind."

He scowled at her with such ferocity that he could mean nothing serious by it. "I am too kind. If I were stricter, you would not be engaged in outright dangerous behavior."

"But we were never in any danger," Chloe protested.

"You were. We all are. When your mother—ah, Phoebe."

She glided into the room with Kieran behind her, and went straight to Tyne. "I told Alicia that Deirdre needs me, so she will see that the cooking is finished. That is not untrue, is it?"

Tyne took her hand. "Not at all. We all need you."

Kieran positioned himself behind Deirdre's chair. He laid his hand on her shoulder, and she knew that she needed him there. *Can't you understand that I owe my allegiance to them?*

She couldn't say it because he couldn't understand. He had given her his name much for her benefit. He had a right to expect her allegiance. She simply could not give it to him.

"Phoebe," Tyne was saying, "I have told our little story to Kieran, as we discussed before I left. May I tell our younger ladies also? They need to understand the gravity of what they did today." He looked at them. "And others?"

"Just once," Deirdre admitted.

"Twice too often." Phoebe pressed her fingers to her lips. "I can't believe you two took the risk. Yes, Garrett, we need to tell them about how I nearly got hanged doing what I thought was right."

Kieran moved his things into the bedchamber adjoining Deirdre's. He should have done so the first night and not gone haring off to London.

Yet if he had not, he would not have cleared his name at least in part and begun to gain an understanding of his father, an understanding that left him feeling less worthy to be his only heir than he had previously experienced. Two things might help him gain Tyne's full respect and acceptance as a responsible successor—the right answer from Greece and keeping Deirdre out of trouble. He felt confident that the former would prove him innocent of debauching Joanna. As for the latter, he did not know what he would do with Deirdre short of locking her up. That was the easy way. That was tempting.

It would make her despise him.

He did not want to face a life with Deirdre despising him.

With that in mind, not knowing how to go about it in the least, he slipped through the dressing room and into her bedchamber. She sat at the dressing table, brushing out her glorious hair. She looked magnificent. Scrubbed clean, her face glowed with rosy health. Her cheeks looked fuller, her whole demeanor softer. Wordlessly, he reached out to her, took the brush from her hand, and began to perform the task for her.

"I still can't believe that Phoebe was a spy," Deirdre said.

"I found it difficult to accept myself. She is so gentle. For twenty-five years I have believed Mama was always the perfect wife. But no wonder she loves my father so much."

"And he her." She blinked several times fast and hard, and he realized she was fighting back tears.

He set the brush aside and began to rub her shoulders through the green velvet of her dressing gown. "I probably would not have gone out as a privateer if I had known, though my father said the only reason he did not disinherit me for doing it was because it has helped show the Crown that the family is loyal to England."

"Except for the American wife you brought home." She hunched her shoulders, shaking off his hands, and turned on the stool to face him. "Do you wish to be rid of me, Kieran? Would that suit the family more?"

"No!" The word emerged with the fear he had experienced in those moments when he thought she had left him.

He dropped to his knees before her and clasped her hands between his. "Deirdre, I—" He swallowed. "I care about what happens to you." He tried a smile. "I rather missed you."

She drew her hands free. "Is that why I received messages from you that were impersonal enough to be from Addison? Is that why you spent your entire visit to London taking my money out of my control and going to dinner parties with other women? Is that why I am now nothing more than a prisoner in a far finer prison than my crew— because you missed me and care what happens to me?" She rose so abruptly the belt to her dressing gown smacked him in the face.

He barely felt the soft fabric blow, but it acted like a whip driving him to his feet. "I did not spend my entire time in London going to dinner parties or anywhere else with other women." He dropped his hands onto her shoulders to keep her from turning away from him. "You know I was trying to clear my name for the sake of my family, and that includes you."

She arched her brows. "In the past two months, I have learned that you have kissed every eligible female in the neighborhood, including Amelia Trilling in a hayloft. Such lovely things to hear about my husband."

Her sarcasm stung.

He gazed at her looking more beautiful than he remembered, and wanted her with an ache clear through him. At least in passion they were of one accord, not locked in an endless battle of conflicted loyalties.

"You know why you can't go to Dartmoor. My family—"

"And what about my family?" She flung up her hands.

"They are the enemy."

"Not to me."

"Yes, Deirdre, to you. You are the wife to the heir of a peer of the realm. That makes you a British subject. Can you not get that through that stubborn brain of yours?"

"Could you give up your family were we in America and your family imprisoned?"

Kieran took in a deep breath and let it out slowly, forcing his muscles to relax and his voice emerge with gentleness. "No, I could not. Nor could I risk the freedom and the lives of people who took me into their family and cared for me."

She opened her mouth as though about to rebut his claim, then brushed past him to perch on the chaise without saying a word.

Not for a moment did he think he had achieved a victory. Victory indeed. As though their marriage was a war.

Feeling as deflated as a balloon without its fire to give air, Kieran dropped onto the chaise beside her. "When will your maid arrive?"

"Soon. The Trilling ladies are staying for dinner, since we didn't expect you and Tyne home for two more days."

"Which is why you went to the prison today. You thought it safe."

"I wanted to take them some Christmas cheer." She leaned into the deep cushion of the chaise and closed her eyes, looking as fatigued as he felt. "So have you cleared your name?"

Accepting that the subject of her visits to Dartmoor was ended for now, Kieran lifted one of her hands and held it between both of his. "I made great strides forward, thanks to my father. He's starting to see me in a different light."

"I'm glad of that." She opened her eyes and gave him a half smile.

Thinking she was sincere, he started to point out that now, more than ever, he needed her cooperation to seal his return into the family's good graces, but her maid arrived and he needed to make his own ablutions before dinner with company. He had plenty of time with Deirdre to work out their difficulties and more.

When he walked into the drawing room an hour later, he realized he needed to add Amelia Trilling to the difficulties with his wife. Kieran knew perfectly well that she always expected him to offer for her. But he had too much respect for and received too much enjoyment from female companionship to settle for a pretty face masking a mean spirit.

But there she sat in one of the more formal drawing rooms, draped over the arm of a chair in an attitude of drooping flower in need of watering. As he held the door open for Deirdre, astoundingly elegant in her midnight-blue silk gown, Amelia swept her gold-tipped lashes upward, looked at Deirdre, then guided the lashes down again.

She had just cut Deirdre dead.

Deirdre pretended not to notice. She crossed the room with her confident stride and joined Mama and Mrs. Trilling.

Kieran headed straight for Amelia. "If you ever treat my wife that way again, I will see to it that you are never invited into this house."

Amelia sat upright. "I have no idea what you are talking about. I did not even see your wife."

"Then you need spectacles." He stalked over to Deirdre's side. "Are gentlemen permitted to participate in the fete, too?"

"Can you entertain children?" Mrs. Trilling asked.

"He has a fine singing voice," Mama answered for him.

He scowled at her.

She laughed. "But you do. Why do you, Jane, and Chloe not practice some music after dinner? Chloe and Jane have prepared some songs, but a male voice will add something special."

"I have not sung much in years. Deirdre?" He looked at her poised on the edge of a chair as though ready to fly. "Do you want to join us?"

"I don't know how to read music."

"You do not know 'The Holly and the Ivy'?" Mrs. Trilling appeared as shocked as Kieran felt.

Deirdre shook her head. "I never heard it before yesterday." She smiled at Kieran in a way that made his toes curl. "But I'll enjoy listening to you sing with Chloe while Jane plays."

How easily she could give him hope of a more harmonious future. He wished the arrangements at the table allowed him to be near her. At dinner, she sat beside his father as the second-highest-ranking female, and appeared to be getting along with him rather well. Because females outnumbered males, Mama had invited the steward and secretary to join the company for a bit more balance. That still placed Juliet and Jane beside one another, which left Kieran with Amelia or the governess. He gave Amelia only enough attention to be polite, while making the middle-aged spinster blush with his attentiveness, and sighed with relief when Mama led the ladies from the room.

"You have found yourself an intrepid bride." His father slid the port coaster across the table. "Keeping her close to home rather feels like caging an eagle, but you know we must."

"I know, sir." Kieran filled his glass, then sat staring into the ruby depths of the wine. "She will despise me for it."

"I am not altogether certain she will." His father offered him an encouraging smile. "She is settling here despite the sojourns to Dartmoor. Phoebe says Deirdre is getting on well with all of them. She loves the dogs. She has a fine head for household accounts, and she is kind to all the servants."

"She is also kind to her crew. If anything happens to a one of them, she will move heaven and earth to betray us and help them." The idea those men came before him in her affections sent a dull knife cutting through Kieran, and he downed the rich, sweet wine meant for sipping, then shoved back his chair. "Shall we join the ladies?"

His father rose, but halted Kieran in the doorway with a hand on his shoulder. "The burden and joy is on you to persuade her otherwise."

Kieran understood what his father was saying, and he held little hope he bore the right skills to accomplish it. Too much depended on the course of the war with America, on how her crew fared in prison, on Deirdre herself. But he could start trying.

The minute he entered the drawing room, however, Chloe descended on him and drew him to the pianoforte. From the corner of his eye, he saw Deirdre sitting quietly by the fire, a pattern of some kind spread on her knees.

"All knitting is concentration," Mrs. Trilling was saying.

"Kieran, pay attention," Chloe admonished. "You can ogle your wife later. Jane, begin again."

He allowed Chloe to pull him into the music. Jane played beautifully, and he liked Chloe's voice. When they finished a set of songs and he sought for Deirdre, she was no longer in the room.

Did he have to tether the woman to him with a chain?

He left and raced up the steps. She was not in her bedchamber either. She stood on the balcony, gripping the railing, a rising wind tugging her hair from its pins and whipping her gown around her legs.

"What are you doing?" he demanded. "It is freezing out here."

She did not look at him. "Do you never feel like fresh air after you have been around Amelia?"

"I feel that way after I have been around a number of ladies, and gentlemen, too." He moved close to her, curved his hands around her upper arms. "Was she unkind to you?"

"Just innuendo." She leaned back against him. "I'm worn to a thread. Must I go back down?"

"No." He rested his cheek on her hair. One of the pins poked his cheek, but her scent of ginger and fresh air filled his senses, and he did not care. "Everyone understands that you need your rest." He slid his arms around her, then drew back with a wordless exclamation.

She laughed, though the sound held no humor. "Did you forget?"

"No, but I did not realize, did not think—" He lowered his hands to her belly, stroking her through the fabric of her gown and petticoat, feeling what the line of the dress had concealed—firmness, fullness, a hint of the roundness to come. "I did not realize that I could notice so soon."

"We've been married for three and a half months." Her fingers clamped on his wrists. "Do you think it's too soon, that maybe it isn't yours?" Her voice was as tight as her grip.

"Deirdre." He held her close against him, giving her knowledge of his reaction to her scent, her nearness. "That thought never entered my head. I am new to this, too. I do not know details like this. But doubt that you came to me innocent?" He began to caress her, noting other changes in her body. "Why would you think that?"

She began to relax against him. "Amelia Trilling suggested that you might prefer society young ladies, so you don't have to worry about your heir being a true Ashford."

"Do not ever believe Amelia Trilling. She enjoys hurting others she deems vulnerable." He slid his hand into her hair, scattering hairpins onto the balcony with pings like raindrops, and tilted her head back so he could kiss her. "I have missed being with you."

She said nothing, but the fervor with which she kissed him back assured him she was happy to give him everything he wanted.

Everything he thought he wanted. Yet afterward, when she lay in his arms breathing with the slow, even rhythm of sleep, he did not feel as much satisfaction as he expected. Despite being weary from travel, he lay wakeful, close to his wife in body, but feeling as though the rough waters of the Atlantic lay between them.

"Perhaps the war will end soon and your crew will be sent home." He rubbed his face on the cascade of her glorious hair.

Another hairpin scratched his cheek. He must have missed one when he pulled them out.

He reached up to remove it—and froze. It was not a hairpin.

It was a twig.

Chapter 21

When she woke, Deirdre found the twig on the chest beside the bed. For several moments, she simply stared at it, unable to think, scarcely able to breathe.

"I had to go down there," she whispered to the telltale twist of wood.

If she had not slipped away from the party to make her way to Blaze's hidey-hole, he would have come looking for her to reassure himself she was all right. Kieran might have caught Blaze and seen to it he was hanged if she remained at the party, stayed safe and warm inside the house playing the role of an obedient, loyal wife.

She should have brushed her hair after racing through the parkland with its low-hanging branches. She should have kept Kieran from getting near her. Letting him think he had edged his way back into her good graces—or at the least her bed—had been a poor idea. It hadn't distracted him from his anger with her over her excursion to Dartmoor. His finding of the twig had made matters worse. Somehow she needed to repair the damage or he would give her not a yard of freedom. With only the vaguest of plans in mind, she slipped from bed, drew on her dressing gown, and picked up the twig. She opened his bedchamber door without knocking. He stood at the dressing table tying his cravat. Their eyes met and held in the mirror.

"Are you well?"

She nodded. "I'm tired a great deal of the time, and if I stand up too quickly I get faint, but mostly I feel wonderful."

"I am pleased to hear that." He finished with his toilette and faced her. "Shall I ring for your maid?"

"Could you play maid?"

His gaze caressed her. "I think not. We are expected for the fete."

She felt like she was melting inside. "I'll ring for her then, but I wanted to explain this first." She held up the twig. "I went outside last night. You were singing with Jane and Chloe, and I'd managed to knit a whole row without dropping or adding stitches, and Amelia was talking about people I don't know. I'm still not used to being inside so much. Please understand that I need exercise and air."

"I do." The heat of desire had left his face. "I also understand that you will put your crew before my family, even knowing that it could endanger all of us, and I have to stop you, for your sake as much as for my family's and mine. You, please, understand that."

"But I'll suffocate under too many restrictions."

"I will ensure that you get plenty of air and exercise." His face tightened. "Do not go outside alone again."

She shivered. "You look like your father."

"Now get yourself ready. We will make the Christmas pudding before we go into the gallery for the fete."

Deirdre had never done anything so astounding as the English tradition of stirring the Christmas pudding. The entire family gathered in the warm, steamy kitchen. With servants looking on, each member of the household took a turn running the spoon around the pudding basin that was as large as a washbowl. It was a rich batter smelling of spices and filled with plums and little trinkets.

"I want the wedding ring," Juliet declared.

"You're only seventeen," Phoebe protested. "It should be Chloe's turn this year."

"I would rather receive the sixpence," Chloe said. "Prosperity for the new year."

Juliet finished her turn at the basin and handed Deirdre the spoon. "This is easier than knitting."

"I've stirred porridge." Deirdre ran the wooden spoon around the edge of the bowl.

"Which trinket do you want?" Juliet demanded.

Deirdre watched the silver tokens wink to the surface then sink again—a button and a thimble, a wishbone and an anchor. She could guess at what they represented—domesticity, good luck, safe harbor. Not one of them fit her life, as much as she longed for the luck to give her crew safe harbor.

"Well?" Juliet pressed.

Deirdre glanced up to a sea of faces gazing at her in anticipation.

She managed a bright smile. "If the crown means I get to call the tune and make everyone else dance to it, then I want the crown." She stepped back from the table. "Who is next?"

Let someone else be under everyone's scrutiny.

Kieran took the spoon from her. "You have stolen my thunder, m'dear. I wanted the crown so I can make Juliet sing for us."

A chorus of protests rose from the family and a handful of the servants.

"You will disturb the dogs with that," Chloe said.

Juliet elbowed her in the ribs. "If I cannot have the wedding ring, I want the crown so I can make you kiss Phillip Lawhorn under the mistletoe."

Chloe looked horrified at the idea.

Having no knowledge of what everyone found so amusing, Deirdre withdrew behind the gathered family to watch the rest of the proceedings. For all Kieran had behaved rather badly in the past, the family caring among the Ashfords proclaimed a love that reduced past indiscretions to mere peccadillos.

Her betrayal of them would not be so easily cast aside.

Her spirit felt as thick as the batter in the basin.

On the other side of his mother and sisters, Kieran held up the spoon. "Does Father come next?"

Stillness came over the kitchen, everyone staring, no one moving except for Tyne, who strode forward, clasped Kieran's shoulder with one hand, and took the spoon with the other.

"Thank you, son." His voice was quiet, the emotion raw.

"He called you Father, not Tyne." Phoebe made no pretense about wiping the tears from her eyes even as she smiled. Deirdre's own throat closed. The sight of the two Ashford men standing side by side filled her with an odd sense of joy for Kieran having gotten what he wanted—full acceptance back into the fold of his family—while dread for herself made her stomach roil.

She could never fight against anything so formidable as the alliance of these two men working to one purpose—protecting the family, the kingdom, centuries of wealth and privilege.

"What a happy Christmas." Miss Pruitt wiped her eyes with a scrap of a handkerchief. "Now then, Martha, do you have the pudding bag ready?"

One of the maids scrambled to produce the bag in which the pudding would be boiled. The spell Kieran's use of "Father" had cast over the room broke.

Juliet dashed up to Kieran and hugged him. "So you do love Papa. I am so, so happy you two will not be fighting all of the time."

Kieran laughed, looking a little embarrassed. "I never said we would not argue a bit. I simply accept that he is my sire and deserves more respect than what I have been giving him."

Respect. Loyalty. A choice between her, his wife, and Tyne, his father.

How could she do that to him?

Deirdre scarcely had time to think, let alone come up with answers. The fete drew scores of children from the countryside, laughing, yelling, gamboling about the gallery at full speed. They sang songs and joined in the Christmas pageant. They ate and drank the refreshments prepared with a liberal hand, and eagerly accepted the gifts the ladies of the parish prepared for them all year.

Through it all, Deirdre stood behind a table laden with bowls of cold lemonade and hot cider and ladled the drinks into earthenware mugs so thick they didn't break even when dropped on the stone floor, which happened often. Her feet hurt. Her back ached. Her smile grew less forced with every small bright face that passed by her. And something odd kept happening to her heart, first a softening, then a genuine pleasure in the noise and laughter and shrieks of joy.

She liked the children.

At the end of the day, certain Kieran would have to carry her upstairs, she rested her head on his shoulder and sighed with contentment. "I never knew I liked children. I haven't really ever been around any."

"Neither have I. I have always managed to avoid the fete in previous years." He slipped his arm around her waist despite the number of guests still present. "But they did amuse me."

"You looked as though you were enjoying yourself with Chloe . . . and Jane."

"They are both lovely, generous girls."

"You should have offered for Jane years ago."

"I would have been bored to death."

"You wouldn't have gotten yourself into so much trouble."

"Hush, Amelia is coming this way."

So she was, gliding purposefully forward like a hawk with a juicy mouse in its sights.

"I am too weary to spar with her further." Deirdre gripped Kieran's arm. "May I plead fatigue and go to my room?"

"I am still needed here."

"But I'm not."

"You may sit in a corner and pout for all I care, but you are not leaving this room without me."

A blow to her belly would not have felt worse than his proclamation. Robbed of speech, Deirdre stared at Kieran, eyes wide, lips parted. For a heartbeat, she feared she would scream, or worse, burst into tears.

Kieran ghosted his fingertips across her cheek, his gaze softening. "I am sorry, and right now I can risk nothing else. But if you truly are fatigued, I will make our excuses and take you to your room. Would you like that?"

She nodded, still not trusting her voice.

"Then let us say good night to everyone."

Doing so was awkward. Looks of surprise and amusement, along with a hissed "That is disgusting," accompanied them on their rounds of the gallery until they reached the door.

By the time they arrived at the first stair landing, Deirdre couldn't hold back any longer. "We can't do that again. If I need to go rest, you have to let me go alone. Now everyone thinks we're going upstairs to-to—mate."

"That is a far better presumption for them to have than the truth."

Deirdre said nothing more until they reached her room, then she turned to him, her hand on the door handle. "The truth being that I am in prison indeed."

"Until I can trust you, yes." He didn't look happy with the idea.

She feared she would make him less happy with their situation. How she wished their circumstances were different, for she acknowledged she did not want to hurt him, even while knowing she would.

The Ashfords celebrated the season with a house full of guests all day, then a ride to a midnight service at the church. Afterward, most of the earlier guests returned to Bishops Cove and the serving of the Christmas pudding.

Addison carried it in, set it on the sideboard, and proceeded to soak it in brandy. The sharp fumes filled the room, then the butler lit the brandy. The liquor ignited with a whoosh, and everyone cheered. Remembering the trinkets in the batter, Deirdre chewed with care, but still bit down on the silver sixpence before she realized she had it in her mouthful. With care, she removed the token and laid it on her plate.

"How shall I prosper?"

She had lost everything, including what little freedom marriage to Kieran should have given her.

The gentleman to her right patted her arm with a fleshy hand. "Your husband has prospered, my dear lady, and that is what matters."

Deirdre ground her teeth, but said nothing.

Along the table, others complained of finding none of the toys or exclaimed with delight over the ones they found. Jane Trilling received the wedding ring, and Juliet the crown that made her queen of the night.

"My first order," she announced, "is for Kieran and Deirdre to lead the dancing."

Deirdre choked on another bite of pudding she had taken to not have to speak. She couldn't dance. The headmistress at school had tried to make her, but she refused to learn. She sent Kieran a helpless look down the table, hating him being so far away so she couldn't warn him.

Kieran rose, his gaze fixed on Deirdre. She tried the slightest shake of her head. The motion caught Juliet's attention, and she began to clap and bob from foot to foot like a child half her age expecting a treat.

"Juliet," Kieran said with mock severity, "what has Mama done to make you forget she is always my first partner in the dance?"

Juliet settled, her brows knit in such exaggerated puzzlement everyone laughed.

"I only thought because you're married now . . ." Juliet trailed off in confusion.

"You're quite right, sweetheart." Phoebe rose and patted Juliet's arm. "I don't mind in the least being replaced." She cast a glance at Deirdre, who caught her cue.

"Dearest Mama Phoebe, I wouldn't dream of taking your place." She swept her gaze over her husband's tall, elegant frame. "Besides, I would rather watch my husband dance."

Her tone, her look, conveyed such a sense of intimacy the guests began to laugh. A few young men, who had imbibed too freely, made some inappropriate remarks, the least objectionable of which was "I'll wager she does make him dance."

Blushing, Deirdre forgot to allow a gentleman or footman to pull out her chair, so eager was she to get to the ballroom and tuck herself into a corner.

With a speed seemingly impossible in the crowd surging from the dining room, Kieran reached Deirdre's side and slipped his arm through hers. "You do not dance?"

She shook her head.

"We will have to remedy that."

"Maybe after—" She glanced down. "But thank you for rescuing me."

"You are my wife." He paused in the doorway to raise her hand to his lips, then led her to a chair not at all in a corner before he slipped through the crowd to collect his mother as the quartet of strings began to play. Once the dancing began, Deirdre moved to the corner where Miss Pruitt sat nodding half asleep. She offered Deirdre a smile, and Deirdre joined her to watch and seethe.

Across the room, Juliet climbed on a chair and herself affixed the sprig of mistletoe above the doorway, preventing anyone from passing beneath it without risking being kissed by the nearest member of the opposite sex. As the refreshments were in another room, a great deal of hilarity arose from the company, Deirdre joining in at the expressions of pleasure or dismay that crossed the victims' faces.

How dare these people celebrate with so much frivolity when not a score of miles away men were suffering in the cold without enough food or proper shelter? Her crew, her family, was suffering, maybe dying.

Unable to bear one more moment of the festivities, Deirdre lunged to her feet and circumvented the room to the door.

Juliet stepped into her path. "You cannot leave."

"Juliet, please." Deirdre caught sight of Kieran flanked by the Trilling ladies, heading in her direction. "Let me go. I'm tired."

"You may leave with the queen's blessing after you show Amelia that my brother does love you."

"Juliet, don't be absurd." Deirdre kept her voice low. "You know perfectly well your brother thinks this marriage was a mistake."

"But it is not. If there weren't a war—"

"But there is, and I am the enemy. Now, please—"

"Kieran." Juliet spoke over Deirdre. "Come kiss your wife."

Despite wanting to turn her back on him, Deirdre knew she could scarcely do so with a room full of guests watching, with Amelia and Jane Trilling at hand. The best she could do was step out from beneath the mistletoe.

"You do not need to ask me twice." Kieran grasped Deirdre's hands and positioned her beneath the waxy, white berries. "How could I have neglected my beautiful wife like this? A whole evening passed, and not one kiss." He touched his lips to Deirdre's.

"Pretend you like it," he said for her ears only, then kissed her with more thoroughness.

She wished she did have to pretend. He was her jailer. Kissing him should not turn her insides liquid.

Amelia's titter restored Deirdre's good sense. "At least this time he is kissing his wife under the mistletoe. A week ago in London, it was poor Liza Cantrell he was trying to—"

The crack of flesh against flesh broke the spell that kept Deirdre frozen. She jumped back from him as though she were the one who had been slapped. But it was Amelia who sported a reddening handprint on her cheek and Chloe who was rubbing her palm.

"It is the truth," Amelia shrieked. "Liza herself—"

"Stop it." Chloe raised her hand again.

Tyne caught it. "That is enough, Chloe. Retire to your room. Mrs. Trilling, please take Miss Trilling home. She has had too much wine."

Chloe stalked out of the drawing room, shooting her brother a glare as she passed. She paused long enough to touch Deirdre's hand. "Come along, Deirdre. I will go up with you."

"I will go up with her." Kieran slipped one hand beneath Deirdre's elbow.

She shook it off. "I am perfectly all right walking on my own." She paced ahead of Kieran and Chloe, head high, back straight, belly feeling prominent, though she knew it didn't show at all beneath the flowing skirt of her high-waisted gown.

Behind her, the revelries continued. Juliet and Phoebe's doing, of course. They could make people do what they wanted them to with smiles and kind words. The incident would be talked about for days, weeks, months. Perhaps no one would blame Deirdre for leaving a husband who had been unfaithful, an odd way to spare the feelings of these kind people, to direct the authorities away from thinking the Ashfords would have anything to do with the disappearance of eleven American prisoners and their dead captain's daughter.

She reached her bedchamber and tried to close the door in the others' faces. No doing with those two. They pushed right in behind her.

"Go away, Chloe," Kieran said.

Chloe settled in one of the sitting room chairs. "Liza is my friend. I want to know what this is all about."

"Ruining me," Kieran said. "Joanna Rutledge's brother wants me discredited. If that means making me look like an adulterer, he'll work on it. Liza kissed me. I did not kiss her." His voice softened. "Deirdre, will you believe me?"

"If only he knew the truth about your wife," Deirdre said, "he wouldn't need to concern himself with trying to make you look unfaithful."

"Deirdre." Kieran closed his eyes and his face twisted. "Can we not call a truce?"

"Will you cease being my jailer?"

"You know I cannot."

"You promised if I wed you I would have more freedom than I would as a noncombatant." Deirdre pressed her hands to her face, fearing the burning behind her eyes, the tightness in her chest. "You broke your promise."

"I did not know at the time about Mama and the long memories of men in high places. Deirdre." He held out his hands to her.

She turned away from the longing in his face and met Chloe's eyes.

"I think," she said, "I need to leave you two alone." She rose, embraced both of them. "I understand why Mama would do anything to see the war end." She departed, leaving Deirdre alone with her husband, the greatest barrier to her freedom.

"If the weather is dry tomorrow," Kieran said, "I will take you to the cliffs for some sea air."

Deirdre accepted the offer for what it was—an offer of a compromise, a request for understanding between them. The gesture was kind of him. To reject that kindness was unworthy of her sense of decency. She had married him of her own free will. She had shared a bed with him of her own free will.

He became such a devoted husband over the next few weeks she began to accept that keeping her a prisoner was not what he would have chosen were their circumstances different. As often as the winter weather permitted, he drove her to the cliffs for fresh air. He walked with her in the gallery on inclement days. He plucked roses from the bushes in the glass houses and left them for her in unexpected places like under her pillow or pressed between the pages instead of the slip of paper she used to mark her place in a book. He assured her warm blankets and coats had been sent to her crew through means he would not disclose.

His performance was so convincing, Amelia stopped her taunts or even flirting with him, and his parents gazed upon him with approval. For herself, Deirdre doubted the coldest of females could fail to thaw, and the part of her that had always liked him warmed toward him much of the time. If she could forget how someone, from her husband to Miss Pruitt, was always in her company, she found Kieran a pleasant, even a looked-for companion. On blustery nights, she certainly welcomed him beside her. But too often wakeful, as he slept with his head on her shoulder, she reminded herself not to care for him or his family. She could not betray those to whom she was devoted. If she cared about Kieran and his family enough to be loyal to them, she betrayed her crew. Her responsibility lay with them first as much as Kieran's lay with his family.

And she remained in a prison from which she could not gain even a minute's parole in order to free others from a prison that contained neither comfort nor kindness.

When a north wind swept down from the moor, finding every crack in the old house to send family and servants alike scurrying to the nearest hearth and reaching for another warm wrap, Deirdre thought about what her men were suffering. They might have blankets, yet she doubted they possessed so much as a brazier for warming their hands. When she ate hot soup and drank hotter tea, both of which she seemed to consume in great quantities, she wondered what kind of meals Ross and Wat and the others enjoyed. And were Blaze and Zeb surviving at sea? The few glimpses of the Channel she caught on the way to church, the only place she went outside of Bishops Cove, displayed an angry sea with ten to twenty-foot swells topped with froth like foam on the lips of a mad dog. They had to be holed up in a French harbor, waiting for finer weather.

Certain Blaze could not still be in England, Deirdre didn't fret over reaching the letterbox. But when the end of February brought a warm spell of sunshine and calm seas, she began to seek a way to slip her leash and take the path through the park in search of a message.

One day in the stillroom, listening to Phoebe's careful instruction regarding how to prepare a potion for treating a digestive complaint, Deirdre remembered Kieran's mal de mer and how she had treated it, and a horrible, wonderful idea came to her. When Phoebe turned her back to blend ginger and cinnamon, Deirdre slipped a bottle of laudanum into her pocket.

If Deirdre were his wife alone and not his prisoner as well, Kieran might have been content, even happy with domesticity. He liked having someone near with whom he could converse or play spillikins or stroll in the gallery without having to be careful how much he flirted for fear of arousing false hopes. He liked having her warmth beside him at night and not waking up alone.

He did not like the truth that she was with him against her will.

Yet she seemed to accept her fate. Occasionally Kieran found her staring out a window with such longing on her face his heart ached. More often than he liked, she chose to sit on the other side of the room from him. But she spoke of her crew only the occasions he paid a Princetown innkeeper to take clothes and blankets to the Americans inside Dartmoor. She thanked him politely, then seated herself by the drawing room fire with Chloe, Juliet, and Miss Pruitt to continue her knitting instruction.

"Nothing," he said to his father, "is a finer sight. She is more beautiful than ever these days."

"She is a lovely young lady." A grimness to his father's mouth belied the compliment in his words.

Kieran turned to him. "Is something amiss, sir? Has more talk cropped up to give us trouble over my marriage."

"Not yet."

A rustle of silk and drift of lilac scent announced Mama's entrance into the room. She took up a position beside her husband, and the two of them hemmed Kieran into a corner.

His heart skipped a beat, then began a slow, heavy march behind his ribs. "What is wrong?"

"That is what we wish to be sure of." Father kept his voice low.

"This is a difficult conversation." Mama rested her hand on Kieran's arm. "But Sally noticed and spoke to her mother, who spoke to me . . ." Her hand tightened.

Kieran's gut knotted. Sally, Deirdre's maid, spoke to her mother, the local midwife. He could make those calculations.

"She thinks something is wrong with the baby?" He managed the words in measured tones.

Mama and Father exchanged glances.

"Not wrong." Mama removed her hand from his sleeve and laced her fingers against her fichu. "She seems too bloomed to be less than six months along."

"I see." He felt sick, more betrayed than he had when finding her and Chloe returning from Dartmoor in boys' clothing, though betrayed by Deirdre or his parents he was not yet certain. "You are convinced the baby is not mine."

"She did agree to marry you with little resistance," Father said.

"She agreed to spare her crew." Kieran dragged his mind back to those days in St. George's Harbor. "She—I nearly forced marriage upon her. I . . . she . . ." He took half a step back and came up hard against the wall. "Why are you doing this to me?"

"We are thinking perhaps we should send Deirdre to Northumberland until after the baby is born." Father propped one shoulder against the doorframe in too casual a pose. "Once the baby is born—"

"After the requisite number of months," Mama interjected.

"We can bring her back here," Father concluded.

Kieran pressed his hands against the cold plaster to stop himself from balling them into fists. "And if the baby is born before the requisite number of months?"

"Adopting it out is far easier up in the north than here where more people know you," Father said.

Kieran stared at him, then Mama, wanting to push himself between them and snatch up his wife, carry her away from them and interfering midwives.

He kept himself still. "And would I accompany her?"

"If you like." Father smiled.

"And if I do not like this plan, what then?" Despite his efforts, Kieran's fingers curled into his palms. "What if I think taking Deirdre's child away from her is barbaric and cruel?"

She had agreed to abandon her children to him in some vague future, but that was before they were married, before she knew she was with child—surely she had not made a fool of him.

"If the child is a boy," Father was saying, "it will be your heir by law being born within wedlock. Do you want a cuckoo in the nest?"

"What I want," Kieran enunciated, "is to keep as much of the promise I made Deirdre as I can. I cannot see to her crew's welfare from Northumberland. The child is mine by law or by blood, does not matter. We are staying here unless you insist we leave, in which case I will find us our own home. Perhaps I should do this anyway, if this is what you think of my wife."

Mama and Father exchanged another one of those glances that said nothing to Kieran but seemed to communicate hours of dialogue between his parents. When they looked back to him, their faces held sympathy, perhaps understanding.

"Don't act in haste, Kieran." Mama embraced him. "You have a little time in which to make a decision."

"Remember we only want the best for you, son." Father held out his hand.

Kieran did not take it. "Excuse me." He turned sideways to step between them, too angry to care how rude was his action.

He looked at neither of them for the rest of the evening. He did not want their pity nor their understanding. He did not want to believe their suspicions were true. He wanted life to continue as it had been— no, better, the war over so his wife would not have to be a prisoner. He wanted harmony between them.

Yet all his wanting did not stop him from bringing up the subject with Deirdre that night.

Though calm, the weather was cold and Kieran and Deirdre lay spooned in the bed for warmth. With his arms around her, he caressed her gently, his hand coming to rest on her belly. "Too many seed cakes?"

"I am getting fat, aren't I?"

"Only here." He smoothed his fingers over the mound. "It is a bit rounder than we expected by now."

"We?" Deirdre propped herself on one elbow so she could twist around to glare at him by the light of a candle secure beneath a pierced canister. "Who is the 'we' you've been discussing my plumpness with?"

"My parents." He met her hostile glare without flinching and related the entire conversation.

She did not interrupt. She did not move, but her body grew rigid, her face taut.

"So we are staying here," he concluded.

"How magnanimous of you." She slipped from bed then. Dragging on her dressing gown, she stalked to the hearth and stooped to build up the fire. She remained crouched before the flames, her hands clasping her upper arms. Not until her shoulders jerked up toward her ears did he realize she was crying.

He joined her at the hearth and wrapped an arm around her shoulders. "Deirdre, I—"

She shook off his arm. "Leave me. Lock me in if you must, or set a guard on the balcony so I don't climb down that way, if you think I can, but get out of my sight."

"But I disagree with my parents. The Northumberland house is cold and damp and—"

She shoved her palm against his chest. "Egad. I am sick of Ashfords and their kindness to my face while plotting against me behind my back."

"It is not plotting behind your back so much as concern about the succession of the title."

"Do you have concerns about the succession of the title?"

"I am more certain than not of your innocence when we wed."

"More certain than not?" Her voice rose to a pitch sure to bring footmen running. "Will you be certain if I tell you I was untouched on our wedding night?"

"I have already said—"

"You can sit there with only a bit of doubt about me, in spite of what I say, yet you became a privateer because your parents didn't believe you over Joanna."

She may as well have kicked him in the belly. He could scarcely breathe. He could barely think clearly, let alone speak.

"Who is the traitor here?" Breath and words not failing Deirdre, she surged to her feet. "Me for wanting to see my crew go free, or your family for saying I am an Ashford now and deserving all that means, while plotting to hide me away like a madwoman and take away my baby?"

Kieran started to point out that her helping her crew go free was treachery under the law, but he held his tongue. In Deirdre's mind it was not. At the same time, she believed claiming she was part of the family while planning actions to separate her from it was a betrayal of the fragile trust they had all begun to build over the past few weeks, trust in her fidelity to their marriage bed, if not England.

For the first time, Kieran faced the possibility of having to choose between his family and his wife. Five months ago—five weeks ago—that choice would have been easy. In that moment, with Deirdre magnificently outraged in all her radiant expectancy, he saw no joy in taking up either side.

With a heavy heart, he paced to the dressing room door, but turned back for one last shot. "There is already a guard below the balcony."

Deirdre turned her back on Kieran and listened to the click of the door latch, the creak of the bed ropes in the adjoining chamber. She huddled on the chaise wrapped in the coverlet for fear she would fall asleep. The minutes ticked by, minutes filled with more tears she refused to shed for a man who had as good as called her a loose woman, a dishonest woman trying to fob off another man's by-blow on him. Imprisoning her for the sake of his family and even his country she understood. Doubting her honesty, her physical innocence, she could not, especially after what his parents had put him through.

When she thought enough time passed, she crept into his room. His even breathing proclaimed that he slept. He did not stir at the click of the door latch. After returning to her own chamber, she hid the vial of laudanum behind a row of books lined up on her desk. She didn't need to use it that night, but it might come in useful at another time.

She would not hesitate to drug her husband or anyone else so she could carry out her mission.

She no longer felt a hint of torn loyalties.

She removed a sealed letter from her escritoire, then slipped into an unused bedchamber across the hall. Shivering in the unheated room, she donned her male garb, then went to the window and pushed it open. This side boasted no balcony, but the ivy growing up the side of the house looked stronger than any rigging she had climbed. Careful not to bump her abdomen against the windowsill, she grasped hold of the ivy and swung her body out of the house twenty feet above the ground.

Chapter 22

*B*y the time she returned up the ivy and slid through the window, Deirdre was panting as though the temperature were not cold enough to freeze the puddles. She didn't feel cold; she felt warm and elated and concerned she would not be able to make this journey much longer. She needed to employ assistance, and Chloe was almost as closely guarded as Deirdre herself.

That was something to concern her in the morning. For now, she could still climb like the sailor she was, and she had a message from Blaze.

Heart racing, she slipped out of her breeches and shirt, drew on her nightgown and dressing gown, and tucked her disguise beneath the empty room's mattress, where no one would ever look for something of hers, she hoped. In her own chamber, she noticed for the first time that her feet were freezing, and built up her fire. After a peek to ensure Kieran still slept, she opened Blaze's message, covered her mouth to stifle a gurgle of laughter over the audacity of his plan, then burned the missive on the flames. Once the fire had consumed every fragment and her hands and feet resumed a normal temperature, she slid back into bed and lay awake until nearly dawn, her heart aching over the idea that she had almost allowed herself to believe she could be happy at Bishops Cove once her crew was free. Now her contentment would all be for show. The one good thing coming of the night's discussion with Kieran was that she was going to feel blameless about betraying him and his family when she got her crew free. Her only guilt lay in the idea of taking his child away from him.

She pressed her hands to her belly, feeling the life stirring within, and knew she could not leave this baby behind no matter what. It was hers, the only family of her blood she knew now that her father was gone.

For the first time, she understood at least part of Phoebe's claim that little in life was better than presenting one's husband with a child. If she could not be happy about presenting her husband with a child, she was happy in that moment to be a woman and be able to create new life.

With that bit of comfort and contentment, she was able to pretend all was well, lull them all into thinking she was settled and forgetting about her crew.

She began with not bringing up their conversation of the night before. Neither did Kieran mention it, nor did anyone speak of the barrier now lying between Deirdre and the family. He remained attentive when she was alone with him, but when she was with his mother and sisters, Deirdre couldn't stop herself from thinking every glance was speculative, questioning. She wanted to feel resentful. Instead, a deep hurt carved its way to her heart. For a while, she had believed they cared about her, that they accepted her.

Kieran began to spend more and more time in the study with his father.

"At last Garrett is letting Kieran learn how to run the estates," Phoebe said one day, her face aglow. "Garrett is talking about giving you Bishops Down in Hampshire for a wedding present. Kieran has wanted to run it for years, but Garrett thought him too irresponsible. And he was. I have never laid a hand on my children in anger, but I tell you, Deirdre, I could have taken a switch to him for going off as a privateer. But now look at things." She gestured to Kieran and Tyne deep in conversation at the far end of the salon. "They don't argue more than once a day now instead of once an hour. All because he had to bring you home."

"Is that why you accept me?" Deirdre asked. "I serve a purpose?"

That stopped Juliet in the midst of her chatter with Chloe.

"We never turn away strangers," Juliet said. "And you are married to Kieran, and you are—well, um . . ." She glanced down, her cheeks pink behind her tumbled black hair. "I am having a party for my birthday next week. Will you be able to attend? Because if you cannot, I need to invite another female. I am so fortunate that Amelia's mama sent her off to an aunt—"

"Juliet," Chloe cut in, "let Deirdre answer your question before you run on to something else." She met and held Deirdre's gaze. "We will be all but obligated to invite Liza Cantrell, now that she is back home, if you do not feel well enough to come down."

Deirdre felt well enough. She had never felt better than she had in the past week.

Feeling the now familiar fluttering in her belly, Deirdre laid her hands there and smiled. "I don't think any gown except for a pannier from thirty years ago will cover this." She smiled, content, mind racing.

"But Liza has become as awful as Amelia," Chloe protested. "Surely with a fringed shawl . . ."

"But Kieran adores Deirdre," Juliet said. "He would never do anything wrong. And I, for one, think a nephew or niece coming is too exciting to hide, whatever polite society thinks. The tenants' wives go about sticking out."

Phoebe sighed. "Where did I go wrong with raising you to be a lady?"

"It was not you, Mama." Juliet jumped up and kissed Phoebe's cheek. "It is having a rakehell for a brother. Or perhaps you are too permissive. So, Deirdre, you will please come to my party."

Deirdre smiled. "I will see if I grow any more between now and then."

"Do not," Juliet commanded, resuming her embroidery.

"Please," she thought Phoebe murmured.

Annoyed, Deirdre stood. "I'm going for a walk in the gallery."

"I will join you." Chloe dropped her needlework onto her chair and rose. "Juliet, Mama?"

They both shivered. "That drafty old place." Juliet hugged her arms. "It is cold enough by the fire with that wind blowing."

"Make sure you take a shawl, Deirdre," Phoebe said.

Deirdre took no shawl. She was never cold these days. Arm in arm, she and Chloe made a complete circuit and a half of the gallery before either of them said a word. Then Chloe stopped at the farthest end from the corridor leading back to the commonly used rooms of the house.

"I have a letter from Ross," Chloe announced.

Deirdre stared at her. "You have a letter? How?"

"Sally's eldest brother. He works for Papa's wine merchant. When he brought a delivery the other day, I gave him a half crown and a commission."

"Chloe, that was dangerous. I mean, for me to do something for my crew is one thing. It's expected. But to endanger your family . . ." Deirdre shook her head. "You shouldn't have risked it."

Chloe wrinkled her nose. "I do not for a minute think that I am endangering my family with a little correspondence with a man who does not even know my name."

Deirdre hoped she was right.

"What did you say? Did he say?"

"I gushed like Juliet." Chloe grinned. "He is, you see, her hero out of a romance novel."

"Ross?" That made Deirdre laugh. "He's a foul-mouthed sailor."

Chloe sobered. "That is not how I see him. He is angry, yes, and he has every reason to be. But he is polite in his language with me—mostly. He is . . . is . . ."

Deirdre leaned against the stone wall, wanting to bang her head against the unyielding surface. "Don't tell me, Chloe. I don't want to know that you have a *tendre* for Ross."

Chloe blushed and turned away. "I do not know him. We have exchanged some correspondences is all."

Deirdre sighed. "So what did these messages contain?"

"I told him about getting caught and being made prisoners."

"That should make him love Kieran more than he already does."

"He did say he was a—well, he did cross it out, but I could still read it. But what is important, Deirdre, is that they are starving in there. Wat's cough never gets better, and Ross got put in a completely dark place for two weeks because he threw a paving stone at a guard who was punching a Frenchman for—well, he did not tell me what the Frenchman was doing."

Ross in the dark was unacceptable. He loved wind and light and open space as much as she did.

Deirdre rubbed her eyes. "I got a message from Blaze."

Now Chloe was the one to be astounded. "How?"

Deirdre recommenced her stroll. "I climbed down the ivy outside the room across from mine."

"What if you had fallen?"

"I have never fallen in my life."

"You could have endangered yourself or the baby."

Deirdre shrugged. "Maybe everyone would be just as happy for that. Kieran could be rid of me and the baby no one thinks is his anyway."

"Did he tell you about that?" Chloe's slippers slapped against the flagstone floor. "I thought something was wrong between you two. Now I am going to kill him. He is a dolt."

"I'd rather know the truth of what he thinks of me. It makes everything easier."

"How's that?"

"Blaze had a plan, but I now have a better one. And I will use my advancing condition to my advantage."

"What will you do now that Papa has patrols on every terrace?"

With the explanation that their proximity to the coast gave him concern for the safety of his household now that England fought two wars, Tyne had set guards patrolling the terraces and guarded the gates at night. During the day, though Chloe and Deirdre could roam the garden and parkland, someone followed them, and should they give that person the slip, guards remained at the gates. Setting foot through one of those portals without an escort was impossible. But a stone wall was nothing for Deirdre to scale even with her expanded middle.

"I will make my excuses and forgo the pleasures of Juliet's party."

"What will you do while we are celebrating?" Chloe whispered.

"Wait and see."

Kieran realized he never should have doubted her, not for an instant, not even with the ladies, including Mama, murmuring about how they had been able to go about in public with no one the wiser of their condition well into the fourth and even the fifth month. Deirdre had been starting to show at three months. Three months after their wedding, which seemed to be the difficulty. Her lack of warmth toward him now made him wish he had left well enough alone and believed her.

She was right, he had treated her as badly as his parents treated him over Joanna. Perhaps part of his heart feared she was like Joanna, trying to foist another man's brat off on him. But Deirdre's spirit held more loyalty than had Joanna's.

A pity she had turned that loyalty from him.

"Your fault," he told his reflection in his shaving mirror.

She had been warming to him, looking content and even happy. His parents wanted the best for the family, as always. The family came first, as always.

Deirdre was used to coming first. Her crew had put her first so plainly they had sacrificed their freedom for her sake there on Bermuda. No wonder she cared more about them than the Ashfords.

Kieran jabbed his cravat pin in so hard he pricked his skin. While ensuring no blood would mar the pristine whiteness of shirt and cravat, he heard Sally in Deirdre's room. Presuming his wife was getting herself ready and would go down shortly, he made his own way to the drawing room.

But she did not appear in a few minutes or several. Guests spoke to him, then glanced past him toward the door, well aware his mate was missing. With the hands of the clock pointed at ten minutes to eight of the clock, Addison was about to announce dinner.

Mama glided up to him and touched his arm to draw his attention. "Kieran, go up and fetch Deirdre. I will tell Addison to have Cook hold dinner for another five minutes."

Kieran nodded and slipped from the drawing room of guests sipping orgeat and sherry. Once the door closed behind him, he took the steps two at a time, his evening pumps slipping on the stair runner.

Surely she would not have gotten up to something in so short a time and with a house full of guests.

He reached the Duchess Suite and shoved open the door without knocking. Deirdre sat at the dressing table. Her hair looked arranged for the evening, twisted and tucked into place with the pearl and silver combs he had given her, but she wore a dressing gown, and did not glance his way.

"Deirdre?" He closed the door. "Are you unwell?"

She shook her head. Tendrils of red hair caught the candlelight like strands of fire. "I am well. But I'm not going down."

"The table arrangements . . . Mama told me to fetch you."

Deirdre told him in no uncertain terms what she thought of the table arrangements. "I am sure you will enjoy yourself with Miss Jane and Liza."

"I do not want to enjoy myself with them or any other females." He paced across the room and stood behind her, trying to read her expression in the mirror. "I want my wife's company."

"No, Kieran, you do not want me to embarrass you in front of your guests." She stood up and let her dressing gown slip to the floor. "Look at me."

She wore only a chemise. The soft, white fabric clung to her, revealing every curve—breasts far larger than when he met her and a taut, round belly.

"I'm too big," Deirdre said, and started to cry. "Even Sally says that her mother never looked this big this far along, and all her children have been plump and happy when they were born. I know it's yours, but how can I convince you now?"

"I should believe you because you say so." He produced his own handkerchief and slipped it into her hands, then wrapped his arms around her. Guilt nearly strangled him. "I never should have doubted you for a moment."

She wiped at her eyes. "But you do doubt me, if you're honest."

"I did not until . . . the talk . . . I do not know about these female things. Joanna was barely showing but had to be five months along when she fainted and I loosened her stays so she could—Deirdre, stop."

Mention of Joanna made Deirdre cry harder. "I am not Joanna."

"I know." He retrieved her dressing gown and wrapped it around her, then held it in place with his hands on her belly.

She curled her hands around his wrists. "Right now I wish this was your neck I had my hands around."

"I know." He stroked her through the silk of her chemise.

The past six weeks of celibacy, sleeping in his own room at her request, began to take their toll.

He groaned. "I wish I could trust you not to do something stupid behind my back. Right now—"

She pushed him away with an elbow to his belly. "You have guests waiting."

"So do you. Without you, we are a female short, and I cannot sit out dinner without offending my sister and the Cantrells."

"Invite Miss Pruitt down. She may as well be bored in company than in her rooms."

"We would rather have you. You are far more enjoyable to grace our presence."

"A female who looks as I do right now is not fit for that company."

"I do not know any female I find more beautiful."

"I understand how you earned your reputation with females if you have always talked like that to my sex." She slipped away from him and shoved her arms into the sleeves of her dressing gown. "Go down and charm the ladies. Juliet will be crushed if you aren't there. She doesn't want me there looking like I swallowed last year's jack-o'-lantern. And tell your mama—discreetly of course—that Madame Blanchette did not make the extra seams quite deep enough on my gown."

Kieran started to protest, but her clock said five minutes past eight of the clock, and Mama would likely send up Father or Chloe if he did not return soon. Besides, Deirdre looked honestly weary as she sank onto the chaise. Dark circles shadowed her eyes, and the corners of her mouth drooped.

"As much as I wish to stay and persuade you to let me back into your bed, I will go." He settled for a chaste kiss on her lips. "I will be back as early as I can."

"I will be in bed."

Hoping she was softening toward him and that was an invitation, he cast her a warm smile and departed.

Mama met him halfway up the stairs. "Is something amiss?"

He shook his head. "She is feeling embarrassed about her condition."

"Of course. I will send up for Miss Pruitt." She drew her brows together. "I should be preparing to take the girls to London, but I dislike leaving Deirdre in these last few months. She could deliver as soon as—"

"The end of June at the soonest." He spoke with finality.

She patted his arm. "Of course, my dear. Let's go down to the company."

He went down. He played the gallant to the ladies present, and all the while he wanted to end the separation from his wife.

He wasn't going to be separated from her that night. He knew it the moment he walked into the bedchamber and saw her in bed curled on her side, her hair spread out on the pillow, not braided. Quickly, he undressed and crawled in beside her.

Her skin was freezing.

"I had to get up." She sounded sleepy. "You know how things are."

"Yes, but—" Suspicion raised its ugly head. "The room is warm."

She inched away from him. "Of course it is." Her tone was as cold as her skin. "I built up the fire before getting back into bed." She nestled against him. "Warm me."

He warmed them both, but for all the pleasure he found in being with her, he could not set aside the burden of knowing something was missing between them.

Deirdre grew to look so burdened in body and spirit the next few weeks he feared the worst. When he tried to talk to her about why she seemed so sad, she said she wished the war would end and that she could at least walk along the sea, if not sail upon it.

Neither seemed likely. The weather was foul and the war showed no signs of ending soon. America had yet to win a decisive land battle, and she had no navy to speak of, yet she had defeated two British naval vessels, and her privateers were decimating Britain's merchant shipping.

Needing something to do, he asked his father if he could take over the running of Hampshire for the spring lambing and planting rather than waiting until autumn after harvest.

"Besides," he concluded, remembering Deirdre's ice-cold skin the night of Juliet's birthday, "she will not need to be such a prisoner that far from Dartmoor. And with the girls in London, we will all be safe from any machinations those two can conjure."

"The girls are not going to London," Tyne announced. "Chloe refuses to go, and Phoebe will not take Juliet without Chloe there to help watch over her."

"Can you not make Chloe go, sir?"

Tyne raised his eyebrows.

Kieran laughed. "No, I can understand that that would not be a wise idea."

"Nor, I think," Tyne said, "would taking Deirdre from here be wise. Her condition seems to be her best jailer at present, and Phoebe wants the midwife here to attend her. She does not know anyone reliable in Hampshire."

"Of course." He had to leave the female details in his mother's hands. "But, sir, I need something to occupy my time. She seems to barely abide the sight of me, let alone want me near her."

The night of Juliet's birthday had been the last time she welcomed him for more than another body in her bed to stave off the winter chill. Tyne's smile was grim. "Just wait until she enters her confinement. Even your mother said some rude things about me then."

Kieran grimaced. "She does not seem to like me overmuch at the moment as it is. How can matters get worse?"

∽✑

As spring touched the countryside with daffodils and crocuses blooming in Mama's garden, Deirdre told Kieran to return to his own bed. "I'm too uncomfortable at night to have someone else about. If I want to sit up, I want to do it without disturbing you."

"You may disturb me all you like."

"Please, Kieran, I don't want you seeing me in my nightgown any longer. I look ghastly."

"I think you look rather beautiful. So . . . well, um—"

"Fertile?" She frowned at her middle. "I feel like a Dutch round ship. Now leave me in peace."

He left her, but whether or not she had peace, he did not know. He did know that he experienced anything but comfort alone in his bed, waking to every creak of a floorboard or draft of air across his face. He expected to stumble into her chamber in the middle of the night and find her gone, though he couldn't imagine how she would manage to leave. Footmen guarded each end of their corridor at night, and groundskeepers patrolled the outside of the house. Yet more than once, he did rise and look in on her. Each time, she at least pretended to sleep, half sitting up against a mound of pillows.

You are a fool, Ashford.

But he could not help himself.

So he welcomed the urgent message his father received in the first week of April requesting that someone post off to Bishops Down in Hampshire, at once.

"Seems that someone is stealing the lambs," Father reported over breakfast.

"That is horrid," Juliet cried. "Why would someone steal lambs?"

"Fricassee," Chloe murmured.

Juliet glared at her. "You are the horrid one. Papa, what shall you do?"

"Go, of course. Kieran?"

Kieran rose. "I will come, too. You can take this opportunity to introduce me to the estate manager."

"But who will be our jailers?" Chloe asked with too much sweetness.

Kieran smiled. "Deirdre is, at present, providing her own jailer. And as for you"—he met and held her gaze—"you will do nothing to endanger this family, will you?"

Chloe did not so much as blink. "I never have."

"That is debatable," Father said.

"You can trust me not to do anything stupid," Chloe said.

"If she thinks the prison is so terrible," Juliet added, "she would never want one of us to end up there."

"Wise child." Kieran rumpled Juliet's hair, kissed his mother on the cheek, and ran upstairs to bid Deirdre to take care of herself.

The morning after Tyne and Kieran departed for Hampshire, Deirdre found a use for the laudanum. She dosed her morning chocolate, then offered it to Sally, who was eager to take the special treat. On the ground floor, Chloe carried mugs of hot, sweet tea and more laudanum to men patrolling the grounds between terrace and parkland. It worked better than had the rum Deirdre gave the men aboard the *Maid* in St. George's Harbor. Later, if Tyne was inclined to dismiss the men for sleeping at their posts, Deirdre would confess what she had done to lay them blameless. Worse confinement for her wouldn't matter after today until the fourth day of June, and she had plenty of time to devise another form of escape by then.

Once the guards slept, Chloe and Deidre wended their way through the parkland with its budding trees providing plenty of shelter, and reached the wall. Carrying a rope Chloe had found in the attic, Deirdre clambered up the stones, with the aid of low-hanging branches, and lowered herself panting and a little shaken onto the turf beyond the boundary.

Chloe, not as adept with finding hand- and toeholds, used rope and branches and tumbled to the ground beside Deirdre. "I am not as agile as I thought I was."

"I'm not as agile as I used to be." Deirdre pressed her hands to her middle, where the Ashford heir or heiress seemed to be practicing tumbling off walls. "This will have to be the last time."

"If we're caught, Papa will build a tower to lock us in and toss away the key." Chloe held a hand up to shade her eyes. "And here is our transport so we won't be caught right away."

She seemed to possess an endless stream of loyal tenants eager to do her bidding with or without the largess of her pin money. The amount of time she spent watching children so tired mothers could rest, or left discreet packages of food on doorsteps of those struggling to fill their bellies, was more likely the reason. Now one of those devotees tooled up to them in a two-wheeled cart, a sad-looking mule in the harness.

"He's old," the farm lad said, "but he'll get where you want to go and back without complaint."

He helped Deirdre into the cart and handed the reins to Chloe, and they were off. At the abandoned cottage, they stopped to don hats and veils to give themselves the vague appearance of widows.

"If they truly wanted to imprison us," Chloe said, "they should have kept us apart."

"Maybe Tyne thinks we are safer getting up to mischief together."

They laughed, but all the way to the gorge, they kept looking over their shoulders.

"If only we could do this at night." Deirdre began to survey her surroundings with attention to the details. "Getting out of the house was sadly easy the night of Juliet's party."

With extra servants in the house due to guests having brought their own maids, pretending to be one of them on an errand for her mistress had made slipping away from the doorkeepers go off without a hitch.

"Celebrations are the key. People pay less attention during a party." Deirdre noted a boulder perched above the track and called a halt. "I'm going to ink an X on this one, on the back, where no one will see it from the track."

"What is it for?" Chloe asked.

"I'll tell you when the time comes." Deirdre started to clamber from the cart.

Chloe took the ink bottle from her. "Let me. You may think you are invincible, but I have known ladies who have stumbled and gone into labor early."

"That would prove everyone's suspicions right, wouldn't it." Deirdre couldn't keep the bitterness from her voice.

Chloe said nothing, but she stomped up the steep side of the gorge and slipped behind the boulder. Once she was back in the cart, she huffed out her breath and flipped back her veil to frown at Deirdre. "Kieran is a beast. How could he doubt you just because Joanna tried to pass some other man's by-blow off on him?"

"So you believe him even though the emissary hasn't returned from Greece yet?"

"I believe him." Chloe's voice grew distant as she gazed at the rising walls of the prison ahead. "Do you?"

Deirdre rested her hand over the acrobatics going on inside her. "Yes."

"Then why does he not trust you?"

"I am the enemy."

They reached the prison, and Chloe said nothing more. Deirdre hauled herself out of the cart and wrapped herself more fully in the quilted cloak that camouflaged her condition. Ross needed to know the truth, since using it was part of her plan, but she feared his reaction.

They had to find him in the market crowd. He stood alone holding a carved box as though intending to sell it, as prisoners were allowed to do. Somehow, he had found the means by which to shave and look fairly clean, though his clothes were patched and dingy, and his hair hung loose over his shoulders, longer than Kieran's, whipping about in the wind.

He looked barbaric and dangerous, and Chloe caught her breath.

"He will make a formidable enemy," she murmured.

"He had made a formidable friend." Deirdre held back, allowing Chloe to approach him.

She didn't know what kind of a friend he was now.

Chloe glided toward him with her mother's grace combined with the regalness of her height. Deirdre watched Ross watching her, caught the gleam of appreciation in his eyes. That was a poor idea, the two of them finding attraction to one another.

"That is fine workmanship, man." Chloe spoke with hauteur. "Do you intend to sell it?"

"Even our barracks are finer than standing here in the wind," Ross returned. "One guinea."

"Heavens. That is robbery." Chloe glanced back at Deirdre. "Is it not utter thievery to ask that price for a little trinket like this?"

Deirdre shrugged, then grabbed for the edge of her cloak. "He is a charity case, is he not? Give him two guineas."

She mimicked Chloe's accent, but Ross started, stared at her, took a step back.

He didn't say her name aloud, but formed it with his lips. "What's happened to you? You look—" Understanding dawned, and he paled. "You won't come with us." He didn't look angry; he looked bereft.

Deirdre shook her head. "I can't. I can't leave my baby behind."

She would not—could not—think about the possibility that Ashford power and money might separate her from her child. That notion hurt so much she couldn't think at a time when she needed to think hardest of all.

"But how . . . ? When . . . ?" Ross appeared dazed. "D—you can't help us like . . . you are."

Deirdre wept behind her veil. "I can." She glanced around, seeking anyone who might be listening. "Be ready on the king's birthday. That will provide one distraction with the revelries in Princetown." She patted her belly. "I will provide the other."

Now Chloe and Ross both stared at her.

"When is the king's birthday?" was all Ross said.

"June fourth," Deirdre said. "Be ready."

"But the baby," Chloe whispered as a guard headed in their direction.

"I will only be starting my ninth month then," Deirdre answered. "We have plenty of time."

Chapter 23

eirdre half reclined in a ground-floor sitting room and squinted at the tiny garment she was attempting to sew. She would allow Phoebe to execute the embroidery, but Deirdre wanted to stitch her baby's christening gown herself. Why, she didn't know. Maybe sheer boredom drove her to pick up needle and thread and commence setting miniscule stitches along the seam of fine, white cambric. She could do little else.

At Phoebe's suggestion, Deirdre had taken over this ground-floor room, normally used as a lady's retiring room during large parties, as her bedchamber so that she could still join the family for meals without having to negotiate the steep and somewhat treacherous steps. With French windows leading onto a terrace and the weather growing finer by the week, Deirdre could enjoy plenty of fresh air and take a short, daily walk in the garden.

No one guarded her closely any longer, and with the easing of external restrictions came a thawing of hostilities between her and Kieran. Either that or boredom drove her to accept his company in addition to that of the Ashford ladies and Miss Pruitt. Her own body seemed to be her prison warden, her middle growing ever larger and larger until she wished that she were in her ninth month instead of her eighth.

"I feel like I'm carrying half the *Maid*'s cargo in my belly," she announced one afternoon in late May.

Kieran, who sat on the floor beside her sofa, rested his head against the mound. "You rather look like it, too."

She yanked on a strand of his hair. "Let us hope it is a big, healthy boy with black hair as pretty as yours."

"I would rather it be a girl with red hair." He touched her cheek. "She will be beautiful if she is only half so pretty as you."

Deirdre turned her face away. She knew why he wanted a girl.

"Have you taken a good look at Chloe lately?" she asked.

"I try not to."

"Why not?"

"She gives my parents grief, refusing to go to London for a Season. Does she want to be an ape leader?"

"She's only twenty. I'm twenty-four."

Kieran shot upright and stared at her. "When did you have a birthday?"

"When you were in Hampshire."

"Why did you not tell me?" He looked distressed.

"You all are making enough fuss over me. Look at this room. It took four footmen to bring down and reassemble my bed in here. And you're sleeping on the sofa, which cannot be comfortable for a man your size, and it's all unnecessary."

And yet the gesture moved her to remember how much she had grown to respect him on the *Maid*, and to like his companionship before he decisively sided with his family over her honesty. But that was a subject they tacitly decided not to discuss.

"Now, about Chloe," she began.

Horses' hooves drummed on the drive, slowing as they neared the house.

"Close the door," Deirdre said. "I don't want anyone to see me."

"I will see who it is." Kieran rose with languid grace and paced to the door. He stepped into the hall and closed the portal behind him.

Through the panels, Deirdre heard the knocker, then Addison answering, and Kieran saying he would see the man back to Tyne's study. He sounded strained. She wanted to follow and discover what news had arrived. But she couldn't move. She was tired and sad and most of all anxious about her plans for the following week.

Chloe didn't look well. She seemed thinner, and shadows rimmed her eyes. Worst of all, she scarcely visited Deirdre.

Deirdre feared that Chloe was having second thoughts about helping with the escape.

As though her thoughts conjured her, Chloe burst through one of the open French windows and slammed it behind her. "It is the emissary from Greece."

"Oh, that." Deirdre shrugged and took three more stitches. "Your parents should have believed him without proof. Will you ring the bell? I'd like some lemonade."

"Lemonade?" Chloe began pacing up and down the room. "You want lemonade when your future will be decided on what is said today?"

Deirdre set down her sewing. "Chloe, what does this man's answer have to do with my future one way or the other?"

"Kieran never told you?" Chloe stopped and pounded on a bedpost. "That man. After Kieran helped clear things up in Hampshire so well—and a fine mess your friend created there—Papa said he would give Kieran Bishops Down outright if Kieran has been telling him the truth about Joanna."

"And he chooses to be loyal to him over me." Deirdre closed her eyes. She was too tired to cry over that any more. "But I would like to go to Hampshire once my men are safe. And speaking of that . . ." She fixed Chloe with a hard stare. "Have you changed your mind?"

"No." Chloe's whole body seemed to speak the denial. "Those men cannot stay there any longer. Wat is so ill the others may have to carry him, and Ross had to spend—" She paled.

Deirdre arched her brows. "Yes? What are all these details about which I know nothing?"

Chloe rubbed her fingers over her lips as though trying to scrub away her words.

"Chloe?"

Chloe perched on the edge of the bed. "I have gone over the wall like you showed me and been back. Twice. I wore a different disguise each time, but Ross always knew me, and we have exchanged some letters . . ." She hung her head. "I am a fool, but I think I am in love with him, and I will likely never see him again."

"Oh, Chloe." Deirdre struggled to her feet and waddled across the room to slip one arm around Chloe's shoulders. "Ross won't ever love an Englishwoman. He despises the English, probably more so now."

"But he says . . . things." Chloe gulped and sniffled. "The war cannot last much longer, and after . . . I'm half American."

When she saw Ross again, Deirdre thought, she would likely scratch his eyes out.

"Chloe." She stroked the younger woman's lovely Ashford hair. "I'm afraid that Ross is leading you on to believe he cares for you so that you will help him escape. He has been my friend for years, but he isn't nice now. Prison has done that to him, and the war will do worse, I'm afraid."

"I am, too." Chloe wiped her eyes. "But it does not matter what he thinks of me. I still want to help him and the others."

"Don't let yourself care, Chloe. Do not trust the enemy, for you are his enemy, too."

"My parents love one another, and you and Kieran seem to be getting on well."

"Your parents are special. Kieran and I . . ."

She didn't know how to explain that the walls of Dartmoor still rose between them, every tidbit of war news, whether good for America or for England, laid another stone on the barricade and left her heart feeling as bleak as the *cacheau* the guards used as punishment. Sometimes, she caught shadows in Kieran's eyes suggesting he felt the same bleakness.

None of that showed now, as he strolled back into the sitting room. His eyes glowed with golden light and his smile was broad.

"Good news?" Chloe leaped to her feet.

He smiled. "The first of September," Kieran said. "I did not meet her until the first of March. And no one considered that this child could be two months early."

"Why, that lying slut," Chloe cried.

Kieran arched his brows. "Language, dear sister. Do not let Mama hear you talk like that."

"But it is true. She is no better than Haymarket wares."

Was that what the Ashfords called her behind her back?

Deirdre pressed her hands to her hot cheeks, feeling like weeping for the first time in months. "At least," she murmured with a twist of her upper lip, "this child can't be two months early either."

Smiles slipped from Chloe and Kieran's faces. From the doorway, Tyne and Phoebe halted, faces turning grim.

Deirdre set her gaze on Kieran, held his eyes. "I always believed you were telling the truth."

"I know." He swallowed and broke their eye contact. "Thank you."

Deirdre didn't know what response she expected, but a thanks and acknowledgment of her belief in his sincerity was not what she wanted. In that moment, she admitted she wanted something more from him than this politeness, yet if he became her friend, if he cared about her, she might feel guilty about what she was planning to do.

"I am so glad it was not you." Chloe filled the silence with chatter worthy of Juliet. "Of course, that all led to you bringing us Deirdre, who is ten times better than Joanna. Will you notify Rutledge, Papa?"

Tyne left the doorway, Phoebe beside him. "I already have sent a message to my solicitor in London. He will notify Rutledge of the consequences of continuing his accusations against Kieran. How are you faring, Deirdre?"

So they were to pretend nothing untoward had happened between her and Kieran. She knew how to play that game after seven months in a nobleman's household.

"Well, sir." Deirdre trundled over to the sofa and sank onto the cushions. "Phoebe, see my stitching? It is improving, is it not?"

Phoebe settled beside her. "It is coming along fine indeed. Are you feeling more comfortable with a needle?"

"Yes, except I can't seem to focus for long."

Phoebe patted her arm. "That will pass. You are well? No pain? No other discomforts?"

"No, ma'am." Deidre tried stitching some more. "I don't even feel worn to a thread all the time anymore."

She seemed to have more and more energy. Maybe that was due to Kieran looking happier. The whole family seemed in lighter spirits. No social cloud hung over the son and heir—except for his American wife, but she was mostly out of sight of anyone and thus seemed to be out of mind, which worked well for her.

So did the family's embrace of approaching summer, finer weather, and numerous fetes and parties on the horizon. Juliet, especially, wearing her hair up, reveled in an invitation to her first grown-up party to celebrate the king's birthday despite the fact that the man was completely mad. Chloe received an invitation, too, but told Juliet she should go on her own to this first event as a young lady stepping onto the marriage mart.

Deirdre herself felt lighter in her spirit. Maybe she felt happier because she was about to end months of guilt and remove one barrier between her and Kieran. He would suspect that she helped in the escape, but she would do her best to ensure that he knew nothing.

Once her crew was gone, he would have no more reason to be her jailer, and when her baby was born at the end of nine months since they married, he, like Tyne over doubting Kieran, could feel like a worm and lavish her with husbandly devotion—or at the least, build some sort of camaraderie between them as they had shared aboard the *Maid*. Until then, she needed him to be gone on June 4.

In the end, that seemed all too easy. She simply told him that he should accompany Juliet to the party in Plymouth.

"I know that Tyne and Phoebe are going, too, but she may like a handsome male escort, even her brother."

"But what about you?" He looked dubious. "If your time—"

Deirdre balled her hands into fists and made herself speak slowly. "Is not until the end of June or possibly the beginning of July. If you don't believe me, then-then—" Something inside her snapped. "Go find another reason to kiss Liza Cantrell."

"Deirdre—" Shock paled his skin.

She turned away from him. "If the child comes too early, you can accuse me of something, I am sure, and have Parliament dissolve the marriage sooner than later. What does it matter if I am socially ruined in this blighted country?"

"Let us not act in haste. Once the war is over, things could be different." He rubbed the small of her back, making her nearly purr in spite of herself. "Perhaps?"

His tone held a longing she understood, a desire for peace if nothing else.

"Go to the party with Juliet," she managed. "Chloe is capable of sending for the midwife if something occurs, and she'll send for you, too."

"All right." Reluctantly, he moved away from her. "I dislike being that far away."

She would be farther.

"You won't be allowed in here if my time does come that night anyway."

Phoebe was adamant about that. She didn't want Chloe or Juliet around either, but Deirdre expected that Chloe would ignore that edict. She had helped deliver babies before, after all.

Now she only needed to pray for fine weather.

She did, and the day dawned bright and clear. She woke with the birds and felt so restless she rose and began to pace about the chamber. Bored with that, she went onto the terrace to smell the roses just beginning to bloom. By that time a week from now, her crew would be smelling roses in France. She hoped they didn't care much about the days they would have to hide in the caves, but they dared not move them into boats the same night they vanished.

She plucked a pink rosebud from the nearest bush and carried it back into the house. With Juliet excited about going to her first party with her hair up and allowed to dance with any gentleman to whom she was presented instead of only a select few, the household would focus on her. They would leave at noon and stay the night in Plymouth.

Chloe and Deirdre would leave at thirty minutes after twelve of the clock, hidden in the back of the home farm delivery wagon, and, unless disaster struck, be home by midnight.

Disaster would not strike. Deirdre felt too well to have anything go wrong.

With her eyes sparkling like sunlight on water, Chloe looked excited, too, though fatigued. Deirdre wondered if she had slept. They ate breakfast and carried on normal conversation, an easy feat with Juliet chattering nonstop.

Deirdre thought nothing of the twinge of pain that rippled through her belly. She had had them before. Phoebe assured her that they were normal and were nothing to concern her. Even the second and third ones that struck moments after the family left the house meant nothing to her. She wasn't due to go into her confinement yet. At least three more weeks, possibly more.

She said nothing to Chloe, who arrived promptly at thirty minutes after twelve of the clock dressed in an afternoon gown of pink sprig muslin and wearing a fetching hat trimmed in roses.

"Ready for a walk?" Chloe asked for the benefit of the servants. "It is warm today. Let us walk beneath the trees."

"Just for a moment," Deirdre said. "I need a great deal of rest." She smiled at Addison in the doorway. "Please make certain no one disturbs me."

He bowed. "Yes, my lady."

Chloe and Deirdre left the house by way of the French windows. Instead of leaving them open, they closed the curtains and the windows, then headed through the trees.

"One chore behind us," Chloe said. "Am I walking too quickly?"

"No." But she was panting.

She dared not tell Chloe that she had just experienced a cramping pain that robbed her of breath.

"We can go faster."

Nothing was wrong. This was unaccustomed exercise was all. They only had a few more yards to go. But they felt like miles. No more pain struck her, yet the burden of her middle weighed her down beneath the lavender sacque gown of half mourning that was all she could wear. Gasping, she stepped from the trees and onto the delivery lane, where the wagon waited out of sight of the house and rear gate. The lads helped them to climb into the bed, then covered them with blankets and a dusting of straw, then set baskets between them and the back. The wagon set off down the road. Chloe clutched Deirdre's hand. A pain seized at her belly, and her body jerked.

"What is it?" Chloe grabbed Deirdre's arm. "Are you in pain?"

Deirdre shook her head. She felt all right now. "False. Your mother told me to be careful."

"You are certain?"

Deirdre nodded to save breath. "Whatever you all choose to believe, it is too soon. Let's hurry this along."

The wagon stopped on the far side of a sheep meadow, where the cart and mule awaited their needs. Feeling quite all right now, Deirdre left the wagon with alacrity and stepped into the cart.

"Hurry," she repeated her earlier command.

Chloe hurried the mule along as fast as he would go. She had cast off her gown to reveal boy's attire. Deirdre wore a veiled hat, though doubted she would fool anyone for long. But they saw no one on a summer Sunday afternoon. Up, up, up onto the moor the cart climbed. Deirdre sat motionless, bracing herself against any more pains. She had to hide them from Chloe. She would turn back if she knew. Besides, they might stop on their own.

When the next pain doubled her over at the mouth of the gorge, then the next left her sick and perspiring mere yards from the prison gate, she could no longer deny the truth.

Kieran wished that he had chosen to ride into Plymouth. He felt too restless to sit still in the carriage with his parents and sister, listening to Juliet chatter with the excitement over the upcoming party. He did not want to go to that gathering either, but Deirdre did not seem to want him around much anymore, and he thought perhaps a day without him as a constant reminder that he was her jailer as well as her husband would make her miss him.

He missed her. He knew it was more than his physical need for her, unfulfilled for months now. It was the belief that she had begun to care for him. Somewhere, that had died.

Somewhere? He knew exactly where.

He closed his eyes and leaned into the corner of the squabs, telling himself that the pain of his own making would recede. Somehow, he would find a way to win her regard, perhaps even her heart, convince her that he adored her regardless of the past.

But whose past? His or hers? His seemed to mean nothing to her. Until today, she never made mean quips about the ladies who seemed to think Deirdre was a temporary inconvenience, not the wife he had married for life.

Except he had not married her for life. He never expected that sort of future with her. She was a convenience, a means to an end he had achieved months ago. Yet her coolness toward him, the way she tolerated rather than welcomed his company, sliced right through him.

He wanted more between them than polite strangers who once shared passion.

He had been such a fool to doubt the truth of her baby's parentage. She did not reject him over Amelia's announcement that he had kissed Liza, and she had always believed him about Joanna. Yet he let his mother's concerns cloud his belief in Deirdre. He excused his doubts over the child's parentage because Mama knew far more about these things than he, naturally. If she thought Deirdre too large for the length of time, then she must be right. Yet could not more lie behind his doubts, a lack of belief that Deirdre would so quickly agree to wed him and share his bed? Joanna had encouraged him to propose to her two weeks after they met. Deirdre agreed within a week. He had believed her innocent then despite her lack of discomfort on their wedding night. Because she lived such an active life, that could be explained. He knew Mama warned the girls, especially Chloe, not to ride astride or climb trees, or participate in other such strenuous activities. So he thought nothing of that with Deirdre—

Until she started sneaking about behind his back. Every time he left her alone even for a few hours—

He shot upright with a groan.

"What is it?" Mama and Juliet both cried.

"We should not have left them alone." Kieran looked at his father. "I know we have guards all over and Deirdre is near her confinement, but Chloe is with her. Why would Chloe not want to come with us?"

"She does not like parties much," Juliet said. "She is so pretty, but she thinks young men are sycophants wanting Papa's money and connections."

"And you know Deirdre can barely walk," Mama said, "let alone get up to mischief."

"Deirdre," Kieran said through his teeth, "can always get up to mischief."

And he did not want her to change that indomitable spirit.

"They did not while we were in Hampshire," Tyne said.

"Did they not?" Kieran ground his teeth. "Do we know that? Did we ask if Chloe took out the pony cart?"

"She did not," Tyne said. "I did ask."

"And neither of them has enough money to be bribing the servants," Mama said.

"No?" Kieran raised his hand toward the check string and have the carriage turn around. "I never found all that much gold out of the strongbox. If Deirdre retrieved those bank certificates from their hiding place, why could she not have hidden the gold somewhere more secure?"

"You are not going to make us go back," Juliet wailed. "We will miss the party."

Kieran stayed his hand, not wanting to hurt his younger sister. Still . . .

"Sir?" He addressed his father, "Why did someone decide to steal our lambs in Hampshire?"

Tyne knit his brows. "I presumed it was Rutledge up to more of his tricks."

Kieran lowered his hand, nearly convinced.

"Kieran," Mama said, "Deirdre could not have arranged for someone to steal lambs in Hampshire. She knows too few people."

"And Chloe?" Kieran asked. "She knows more people than I."

"She would still need to know someone who could travel that far," Tyne pointed out, "and none of our people were gone long enough."

"Please stop this," Juliet begged. "It will be my first real party not at our house, and now that you are no longer considered to be bad *ton*, I can start seeking a truly eligible husband."

"Not quite yet," Mama said on a sigh. "I still need to marry off Chloe."

Talk turned to possibly taking the girls to London in the autumn for the Little Season. Kieran sat staring out the window, not caring about where Chloe would spend October. He wondered where he would spend it. Hampshire with his wife and baby? His baby? Of course it was. His family doubting him made him doubt himself, doubt how a lady as wonderful as Deirdre could want him because she cared about him. Yet his family was attempting to make up for their doubts. He raised his hand to the check string again. They were close enough to Plymouth he could hire a horse and return home.

The coach stopped before he touched the signal to the driver. The hatch opened and the coachman's wind-reddened face peered down. "There be a vehicle comin' up fast, m'lord. I thought to let 'em pass afore—" His head disappeared.

Kieran let down the window, letting in a blast of cool, sea-scented air, and poked his head out to see what had drawn the coachman's attention. "What the—" He stared. "It's a mule-drawn cart."

The lighter vehicle swept around them as though it were a phaeton and rocked to a halt.

"He's blocked the road." Kieran reached for the door latch.

"My party," Juliet moaned.

Kieran shoved open the door and leaped out without letting down the steps—and came face to face with Chloe in breeches running from the other vehicle.

She grabbed his hands. "It is Deirdre. Her confinement."

"Then why did you leave her?" Kieran all but shouted at her. "You left her alone with servants? What if—"

"Calm, my dear." Phoebe rested her hand on his shoulder, then leaped to the ground with the grace of a young girl. "How long, Chloe?"

"I do not know." Chloe's eyes were wild. "Two hours?"

"Two hours?" This time, Kieran did shout. "It took you two hours to come?" He wanted to shake her.

He was shaking, shattering inside. He was about to believe in Deirdre, but now nature had proven her a liar. Weeks early.

"We'd best be on our way." Mama was still calm. She turned back to the coach. "Garrett, my dear, will you continue on to Plymouth with Juliet? I think she is best off out of this."

Kieran glanced at his father. When Tyne leaned from the carriage to squeeze his shoulder, he thought perhaps his face gave away some of his agony.

"Learn a lesson from us, my son," Father said in a low voice. "Do not leap to conclusions without all of the information."

Kieran simply nodded. His throat felt too constricted for words.

"Why are you in this cart?" Mama asked.

"Why," Kieran asked Chloe in a voice tight with control, "did you take two hours to reach us?"

"Because—" Chloe covered her face with her hands. She was shaking and gasping as though she had run to fetch them. "Because we were nearly to Dartmoor when she told me."

Chapter 24

"You were nearly at Dartmoor." Kieran stalked to the cart and gathered the reins so he did not strangle his sister. "Get in wherever you can fit."

Mama settled onto the seat beside him and bowed her head as though she were praying. If she were, he hoped that the Lord had mercy on Chloe and his wife; he could not. She had betrayed his country, his family, and him. She had lied to him.

He shoved his fingers into his hair and gripped the sides of his head as though that could push the thoughts away—or hold his heart together.

"Tell me," he managed to get out without bellowing. "Everything. No, wait until we're moving again." With Chloe perched in the narrow bed of the cart, he started to turn the vehicle toward Bishops Cove.

"We need to head up the road to the prison." Chloe sounded like she was being choked.

"Indeed." Kieran lifted the whip from the box and cracked it over the mule's back.

The beast shot forward, and Chloe began to talk. She spilled everything as the cart began its climb away from the sea—the visit in April, the plans, the manipulating of circumstances that day.

"She planned to pretend to be going into her confinement to create a distraction," Chloe concluded. "With the new clothes the men have been able to purchase and hide with the gold we have smuggled in to them, they could pass as persons with wares to sell and leave while the guards were distracted with Deirdre and walk out. There is a boulder halfway down the gorge. Deirdre marked it in April, and I have gone back in the night to work around it with a spade. It is loose enough that a push will bring it coming crashing down and block the track from pursuit long enough for me to get the men away to hide in the caves until boats can get them away."

Kieran barely heard this explanation through the rush of blood in his ears. At that moment, he thought he could have outrun the mule. He hoped Chloe could outrun him. At the least, he would lock her in her bedchamber. She deserved to be in Newgate or transported to New South Wales.

"And were you going to leave Deirdre there to suffer the consequences of your treason?" Mama asked.

"You left my wife in a prison." Kieran thought he would strangle from the effort not to shout at his sister. "That baby is going to be born in a prison?"

"As though she were not already in a prison as your wife," Chloe shot back. "I did what I thought best."

"Best would have been to stay—"

"Children." Phoebe flung up her hands, palms forward. "Chloe did the right thing. First babies rarely come quickly, but bumping about in a cart could hasten delivery, and Chloe is ill-equipped to manage such a thing." She turned to Chloe with a smile. "Continue telling us about your plans. You were not going to leave Deidre in the prison after her men escaped?"

"No, Mama." Chloe's hands opened and closed on her nankeen-clad knees. "She would ask to be taken to the inn at Princetown, and of course the guards would comply for a lady in that condition. And she could escape from there."

"Is that what you did?" Kieran asked. "Did the guards take her to the inn?"

"I have no idea," Chloe wailed. "I had to leave her. She was not supposed to go into her confinement."

"Then you should not have waited so late in the season," Kieran bit out. "We have been expecting it any day now."

Chloe thrust her face between Kieran and Mama and glared at him. "How dare you make accusations against her?"

"How dare she betray me in favor of those men."

"Because she knows her crew loves her. They have been more of a family to her than we have and longer. They know this is all your fault."

"My fault—"

"Children." Though soft, Phoebe's single word shut Kieran and Chloe up in an instant from a lifetime of experience. "This isn't helping Deirdre any."

Chloe's face twisted up, and tears ran down her face. "I tried to stop her once I knew. I could not stop her."

"And why was my sister there, too?" Kieran demanded. "Aiding and abetting—"

"Kieran," Phoebe interjected.

Chloe wiped her eyes on her sleeve. "Ross . . . Trenerry."

"For the love of—"

For the first time in his life, Kieran wished he were a female so he could dissolve into tears. They had to feel better than the churning agony tearing his insides to shreds.

"My wife led my sister into treason *and* introduced her to the man who . . . who is—" He could not say it, could not voice his fears.

"Oh, Kieran." Chloe wrapped her arm around his shoulders. "Do not be such a widgeon. Ross Trenerry is not that baby's father nor is anyone else in that crew. He was devastated when he realized her condition. I saw his face, and he knew it meant she would not go with them. Would he assume that if he had a prior claim to the child?"

"It would have a better life with us."

"He would not think that, not the way he hates us English." Chloe was sobbing now, and Kieran took the reins on one hand so he could press her head against his shoulder. "It is not Deirdre's fault that I . . . care for him. And I asked her if I could help. The conditions there . . . And it is an Ashford's fault that her men are there. I had to help even after learning Mama's story."

"But Deirdre is betraying me." Kieran spoke the words, then realized that that mattered more to him than her treachery to England.

"Loyalty to those we have loved the longest is a powerful lure," Mama said. "I knew what I did was wrong, but I'd known Charlie, my fiancé, all my life in Savannah. I couldn't dismiss him simply because I knew he wasn't the loving man I'd always thought him."

"And Deirdre's crew does still love her," Chloe said. "Ross is angry, but that is because he is hurt that she loves someone else and an Englishman at that." She poked Kieran in the chest. "You."

"I wish—" He heaved a sigh in an attempt to relieve the restriction across his chest. "Her baby . . . Risking you all for her crew . . . I mean nothing to her."

Beyond the rumble of the wheels and clatter of the mule's hooves on the hard-packed track, the world seemed unnaturally still. Mama and Chloe said nothing. Kieran could think of nothing to say. Then the wall of the prison hove into view.

"What do you intend to do?" Mama asked.

He wanted to cry out, "She can deliver in a gutter like a Covent Garden whore for all I care about what happens to her or her brat."

But he did care about what happened to her. He loved her even now that he knew of more lies from her, more acts of treason and deceit. He loved her enough that he did not care who had fathered her child. Since it came from her womb, and if it grew to inherit only half of her spirit, he would be unable to do anything else but love it.

"We have to fetch her home before she delivers our baby," he said. "If there is time."

"Will you go get her?" Mama asked.

"What about her crew?" Chloe asked. "Do we leave them to languish even longer in that hellhole?"

"Chloe, your language," Mama murmured.

"We have everything arranged." Chloe continued, her words tumbling over one another in her haste. "We have everything planned. A trap. Ponies on the moor. Provisions in one of the caves."

Kieran stopped the cart. He held up a hand to stop Chloe, then pulled out his penknife. "Her crew will not escape if I can help it."

As far as he was concerned, they could rot in prison for letting Deirdre risk her life and his family's to get them out. As soon as she could travel, he would take Deirdre to Hampshire and too far from Dartmoor to do anything for them.

But he had put them there.

And had nearly lost his family's regard for doing so. Now that he had rebuilt their respect and begun to realize that his father did love him, he could not risk it all for strangers.

He began to saw at his hair with the knife. "We need disguises, Mama."

With his hair rough-cut like a laborer's, divested of his fine coat and with his shirt sleeves rolled halfway up his forearms, he had done the best he could to mask his true identity. All Mama could do was tilt her hat brim to obscure her face and remove her gloves. But she could stay with the cart out of sight of the guards.

Kieran and Chloe approached the prison. Austere gray walls and the smell of corruption made him ill. Human beings lived inside there. Died inside there. The guards looked stolid and bored where they stood near the gate.

One barred their passage through the gate with an upraised musket, bayonet affixed. "You ain't got naught to sell. You can't go in."

"I think my widowed sister is here," Kieran said in the broadest Devonshire accent he could produce. "I told her not to come, as she's near her time, but she never listens. My brother-in-law is lucky he died and don't have to live with her." Kieran felt in his pocket and found half a crown. "Just let me in to fetch her, will you?"

The guard glared at him. "Do you be tryin' to bribe the king's soldier?"

"No, sir." Kieran thought fast. "I thought you could pay a body to fetch her out for me, if she's here."

"Aye, she's here, caterwauling about going to the inn, but ain't nobody gonna carry a female that big all that way." The guard took the silver coin. "Go on with you." He lowered his bayonet.

Imagining that length of steel entering his back, Kieran shook his head at Chloe and went in alone. He spotted two of the *Maid*'s crew at once—Old Wat and a man whose name he did not know. Both looked ill. They stared at him, their eyes alight with recognition. He turned away, seeking Deirdre, seeing other men he knew—including Ross Trenerry.

Trenerry stooped beside Deirdre, who sat on the ground, her arms wrapped around herself. A veil hid her face, but the bow of her body spoke of wracking pain.

Kieran stalked over to them. "Get away from my wife."

Ross rose and stepped back. "Get her to safety. She needs to go where she can have help and forget about us."

"Can't." Deirdre was panting. "I'll give birth here before I'll let you all down. You know the plan. I'll start screaming again—"

"You are going—now." Kieran knew he could not carry her. She was a big girl even without her burden. "If you help me carry her, Trenerry, you can go free."

With one crewman released, Deirdre might find some tenderness toward him eventually.

Yet was some enough?

"I'll help you carry her out of here," Ross said, "but I won't run without the others."

"I'm not leaving. Can't—" A moan replaced Deirdre's protest.

Together, Kieran and Ross lifted her and headed for the gates. She began to sob. The guard paid little attention to them as they were leaving. Ross could escape now with or without Kieran's assistance.

Ross helped Kieran settle Deirdre onto the seat of the cart, then turned and walked back through the prison gates.

Deirdre cried out in protest.

Mama scrambled into the back of the cart behind Deirdre. "We better be going."

She was right, but Kieran kept staring at those gates where Ross had returned to being a prisoner.

Loyalty and love.

Ross had just given up his hope of freedom for the sake of his crewmates. Deirdre was willing to have her baby in a prison yard to give those she loved a chance at freedom. Kieran knew he condemned all of them to more imprisonment because he was afraid that he might lose love. Yet he had done nothing for anyone he claimed to love. He had caused his family years of embarrassment and even shame for his rakehell ways because they did not treat him with the respect he thought they should, yet he said he loved them. He had humiliated Joanna before the *ton* because she had let herself get seduced by some man who abandoned her yet claimed he cared enough to spend his life with her. Now he intended to keep Deirdre and eleven men prisoners because his family might stop loving him, not because he believed they faced much danger unless outright caught. Yet he expected Deirdre to believe she should ally herself to him and his family. For what? A marriage that mostly benefited him, passion that would produce more children and curtail her freedom? A husband who distrusted her as much as he lusted after her, but did not claim to love her? He should expect nothing less from her than disloyalty when he had given her so little of himself to love.

Chloe grasped his arm. "What are we going to do? The cart will never carry all of us."

"I see that." Kieran took the reins from her and handed them to Mama. "You will need to drive home. You will get there faster without all our extra weight."

"How will you get home?" Mama looked around at the trickle of people leaving the prison yard.

"Chloe and I will manage something. We can likely hire horses in Princetown."

"All right." Mama compressed her lips, then lifted her head as though about to say something more, but Deirdre groaned, and Mama merely nodded before setting the cart into motion.

Chloe turned toward the track into the town. "I hope you are right about hiring horses."

"We have no need of them from town." Kieran took a deep breath. "Did you not say you and Deirdre arranged for ponies to await you all on the moor?"

&

Deirdre couldn't stop crying. She had failed her crew—again. After this escapade, Kieran would have every right to lock her in a room and throw away the key, maybe even take away her baby. Her crew would die. She had seen Wat in the prison yard. He was gray and gaunt, consumptive. Dying, while she now lay in a feather bed with a fire burning despite the warmth of the June evening.

"Deirdre, you need to calm yourself." Phoebe sponged her face with a cool, damp cloth. "The pain won't be so bad if you relax."

"I don't care about the pain." She deserved every bit of it. "It's the future . . . My baby . . ."

That gave her more to cry about—her baby's future. What kind of life would he or she have with a mother who couldn't take care of her own and a father who didn't believe he was the father? It didn't deserve that kind of life. It deserved to be loved.

Resting on her side between contractions, Deirdre thought about the life she was about to bring into the world as what it was—a real son or daughter who would need to be nourished and taught, disciplined, and, most of all, loved. She had always known this, especially from the first quickening. Yet she had thought of the baby more as a nuisance, a weakness of her sex having to pay for passion's fulfillment with such a burden. Then she thought about the child as a means to an end. A woman with child could get away with a great deal, like excusing herself from parties or creating distractions in prison markets. But this was far more. It was a creature demanding that she take notice and give it breathing life.

She lay her hand on the mound of her belly and tried to send the being within a silent message. *I'll do my best not to fail you. I will love you no matter what happens.*

The next contraction left her gasping. When it passed, she lay drifting into a half sleep, thinking about her mother. How she must have loved her father to give birth on a ship, then stay aboard with her child. This then was why Deirdre did not include herself in plans to get her crew out of England, despite Kieran's doubts regarding the baby's parentage, in spite of him keeping her as imprisoned as he could, regardless of him putting his family before her. She had her mother as an example of true devotion.

Devotion and love. Heaven help her, but she loved her husband. She probably had for months, since before he questioned their baby's paternity. His betrayal would not have hurt so much if she cared little for him.

So had her betrayal, setting her crew ahead of him, hurt him? He would have to care for her, maybe even love her, to be hurt and not merely angry that she endangered his family's reputation or even freedom.

Suddenly needing to know where his heart lay toward her, she opened her eyes, glancing about the room. "Kieran?"

"I'm certain he's about somewhere." Phoebe held up a glass. "Drink a little water, child."

"But he doesn't want to see me?"

"This is women's work, my dear. Men don't know what to do."

A shiver ran through Deirdre. "Was Tyne there for your children?"

"When Kieran was born," Phoebe said with a laugh, "Garrett fainted when I screamed."

"Tyne fainted?" Deirdre shook her head on the pillow. "I can't believe that. Does Kieran know? Is that why he's staying away?"

"Oh, I never should have mentioned that I screamed." Phoebe began to fidget with items laid out on a bedside table—water glass, carafe, clean cloths. "I don't want you to be frightened. This is all perfectly natural, and you're a big, strong girl. But if the pain is bad enough, you go right ahead and scream. Mrs. Barnes is here. She and I both know—"

"It's because he doesn't think this baby is his, isn't it?" Deirdre interrupted.

"Kieran will be a good father—"

"It is his." The words emerged as the next contraction struck, turning them into a cry of anguish. "His. Oh, why isn't he here?"

"I'll go look for him." Phoebe sprang from her chair and bolted from the room. She returned a few minutes later with the midwife instead.

Mrs. Barnes strode to the side of the bed and took Deirdre's hand in hers. "How long since your pains began?"

Deirdre glanced at the darkening window. "Eight or nine hours."

"It's your first? They can take a bit longer." She rested her small, blunt-nailed hand on Deirdre's belly. "We can get you moving a bit and help things along."

She kept up a stream of cheerful chatter as she helped Deirdre move about the chamber, having her lean on the mantel, a wall, a bedpost when the contractions struck.

Through it all, the midwife scarcely ceased speaking. "My mother delivered your husband and his sisters, you know. The women in my family have been midwives for generations. The tales that have been passed down—ah, now we're getting somewhere."

Warm liquid ran down Deirdre's legs to puddle on the floor. She wanted to shrivel with humiliation. She leaned on the bedpost, gasping through another contraction. "I'm going to kill him . . . for doing this . . . to me."

"Who, my dear?" Phoebe asked from near the fire, where she was spreading freshly laundered and aired quilts in the bottom and along the sides of a cradle that had rocked Ashfords for generations.

"Your—" The next contraction hit so hard she sank to her knees. "Your son."

"I think," Mrs. Barnes said, "we need to get you onto the birthing chair."

"What's the time?" Deirdre asked, not moving.

"One of the clock," Phoebe said.

"Kieran?"

Phoebe looked concerned. "I'm sorry, Deirdre, he isn't here."

"Up you go," Mrs. Barnes said too brightly.

Deirdre fell forward onto her hands and was sick with the next contraction. She felt as though the pressure inside her womb would tear her in two and couldn't stop the cry that erupted from her lips.

"Your son," she said between gulps for air, "is a misbegotten son of a mangy cur. He did this to me and now runs. He denies . . . responsibility. I'll snatch him bald. I'll—"

She couldn't speak any longer. The pain was too intense, each spasm too close together.

"Lady Tyne," Mrs. Barnes said as though Deirdre hadn't just insulted her mother-in-law along with her own spouse, "please help me get her onto the chair."

Among the three of them, Deirdre ended up safely settled onto the birthing chair with solid oak arms for her to grip, sloping back to support her, and cutout seat for the baby.

The baby. It was about to enter the world with a father who couldn't bother to be there and who probably wouldn't care when he couldn't avoid staying away any longer.

But I'm here, little one. I care.

At that moment, she wasn't so sure about caring about the father after all. Not then with the midwife and her mother-in-law crouched before her, giving her softly spoken instructions to bear down, to push, then not to push. The pressure so great she didn't bother to suppress her moans, nor invectives against Kieran for putting her through the agony.

Then the pain eased and Mrs. Barnes and Phoebe were exclaiming in tones of joy, nearly drowning out a high, thin wail.

"It's a boy," Phoebe cried. "He's small as early children are, but he's perfect. Oh, Deirdre, my daughter—" Her voice broke on a sob.

Deirdre opened her eyes and stared at the protesting bundle of smeared, red humanity in amazement. "He's mine? I produced a son?"

Phoebe laughed. "Yes, my dear, an Ashford heir."

"I'd like to hold—" Another wrenching spasm gripped her, and she cried out. "What's wrong?"

"Nothing, my lady." Mrs. Barnes massaged her belly. "All is well. It's just the—hello. Keep pushing, my lady. Come on, my lady. Harder. Don't stop—"

"I can't. No strength."

"You must. You—"

Through a haze of blinding pain, Deirdre heard Phoebe exclaiming and Mrs. Barnes declaring, "This explains why you went into your confinement early."

"Someone stole my purse." Shrieking the accusation, Chloe charged into the prison yards. "Who was it? Who was it?"

"Get back here." Kieran paused at the startled guards and offered them an apologetic smile. "Our mam spoils the brat."

The nearest red-coated militiaman sneered. "We don't care. Just get 'im outta here. We gotta be closin' the gates."

"Yessir. Right away, sir." Head down, Kieran charged into the middle of a hundred enemy combatants.

He could not see Chloe, but he could hear her, yelling about her purse, about pickpockets, about ungrateful Yankees. All too conscious the men nearest him babbled in French, Kieran sprinted for the ruckus. On the far side of the yard, Chloe gripped Ross's shirt and shook it like a terrier attempting to move a wolfhound.

"Stop it." Kieran yanked her away. "Your purse is gone and you need to come along if you don't wanta get locked in with these scurvy knaves." He cast Trenerry and the other Americans a meaningful glance.

At least he hoped they caught his meaning.

A nod from Ross said they had, and Kieran tossed Chloe over his shoulder to make her shout again.

"Let me down." She pounded his back with more force than necessary. "I want my purse back."

"Stop being so lazy and earn the money back." Kieran raised his voice to match Chloe's. Beneath his breath, he muttered, "And stop hitting me so hard or I will leave you inside here."

"You would not dare."

"Do not tempt me." Kieran strode toward the now grinning guards.

Chloe kicked her legs and continued to beat at his back. Around them, Somerset militia and prisoners alike laughed and called advice as to how to handle the recalcitrant youth. At the gate, Chloe flung herself off Kieran's shoulder, knocking into the guards. They landed in a heap of arms and legs and muskets flung aside.

"A thousand pardons, sir." Kieran extended a hand to the closest guard.

"It's his sister," the other redcoat shouted, getting an armful of Chloe. "Brazen hussy. If you're wanting to refill your purse—"

While scrambling away from him, Chloe managed to drop one knee into his middle. The soldier released her with a whoosh of expelled breath. "Assaulting an officer. I could have you arrested—"

Chloe, Kieran, and a throng of visitors to the prison set off toward Princetown. Eleven American prisoners headed down the gorge toward freedom.

"We did it." Chloe flung her arms around Kieran's neck. "We got them out."

"We have not done anything until they are in the caves at the least."

Out of England would be better, but that was days off.

"They are straggling." Kieran pressed a hand to the small of Chloe's back. "We need to get them out of here faster."

"Lead the way."

They loped after the prisoners. Kieran shouted to the slowest ones, urging them forward. He commanded Chloe to go ahead with him. They needed to be on the moor in the right place or who knew where the Americans would end up. Likely in British hands.

Kieran charged ahead, calling encouragement and threats in equal portion. He scrambled past the boulder Chloe had pointed out, and up the side of the gorge to help the first of the escapees.

Thanks to Chloe's machinations, moorland ponies awaited. The weakest of the Americans would ride the ponies in a circuitous route across moorland and down to the cliffs and the caves beneath. Kieran had marveled at Chloe and Deirdre's planning. Now he thought of everything that could go wrong.

Thus far, nothing had gone wrong. Three prisoners reached the rendezvous along with Kieran. He turned back to assist a fourth and look for Chloe—and the clang, clang, clang of a bell began to toll across the land.

The faces of the Americans whitened.

Chloe staggered to a halt in the midst of five more men. "The alarm. That's the alarm."

"They know we're out." One man began to spin in circles.

Kieran grabbed him and pointed. "Go. I will catch up with you. Chloe, you can lead—"

But Chloe was gone, leaping back down the track toward the last two prisoners—Ross Trenerry and Wat Drummond.

"Just go." Kieran shoved the nearest prisoner in the right direction. "Take two of the ponies for the weakest of you."

He did not like leaving the Americans on their own, but he could never leave his sister behind to be caught. That would condemn his family for sure, Deirdre and his baby included. As for Ross and Wat, Deirdre would never forgive him if he let them fall into the hands of the soldiers.

And soldiers were coming. Sprinting in Chloe's wake, he glanced up the gorge. Someone had to have noticed the *Maid*'s crew leaving, had sounded the alarm. Now, more than half a dozen men from the Somerset militia who guarded Dartmoor were marching down the gorge.

"Where are you?" he cried out in anguish. "All of you."

Something flashed well ahead of the soldiers, three of them running, Chloe going toward the others, one lagging behind the other. Wat, of course. He seemed to be stumbling forward more than racing—stumbling and falling against a rock.

"No." Kieran started down the steep side of the gorge. "Less than two minutes until the soldiers catch up with us."

Ross stopped, turned, ran toward Wat.

"Keep running," Kieran shouted to Chloe and Ross.

Of course they could not hear him. Of course they would not obey if they could. He would not expect them to. Trenerry heaved Wat over his shoulder. It slowed him down; prison had weakened him, too. But the soldiers were strong and well fed. They pressed on, marching faster.

Then a shot rang out. Trenerry fell, Wat slipping to the ground, the wound on his back so terrible he had to be dead.

"Get up." Kieran headed down the slope to the gorge floor. He had to help his sister escape. Trenerry, too, though that was harder. Trenerry and Deirdre . . .

He would not think that. He would get them out, free her men as a gift of love to his wife.

Below, Chloe reached Trenerry and helped him to his feet. They ran together down, down, down to the rock Deirdre prepared. But another soldier raised his musket. Muskets were so inaccurate. He could hit Chloe.

The musket ball struck Trenerry. His body jerked, but Chloe's arm around his waist seemed to be holding him upright.

"Get out of there." Kieran could not shout the admonition. He could not make a target of himself when Ross and Chloe would be unlikely to hear him anyway.

Kieran ran toward Chloe and Trenerry. Keeping low, Chloe and Ross from one direction, Kieran from the other, slipped and staggered on the steep hillside toward the marked boulder, the gate to safety.

The soldiers drew nearer. They aimed. The report of musket fire reverberated through the gorge. Dust sprang from the boulder Chloe, Ross, and he were trying to reach, needed to reach.

Not fast enough. They could not keep out of view and move swiftly. Another minute and the soldiers would be upon them. They would be caught. The Ashfords would lose property, perhaps their lives . . .

Chloe and Ross reached the boulder, shoved. It did not move. They were too late—

Kieran risked exposure to increase his pace. Half a minute. Only half a minute until the soldiers reached Trenerry and Chloe.

A rumble joined the clamor of alarm bell and more musket fire. The boulder began to tilt, fall, roll. The soldiers checked, shouted warnings, staggered back from the avalanche of rock, shrubbery, and earth raining down from the hillside.

And Ross Trenerry grasped Chloe's shoulders and kissed her.

Kieran reached Chloe and dragged her away. "Get moving. That landslide will not hold the soldiers forever."

Trenerry nodded and turned to the moor where a straggly line of ponies headed toward the sea. Chloe started to join him, but Kieran caught hold of her arm and swung her away.

"Go home, Chl—Juliet."

She merely looked at him and snorted before fixing her attention on Trenerry.

Not liking the way the American gazed upon his sister, Kieran glowered at the younger man. "As for you—"

"Later," Trenerry said.

They ran, a hail of musket balls and curses raining behind them.

Kieran and Chloe knew the moor. They had grown up there. The soldiers had not. Kieran and Chloe could navigate the tumbled rocks and treacherous marshes in the dark. The soldiers could not. As darkness descended upon them, the soldiers fell behind.

The *Maid*'s crew began to falter, stumble, fall. They took turns with who rode the ponies, except for Ross. He was bleeding badly but would not let them take the time to stop and bandage his wound, so he rode a pony all the way. Chloe held the reins to guide the mount. To stop himself from dwelling on the way his sister's face glowed each time she glanced at Trenerry, Kieran concentrated on shepherding the others toward the cliffs and caves beneath. That way he was not tempted to push Trenerry off the highest peak and directly into the sea. He was shaking with his need to lash out at the man for loving Deirdre, for toying with his sister.

With thoughts of Deirdre in travail nearly a month early.

Once beyond the opening to the caves, so narrow only those who knew about it could find it, Chloe dropped back from the head of the line. "I will lead them inside. I know where I have hidden lanterns and strike-a-lights."

"And food and blankets?" Kieran made no effort to disguise an edge of bitterness that this had all happened behind his back.

Her teeth flashed in the darkness. "Of course."

"All right, go, but stay away from Trenerry."

Chloe simply laughed and darted forward.

"Minx."

But a good companion in a crisis. A sister to be proud of.

She vanished into the cliffside like the Pied Piper, followed by the men. Kieran remained outside, straining to hear above the hiss of the sea at low tide and whistle of the wind overhead for sounds of pursuit. Nothing. Silence. Safety.

He slipped through the slit in the rock and followed the pinpricks of lights ahead. He guessed where Chloe would take them—caves deep beneath the cliffs, but with exits in two other directions. With food and water they could live there for days. Kieran did not know how they were supposed to get the men away to France or return the ponies to their owner, but he guessed that Deirdre had worked that out, too. The risk to the Ashfords was far from over, but lessened as long as the men stayed put until time to leave.

Kieran walked into the cavernous chamber that would be the men's new prison for a while . . . and came face to face with Ross Trenerry.

"Thank you for your help," Trenerry said in his thick-as-treacle accent. "We won't forget it."

"I'd rather you did, and the rest of the Ashfords, too. That includes Deirdre." Kieran stepped forward—

And ran into Trenerry's fist slamming against his jaw.

Chapter 25

$\mathcal{K}$ ieran reeled back against the stone wall, tasting blood where he'd bitten his tongue. "What the devil—"

"Ross," Chloe gasped.

Ross grabbed Kieran's arms with surprising strength and leaned in close, pinning him to the wall. "That's for thinking a woman like Deirdre would ever give herself to any man but her husband. If you don't love her enough to believe that, you don't deserve her, and I'll take her away."

"You try to," Kieran said with deadly calm, "and you will not find a corner of this world safe. Understand?"

"You two are acting like children," Chloe protested. "Ross, let go of my brother."

Ross did. He stepped back and smiled. "I understand. I think you're a"—he glanced at Chloe—"rotten Englishman, but Deirdre loves you."

Kieran rubbed his swelling jaw. "I can't even begin to hope you are right in that. All I can hope for is that this is enough to show her that I love her."

"We should get back to her," Chloe said. "Perhaps she has given you a son."

"A son?" He saw stars for a moment, an overwhelming wish to be with his wife, with his baby. "Yes, my son." He held out his hand to Trenerry. "Thank you."

Ross shook it. "Take care of her."

"You take care of these men. And I'm sorry about Old Wat."

Pain twisted Ross's face. "Don't tell Deirdre straightaway. It'll break her heart. He was there when she was born."

"I will wait." Kieran clasped Chloe's elbow. "Someone will be back to see that you have everything you need. I doubt the soldiers will find you here. If they come, though, scatter."

"We have our plans," Ross said.

Chloe told Kieran about Blaze on their way back to Bishops Cove. "You will not try to catch him and hang him for nearly killing you, will you?"

"How could I?" The nearer they drew to the house, the more excited and the more anxious Kieran grew. "Had he not done that, Deirdre would have got away from me."

They crept into the house and up to their rooms. Kieran took one look at himself in the mirror and knew he had to do something about his hair in the event that prison authorities began to make the rounds of local houses asking questions about escaped prisoners. He wanted no one to recognize the ragged mane now spilling around his face. Chloe could manage it, he knew, but that would take so long, and Deirdre—

No, he had to wait. She was an Ashford. Her safety depended on him looking as usual as possible. But he swore he heard a cry from below. It made his heart race and tugged him to the door.

Chloe met him there with shears in hand. "You look terrible. A few snips to make you look more like a lord than a laborer."

"But Deirdre—"

"Is inclined to geld you at the moment, according to Sally. Now sit. You know as well as I that soldiers are likely to make an appearance here soon."

"We have just committed treason."

"More like helped justice. Now sit."

Kieran sat, but the few minutes Chloe spent shaping his hair into something resembling respectability felt like an hour. When he heard a scream, he jumped and nearly lost a chunk out of his other ear. He could not bear the idea of her suffering because of him, because he had used her for his own ends.

"But I love her."

"I know." Chloe brushed up the hair and dumped it onto the fire. "And she—"

Another cry ripped through the night.

Kieran sprang to his feet and raced for the door. He took the steps two at a time, then vaulted over the banister halfway down the last flight and landed on the hall floor just as pounding sounded on the front door.

The soldiers arrived as he heard the cry of his first newborn baby, a baby he might never see.

Waving Addison and half a dozen servants back, he stalked to the door and yanked it open. "You had best have good reason for this interruption, sirrahs."

"We do, man." A young man with lieutenant's epaulets on his shoulders stepped forward. "Where is your master?"

"I am Lord Ripon. Who is your master?"

His ears strained to hear another infant wail, for signs that all was well inside the birthing chamber.

"My lord." The lieutenant saluted. "Where have you been all evening?"

"I beg your pardon? How is that any of your business?"

"It is the king's business, my lord." The lieutenant spoke in staccato bursts. "We have received information that if trouble occurs at the prison we should make certain all the Ashfords can account for themselves."

"And who, pray tell," Kieran drawled, trying to sound indifferent, "would tell you such a Banbury tale?"

"None of your concern, my lord." The lieutenant laid his hand on his small sword. "We need all of you Ashfords to account—"

Another shriek resounded from the birthing chamber.

Kieran shot upright. "My wife!"

Why would she do that if the baby were already born? Something had to be wrong.

Going cold all over, he started to slam the door in the lieutenant's face. "My wife is in childbirth. You must go."

The lieutenant pushed his way into the hall. "What I must do is discover . . ."

"Discover what, Lieutenant?" Chloe, looking positively wanton wearing a silk dressing gown and with her hair spilling down her back, glided down the stairs.

"Um . . ." The man gulped.

Kieran leaped for the door to Deirdre's chamber. He heard a baby's cry, the low murmur of voices, and nothing else. Good or bad? Women died in childbirth. But not Deirdre. Not Deirdre.

He turned the door handle. Locked. He began to pound on it.

Behind him, Chloe flirted outrageously with the lieutenant, talking about Tyne and Juliet in Plymouth—"You do know Admiral Barrington, do you not?"—Deirdre and Mama "seeing to ladies' business," and her brother and herself banished until the business was over.

Kieran pounded on the door again. "Deirdre? Mama? Someone let me in."

The key turned.

"What is all this about, Lieutenant?" Chloe asked.

"We do not like to say, my lady," the lieutenant said.

Mama opened the door and, though small, managed to block the entrance. "You can't come in here yet."

"Please." Kieran felt like a schoolboy begging for a holiday treat. "I want to see my wife."

"She doesn't want to see you," Mama said. "What are these men doing here? And Chloe, you're in your dressing gown."

The lieutenant turned on Mama. "You are American."

Mama stepped into the hall and closed the door with a firm click. "I am Lady Tyne and just happened to be born in America when it was under the Crown. Now how may I help you, man? Speak your mind and be gone."

"You have blood on your gown," the lieutenant said. "And we killed one of the escaping prisoners and may have wounded others. If you have a wounded man in there—"

"That blood," Mama overrode him in her gentle voice that somehow always managed to supersede anyone's bombast, "is my daughter-in-law's."

Deirdre's blood? Kieran looked at the patches and streaks on the apron Mama wore over her dress, and spots danced before his eyes. He took a long, deep breath and leaned against the wall. Men did not swoon, but he felt lightheaded enough to do so.

"She has just given birth," Mama continued. "And no, sirrah, before you even consider it, you will not go in there and look."

The mewing wail of an infant penetrated the door as though even the new Ashford intended to proclaim that they were all too occupied that night to be up to mischief—or treason.

His child.

Kieran regained his equilibrium and smiled. "Leave our house at once, Lieutenant. If you do not, I will have you forcibly removed."

"You cannot treat an officer of the Crown in such a manner, lordling or not." The lieutenant made the declaration as he edged toward the door, glancing between Phoebe's blood-streaked clothes and Chloe's dishabille. "I was merely doing my duty."

"Of course you were," Chloe purred. "We are sorry you were misdirected."

"Perhaps," Kieran said, "you should look in the cove before the fishing boats go out at dawn. Any escapee worth his salt would head for the sea, would he not?"

"Of course. Of course." The lieutenant bowed. "And, um, congratulations, my lord."

Kieran stalked behind the man until he and his underlings were outside the door, then he shot the bolts home and turned to his mother. "Why can I not see my wife and child? Does she . . . despise me so?"

Mama smiled. "She hasn't been paying you compliments for the past hour or two, and my vocabulary has increased tenfold. But no lady would have her husband see her looking her worst."

Kieran glanced at the door that he knew to be unlocked. "I do not care what she looks like."

"My dear." Mama laid her hand on his arm. "We have enough to do in there without having to revive a man your size who has just fainted."

He felt his cheeks heat. "I would never."

Chloe snorted. "You nearly did at the sight of Mama's apron. Just imagine seeing Deirdre. Childbirth is a bit messy."

"You shouldn't know that, young lady," Mama exclaimed. "And you should be dressed if you're coming down here. You, too, Kieran." Mama squeezed his arm. "At the least change your shirt. By the time you get back down, you can see your wife and babies."

"Yes, ma'am." Kieran charged up the stairs. On the landing, her words nearly knocked him flat, and he spun back toward her, noting that Chloe wore a look of shock that must mirror his own face. "Babies?"

She laughed. "Yes, Kieran, it's twins."

Deirdre had never been more exhausted in her life. Hauling lines in a hurricane had been less of a struggle than giving birth. But the results were worth the effort, she knew the instant she held her son in her arms. He was tiny and wrinkled and red fuzz covered his scalp, but he was warm and breathing and perfect in every tiny finger and toe. She didn't know she possessed so much tenderness inside her until this being her body had produced rested in her arms.

Then she saw her daughter. She had black fuzz on her head and hadn't yet stopped complaining about entering the world since a surprised midwife had eased her into it. That made Deirdre smile and cry.

"She's got black hair like her father."

But Ross had black hair, too. Would they think—would Kieran believe—that another man sired these babies?

Her babies!

"We should try to feed them straightaway," Mrs. Barnes said. "Do you have a wet nurse, since the babes are early?"

"No wet nurse." Deirdre made the proclamation without even looking for Phoebe's guidance. "They are mine to nourish."

"Hmm." Mrs. Barnes sniffed. "Modern girls. But it's your place to guide her, Lady Tyne."

Deirdre looked at Phoebe then, wondering if she would disapprove. She nodded. "We'll find a wet nurse if her milk isn't sufficient for both."

"Then you should try straightaway," Mrs. Barnes said. "But let us get you cleaned up first. Lord Ripon wishes to see you."

Deirdre's head shot up. "He does?"

She vaguely recalled pounding on the door, but had been in too much discomfort still, not to mention shock over learning she had been carrying two babies, to pay much attention.

"What does he want?"

"To see his babies, of course," Mrs. Barnes said.

"But he—" Deirdre looked down at her daughter and stroked one red cheek. "What does it matter what he thinks?" she murmured to the infant. "You have me to love you." Aloud, she said, "He puts me through all the work, makes me go through the pain, and wants to trot in here to—what?—play the proud father now that it's all over? No thank you. He can wait until perdition is an iceberg."

"He wants," Phoebe said, taking the baby girl from Deirdre, "to see the wife he loves, as well as his children."

Deirdre turned away, her tears now stemming from pain in her heart rather than the joy of seeing her children. "He doesn't love me."

"You need rest," Mrs. Barnes said. "You'll feel better about things in a bit."

Deirdre didn't believe her, but she allowed herself to be bathed and dressed in a fresh nightgown, then tucked into the bed. Two of the older maids arrived to help clear away any signs of the birth except for the two infants in the cradle. When she woke, both were crying, and she nursed them for the first time. The boy had to be shown what to do, but the girl latched on at once. That made Deirdre laugh.

"My daughter. How am I going to raise a daughter?"

But she knew. In the past eight months, she had learned that being a female carried special rewards of friendship and giving she would never trade away.

"But you're still going to learn to sail."

Phoebe laughed and took the now sleeping child from Deirdre. "Will you see Kieran now? He's been cooling his heels in the hall for hours, and wearing grooves in the stone with his pacing, I have no doubt."

Deirdre sighed. "I suppose it can't be avoided." She lay back against the pillows and closed her eyes. "Send him in."

Through her lashes, she watched Phoebe lay the baby in the cradle, then go to the door. Deirdre closed her eyes. Maybe he would think she was asleep.

But when the door opened and closed and she heard a heavier tread than Phoebe's on the floor, she raised her lids enough to watch him enter.

He glanced toward her, then went to the cradle. He stood there in silence, head bowed, hair—heavens! What had he done with his hair?—falling over his cheek. His shoulders rose and fell, and the next breath he exhaled emerged in a ragged sigh. When he turned toward Deirdre, she saw that his cheeks shone with tears.

Her eyes popped open wide. "Kieran?"

Wordlessly, he paced across the room and sank onto the chair beside the bed. "My dearest wife—" His voice broke, and he took her hand in both of his. "I . . . Deirdre, I . . ."

All the pain and anguish he had put her through in the past eight and a half months, especially the past twelve hours, slipped away beneath a tide of love so profound she thought her heart would burst. She didn't care if he doubted her. She would spend a lifetime convincing him of her love and faithfulness. She owed him that much for all the games she had played to free her crew.

"Will you forgive me," she asked, "for what I tried to do? I haven't been a good wife, so it's no wonder you think me faithless, but I love you dearly and will try—"

He cut off her flow of words with his lips. When a drop of moisture splashed onto her cheek, she reached up her hands and cupped his face, wiping away his silent tears that had to be costing him every ounce of Ashford pride he possessed, yet he was making no move to conceal them from her.

"What's wrong?" she asked. Then her heart skipped a beat. "The babies? Is something wrong with them no one's telling me?"

"No." He raised his head and swiped his sleeve across his face. "They are perfect like their mother."

"And their father." She stroked his cheek with her fingertips, came up short at the swelling on his jaw. "What happened?"

He smiled. "Ross Trenerry hit me for thinking you would give yourself to any man but your husband."

"Ross? In the prison yard? They'll put him in the black hole again and he—"

Kieran kissed her again. "No, dearest Deirdre, he did it in the caves beneath the cliffs."

"But how?" Her head spun. "I couldn't help them find their way there."

"I could. Chloe and I could."

"Not possible. It's treason. Your family. Your father may disown you."

"He may." Kieran gazed at her with those sleepy eyes that would, she did not doubt, seduce her for the rest of her life. "But I could think of no other way to show you how much I love you than to help your crew escape."

"Oh." She began to sob. "I thought you abandoned me. I thought you wanted nothing to do with the babies because it has been barely over eight months and I've lied to you and led your sister into danger and—why are you laughing?"

He slipped his arms around her and rested his head on her shoulder. "What a pair we make. I have been such a fool. If you hadn't tried to save your crew, I doubt I could love you so much. As for Chloe, she will get over her *tendre* for Trenerry now that he will be far away from England. And as for the other . . . Trenerry did not need to hit me. I already knew I had been making a terrible mistake. Will you believe me, that I love you?"

"Yes." It was all she could say for a few moments. She stroked his shorn hair. "What happened?"

"It was the best disguise I could manage in a hurry. Shall I keep it this way? It covers my ear except when the wind blows."

"I don't know. I think I like it long. You made a perfect pirate."

"I was never a pirate. The only thing I stole was your heart."

They were laughing over this, Deirdre complaining doing so hurt, yet unable to stop, when the door burst open.

"There you are, Kieran," Juliet cried. "Is it true there are two of them? This is so wonderfully exciting. But, Kieran, you are—oops."

The babies began to cry.

"Juliet," Kieran said, "Will you please affix brakes to your tongue?"

"Will you fetch Phoebe?" Deirdre asked. "I need my babies."

"I will bring them to you." Kieran rose. "Juliet, leave us. You should not be home for hours yet anyway."

"We risked traveling before dawn once we received word of the births," Juliet explained.

Tyne, Phoebe, and Chloe appeared in the doorway behind her.

"We had some interesting callers in the middle of the night," Tyne said. "An overeager lieutenant. Would you know anything about this escape, Kieran?"

Kieran didn't answer. He busied himself bringing the boy to Deirdre. She wanted to nurse him, but didn't know how with the room full of people. Yet she didn't want them to go. Whatever Tyne did to Kieran, she needed to be there with him.

"Here you go, child." Phoebe pulled the Norwich silk shawl off of her shoulders and draped it around Deirdre's. "I would have kept them out, but I thought perhaps you would want to be in on this little family row."

Little? Deirdre hadn't seen Tyne so angry since the day Kieran brought her home.

"Who tattled on us?" Chloe asked.

"Rutledge." Tyne closed and locked the door. "He seems to have been spreading a bit of gold about to learn Ashford family secrets."

"He will have the wind taken out of his sails now," Juliet declared. "Admiral Barrington told him to leave the house right in front of everyone."

"He is a worm," Chloe declared. "He cannot win against us."

"He came a bit close." Tyne's mouth hardened. "Thank you, Deirdre, for choosing last night to present me with my first grandchildren. No thanks to their father and aunt, they should grow up to enjoy the privileges of being Ashfords." He skewered Chloe and Kieran with his lapis eyes. "As for you two, you deserve a month or two locked up for daring—daring!—to risk our safety and freedom for strangers, for our enemies, for what? Excitement? Pure rebellion? I thought you had gone beyond that kind of behavior, Kieran. I thought you respected me enough and wanted my trust enough to act like a responsible husband and father."

Watching Tyne, Deirdre realized that he wasn't so much angry as hurt.

"Sir," she began.

Kieran squeezed her shoulder. "Wait." He stalked forward and faced his father. "What is more responsible than performing the one act that will show the woman you love that you hold her in the highest regard?"

"Oh." Juliet clasped her hands to her heart.

The others stood staring at him in wide-eyed silence. Deirdre wished she could climb out of bed and stand beside him. She cuddled her sleeping baby instead and hoped Kieran could read her love in her eyes.

Tyne cleared his throat. "You knew I could disinherit you of everything but Tyne Hall and the title?"

"Yes, sir."

"And deny you the right to ever see your mother and sisters again?"

Kieran grinned. "And yourself the right to ever see your grandchildren."

Tyne looked stony-faced for a full minute. Then he started to laugh and embraced his son. "Then I am proud of you. But if you ever pull a prank like that again . . ."

Laughing, too, Kieran led Tyne to the cradle. "Our daughter. Do you think she will favor her mother or me?"

"Her mother, I hope." Tyne smiled at Deirdre from across the room. "And the lad, too."

"Hey," Kieran protested. "I have done well for myself."

"Not so well as I have," Deirdre said. "I got a whole family out of this."

"Bringing you home," Tyne said, "is the best thing my son has done thus far, is it not, Phoebe?"

"I always told you he would settle down once he met the right lady."

"I suppose I'd better learn how to be one." Deirdre looked at Kieran. "I can't go around embarrassing my children by hanging upside down off balconies."

Kieran paled. "You did what? When?"

"How do you think I managed to hide a thousand English pounds of gold?"

He paced to her side again and stood frowning down at her. "I knew it had to be somewhere. Have you spent it all?"

"I'm afraid so." She let the shawl fall back enough to expose the baby's red scalp fuzz. "Are you angry?"

"It was only gold." He touched the baby's cheek with a forefinger. "This is life and love and—what do we name them?"

"I think you should name them—"

Chloe clapped her hand over Juliet's mouth and steered her through the door. "You need your beauty rest, younger sister. You look positively hagridden."

Tyne and Phoebe followed, closing the portal behind them with a gentle click.

Deirdre started to look away, then held his gaze. "I was afraid to think about that. I wanted to name a boy for someone in your family, but you might not have liked that. I mean—" A twinge of lingering uncertainty roughened her voice. "If you thought he might not truly be the heir."

"Oh, Deirdre." Pain clouded his eyes. "I have been a blackguard, have I not?"

"Well, a bit." She grinned at him. "But I forgive you."

He tweaked her nose. "You, my wife, have not been a saint."

"Give me another year or two, and I will be a staid, quiet matron like your mother. I'm even learning to sew."

"Do not work at it too diligently. I would not want you to be a bad influence on the children." He glanced at the cradle. "What was your mother's name?"

"Sophie. Why?"

"She had to have been a brave and devoted lady to go to sea with her husband and bring you into the world. I would like our daughter to carry that legacy. As for this one . . ." He lifted the boy from her arms and gazed down at him with unabashed pride and love. "Garrett for his grandfather? Though he looks a bit small to be the future ninth Earl of Tyne."

"He has decades to grow into the role."

Gazing at Kieran holding their son, Deirdre felt the last of her uncertainties slip away like waves beneath a keel. Before her stretched a vista of love and passion and friendship far more beautiful than anything she had ever observed from the crosstrees.

A PREVIEW OF BOOK 2 FOLLOWS.

TRUE AS FATE

The Ashford Chronicles:

Book 2

LAURIE ALICE EAKES

Waterfall
PRESS

Chapter 1

Devonshire, England
Sunday, June 4, 1813
8:00 p.m.

Seventeen miles of barren moorland lay between Ross Trenerry and freedom. Less than a mile lay between him and Dartmoor Prison, and the alarm bell was beginning to ring. The Somerset militia guarding the American and French prisoners of war had discovered that eleven of those men had escaped.

"Too soon." Ross glanced over his shoulder, feeling the iron bands of shackles holding him down, as they had too often since the American merchantman on which he served as first mate had been captured by a British privateer. Or maybe this second capture would simply get him hanged.

Instead of darkness, sunshine slanted across the rocky gray-black landscape in the late spring evening, and Deirdre, his friend, his dead captain's daughter, wasn't there. She was giving birth to their enemy's get, and that enemy, her husband, Kieran Ashford, raced past the ragged prisoners, prodding them along with curt commands and glares from his eyes, their bright amber glow more obvious for the dirt rubbed on his face to blur his features. Another Ashford, the stunning sister in male attire, sped along with them, as agile on the rocky path as a gazelle.

But the soldiers were marching. The escaped prisoners and their enemy guides needed wings to get free.

"Trot, lads," Ross said.

The men glanced at him, then tried to move faster. Ross saw the effort in their gaunt faces running with sweat despite the chilly evening, the straining of limbs robbed of once formidable muscles from hauling lines and climbing rigging and lifting cargo aboard the merchantman *Maid of Alexandria*. But the uneven stone path and eight months of near starvation had weakened all of them, especially Wat, already an old man before the English had captured their schooner and they'd all ended up in Dartmoor.

Now Kieran Ashford, that privateer owner, was helping them escape for the sake of his wife, Deirdre. At least that's what he claimed. With the alarm bell clanging its warning that prisoners had escaped, Ross suspected a trap, a betrayal.

He flashed a glance at Ashford. "Who knew besides you, Deirdre, and your sister that we planned this?"

Ashford either did not hear or chose to ignore Ross. The sister, the lady who had brought him food and blankets and promises to keep him going through the months at Dartmoor, glared at him, and said nothing except "Faster."

"Faster." Ross repeated the admonition above the persistent clang, clang, clang. "Come on." He slipped a hand beneath Old Wat's elbow.

Wat shook his head and slumped against a boulder beside the narrow track cutting through the gorge. "Can't. Go on without me."

"A little farther is all." The sister spoke, lagging behind for a moment. "We've traps set and ponies waiting."

The drum of running, booted feet joined the rhythm of the bell.

Ross froze, refused to look, to watch the enemy bear down upon them. He knew what would happen if the soldiers caught them—worse confinement in the *cacheau*. Darkness. Fetid air.

"Run," Ashford called. "A hundred yards and we can trap 'em."

The men picked up their pace to a trot. Bare feet slapped and rattled against the rocky path. Their breaths wheezed. Ross's breath chilled in his lungs. None of the men could move any faster, and pursuit sounded louder, closer. Too close. The soldiers couldn't achieve more than a trot on the stony, uneven ground, but they surely moved swiftly enough to overtake the Americans within minutes. Despite himself, Ross glanced back. He counted eight men, seven with bayonets affixed to their musket barrels. Too close to get the men away unless they found the strength to run.

"Go. Go. Go." His voice was hoarse. He counted his men. Besides himself plus Ashford and his sister. Only twelve.

Ross halted. Old Wat wasn't with them. Turning, Ross caught sight of the man still slumped against the rock, his face gray beneath the layer of dirt they all wore.

And the soldiers drew closer, close enough for Ross to see faces behind the muskets. Five minutes' grace was all Ross figured he had to get free with the others.

Wat pressed one hand to his chest and waved Ross on with the other. "Leave me."

Ross glanced at the approaching soldiers, then down the hillside toward the crew and freedom. Wat was his mentor, a surrogate father.

Ross sprinted back to the old man. "Come on. Ashford set a trap down a bit." Or so he claimed.

"No, lad—"

"Don't argue." Ross lifted the old man over his shoulder and headed downhill. His legs felt like year-old carrots. Wat sagged against him, dead weight. No, not dead. Not—

Muskets cracked above the drum of footfalls, drum of heartbeats. Ross tasted tin, the bile of fear. Soldiers were still too far away to fire with accuracy. But soon, too soon, a minute or two, he'd be in range.

Run faster!

He staggered under the old man's weight, slight though it was.

More muskets resounded. Wat jerked, and Ross smelled the metallic stench of blood.

"God, please, no!" He forced himself into a run. Fire blazed in his lungs. More gunfire rattled, and pain slugged into his shoulder. He stumbled over an outcropping of granite, then landed on his knees. Sharp pebbles cut through the frayed cloth of his woolen breeches, and Wat slid onto the ground, dead. No one survived a wound like the one gaping on the old man's back.

Ross closed his eyes, willed his body to find the strength to rise, keep going. The soldiers grew louder, nearer. Another minute, another shot. Ahead, nothing of the others echoed down the gorge. Good, they were away . . .

Running footfalls pounded on the path, quicker, lighter than those of the soldiers.

Those footfalls thudded toward him. He lifted his head, stared. He wasn't mistaken. Someone ran toward him, Lady Chloe Ashford, who had corresponded with him against even Deirdre's will, who had visited him, who had given him hope that all the English weren't scoundrels, that the war would not last forever. As in a dream, she swept toward him, leaping over the rocks with the long-legged grace of the deer back home in Carolina.

"Sir." Her face still obscured beneath the floppy brim of a hat, she dropped into a crouch before him. "Let me help you." Her voice was soft, melodious.

"No." Ross shook his head. "I'm hit—"

"I can get you up." She held out narrow, long-fingered hands. On one finger, a ring glowed like a slice of moonlight with sparks of blue and green. "I'm stronger than I look."

"But you're a woman." And what those approaching soldiers would do with a female, he didn't want to consider.

She laughed. "And I won't leave Deirdre's best friend to my countrymen." She moved closer, close enough to slip her hands beneath his elbows, close enough for him to smell lily of the valley and violets above his prison stench.

The sweetness of the girl swirled through his head, springtime incarnate, dizzying. No, blood soaking down his arm made him dizzy. His head throbbed like boot heels on stone. Soldiers nearer. Musket blasts.

He grasped Lady Chloe's arms and lurched to his feet. "Wat?"

"I'm sorry." She slipped her arm around his waist. "We have to leave him."

"I tried—" His throat tightened.

"Save your breath." She propelled him forward.

The ground rocked beneath his feet like an earthquake. The sides of the hill seemed to draw nearer, sway, dim. He reached for something steady and found his arm going around the girl's waist. She was warm, slender but sturdy. His other arm wouldn't work. He was cold on that side. Numb. The girl warmed his other side, kept him going. Faster. Faster. The ground slipped beneath his feet. Thumping reverberated through his body from the wound, through his ears from the soldiers' feet. He glanced back and saw the soldiers' faces. He shook his head, certain he was seeing things. Blood loss was making him hallucinate.

"Here." The girl rounded an outcropping of blackish granite, and the faces vanished. "We've got to climb."

Ross stared at the steep bluff, lower than the gorge sides where the soldiers still marched, but still formidable to a weakened man. He noted the broken scrub pine, earth scored where rocks had lain. "The others went this way?"

"Yes, we've sturdy moorland ponies on the other side of that ridge."

"But the soldiers will catch us."

"Not if we create a little diversion." She grinned. "Deirdre planned a trap. It's up to us to carry it through." She spun away from him to lean against a boulder. "Help me push this if you can."

"Of course I can." With one hand he could. He'd do anything to remain near her warmth, her courage.

They shoved the rock. Pain sliced through his shoulder. The rock remained immobile, and the soldiers sprinted forward. Half a minute would bring them abreast. They'd capture Lady Chloe and Ross.

Ross pushed on the rock again. Lady Chloe joined him. The boulder moved perhaps a handspan.

A volley of musket fire sent splinters of granite spiraling into the air. Ross thrust both hands against the rock. Blood gushed down his arm. No pain. Cold seized his body. Darkness clouded his sight. His ears roared. Taking a deep breath to gather more strength, he found dust and gunpowder filling his nostrils. But the next thrust worked. The boulder tilted, swayed, rolled. Cries of alarm rose from the soldiers.

As the hillside began to collapse, barring the soldiers' way, a cry of triumph rose from Lady Chloe. "That'll stop them long enough." She grabbed Ross's hand and started climbing. Rock fragments, earth, and bell heather showered them, stung Ross's wound. He bit down on a blossom in his mouth, tasted bittersweet.

No more gunfire roared behind them. The soldiers were eerily quiet. As one, Ross and her ladyship paused halfway up the side of the gorge to glance back. The redcoats swarmed around the far side of the boulder, pushing, shoving, and making no forward progress. Two men tried to climb the steep sides of the gorge.

"We did it." Lady Chloe's voice was soft but so full of triumph she might have shouted.

Ross couldn't stop a grin from curving his lips. Nor could he stop himself from succumbing to the temptation of her ladyship's smiling mouth. Briefly, for no more than a heartbeat or ten, he kissed her, reveling in the human contact, the softness of her lips, the sweetness of her mouth.

Then a shout drew his attention away from Lady Chloe kissing him back with abandoned fervor. Stunned, Ross stared back.

Ashford grasped his good arm. "Get moving. That landslide won't hold the soldiers forever."

Ross nodded and headed across the moor where a straggly line of ponies headed toward the sea. Lady Chloe started to join him, but her brother caught hold of her arm and swung her away.

"Go home."

"I cannot. You need my help."

Ashford's mouth pursed, but he gave a brusque nod of acknowledgement and stalked away.

"Come along, Mr. Trenerry." Lady Chloe grasped his arm. "I will see you get to freedom."

She helped him and the others get off the moor and into a rabbit warren of caves, and after that, Ross's memories grew dim, as loss of blood and wound fever took over his existence. When he regained his senses, the ret of his crew was gone. Nor was Lady Chloe anywhere in sight. Instead, her beautiful younger sister, Lady Juliet, sat holding his hand, while she read to him from Shakespeare's sonnets.

"You are awake," she cried. "This must be the happiest day of my life."

In that moment, as weak as a kitten and with no idea how long he had lain senseless, Ross believed that moment might be his happiest as well.

ACKNOWLEDGMENTS

Without the prompting of many people, this story would still be residing on a backup drive where I stored it after writing it while my husband was in law school and I spent about sixteen hours a day alone after getting laid off from my job. Indeed, I have probably forgotten half the people who persuaded me this is a story worth letting others read. Besides my agent and editor, these lovely ladies include Marylu Tyndale, Patty Smith Hall, Louise M. Gouge, and Kathy Davis.

Call me crazy, but I have to thank my cats as well. They lie on my desk, entice me away to play, and just offer me cuddles when I need to calm. In memory of my foot-warmer, Tangelo, who was taken from me much too young, to Chili Pepper, my most faithful desk-sitter, and to Ford, for coming into my life with such youthful exuberance, even if that means I often end up with weird messages in the middle of my manuscript from your attempts to help me write. Most of all, I thank my husband, who solves my computer issues and is the reason I can write romances with sincerity.

ABOUT THE AUTHOR

Photo © 2015 Marti Corn Photography

Laurie Alice Eakes lay in bed as a child telling herself stories and dreaming of becoming a published writer. She is now a bestselling, award-winning author with nearly two dozen books in print. *Romantic Times* writes: "Eakes has a charming way of making her novels come to life without being over the top."

Laurie Alice has a degree in English and French from Asbury University and a master's degree in fiction writing from Seton Hill University. She lives in Texas with her husband and sundry pets. She loves watching old movies with her husband in the winter and going for long walks along Galveston beaches in the summer. When she isn't writing, she's doing housework, which she considers time to work out plot points, and visiting museums as a recreational activity. For more information about Laurie Alice and her books, visit www.lauriealiceeakes.com.